KILLING
STREAK

MERIT CLARK

This is a work of fiction. All of the characters, organizations, and events portrayed in this novel are either products of the author's imagination or are used fictitiously. Although many of the places in this book are real, I have taken great license with landmarks, geography, and most particularly with the boundaries of the City and County of Denver, in order to create a world of my own design. Any resemblance to actual persons, living or dead, events, or locales is entirely coincidental.

www.meritclark.com

ISBN: 1482512521
ISBN-13: 978-1482512526

For Byron Clary, wherever you are, for leading me on the journey.

ACKNOWLEDGMENTS

If self-pity paid by the hour I'd be retired and living on an island somewhere, for example, New Zealand. Writing can feel very isolating, and it's all too easy to forget that I'm really not in this alone. Compiling these acknowledgements has reminded me of what a wonderful support network I have, and of how many people have helped and inspired me over the years.

First I'd like to thank all of my law enforcement contacts who were instrumental in my not making some very dumb mistakes, although I'm sure I've still made some. If I have they are mine alone. I'm more grateful than I can say to these very busy individuals who took time—in some cases lots of time—to meet with me and answer my questions. A special shout-out to:

Forensic Imaging Specialist Michael Bush with the Denver Police Crime Laboratory

Elizabeth Ortiz, Medical Investigator

Officer Chad Read

Deputy Howard S. Thevenet with the Bernalillo County Sheriff's Department

Sergeant Sam White with the Bernalillo County Sheriff's Department

Next up, my magnificent cover artist, Scott Baird. You far exceeded my expectations.

Kristi Yanta, my hard-working, amazing editor who has an uncanny ability to hone in on every single spot where I struggled in the manuscript. Invariably, where she said something like, "this doesn't sound like quite the right word," she'd stumbled upon an awkward passage that needed complete reworking. I'd like to think I now know how to use commas, but I'd be deluding myself.

Harlen & Donna Campbell, for over the top moral support, brilliant writing critiques, encouragement, emergency curtain alterations, and gourmet meals—a girl's gotta eat after all.

Frank Gryglewicz, for providing truly invaluable introductions to law enforcement contacts. There is no way I would have gotten a lot of the information for this book without your help.

Kendell Murphy, for somehow seeing and cheering my intentions through the murk of my truly dreadful first drafts. And, not incidentally, for having stellar taste in men, food, wine, and historical dramas.

Page Lambert, for horseback riding retreats in Wyoming, and writing workshops, and for being one of the most warm and supportive people I know.

Jeff Boxer, it is not an exaggeration to say that at the beginning of this process I did not know a shell casing from a sausage casing. Jeff explained the difference, along with many other fine points of firearms and ballistics.

Sally Kurtzman, for—this could be a long list. For being one of my first writing coaches, and my friend, and opening her house to both me and my husband whenever we needed a place to stay—not to mention for storing our stuff when we moved before our new house was ready. For hooking me up with her brother's guest house on Molokai (I'd really love to work on book two there, hint, hint). For book club, and unlimited hospitality, and rescuing me more times than I can count. Thank you, Sally!

John Hutchins & Suzanne Balvin, for being my fearless beta readers.

Jodi Warter, for always being positive, encouraging, and brilliant.

My friends Jodi Escalante, Connie Schafer, Cheryl Robinson, Ellie Petrini Skriletz, and Anne Durrant. The best hiking, skiing, and/or drinking buddies ever.

Caryl Farkas, for being the person I can always call in the midst of a crisis—existential or otherwise—since I was 5 years old. Or maybe 4. There's some debate about the age we first met.

And last but definitely not least, my long-suffering, patient, awesome husband Jim Ure who heard about the book ad nauseum for years, read some of those really awful first drafts, and through it all somehow managed to stay upbeat and supportive. Everyone agrees he's much nicer than me, and they're right!

KILLING
STREAK

CHAPTER ONE

Evan Markham's wife called three times while he was busy with Vangie. He always looked, in case the calls were important, and then dropped the phone back onto the rumpled bed next to them. Corie could wait. The girl beneath him could not. She lay face up, blindfolded and gagged. Her knees were spread wide and he'd tied her ankles high on the bedposts so her ass was in the air. Her arms were behind her back with the wrists handcuffed together. It looked very uncomfortable, not that she seemed to care. Instead, her focus was on the vibrator he used to touch her instead of his hands. The toy made soft humming sounds and she made high-pitched whimpers each time he took it away.

Every time his phone rang, she shook her head violently from side to side as he broke contact to check it. Her frustration amused Evan. He considered calling Corie back, having a long conversation while he touched the bitch just enough to keep her hanging, one stroke short of release. But it was eleven thirty and he only had another half hour to play before he had to clean her up for lunch with new clients at one.

Vangie had asked for this in the emails she wrote, very explicit pornographic messages in which she detailed in fractured prose exactly what she wanted Evan to do to her. For two years she stalked him like a corporate groupie, squeezed into cheap animal prints at conferences and sending provocative pictures of herself in black leather thongs straddling a Harley. She promised to be a willing slave if he gave her a chance, and at least she hadn't lied about that last part.

But Vangie Perez was a business contact and Evan was scrupulous about keeping the different areas of his life separate. His wife, Corie, was beautiful, intelligent, loyal, and sexually curious. He had no need for Vangie. Until recently.

He took what he wanted silently and then Evan was struck with an inspiration. Ignoring Vangie's frantic head shaking and groans, he left the bed, walked into the small kitchen, and got an ice cube. That was something Corie used to like, being touched with cold ice at precisely the right moment.

It was hard to believe now that he used to do these things to Corie. He'd maneuvered his wife past her comfort zone gradually, over the course of years, but in the end he'd pushed her too far. It was exciting, taking someone classy and innocent like Corie to so many dark places. Although it came at a cost.

When he untied Vangie's ankles her legs flopped awkwardly onto the mattress. He released the handcuffs but she still didn't move. Evan was overcome by a rush of memories and felt the old, familiar tingling anxiety in his gut at the sight of a lifeless woman. Other than the fact that there was no blood . . . Evan felt dizzy. His breathing grew harsh and then he was angry with her. "Get up. You need to take a shower. I'll pick out something for you to wear." He slapped her thigh to get her moving, nothing soft in his voice or his touch.

Where Corie was fashionable, Vangie had trailer park written all over her. Her hair had been bleached too much and looked cheap so he sent her to his stylist who dyed it dark brown and changed the style to a straight, sleek pageboy. She hadn't minded the makeover, just as she didn't mind anything he did. He was already bored.

From the closet he selected one of the expensive designer suits he'd bought her, hung it on the doorknob, and set out a pair of peep-toe high heels. She'd probably complain about wearing the pale blue wool because it was too scratchy and hot. Tough. He pulled out a suit for himself, too, from the clothes he kept in the grimy duplex he'd rented quickly for Vangie when she'd left the husband she wasn't supposed to have and showed up in Denver. Instead of bondage and discipline they were supposed to be preparing for an important lunch meeting, but Evan didn't really need any preparation. He knew forward and backward what he was going to say. What he didn't know was what he was going to do about Vangie.

When he heard the shower running he called his wife back. Instead of Corie a man answered. "Who is this?" Evan asked.

"Mr. Markham?"

Evan considered for a moment before he answered. "Yes. Who is this? Where's Corie?"

"Mr. Markham, this is Detective Jack Fariel with South Metro. There's been an incident at your house and we need you to come home immediately."

Evan's grip tightened on the phone. "An incident? What happened? Where's my wife? Is she all right?"

"We need you to come home," Jack repeated. "How far away are you?"

"I'll be there as soon as I can. Within the hour." Evan ended the call. Why was a detective answering his wife's phone? He glanced around the room, saw the ties he'd used to restrain his girlfriend now hanging limply from the bedposts and the various implements of pain—or pleasure, depending on your point of view—on the nightstand. What kind of incident?

He joined Vangie in the shower. "Move. I'm in a hurry."

"We have plenty of time," Vangie said.

"I've decided you should take the meeting on your own."

"What? Why?"

3

He showered quickly, got out, looked in the mirror, and rubbed his face. He could get by without shaving. "I've set out your clothes."

"What happened? It's your wife isn't it? What does she want this time?" Vangie stepped out of the shower and started drying off.

He regarded her naked body critically. Full, perfect breasts he'd paid for, brownish nipples, round belly, striping from the punishment he'd inflicted on her back and fat ass that wouldn't show once she was dressed, long, wet hair framing a pudgy face. "Make sure you do your hair and makeup the way I showed you," he said. "You need to look professional."

"Evan, I don't want to take the meeting on my own. Why can't you stay?"

"Something else has come up. You'll be fine." He combed his hair and applied some cologne.

"I'm not fine. Why won't you tell me what's going on?" Vangie's whining tone grated on his nerves.

"Look." He turned away from the mirror and faced her. "I wouldn't leave you on your own if it wasn't important. That's all you need to know right now." He left the bathroom and started dressing in a dark blue pinstriped suit, white shirt, and carefully knotted, red silk tie.

Evan wasn't a lawyer himself but he made a lot of money off of them. His consulting business specialized in helping resorts defend against lawsuits. Ski resorts in particular benefited from his services and Evan had recently helped one in Utah avoid a hefty settlement. In this particular case a ski instructor had crashed into a guest while performing an aerial trick at high speed. The guest suffered broken bones and the force of the collision sent her skidding into a tree. With Evan's help, the resort had managed to dodge any financial responsibility. He was skilled at reconstructing these kinds of accidents and testifying about them in court. He also knew how to present himself as a very likeable guy juries could relate to.

Now representatives from another big resort had flown to Denver to meet with him and Evan was going to have to miss lunch and send Vangie on her own. It would have to do. He'd laid all the groundwork. All she had to do was show up and be pleasant. He would circle back with them later that afternoon.

Vangie followed him into the bedroom and watched him as he dressed. "Is there anything in particular I should say or do?"

Evan thought that the less she said the better, but he didn't need her all pissed off. "You know what to do. You've been in dozens of these meetings with me." It was true. To explain her presence he'd passed Vangie off as his assistant and had been including her in business functions when Corie wasn't around.

"You're ready." He walked over and put his hand under her chin. "Don't you trust me?" He looked down at her—he was six foot and she was maybe five-three—and forced himself to smile.

It worked. She beamed back up at him. "You really think I can handle it on my own?"

"I do." He kissed her quickly on the forehead—never on the mouth—and then critically examined himself in the full-length mirror. A detective would notice everything. Evan's blond hair was still damp, but it was short and would dry quickly on the drive home. There wasn't a mark on him—no scratches, bite marks, or other incriminating signs. He looked like a successful businessman in his Brioni suit, well-shined Allen Edmonds shoes, and custom-made dress shirt. And that's exactly what he was. Among other things. He wore a gold wedding band on his left hand and a Cartier watch on his wrist. Other than that, no adornment. Evan loathed jewelry on men. His hands were neatly manicured. With his blue eyes and smooth skin he looked safe and conservative. A man you could trust. His looks had always served him well.

At his house he found chaos—several police cruisers, an unmarked sedan, and a crime scene van. This was major. The police had secured a perimeter and set up a command post where an officer stopped him and asked for identification. Evan kept asking about Corie but no one gave him any information.

"Mr. Markham?"

A tall man, well over six feet, in a charcoal gray suit approached Evan. He was in his mid-thirties and moved with the loose, easy grace of an athlete. He wore his dark brown hair a little longer than most of the other cops, who seemed to favor buzz cuts, and he was clean-shaven. None of those goatees or soul patches or other facial hair configurations Evan found so silly.

The detective flashed his badge and introduced himself. Jack Fariel. The man who answered Corie's phone.

"Where's my wife?" Evan asked, for what felt like the twentieth time. "I want to see her."

"Your wife is fine. I need to ask you a few questions before I let you see her." Jack indicated the unmarked sedan. "We can talk in my car."

Evan didn't know where they had sequestered Corie. Perhaps in the big police RV parked at the top of the curving drive. He knew they wouldn't let him see her until after he'd given his statement. The cops wouldn't want the two of them collaborating on a story. But sitting in a police car was as good as being in custody. In the backseat of a cruiser you were essentially a prisoner, locked in with no door handles. Evan wasn't sure about unmarked cars but he balked all the same. "Is there some other place we could talk?" he asked.

Jack's eyes, under heavy dark brows, were flat and expressionless. "You can come down to the station if you prefer and we can talk there."

That would only delay things further. Evan wanted to see his wife. He didn't want to waste the rest of the day waiting in an interview room until the detective got around to him. "Car I guess." Evan slid into the front passenger seat and Jack didn't object. Probably figured he had plenty of backup nearby if Evan tried anything hinky.

"When was the last time you saw Brice Shaughnessy?" Jack asked.

"Brice?" Evan blinked at him. So that's what this was about. "Last night."

"What time?"

"Nine thirty," he said after a short pause. It was best to be as specific as possible. Cops got suspicious when you were vague.

"You didn't see him this morning?"

"No."

"Did you see anyone else other than your wife on the property this morning?"

"No." It wasn't technically a lie.

"Where were you early this morning?"

"What time exactly?"

"Why don't you explain your whereabouts from nine thirty last night until now?"

Well, it was a nice try. Evan took a steadying breath and spoke carefully. Corie didn't know about Vangie and it wasn't like he could count on a cop to be discreet. "I normally go for a run very early, before it even gets light. But today I had an important meeting so I skipped the run and was working with a colleague to prepare."

"We'll need his name." Jack pushed his notebook towards Evan along with a pen.

"Her name."

Jack didn't say anything but there was the slightest narrowing of those flat, dark eyes. He watched Evan write on the pad. "What time were you with your colleague?" To his credit he spoke without a trace of irony.

"From midnight until an hour ago. I left right after I talked to you on the phone." Evan watched the detective for a moment to let that sink in. The other man didn't react. "Except for a couple of hours when I left to play golf with a client."

"What time did you play golf?"

"We had a six-thirty tee time." He told the detective where they played and wrote down all of the pertinent information. He didn't want to involve Roger D'Ambrose but it couldn't be helped. "My clients are very important people. I consult with them on lawsuits."

"Uh-huh."

"The reason I mention it is that we discuss confidential information. Sensitive information."

"Are you a lawyer?"

"No." Therefore attorney–client privilege didn't apply. Evan was more worried about the revelation of Vangie than he was about trade secrets, but there was no reasonable way to ask the detective to keep that quiet. His wife was going to find out. He was going to have to deal with it. Humiliating that it was Vangie.

Jack looked at the information Evan had written, and if the cop recognized D'Ambrose's name, he didn't give any indication. His gaze returned to Evan. "So when I go to the club and view their security footage from this morning, you'll be on there?"

Evan met his eyes. "Of course."

"Do you have any plans to go out of town?" Jack asked.

"No. May I ask what happened?"

"How would you describe your relationship with Mr. Shaughnessy?"

Right. Only one person got to ask questions. "What do you mean?"

"It seems to me that's a pretty straightforward question, Mr. Markham."

"He's a friend of my wife's. We're letting him rent our guesthouse month-to-month while he looks for a permanent place to live."

"Do the three of you spend a lot of time socializing?"

"Not really."

"But you saw him last night."

"Yes."

"Why?"

"My wife suggested I join them in the guesthouse for a drink and I did, to appear friendly." The moment it was out of his mouth Evan regretted it.

Jack watched him. "Mr. Markham, I'm sorry to have to inform you that Brice Shaughnessy is dead."

"Dead?" Since he'd let it slip that he only "appeared" friendly there was no reason for a phony display of grief. "How did it happen? Is Corie all right? She's much closer to Brice than I am."

"We're trying to figure out exactly what happened. Your wife wasn't harmed."

"Can I see her now?"

The detective took a moment before he answered. And it wasn't an answer, it was a request. "We'd like to take a DNA sample and fingerprints from you. For elimination. Your wife already gave us hers."

"Do you have a warrant?"

For the first time Jack's face shifted out of neutral. He smiled. "As a matter of fact I do."

CHAPTER TWO

Jack yanked at the metal latch securing the RV door and simultaneously let out a disgusted sigh. The door was jammed. As usual. "Great." He yanked harder and took an abrupt step backward when the door suddenly gave. He almost knocked his new partner, Serena Owen, down.

"Jeez Jack, I'm sure she'll keep."

He grunted in response and took the two short steps up in one long-legged stride. Serena followed him inside where there were too many people for Jack's taste, including his lieutenant, Danielle "Dani" Hayes, a stubby woman closing in on fifty. Jack's eyes slid past everyone seeking Corie Markham, but Dani insisted on a word.

Command turned up, especially in a case like this—a murder in a neighborhood of million-dollar homes. The high profile denizens of the Aspen Ridge subdivision would want to know how chaos, in the form of a shooting, could have scaled their brick walls and sullied their manicured existence.

"You know who the Markhams are?" Dani asked.

Jack had worked with Dani for two years and their relationship was solid if not exactly friendly. But then, he didn't know anyone who was really friendly with Dani. The lieutenant didn't join in on most of her team's lunches or go out drinking with them after work. Maybe she was one of those rare cops who actually had a social life outside of law enforcement.

Or maybe his boss was watching him out of simple concern. This was his first week back from medical leave and Jack found himself uncharacteristically self-conscious. He felt as if everyone were waiting for him to keel over, as if he needed to prove himself all over again. He himself had been hoping for a quiet first week catching up on paperwork and easing back into the routine. The citizens of Denver had managed to oblige until Thursday. Now, not only had he caught his first post-operative case, so to speak, but it involved a woman he loved. *Used to love,* Jack corrected himself. It was a lifetime ago in another, younger life. None of which he was about to share with his lieutenant.

Jack kept his gaze bland and expectant. Or so he hoped. "Just talked to Mr. Markham."

"Evan Markham sits on the board of several high-profile charities," Dani said. "On some of them with the chief and the mayor."

"How nice that he's involved in the community."

"Thought you should know. He can be a pain in the ass."

Jack poured himself some coffee from a machine set up on a folding table. Probably not the best thing for his stomach, but he was finding Dani's scrutiny uncomfortable and needed a distraction. He was also stalling. Serena had told him Corie was cooperative, had offered to help, and asked why they needed a warrant. That sounded like her. If it was the same her.

Serena hung back and let him deal with the lieutenant.

"Paul and I will be handling all of the media," Dani said.

"Fine with me," Jack said. Paul Diamond was the chief of police. He and Dani were welcome to talk to the press. News vans were already clustered outside the gates with neatly groomed reporters getting ready to do their first remotes. Everyone would want answers, preferably before this led off the five o'clock news. No pressure or anything. Jack poured powdered creamer into his coffee that immediately congealed into oily clumps. He poked at them with a plastic stir stick.

"Delgado's bringing in a team to process the main house," Dani said. Mike Delgado was Jack's old partner.

"He'll like that."

Dani finished up with a terse, "Let me know what else you need," and Jack wondered if he'd been too abrupt. He'd found himself monitoring his behavior, trying to remember how he used to act, almost as if he were putting on a performance. Which sucked.

No delaying any longer. Jack walked the few short steps to the back of the RV where Corie Markham sat at a table with her back to him, giving him a few seconds to process his reaction. He felt as if someone had struck him in the solar plexus. There was the long, lush, untamed strawberry blond hair he'd always wanted to bury himself in; the same slim build. He would have known her instantly.

"Mrs. Markham?" This couldn't be happening. Not now. Not on his first case back.

Corie looked up. She was dressed casually in a peach-colored t-shirt and faded jeans. Not work clothes. No makeup. No jewelry other than her wedding and engagement rings. Her eyes were puffy and red, like she'd been crying, but for the moment she'd stopped. Several crumpled tissues were on the table. Jack tried to hold her gaze but couldn't and stared at a point somewhere over her right shoulder. The expression on her face was distant and unfocused, a look he knew all too well. He and Serena sat down at the table with her.

"I'm sorry for your loss," Jack said. The words felt as inadequate as always.

Corie nodded once, bit her lip, and appeared to be trying not to cry again. Something in Jack's stomach twisted in response.

"I'm Detective Fariel. Jack. I believe you've already met Detective Owen. We need to ask you some questions." How strange to be introducing himself to her. And how awful for her to look at him with no sign of recognition. He ordered himself to get a grip. It had been a long time. She'd had a terrible shock. In his mind Jack saw her in high school, laughing up at him, her smile bright, in horrible contrast to the misery in front of him. So she'd gotten married. How could he possibly be surprised by that?

Corie recognized the young, black detective from earlier. "Serena, right?"

"How are you doing, hon?" Serena touched Corie's arm reassuringly for a moment.

Corie shook her head. She started to raise the cup of coffee to her lips, then changed her mind and set it back down.

Jack still couldn't hold her gaze. He fidgeted with a digital recorder on the table and cleared his throat. "You were the one who found the body?"

"Jack?"

His left hand, holding a pen, froze poised above his notebook. "Yeah," Jack finally managed.

"Wow," Corie said.

Serena's face was neutral but her dark brown eyes were alert. "You two know each other?"

"You're a cop now?" Corie stared at Jack, who forced himself to meet her eyes.

"Yeah." His powers of speech were welcome to return anytime.

"I mean obviously you're a cop. Sorry." The look on Corie's face was somewhere between shock and amazement. "How long has it been?"

"Almost twenty years." *Eighteen years and four months almost to the day, but who's keeping track?* "I'd ask how you are, but under the circumstances . . ."

"Yeah."

"Corie, I know this is all pretty upsetting." Jesus, he really had developed a talent for understatement. "Just take your time and tell me what happened."

He saw her eyes fill, although she fought the tears. "Jack, it was awful. I have no idea how to even describe it."

So pretty. Even with the puffy eyes and red splotches highlighting her pale cheeks. "You're the one who called 911?"

She nodded, then added, "I can't believe you're a cop."

"Homicide detective." Jack tried to smile and instead cleared his throat again. "Corie, what happened here this morning?"

"I don't know. I don't understand. I don't know how any of this—" She choked back a sob and made a helpless gesture in the general direction of the guesthouse with her right hand.

"It's all right," Serena said. Corie and Jack looked at her as if surprised to see her there. "Answer our questions in your own words."

For the first time in their short partnership Jack was grateful for Serena's presence. Emotions warred within him. He wished himself off the case; a sense of unreality clung to everything. *Focus. Do your job.*

"Tell us about your relationship with Brice," Serena asked.

Corie told them she'd enrolled in two courses at the University of Denver about a year ago thinking she might pursue a master's degree in psychology. Her mother-in-law, Jessie Markham, had encouraged her although her husband had been lukewarm about Corie going back to school. She'd met Brice in one of the classes and they got to be friends. As far as Corie was aware, Brice didn't do drugs and only engaged in social drinking. He was new to Colorado and didn't know many people yet, so when he lost his apartment Corie volunteered the guesthouse.

"How did your husband feel about that?" Jack asked.

"Evan's always jealous."

Jack thought of the cold, unfaithful man he'd just interviewed and didn't react to the irony.

Corie gave a small, defiant shrug. "It's my house, too. Besides, Brice is gay."

She didn't seem to notice that she used the present tense. "Did Brice have any visitors in the last couple of days?" Jack asked.

"No," Corie said. "He keeps—" She bit her lip and her voice faded. "Kept to himself."

Jack thought about what they found in the guesthouse. Maybe Corie had been too upset to notice.

She seemed eager to defend her friend. "He offered to let us run a background check."

Jack looked up from writing. "Did you?"

"No. Evan wanted to, but I didn't see the need. I know that seems . . . dumb, but I trusted Brice."

"Where was Evan this morning?" Jack's neutral expression felt frozen on his face.

"I didn't call him right away, and when the officers showed up they took my cell phone."

That wasn't an answer. "That's standard procedure now, Corie." *Markham. Of course.* Jack's mind started to connect the dots as memories resurfaced. He found it especially curious that while Evan couldn't stop asking when he could see Corie, she hadn't asked once if she could see her husband.

"Tell us about Evan," Jack asked.

"What do you want to know?" Corie asked.

"How would you describe his relationship with Brice?"

"Evan would have preferred it was just the two of us in our new house for a while." Corie gave another small, defensive shrug. "Evan's gone a lot for work, and it was nice to have someone to—" She stopped and looked down at the coffee, blinking furiously.

Jack's chest felt tight, seeing her in pain. He spoke as gently as possible. "Tell me what happened this morning."

When she looked up at him, her dark blue eyes were sad. "Brice and I got into a routine where I went out there after I got up and had coffee with him. On the way this morning, I let Murphy out of his pen."

She hesitated and then the words came out in a headlong rush.

"I'm so sorry about the dog—it's just that Murphy usually goes with me. He ran ahead and the guesthouse door was open, so he went right inside. It took me a minute to catch up to him. I didn't think. I pushed the door open further with my hand. I called Brice and then I called Murphy. He came running back tracking something, you know, with his paws. I know now it was blood, but I thought at first maybe he'd gotten into something. I called Brice again, but of course he didn't answer. When I saw him, I let go of the dog. I was—it didn't make sense."

And then Murphy had sniffed the body and walked in the blood. Sacrilege on top of the unspeakable. Corie made a praying motion with her hands and then covered her face with them for a moment. Jack and Serena waited.

"All I could think about was calling 911," Corie continued. "I waited outside until the cops came. I know I should have checked to see if Brice was okay, but I just couldn't."

"He was already dead. There was nothing you could have done," Jack said.

Serena did what Jack couldn't and patted Corie's arm reassuringly. "Did you see anyone around when you went to the guesthouse this morning?"

"No."

"Any strange cars parked out front?" Jack asked.

"I don't think so. But I wasn't really looking." Corie put her hands flat on the table and stared at them.

Jack caught his partner's eye. "Did you hear anything unusual?"

"You probably wonder how I slept through gun shots." Corie was still staring at her hands. "I wonder myself. But I took a sleeping pill. I never do that, but last night I got one from Brice. I must have slept like the dead." She winced as soon as she said it.

"Tell us about the last time you saw Brice alive," Jack asked.

"I've been thinking about that. It was nine or nine thirty last night, at the latest. We had a drink with him in the guesthouse, me and Evan."

Jack mentally reviewed Evan's statement. "Why was that?"

Corie leaned back in her chair and played her thumb along the rim of her coffee cup. "I went over there first, right after dinner. And then we called Evan and asked him to join us. He had a Scotch." Another evasive answer.

"What did the three of you talk about?" Jack asked.

"Personal things."

"Corie—"

"I know. I know I have to tell you. It's embarrassing. I confided in Brice about some problems with my marriage." She looked at him, then away again, took a deep breath, and let it out. Her voice faded. "This can't be relevant."

"There's no way for me to know that yet." Jack's throat was so tight he was amazed his voice sounded normal.

"Brice had this idea that maybe the three of us could sit down and talk, but it was a really dumb idea. I mean, you can imagine how well that went over."

"How well did it go over?" Jack asked.

For the first time Corie displayed signs of irritation. "On a scale of one to ten? Look, I know this sounds really stupid now but it seemed like a good idea at the time. Evan came in, caught wind of what we were up to, and left. That's it."

Fight with friend in the evening. Friend dead in the morning. You didn't have to be a detective to connect those dots. "Was there anything physical? A fight between your husband and Brice?" Jack asked.

Instead of answering she stared into her cup as if trying to divine a solution.

Jack persisted. "Were there any threats exchanged?"

"There wasn't a fight."

Jack changed tacks. "How late did you stay in the guesthouse?"

"I left with Evan."

"You didn't stay and talk more with your friend? I know I would have been pissed if my husband acted like that," Serena said.

"No." Corie looked at Serena and the irritation drained back out of her voice. Now she sounded defeated. "It wasn't like that."

"Is it possible your husband saw Brice again last night or early this morning?" Jack asked.

"No."

"You sound sure," Jack said.

"Not that I know of," Corie amended.

"When you and Evan went home last night, what did you do?" Jack asked.

An edge of panic crept into her tone. "Do? What do you mean?"

"We're trying to get a picture of where everybody was," Serena said.

Corie nodded and took a steadying breath. When she spoke again her voice was calm. "Evan went into the family room and started watching TV. I went to bed."

"What else happened?" Jack's gut felt tight.

"Look, I told you." Corie sat up straighter and leaned forward, although she kept her voice soft. "It was a dumb idea ambushing Evan and expecting him to talk. Evan's a very private man. He had every right to be annoyed. We argued, like all married couples do. That's it."

His eyes locked with Corie's for a long moment and Jack decided to let it go. For the time being. "Do you know if Brice owned a gun?" he asked.

"I don't think so but I don't know for certain," Corie said.

"How about you and your husband?" Serena asked.

"Yes." Corie told them where to find several rifles locked up in a gun safe.

Only now she wouldn't meet Jack's eyes. "Anything else? Besides the rifles?"

Her voice faded. "I also have a nine millimeter. Evan bought it for me. But—"

The sour feeling in Jack's stomach intensified. "But?"

"I'm not exactly sure where it is. It might be up at our cabin but I'm not sure. I haven't seen it in a long time."

CHAPTER THREE

"Always nice catching up with old friends," Serena said when they were on their way back to the crime scene.

Jack didn't answer. He led the way briskly down the flagstone path to the guesthouse and Serena had to trot to keep up with him.

It was a relief to be done talking to Corie, to get away from those sad blue eyes, indicting him for past mistakes. Except of course that wasn't true. He was an arrogant jerk to even think she cared after all this time. She barely remembered him, and he couldn't afford the luxury of paranoia and self-absorption.

"How's the canvas coming?" Jack asked.

Several other detectives were making the rounds, talking to the neighbors, the mailman, the Comcast guy whose van was parked down the street—all the usual constituents in a residential neighborhood on a sunny weekday morning.

Serena brought him up to speed efficiently and then Jack took a last, deep breath of the fresh outside air before ducking into the guesthouse. He pushed Corie out of his mind as he absorbed everything he could about the scene: how it smelled—bad, after being closed up for hours on an unseasonably warm morning—how it sounded, how it felt, even how the air tasted. He saw evidence of her touches everywhere, in the comfortable furniture, the artwork, the fabrics, the muted color palette. She'd designed the place to be a sanctuary for her friends, serene and soothing; it sure as hell hadn't worked out that way.

Frank Yannelli, the investigator from the Office of the Medical Examiner, was finishing up his preliminary examination. Frank was a gentle man in his fifties, impeccable at his job, and Jack was glad to see him.

In the bedroom, Brice Shaughnessy had fallen onto his right side with his left arm extended in a frozen, futile gesture of supplication. There was something grotesquely unnatural about bodies that had undergone violent death, utterly graceless, robbed of all humanity. Perhaps those who died a natural death in their beds at ninety-five looked peaceful. None of Jack's victims did. He swore they were still looking at their killer, if only he knew how to read the meaning in their horrified stares.

The dead man had turned thirty a week ago, according to his driver's license. He was naked and his brown eyes were open, bisected horizontally by an angry, garish, tache noire stripe. That blood-red band wasn't unexpected but it was still jarring. Years of dead eyes had caused Jack to develop an aversion to eating fish with the head attached, or any other entrée that stared back at him.

"Corie Markham walked in and stood here." Jack approximated her position in the doorway, attempting to see the room as she had.

The bed was a rumpled mess. Someone had pushed the covers back on each side and the pillows were mangled by more than one head. They'd found semen on the sheets.

It was possible all Corie saw was Brice. He'd fallen in such a way that he blocked the bedroom doorway. She'd been trying to get the dog out of the blood and away from the body. She'd been shocked, confused, panicked.

Frank indicated a gunshot wound on Brice's chest. "There appear to be three anterior defects and two posterior." That meant three bullets had entered and only two had exited. One of the gun shots or "defects" had hit the victim's shoulder. That one hadn't been serious.

Frank continued. "No apparent defensive wounds. There are indications of anal penetration."

"Corie told us he didn't have any visitors," Serena said dryly.

Jack snorted. They'd found used condoms in wadded-up tissues on the nightstands, their wrappers on the floor. A whiskey glass on one nightstand, a wine glass on the other. Clothes scattered about. A small table had toppled, perhaps during a struggle, and the plant that had been on it spread dirt across the off-white, wool Berber carpeting. A man's bathrobe—*Brice's?*—was on the floor at the foot of the bed.

"Didn't expect you back yet," Frank said.

A second woman's voice spoke. "He's tougher than most folks."

Jack turned and looked at Tiffany Quintana, one of the evidence techs processing the scene. Another friendly face.

"Can I assume since you're back so soon that things went well?" Frank asked.

Frank had a full head of gray hair, a mustache, and the demeanor of a kindly grandfather. If someone had to dissect your loved ones you'd want it to be Frank. But Jack was excruciatingly self-conscious. He wanted to work. He *had* to work. And he needed his team to focus instead of worrying about him. "What about time of death?"

Frank took the hint. "Best preliminary estimate I can give you without a full exam is seven to ten hours, possibly a little longer. Rigor appears to be advanced. Lividity appears fixed with minimal blanching." So Brice hadn't been moved since he was killed, which was consistent with the presence of a sunburn-like color staining the half of his body closest to the floor.

"He died early in the morning then, maybe five, six o'clock at the latest." Serena made a note.

Jack fingered a bottle cap in his pocket as he looked around. He hadn't given lunch a second thought. While they were waiting around for the warrant, he'd sent a uniform out for sandwiches. Now the turkey wrap threatened to come back to haunt him. Literally. He couldn't imagine anything more embarrassing. Jack never ran outside, not once, not even as a rookie. And this scene was a vacation compared to some he'd worked. His body did whatever he demanded of it, functioned on sporadic food, less sleep, and ran a seven-minute mile. At least until recently when it got him good with one large, mutinous malignancy.

"Don't expect this kind of heat in October, huh?" Frank spoke as if he knew exactly what Jack was going through.

"What's up with the dog?" Tiffany asked.

Frank's gaze took in the bloody paw prints. "I was curious about that, too."

"Corie Markham came in with her dog," Jack said. Still felt strange to say that name. "Says she grabbed him right away."

Frank whistled. "Couldn't have grabbed him too fast, based on the looks of things. At least he didn't help himself to a snack. It's bad once they get a taste of human flesh. You can never trust 'em again."

"Yuck." Tiffany walked to the bedroom windows, which were closed. "Got some usable prints from the windows, most likely the vic's." She was a looker in her late twenties with long dark hair and a smooth olive complexion. When they first met, she and Jack had tried dating a couple of times but found they worked much better as friends. At least that's what Jack concluded.

Jack looked at the tightly closed windows. "Hot night. I'd have wanted the windows open. Apparently there's no AC in here, only in the main house."

"And the drapes are open." Tiffany wrinkled her ski-jump nose. "What kind of imbecile sleeps with the drapes open?"

Jack felt a bitter smile tug at the corner of his mouth when he looked at the fabric, a cheerful pattern featuring horses and horseshoes, neatly pulled back on either side of the large picture window. Corie loved horses. "Well I don't, but you never know. Maybe he was an exhibitionist."

Tiffany gave him a wry look. "Or maybe somebody was trying to get a little more light in here without being obvious."

"What else you got so far, Tiff?"

"The fan wasn't on but we got some residue off the buttons." She shrugged. "Maybe the killer turned the fan off for some reason? And the shell casings we found are nine millimeters."

Jack abruptly turned away and walked out of the bedroom. A lot of people owned nine mils. It was a popular gun. It didn't mean anything. He didn't know enough yet to jump to conclusions.

Tiffany followed him into the living room and drew his attention to the couch. "A hole's blown out of a cushion, consistent with someone using it to muffle the sound of the shots."

"Well that narrows it down to anyone who's ever watched *CSI.* Or *Perry Mason* for that matter." Jack walked over and stared at a row of framed pictures on the living room wall.

"Wanna know what else we found?" Tiffany asked.

"Nah, I thought I'd wait for the movie."

"You okay?"

He glanced at her and saw her smooth forehead creased with concern. He realized he was turning the bottle cap in his pocket over and over with his fingers. Great. He was becoming OCD on top of everything else. The cap was from a bottle of iced tea he drank with lunch, and for some unknown reason he'd read the saying imprinted inside the lid: "An undefined problem has an infinite number of solutions." It struck him as ironic, or maybe he was superstitious after all.

"You said you found something else. What is it?" Jack asked.

She held up an evidence bag proudly. "A woman's ring. Found it under the bed not too far from the body."

Jack took the bag from her and couldn't quite suppress a disgusted sigh.

Serena had followed them into the living room and was watching him. "You don't look happy."

"What's happy got to do with anything?" He turned back toward the artwork on the wall, framed abstract prints hung at evenly spaced intervals. "This reminds me of those puzzles; see if you can spot the ten differences between these two pictures."

Tiffany laughed. "I used to be good at those."

There was a gap where a picture should have been to maintain symmetry. Jack's fingertips traced the lightly textured wall and he found the small hole made by a nail. Evan Markham's voice rang in his ears: 'I joined them to appear friendly.' *Right.*

Jack crouched down and found a small piece of glass wedged between the edge of the carpet and the wall. "Tiff, can you get this for me?"

She carefully picked up the shard with tweezers and put it in a bag. "That could be anything."

"Always thinking positive, aren't you? See if you find a picture anywhere with broken glass. Have you guys gone through the trash yet?"

"Aaron's working on it."

Corie said Evan was a stickler for keeping the guesthouse perfect and that Brice complied. But they found the remains of a joint in a makeshift foil ashtray on the kitchen counter, along with an open bag of potato chips, a tub of some kind of spreadable cheese, and a box of bakery cookies. There were dirty dishes in the sink.

A power supply for a laptop computer also sat on the counter. The computer itself, along with Brice's cell phone, was missing.

"Keep me posted, Tiff." Jack paused on his way out the door. The beveled glass panes of the elegant door were intact and the jam wasn't splintered. If it was a break-in, it was the neatest Jack had ever seen.

Serena followed him outside. "There are several sets of footprints leading from the front door to the parking space out back. If the killer parked in back it might mean they were familiar with the property."

"Maybe. Wonder if the place was cleaned recently?" Jack made a note in his pad as they walked. "Cleaning crew could have made some of the footprints outside."

"Now who's thinking positive?"

There were two entrances from the road onto the property: the curving driveway that snaked along next to the main house and led up a slight incline to a three-car garage, and a second, shorter, gravel drive that ran behind the guesthouse. When Jack first arrived he'd quipped to Serena about how maybe they were supposed to use the "service entrance," which is what the second driveway appeared to be at first.

That was where they found Brice's car with the trunk open. The trunk didn't appear to have been jimmied and they found a set of keys on the ground.

He and Serena were halfway up the flagstone path when Tiffany called his name.

"I'll go on ahead and check on the processing in the main house." Serena left.

Tiffany walked up, shaded her eyes from the sunlight with one hand, and peered up at him. "How're you really holding up?"

Jack couldn't quite muster a smile. "Haven't puked on anybody's shoes yet."

"No one would care if you did. Everybody knows what's going on."

"Great."

"I meant . . . the department's the worst place for keeping a secret. It's like a big, dysfunctional, armed family. You know that."

"I've got a lot of work to do, Tiff." Jack felt a twinge of guilt. He had rebuffed her offers to help over the past weeks, preferring to puke and enjoy his misery without an audience.

"I know." She hesitated. "Wanna grab something to eat later? Whenever you're done?"

"Who knows when this day's gonna end," Jack said. "And I've still gotta manage to swing by the doctor somehow."

"I know," she said again, "but you're not going to feel like going to the store after a long day, so let me know if you decide you want to get something."

"Will do." He turned and jogged up the rest of the steps.

CHAPTER FOUR

It should be a good thing that Jack knew Corie, right? They had a shared history and conventional wisdom said that should make Corie more inclined to open up to him. Except that in this case their shared history involved actions on Jack's part that, if anything, would make Corie inclined to shoot him instead of Brice. In addition to Brice. If she shot anyone. He felt that, even in light of fourteen years as a cop including six as a detective, this strained credulity. Which was a problem.

Perhaps some recalled high school with fondness or nostalgia, but Jack wouldn't be that confused teenager again for anything. Corie's maiden name was Farantino. They originally met because students were seated in homeroom alphabetically: Farantino, Fariel. When he first saw her, Jack was fifteen and he thought she was the prettiest girl he'd ever seen. He sat behind her in class and stared at that hair and sometimes had to sit on his hands to keep from touching it. A few years later, by some miracle, they started dating. But they'd barely gotten started when Jack succumbed to temptation in the form of Corie's best friend—and Evan's baby sister—Hennessy. At eighteen, he had no defenses against seduction. And no sense. And absolutely no awareness of how one mistake could change the course of your life.

Instead of following Serena to the main house, Jack decided to talk to Corie again, alone. He found her still sitting at the table in the RV with what looked like the same cup of coffee, now cold, in front of her. "Corie, if you're in trouble, you need to tell me."

She looked up at him, startled. "What?"

"Where's your gun?"

"I told you, I don't know. I know it looks bad."

Jack didn't answer. He approached the table but he didn't sit down. "Why didn't you tell me Brice had a visitor?"

"I wasn't sure."

"You didn't find that noteworthy? That he might have had company?"

"Brice was entitled to a personal life." Corie didn't exactly wilt under his scrutiny.

"So you do know who it was."

"No."

"Look, Corie. You can't hold out on me because of—" Jack hesitated. "Because of anything that happened in the past."

"I have nothing to hide."

"Corie *Markham*?" He emphasized the last name. She froze and then started picking at the rim of the Styrofoam coffee cup. The silence lengthened and, with an effort, Jack waited her out.

She finally said, "I know."

"You know what?"

"I know it seems . . ." She looked up at him and her eyes searched his face for a moment. "I don't know how it seems."

"So it is the same Markham." Evan had already gone to college, so Jack had never met him, back in the day.

"Hennessy died you know."

"I know. Corie, what the hell is going on?" It wasn't that strange she married her best friend's older brother. It did complicate things that Jack had slept with that very same friend, which meant, in light of current events, that he'd also slept with a suspect's sister. A very long time ago, way before he became a cop, but still.

"I don't know." She looked down at the Styrofoam shreds she'd created and started pushing them into a neat pile.

"You better start knowing something. How a dead body wound up in your guesthouse would be a great beginning." He set the evidence bag down next to the pile of white bits and showed her the ring, a delicate silver snake swallowing its tail with small rubies for eyes.

"What is that?" Corie frowned at the ring as if she found it distasteful and then looked up questioningly.

"You don't recognize it?"

"No. Where'd you get it?"

Jack watched her for another long, disheartening moment. "How well did you really know Brice?"

"You really think this is because of something Brice was involved in?"

"You tell me."

"I can't. I'm sorry."

"Tell me about Evan."

"There's nothing to tell."

"How did he feel about you going back to school?"

"You asked me this already."

"And I'm asking you again. Here's a simple one: How long have you been married?"

"It's very hard to tell what's a cop question and what's a Jack question."

Jack let out a frustrated groan and leaned forward with his hands on the table. "Corie, you've got to start giving me some answers. You don't know where your gun is, you don't know where your husband is, and you don't know very much about a man you allowed to live in your guesthouse."

He stood up again and fought to get a rein on his impatience. He was trying to help her. Didn't she see that? "Headlines'll do.

Married how long? What kind of business? Where's Evan's office? Who're Brice's friends? Just the facts, ma'am."

She took a shaky breath and looked away for a moment. Then she seemed to make a decision because, when she turned back to him, she was defiant. "Just the facts? Sure, here are some facts: married almost five years, or it will be next May. Don't think we're gonna make it—not if I have anything to say about it anyway. I realize how that sounds. I realize I'm not giving you the answers you want. Sorry. I realize I'm not exactly rushing to Evan's defense. Again, sorry. The business does consulting. For resorts. We work from home. Evan's an expert witness helping high-end resorts defend themselves against lawsuits. Successfully I might add. Keep that in mind—he makes a great witness."

"Jesus, Corie."

"Want any more facts?"

"Who killed Brice?"

Her voice rose in frustration. "I don't know! If I did I would tell you. I cared about Brice. I couldn't hurt him. I know you haven't seen me for a long time but do you really think I'm capable of murder?"

"Is it common for you to not know where Evan is?"

She gave a bitter laugh but she answered. "Yes. Lately it's common."

It was possible she didn't know about the girlfriend and he decided he wasn't going to tell her. Yet. He was stung by the irony of having cheated on Corie himself years ago. "What kind of problems are you having?"

"Shouldn't you be more interested in why he's not a murderer, instead of all the gory details about my marriage?"

"At this point I'll be happy if you answer any question at all. Why isn't Evan a murderer?"

Corie hesitated too long. "He just isn't."

Was she trying to cover for Evan or make him look guilty? What was she hiding? "And you were here—alone—sleeping like a baby while your friend was shot not once, but three times?"

"I told you, I took a sleeping pill."

Her voice was miserable and strangled; Jack hated himself for losing his patience. "Corie, I know it's been a rough day for you. But can you help me out here a little bit?"

"I don't want to get a lawyer because I didn't do it. But I will. We have a very good one on retainer." She lifted her chin. "Do you have any more questions? If not, I'd really like to know when I can go back inside my own house."

It was unfair but he couldn't resist. "You can't go back in your house until we finish processing it. But you can see your husband now. If you want to."

"What does that mean?"

Jack's voice was silky. "Don't you want to know where he is? Because you haven't asked. Evan, on the other hand, is desperate to see you. He must have asked me a hundred times where you are."

During the long, miserable moment that followed, he saw her swallow.

CHAPTER FIVE

When Evan saw Corie emerge from the RV he called her name, rushed to her, and took her in his arms—or tried to. She didn't seem at all happy to see him and he suddenly felt foolish and self-conscious. The cops pretended not to watch but they noticed everything.

"Corie." Evan touched her hair but she wouldn't look at him. Corie's affect was completely indifferent. No relief, no tears, no reaction at all.

His wife depended on him. He was the one she turned to in a crisis. Except that clearly wasn't true anymore.

She tolerated his arm around her shoulders, though, and within his awkward embrace he felt her trembling. "How was it?" he asked. "The police," he added pointlessly, then led her away from the RV out of earshot of the officers.

Had they treated her like a suspect? Maybe that's what was bothering her. Evan was desperate to know what they'd asked her. Did Corie suspect him?

That thought unsettled him most of all and Evan found himself babbling, off-balance around Corie of all people. "The detective spoke with me already. You probably know that. You're smart enough to realize they wouldn't let us see each other until we'd each given our statements individually. Are you sure you're all right? You're very quiet. Have you eaten anything today? Do you feel ill? You're shivering. Do you need to sit down?"

He couldn't seem to shut up. She kept her unfocused stare toward the street. Then a car door slammed and Corie stiffened. He looked to see what—or who—had finally gotten a reaction out of her and saw his mother-in-law, Violet, emerge from a dark red BMW at the curb. Was it possible to get out of a car indignantly?

"What on God's green earth is going on here?" Vi's shrill voice carried clearly.

Corie spoke her first words: "Shit. I can't deal with this right now."

Evan kissed Corie on the cheek and gave her shoulders a little squeeze. "I'll take care of her. Don't worry." Why was he putting on a show? And for whom?

Vi, dressed stylishly in dark wash, slim-fitting jeans, teetered a little in her spike-heeled boots. Her cream-colored silk blouse had flared sleeves and an elaborate flounce down the front. Chunky gold jewelry adorned her neck, ears, and wrists. Her hair was bleached blond with expensive highlights and cut short in a faux windswept style.

Evan intercepted her halfway up the long driveway.

"What the hell is happening here?" Vi's face contorted into an outraged grimace. "Why are police cars blocking the drive? Where's Corie going?"

Her voice set Evan's teeth on edge. "Violet. I am afraid something awful has happened."

"What? Is something wrong with Corie?"

"I need you to stay calm. There has been a shooting. Brice is dead."

She planted her manicured hands on her hips. "I told you having that man stay here was bad news."

That was the first thing that popped into the unsympathetic bitch's head?

Vi looked smug. "What was it? Some drug deal? Maybe a quarrel with one of his gay lovers?"

"Violet." Evan grasped her roughly by the arms. Too bad there were so many cops around. His hands itched to smack her. "They don't know what happened yet. Brice is dead and Corie found him. She's a mess."

"She found him? Dead?"

"That's what I said." Evan let go of her arms.

Some of the wind went out of Vi's malicious sails. "How?"

"Don't know yet."

"When did it happen?"

"Don't know that either. The police have been here all day. CSIs, detectives. It's been quite the circus. Corie's devastated. What are you doing here anyway?"

"You invited me for dinner. I came early to help."

Belatedly, Evan noticed Vi was holding a shiny paper bag, the right size and shape for a bottle of wine. "Crap. I completely forgot. I'm sorry you wasted a trip."

"It's all right." Vi looked toward the RV. "How is she?"

"The detectives spent quite a bit of time with us today taking our statements."

"They did?" Vi's voice rose to a high-pitched, excited whisper. "What did they ask you?"

Evan shook his head, half in wonder, half in dismissal. "They'll probably need to talk to you as well." He added that last bit spitefully but her eyes glowed with a feral excitement.

"Were you here when . . ." Vi licked her lips. "When it happened? When Corie found the body?"

"I'm afraid not. I had a busy day meeting with clients."

"Corie was on her own? Why didn't she call me?"

The answer seemed so patently obvious. Vi never gave Corie anything but grief. "She's been rather busy with the police."

"Poor Corie."

"Yes." He took in the rare, albeit brief, display of empathy. "So you'll understand that she's not in any shape to make dinner. We don't even know when they'll let us back in the house."

"The house? Is that where it happened?"

"No. But the entire property is a crime scene right now. We'll have to reschedule."

"Of course. But I want to go check on Corie."

"I don't think that's a good idea."

"Why not?" Indignant again.

"Violet, you and Corie don't get along under the best of circumstances. She doesn't need anything else to upset her."

"I'm still her mother, Evan."

Evan glanced over his shoulder to see who was nearby, then leaned in close to her. Usually he played the good son-in-law but he figured the circumstances gave him an excuse. "I know the kind of petty, vindictive shit that comes out of your mouth and, I swear to God, Violet, if you say one nasty word . . ."

"I won't. What on earth is wrong with you?"

"Seriously, Violet. Not one word. She's been through hell."

"A hell of her own making."

"Like that right there. If I hear you make one comment like that in front of Corie, I promise I will throw you out on your saggy ass."

CHAPTER SIX

"Jack Fariel. Who would have thought you'd wind up on the right side of the law?" Vi's conversation was paced and littered with pauses, as if she was taking a drag even when she didn't have a cigarette in her hand. Perhaps she thought it lent itself to better drama.

Jack found it annoying. "Mrs. Farantino. Please, have a seat."

"It's Bellenger now." Vi extended her left hand. The nails were pink and white acrylic, meant to look like a French manicure.

Jack's eyes found the giant diamond on the fourth finger, as the gesture intended. *Like mother, like daughter.* "How about I call you Violet? It's been a rough day for everyone."

"All right." Vi's smoker voice sifted through gravel. She told him she'd never thought it was a good idea to let Brice live there. "I love my daughter. But she's too trusting."

"Did you express your concerns?"

"Naturally."

"What were they, specifically?"

"I had a feeling. Third wheel and all that. Bad dynamic." Vi casually examined one of those manicured nails. "I'm sure you know what I mean."

Jack seethed inwardly. "How upset were you about Brice renting the guesthouse?"

She laughed. "You think I killed him? Not a bad idea. Too bad I didn't think of it."

"Violet, do I need to point out how serious this is? If you have any specific knowledge of a threat toward Brice, you need to tell me."

"No, I don't specifically know of one."

"He has no record. From all appearances he was law abiding, quiet, and a friend to your daughter." Sometimes it felt like Jack was the only one who ever stood up for his victims. "You know they were in grad school together?"

Vi grunted. "Huh. School."

"You don't sound happy about that."

"Nothing to be happy about. Yes, I knew they were in a couple of classes together. Pretty strange stuff, too, if you ask me."

"Strange how?"

"Specifically?" She arched two carefully penciled brows. "I didn't understand why Corie was dabbling in psychology, of all things, when she had a successful business to run. She's too young for a midlife crisis and I didn't understand why she was wasting her time. I figured there had to be a man involved."

Like mother, like daughter again? "Was there? Other than Brice?"

"I said 'a man,' honey. He wasn't interested in my daughter."

"Were there any other men Corie was involved with?"

Vi stared at him and Jack was afraid for a moment of what she was going to say. But all she said was, "Not that I'm aware of."

"Where were you after midnight last night, Violet?"

"At home."

"Can your husband corroborate that?"

"I was alone."

"I see."

"I talked to Corie about ten and then went to bed. I was in the office this morning by eight. Some of the other realtors could corroborate. I have a new listing I'm marketing and I had some work to do in the MLS. Anything else?"

"Do you own a gun?"

It turned out that she owned a Walther PPK/S. What a well-armed family. "Can I see one of your shoes, please?"

Vi stared at him for a moment. "Oh, come on. You're serious? I don't suppose you have a warrant?"

Her tone was confrontational but Jack smiled. "What I'd like to do, with your permission, is take an impression from one of your shoes so we can eliminate any you've left when you visited. Since you and Corie are close I'm sure you're here *quite* often."

Vi stared at him some more and then bent down, pulled up her right pant leg, and unzipped a high-heeled boot. "Fine. I didn't kill him." She glanced up at Jack. "Do you care if it's the right or the left?"

"Nope. Were you wearing these last night?"

Vi started to say something sarcastic, then stopped. "You know, as a matter of fact I was. I met a friend of mine for drinks at a bar in Cherry Creek. I was wearing almost this same outfit. Different shirt. So yes, I was wearing these boots. Knock yourself out."

"Wait here, please."

Jack was gone for about thirty minutes. When he came back, Vi was drumming her synthetic nails on the table and the look on her face was murderous. "Took you long enough. I almost opened this." She held up the wine. Then she snatched the boot from his hand and examined the bottom. "These are very expensive. You better not have damaged it doing whatever CSI voodoo you felt was so necessary."

"I appreciate your cooperation."

"I know your boss, you know." Vi got up to leave.

"Dani?"

"No, Paul."

"Ah." Even higher. "I'll tell him you said hello."

CHAPTER SEVEN

Vangie Perez's duplex was near the intersection of Broadway and I-25, not far south of downtown Denver. It was a small house with peeling white paint and a weedy front yard. There were bars on the windows and a minivan with Texas plates in the driveway. She wasn't trying to hide; the house and the utilities were all in her name.

The woman who answered the door for Jack was in her late twenties and Hispanic, with olive skin and dark hair. She wore a stretchy, low-cut, animal print top which displayed lots of cleavage, and a tight pencil skirt, along with heavy makeup and lots of jewelry. She carried maybe an extra fifteen pounds on her short frame, although her legs weren't bad. She offered him a cup of coffee, which he declined.

"This won't take long." Jack glanced at his phone. He might actually make his five o'clock radiation appointment, which was why he came to interview Vangie alone. He told Serena he wanted her to stay and supervise the crime scene. That way he could sneak off to the doctor without anyone knowing. What he really wanted was to bag the doctor, go to a baseball game, have a beer, and pretend everything was normal.

In the living room Vangie sat down on a faded, brown couch. The tight skirt hiked up her legs and she tugged at it nervously.

The small room felt crowded with the couch, a side chair, end table, and an assemble-your-own entertainment unit holding a flat screen TV.

Jack sat in the chair and pulled out a photo of Evan.

Vangie identified him and asked, "Is he in trouble?"

"It would be really helpful if you could remember the last time you saw him." Jack was all friendly and ingratiating.

Vangie was a bundle of nervous energy. Her eyes darted around the room and she shifted in her seat. She wore enough jewelry to set off a metal detector—rings on multiple fingers, bracelets, heavy gold earrings. Her fingers worried the beads on one of several long necklaces, turning the golden baubles around and around.

"I know about the shooting on his property. How awful." Vangie finally sat on her hands to force herself to be still. "Evan told me to cooperate. Whatever you need. He called me a little while ago to let me know you were on your way."

She looked up at Jack wide-eyed and breathless. Apparently she didn't realize how bad that sounded.

"I need you to be as specific as possible about when you saw Evan," Jack said.

Vangie nodded eagerly. "Oh, of course. Evan came over last night around midnight. He was here the whole night."

"Does he often spend the night here?"

"Sometimes." A smile played across Vangie's face which she tried—and failed—to suppress.

Jack's demeanor remained neutral but it was hard for him to reconcile how any sane man could have Corie and still want the woman sitting on the couch. "Is it possible he left sometime during the night, maybe when you were asleep?"

"No. We have an alarm. It chimes when a door is opened. I would have heard it."

Nice use of the word "we." "What time did Evan leave this morning?"

"He left around six fifteen. He had a golf game with Roger D'Ambrose." Vangie frowned, as if mad at herself for volunteering information.

"You were awake when he left then?"

Even with her dark olive skin he could see her flush. "Evan woke me before he left because he wanted to make love. He likes to do it in the morning. Well, he likes to do it all the time, but he really likes the morning. He says that—"

Jack interrupted her. "What time was that?"

"Five thirty." Vangie knew that for sure because she'd looked at the clock. But Evan always set clocks ten minutes fast so maybe it was really 5:20.

"Is it possible he'd gone out somewhere, maybe for a run or to work out?" Bad timing for Markham's habitual early morning jog.

"No."

"You sound sure."

"I told you because of the alarm." Vangie's fingers started worrying the beads again. "We were up late, if you know what I mean. But Evan doesn't need a lot of sleep. Usually only around four hours."

"And you saw Evan again after his golf game?"

"Uh-huh. He came back around nine. We had a lunch meeting scheduled and needed to prepare. Evan and I are teaming on a very important project. He came back here, took a shower, and then we got down to business."

I'll bet you did. "Wouldn't he have needed to go home and change?"

"He keeps clothes here because he's here a lot. And he really needed the shower, you know, after golf and after—well, you know." Vangie gave Jack a meaningful look. "We got kind of sweaty if you get my drift. A couple of times."

For once Jack wanted a suspect to *stop* talking. "If I have this right, Evan was gone for almost three hours this morning?"

"You make that sound bad. He was playing golf. Ask Mr. D'Ambrose if you don't believe me." She tossed her hair and sat up straight, further deforming the leopard print pattern straining across her chest.

"Did Evan get any phone calls this morning?"

"Of course. He gets lots of phone calls. Some of the calls were from you and his wife about the—about . . . you know." Her legs had been crossed and now she uncrossed them, stretching one high-heeled foot out in front of her. She tugged at the skirt again.

"Even after he found out about the murder, Evan stayed here working with you?" It was almost impossible for Jack to say "working" with a straight face.

"No, he left as soon as he found out. I was in the shower and he got in with me and told me he had to hurry because there was a problem at home."

An awful lot of showering going on. "That's what he said? You're sure of the exact words?"

She thought about it for a moment and the strain formed a vertical crease between her heavily made-up eyes. "I said, 'Is it your wife?' and he said, 'Yes, something's come up and I have to go right away.' I was nervous about the client lunch but he said I'd be fine."

"Did Evan say anything else about the problem at home?"

"No. And I did take the meeting on my own. Does that surprise you, Detective?"

"How'd it go?"

"Very well, thank you. Evan trusts me. He has confidence in me. I'm his partner." Vangie beamed.

Jack stood. "Do you mind if I use your bathroom?"

"It's through there." Vangie pointed toward the back of the house.

Jack saw three doors, all open. He walked through the first one which turned out to be a bedroom. The bed was unmade and leopard print ties of some kind were still attached to the bedposts. Fond of the animal prints, wasn't she? Handcuffs sat out on the nightstand along with a variety of massage oils and some sex toys Jack didn't recognize—and it wasn't like he'd led a sheltered life.

"Not that one, the one on the left," Vangie called out sharply.

"Sorry." In the bathroom Jack turned on the exhaust fan and rummaged quickly through the medicine cabinet. Found quite the collection of painkillers and sedatives—Oxycontin, Vicodin, Atavan, Xanax. An expensive men's electric razor was plugged in by the sink along with a bottle of Ted Lapidus aftershave. Apparently Evan liked to freshen up after his S&M sessions.

"Are we done?" Vangie asked when he returned. "I hate to be rude, but I have someplace I need to be."

Jack favored her with another bright and friendly smile. "I only have a couple more questions. I know you don't have to talk to me and I appreciate it. You said you and Evan were like partners. Did he promise you half of the business? Because that belongs to his wife, you know, community property and all that. Not to mention that she's worked building the business for years."

"Her? Work? Hah!" Vangie practically spat the words.

Jack raised his eyebrows. "You don't sound especially fond of Mrs. Markham."

"So?"

"So you'd think with Evan's money he could have found you a nicer place to live."

"He loves me. He tells me all the time. He said that we needed to keep a low profile. Only until—" Vangie stopped abruptly and sat on her hands again.

Jack continued the thought for her. "Until he leaves his wife? Or until he gets rid of her some other way? Because if he's capable of shooting one person, he's capable of more."

"He didn't do it! He couldn't. You've got it all wrong."

"What exactly do I have wrong here, Vangie? The two of you are in love; you have this little love nest to hang out in. Evan is pulling off an important deal that he's not telling his wife about so he can hide the profits from her. In fact, I'll bet that's where you come in. What'd you guys do? Set up a new company? Or maybe all of the profits are going to be funneled through *your* company, what is it, Perez Associates? And then you'll split it with him. Am I warm?"

"It's not like that." Vangie looked like she was going to cry. "You're just guessing."

"And from the look on your face I'm guessing well. So then what? Evan divorces his wife and the two of you live happily ever after?"

"He's going to tell her. I know he is because he told me not to lie." She said that like it was a good thing. "It's his wife's fault. She messed everything up. She invited that friend here and he started meddling."

"You're talking about Brice Shaughnessy?"

Vangie nodded. "Uh-huh."

"How did he mess everything up?"

"He's a busybody."

"You mean he was."

"What?"

"He *was* a busybody. He's dead, Vangie. At least show a little remorse."

"What do you mean?"

"You don't seem especially sorry he's dead."

"I hardly knew him."

"I wasn't aware you knew him at all." *This is too easy.*

"I don't. I didn't. You should go." Vangie was one of those women who didn't cry in a pretty way. Her face was getting red and mottled. "I don't think I should say anything else."

"You're right. Evan might get mad at you, like he got mad at Brice."

"No!"

"He was mad at Brice, I take it? That's what you don't want to tell me?"

She looked down and played with her necklace again. "He wasn't mad."

"Why was Brice a busybody, Vangie? Why were you and Evan mad at him?"

"I don't know."

Jack leaned back in the chair and watched her. "I think you do. Brice was sticking his nose in your business. Brice being on the scene made it harder for you two lovebirds. You had to find another place to meet." Jack made an expansive movement with his arm. "So here we are. No wonder this is such a dump. You were in a hurry."

"He saw us together." Vangie's voice was low. "He saw me. I rode over there once with Evan and I waited in the car while he went into the house. This man came walking up and he had that dog with him. He looked right at me in the car. That's it. I never even talked to him."

"And you were afraid he was going to tell Corie." Maybe one of them shot the messenger.

"I don't want to talk to you anymore. You need to leave."

"I only have one more question: Do you own a gun, Vangie?"

"Am I a suspect now?" Defiance crept back into her voice.

"I can get a search warrant. Really fast. I'll sit right here and wait. And I can check gun registrations from the car." Jack gestured toward the window with his thumb.

"I didn't say I had a gun."

"It is registered, isn't it? I mean, you wouldn't want to break the *law*. You need to tell me the truth like Evan said. He's a smart guy. You should listen to him."

"It's totally legal. I have a gun for protection, a nine millimeter. I live here by myself and you can see it's not the best neighborhood. Like you said, it's a dump."

"Can I see it?"

"I have to go into the bedroom. I keep it in my bedside drawer."

Right next to the dildos and cock rings. Talk about unsafe sex. "Show me where it is but don't touch it." Jack walked with her into the bedroom and she pointed to a drawer. "I don't see a gun, Vangie."

"What? No!" She looked over his shoulder. "No, that's not right. I haven't used it in a couple of weeks since we went to the firing range."

"We?"

"Me and Evan. He bought me the gun for protection and said I should learn how to use it. He's very careful."

"Vangie, we're going to go for a ride now."

"What? What did I do?"

"Or Plan B is you can tell me where to find the gun."

"I don't know!" She started opening the other drawers and throwing the contents out onto the floor.

Jack grabbed her arm and stopped her. "That's okay, we'll look for you. And we'll be very thorough."

"What are you doing? That hurts!" She started to cry in earnest.

"A nine millimeter, Vangie. Guess what kind of gun was used to shoot Mr. Shaughnessy? I'll give you a minute."

"But this gun hasn't been used! I swear. Someone must have stolen it. I haven't touched it in weeks."

"Has anyone else touched it?"

"What? Who? You mean Evan? No, he bought it for me. He was worried about me."

"What a great guy," Jack said.

"I want a lawyer," Vangie said.

CHAPTER EIGHT

One of the male radiation technicians Jack liked, Dom, retrieved him from the hospital waiting area. Jack changed into the ridiculous gown and got into position on the cold, metal table. He was close to being done with his treatment regimen for testicular cancer; only a few more sessions of being bombarded with highly excited ions. Dom tapped a few keys and laser pointers formed a cross on Jack's lower abdomen. *X marks the spot.* They protected his good, remaining testicle with a clamshell-looking thing that would have been right at home with the paraphernalia on Vangie Perez's nightstand. The first time Jack saw it he thought, *hell no*, but it didn't hurt. Much.

Clicking, whirring, and automatic positioning courtesy of the computerized lasers. The whole appointment generally took less than thirty minutes and tonight was no exception. They irradiated him from four different angles and then he was done, Dom cheerfully counting down the sessions. Two more to go. Word.

Jack appreciated his loose dress slacks. Radiation created what felt like a kind of sunburn down there, in the most private of places. And the nausea from the "treatments" had been getting worse. Dosage achieving critical mass or something. They'd given Jack some anti-nausea medication but it made him sleepy so he didn't take it. Usually he had at least two hours before the nausea hit in full force. Maybe somehow he'd manage to puke at home, but if not, he'd worked through being sick before and he could do it again.

His cell phone rang before he was halfway across the hospital parking lot. Serena said Roger D'Ambrose could see them at his office if they could get there by seven. Jack met her at headquarters so they could drive together.

"What's up with you and Mrs. Markham?" Serena asked when they were in the car.

"What do you mean?"

"I was wondering about the history between you two, since it came up in the interview."

"There is no history. We knew each other in school. It was a long time ago."

Serena pressed the point. "High school or college?"

"I guess you could say both because we wound up at the University of Colorado at the same time, but we weren't really close." Jack stopped himself from adding "by then."

"Were you close in high school?"

"Jesus, Serena, are you interrogating me?"

"I'm trying to get an idea of the relationship."

"There is no goddamn relationship." Jack drummed his fingers on the steering wheel. He wished he could confide in her. He wished he could say, 'My first case back and it's a fucking mess.' Or, 'I feel like high school just blew up and I'm in the middle of a goddamn soap opera.' He couldn't say any of those things but he didn't need to chew her head off either.

He was touchy about everything right now and Serena didn't know him well, didn't know the warning signs and when to back off like his former partner, Mike, did. By the time Jack came back from medical leave Delgado had been reassigned. Serena wasn't an inexperienced cop but she was new to homicide.

Jack blew out air. "Corie Farantino—Markham—was someone I went to high school with. I haven't seen her or had any contact with her in almost twenty years. She was never even my girlfriend or anything like that. If I thought there was a need to recuse myself I would. Any other questions?"

"No."

"You're sure? Because this is a onetime deal."

"Got it."

Jack glanced over at her. "Where'd you go to high school?"

"I moved here from St. Louis."

"I grew up here. If I recused myself every time I contacted an acquaintance, I'd never work."

They fell silent after that. It wasn't far from police headquarters at 13th and Cherokee to D'Ambrose's office, but between rush hour and the Rockies game, the downtown streets were gridlocked.

Denver was a young city and it had always been a boom and bust town. There was no continuity and very little history, just a jazzy, frenetic, youthful energy, as if the city didn't know which way to go.

Denver didn't have the charm of a Charleston or a San Francisco and it certainly wasn't laid out according to some master plan like Jack's favorite city, Paris. Denver was more like a neglected plant that got occasional jolts of fertilizer and had grown in leggy, disconnected spurts. That lack of planning resulted in horrible traffic and the city was forever playing catch-up when it came to road construction. A frustrating place to try and get from Point A to Point B.

But it was this patchwork, disjointed quality that appealed to Jack and gave Denver a sense of both mystery and of history being written before your eyes.

Serena broke the silence. "You know this guy, D'Ambrose?"

Jack gave a short laugh. "Serena, you've got to keep up with current events better. He's one of the richest men in the state. A developer. Involved in getting big new resorts off the ground."

"Oh great, another arrogant rich guy. I guess it makes sense Markham works with D'Ambrose since Markham's business is consulting for resorts."

"Getting them out of lawsuits."

"Getting them out of *losing* lawsuits."

"Apparently it pays well." Jack cursed at the driver of a pickup truck who cut them off.

"I wonder if he gets a percentage. You know, like if they're being sued for ten million dollars and he helps them win, he gets a cut."

"I wonder how he helps them win."

"You think he crosses lines?" Serena braced herself with one hand on the dash.

"Don't worry, my driving hasn't killed any of my partners. Yet. People like Evan always cross lines. It's a matter of which ones."

Before she could respond, the dispatcher's breathy voice spoke from the radio: "Base for Detective Owen?"

"Owen. Go ahead."

"I have an Officer Paulk on the line," the dispatcher said. "He says he has some information about a case you're interested in. Should I put him through?"

"Affirmative," Serena said, as Jack looked at her and arched an eyebrow.

"From the background check," Serena explained. "I learned that a woman named Jennifer Suarez filed assault charges against Evan a couple of years ago and then dropped them. Paulk took the report."

Officer Reggie Paulk's voice came out of the radio: "Hear you guys are interested in the Suarez assault. I pulled the file but I really didn't have to. Remember her clearly. What're you interested in?"

"Evan Markham's a person of interest in a homicide," Serena said.

There was a pause before Reggie's disembodied voice continued: "This one always kind of bugged me. Ms. Suarez was in pretty bad shape when she made the complaint. Knocked around pretty good. Claimed he tried to rape her. And then all of a sudden changed her mind."

"Too sudden?" Jack asked.

"Seemed that way to me."

"Thanks, buddy." Jack signed off. "I wonder what else we'll find excavating Markham's past."

He parked in a loading zone in front of D'Ambrose's building. The guard at the desk in the marble-tiled lobby made a phone call and then directed them to the top floor of the building. They emerged from the elevator into a carpeted hallway lined with dark wood paneling. Oil paintings, each individually lit with a brass light, were spaced at regular intervals, as if in an art gallery. Their feet made no sound in the dense carpet as they turned left and made their way to a door at the end of the elegant hallway.

"This is more like being in a museum than an office," Serena said. "I'll make sure I say 'please' and 'thank you' and wipe my feet before I go inside. Hold my little pinky out in the air and all that."

Jack laughed. "What have you got against rich people? They get killed like everybody else."

A tall, very attractive dark-haired woman in her twenties opened the heavy wooden office door. She wore a pale gray, elegantly cut suit that hugged her curves. The skirt stopped just above her knees, long enough to be respectable but short enough to show off long legs made longer by black leather stiletto pumps. "You must be the detectives who phoned." She extended her hand to each of them in turn. "I'm Aranda Sheffield, Roger D'Ambrose's assistant. Please, come in."

In the luxurious reception area, Aranda indicated a sumptuous leather couch along one wall. "Mr. D'Ambrose is finishing up on a conference call. He promises he'll be with you as quickly as possible. In the meantime, can I get you anything? Water? Coffee? We have an espresso machine."

"A double espresso would be great," Jack said.

"I'm good, thanks," Serena said.

Aranda nodded and walked over to the espresso machine which was located on an elaborately carved buffet along one wall. Jack watched her go. He leaned back against the couch and crossed his legs, his left ankle on his right knee, the very picture of relaxation. Serena, on the other hand, was perched on the edge of the couch as if she wanted to get up and bolt from the room.

"I'm sure none of them will bite," he said quietly.

Serena gave him a dry look. "Considering the way you drive, maybe you should stick to decaf."

Aranda came back with his espresso, bending a little lower than necessary to place the cup and saucer on the coffee table in front of him. There were two sugar cubes perched on the rim of the saucer and a sliver of lemon peel.

"Thanks." Jack didn't look up at her.

"Let me know if that's all right," Aranda said.

"I'm sure it's perfect."

"Are you sure I can't get you anything, Detective?"

Serena shook her head.

"Please let me know if there's anything else you need." Aranda looked at Jack and then walked to a large desk and slid gracefully into her chair, turning her attention to her computer.

Serena raised an eyebrow but her partner was intent on stirring his coffee. After a couple of minutes, Jack got up and walked around the spacious reception area with his espresso. He stopped in front of a large oil landscape. "That's a Bierstadt, right?"

Aranda stopped typing. "It is."

"Great landscape painter. I really like the way he used light, for example in these storm clouds."

"It sounds like you know something about art."

"A little." Jack shrugged. "I have to confess that I'm more of a fan of the modern southwest painters: Peter Hurd, the Taos Six, stuff like that. Bierstadt's a little romantic for my taste."

"I see." Aranda looked at him appraisingly.

"What about you?" he asked. "Which are your favorites?"

Before Aranda could reply, an office door opened and Roger D'Ambrose summoned them. "Detectives, sorry to keep you waiting. Please, come in."

The same lush carpet extended into D'Ambrose's private suite and was topped in several places by expensive-looking oriental carpets. Brass sculptures, mostly in western themes, adorned several wooden pedestals and the walls were lined with more paintings. The best thing about D'Ambrose's office, however, was the view. A wall of windows behind his desk faced west providing a jaw-dropping view of the sunset over the Rocky Mountains. It was hard not to stare.

D'Ambrose was around sixty with thinning red hair going gray. His hands were freckled and his skin had the weathered look of someone who spent a lot of time in the sun. Dressed casually in a Coogi sweater, khakis, and loafers, D'Ambrose appeared friendly and relaxed.

"I'm investigating a murder that occurred early this morning on the property of one of your business associates, Evan Markham," Jack said.

"This morning? How awful. I had no idea. Evan didn't mention anything about it to me when I saw him."

"What time was that?"

"Too early this morning. Evan has a tendency to get up at the crack of dawn. Let's see." He consulted his Blackberry. "We had a six thirty tee time."

"Where did you play?" Jack asked.

"Cherrybrook. I'm a member," D'Ambrose said.

"Nice. What time did you finish up?"

"Each of us had meetings to get to so we only played nine holes. We finished up around eight thirty or quarter to nine. I know I was back in my car by nine."

"Did Evan play the entire time with you?"

"Yes. We usually talk some business while we play and this morning was no exception."

"And he met you there at six thirty?" Jack asked. "Is it possible it was later?"

"Well, he was a few minutes late, but if my wife looked like his, I'd find reasons to be late, too," D'Ambrose said.

"I hear she can be kind of wild," Jack said.

"I don't know where you get your information, Detective, but I've never seen Corie Markham be anything but a perfect lady." He almost seemed offended.

"Have you seen Evan since this morning?"

"No. And it's unusual not to talk to him once or twice a day, but considering what you've told me I understand why."

"Can you tell me if you know a woman named Jennifer Suarez? Her name came up in the course of the investigation and we're attempting to locate her."

D'Ambrose seemed to freeze for a moment before he answered. "She was Evan's assistant for a while. Has something happened to her?"

"Was?" Jack asked.

"It's been a couple of years since Jennifer worked for Evan."

"What can you tell me about her?" Jack asked.

"Not much. She was Evan's assistant, not mine. I'm not sure why he became dissatisfied. He told me he had to let her go and I had no reason to question him about how he runs his own business."

"Do you know how we could get in touch with her?"

"I don't but Aranda might."

Jack closed his notebook. "I appreciate you seeing us so quickly."

When they emerged from D'Ambrose's office, Aranda got up and closed his door behind them with a solid thunk. "Will there be anything else?"

"As a matter of fact, yes," Jack said.

Aranda tilted her head to the side curiously and waited.

"We're trying to locate a former assistant of Evan Markham's, Jennifer Suarez. Roger said you could help us with that."

As with D'Ambrose, there was a small hesitation before she answered. "Of course." Aranda sat down and pulled up some information on her computer screen, then wrote on a piece of paper which she handed to Jack.

"Who's this?"

"A private detective." She bit her plump lower lip for a moment. "Roger is very particular about who he works with."

"Uh-huh." Jack watched her.

"He has his business associates checked out."

"By this guy."

"Yes."

"And would he also be able to help me locate Jennifer?"

"I believe so. After she—after Evan fired her I called and asked her to lunch, you know, to be friendly. She declined but assured me she was doing well. Commented that she'd simply had a personality clash with Evan."

"You usually keep in touch with the fired employees of your business associates?" Aranda didn't respond right away and Jack persisted. "Why were you worried about her?"

Aranda thought about it some more and decided to answer. "One night I was out to dinner with Roger and Evan. He had quite a bit to drink. Well, we all did. Anyway, at one point Jennifer's name came up and Evan said horrible things. Just went off. Calling her names—you know the kind of things some men say about women."

"I do," Jack said quietly. "It's wrong."

"It was vile. Roger was furious. Told Evan that he better stop, and if he ever talked about a woman that way again, they'd never do another deal together. That shut him up."

"But that wasn't the end of it?" Serena asked.

"Roger is a really nice man. He apologized profusely to me for Evan's behavior, even though it wasn't his fault. I know that no one believes a man can be rich and successful and also ethical, but he is. It bothered him, the way Evan acted and Jennifer suddenly disappearing, so he had it checked out." She nodded toward the piece of paper. "The investigator can tell you a lot more than I can."

"You've been very helpful." Jack folded the paper and put it in his pocket.

She got up from her desk again to walk them out. As she opened the door to the hallway she turned to Jack. "If you have any follow-up questions or we can help in any way, please let me know." Aranda extended a slim hand and Serena saw a flash of white as she smoothly handed him her card.

CHAPTER NINE

Vangie was on the phone. And she was hysterical. Evan looked at Corie. They'd finally been allowed back inside their house and Corie sat listlessly at the kitchen counter. Vi, martini in hand, was trying to coax her to eat something. Evan took his glass of Bordeaux and walked outside onto the front porch.

"Evan, it was awful. They treated me like a criminal. They want to search my place." Vangie sobbed so hard she choked. "They think I did it! Me."

"Stu called you, right?"

"Yes, but—"

He cut her off. "I told you I'll take care of it. You can't keep calling me."

"I need someone to talk to. I don't know anyone else here. Please come over. Please."

"We've been through this." On the porch Evan paced. Corie had arranged the outdoor furniture in groups meant to facilitate conversation. It struck him now as charming and innocent.

"We haven't been through this." Vangie's voice grew shrill. "I did my part. When are you telling your wife?"

He glanced through the front windows into the house. "Christ. Her friend was just murdered. What the hell is wrong with you?"

59

"What's wrong with me? I was dragged to a police station."

"As long as you didn't say anything, it will be fine."

"It would be your own fault if I did. That detective was obnoxious."

"You're not making any sense." Evan was sure no one could hear him but he lowered his voice anyway. "Look, I have to go. Sit tight tonight. Relax. Take one of the pills I left you."

Vangie's voice shrieked out of the phone. "I didn't tell the police anything. But I could tell them lots."

"Vangie, I know you're upset and you don't mean to say something you'll regret. I said I'll take of care of you and I will. Tonight, I need you to be a good girl."

"I'm sick of being a good girl. I'll let you go so you can go back and comfort your wife. I have to call the detective anyway."

And she hung up on him. The slut actually hung up. Evan stared at the phone in disbelief, then quickly placed a call to his lawyer, Stu Graber. "Meet me at Vangie's." Evan would have texted but Stu was old school.

"Now?"

"Yes, now." Evan's voice was a snarl. "How fast can you get there?"

"Ten minutes."

"Make it five." Evan didn't wait for an answer. Stu worked for him. So did Vangie. They all worked for him. So why did he have to do everything himself? He composed his features before he went inside to look for his wife. Corie and Vi were sitting on the deck off of the kitchen. *Shit.* They were outside. Could they hear him? Had he used Vangie's name?

Corie looked up as he opened the sliding glass door from the kitchen. She was still wearing the same t-shirt and jeans that she'd had on all day and she looked very pale.

"Sorry about that." Evan walked over to his wife and put his hands on her shoulders.

"Everything all right?" Vi took a healthy sip from a freshened martini.

He saw her cigarette. That was why they moved outside. "My lawyer. I'm afraid I have to go out for a little while." Corie stared off into space in the general direction of the deck railing. Evan massaged her shoulders.

"Now? I don't understand why you have to deal with this tonight." Vi's eyes flicked quickly to Evan's face and she stubbed her cigarette out.

"The police don't take the evening off, Violet. Everything is fine. I have to meet briefly with Stu and I'd rather not upset Corie any more than necessary." Evan buried his hands in Corie's long hair and lifted it off of her neck.

His wife looked up at him. "Tell Stu to come here. It's not as if anything could make this day worse."

"I think it's better all around if I meet him at his office." Evan kept his hands in her hair.

"With the life that man led it's no surprise he's dead," Vi said. "They better not hound us. I won't hear of it."

"We're all suspects, mother."

"Corie." Evan's fingertips brushed her neck.

"No. It's true. We are. It's how this works." Subtly, Corie pulled away from Evan's touch and leaned towards her mother. "I don't mind talking to them. Brice was my friend."

"I'm not going to let the police run me ragged because they're incompetent. I know people."

The disgust in Corie's voice was palpable. "Oh, please. You're going to call Nancy? You need her to protect you?" Her mother was friends with the mayor, Nancy Thorne, as well as assorted congressmen and other Colorado luminaries. "Did you kill him, Mom?"

Vi's voice squeaked. "How dare you."

"Then I don't understand what the big fucking deal is about talking to the police for five fucking minutes."

"You are so naïve." Vi made a dismissive motion with a manicured hand.

"That's your stock answer for everything. It's such bullshit."

"Violet." Evan's voice cut through their squabble. "Corie's had an extremely hard day." Apparently she'd forgotten their earlier conversation in the driveway. "I think it's best if we all cooperate with the police. The faster they resolve this the faster we can all move on with our lives."

Corie looked up at him. "How long will you be gone?"

"I hope not long." He leaned down and kissed her and Corie let him. "You two really should be nicer to each other." That last comment was directed at Vi, who had trouble holding his gaze.

He heard Corie mutter, "In what universe," as he retreated back through the kitchen door.

Evan parked his silver Mercedes a couple of blocks down from Vangie's after taking note of the unmarked car across the street from her house. He'd watched for a tail on the way there but hadn't spotted one. Still, best to be careful. Evan was grateful for the alleys that ran behind the houses in these older Denver neighborhoods. He made his way to her back door and let himself in using his key. The moment she saw him Vangie let out a squeal of delight, ran to him, and threw her arms around his neck.

"I knew you'd come. Oh Evan!"

He pushed her away. "You better not have made a phone call. Where's Stu?"

"He's not here. Why would he be?"

Evan strode to the bathroom, shook out a pill into the palm of his hand, and returned to the kitchen. A wineglass filled with pink liquid sat on the counter. Probably from a box. Evan grimaced and handed the glass to Vangie along with the pill. "Take this." Evan clenched his teeth. When exactly had he lost control?

"I don't want a pill. I want you."

Evan stared at Vangie. Her face was blotchy from crying and her makeup had run. He took in the tacky jewelry, the animal print blouse, and long, two-tone acrylic nails painted in a reverse French manicure with the darker strip at the tips—the style, apparently, if you were a trashy minimum-wage slave or a hooker. He saw her for what she was: a tasteless, stupid, greedy woman. What the hell was he thinking? Evan grabbed her by the chin. "Do I need to force you? I'll shove it down your throat if I have to."

"What's wrong with you?" She yanked her head away.

"You asked for my help. If you don't want it, I'm happy to leave."

"I don't want a pill. Besides, I've been drinking wine."

"That Kool-Aid you like isn't even real wine. You're going to take the pill. You're going to tell me who you called. Then you're going to wash your face and get ready for bed."

Someone rapped on the front door and Vangie's eyes grew wide. "Who is that?"

"Your lawyer. Do you want him to see you like this?"

Stu knocked again.

"Aren't you going to let him in?" Vangie asked.

"That depends. Are you going to cooperate? Or are you going to get your own lawyer? They're very expensive, you know."

She put the small round tablet in her mouth and followed with a healthy swig from the wineglass. She made a face but she swallowed.

"Good girl. Now open the door."

"Hello, Vangie." Stu walked into the living room and closed the door quickly behind him. "Got some surveillance going on out there."

Vangie stared at Evan wide-eyed. "What? What does that mean?"

"Go get ready for bed." Evan waited until Vangie had disappeared into the bathroom and then turned on Stu. "Ten minutes? You better not fucking bill me for the last hour."

"What couldn't wait?"

"I need some damage control." He prowled the small space and wound up next to a bar set up on one side of the dining area. Evan poured two fingers of Scotch into a glass, then sat down on the couch and nodded toward the chair Jack had occupied a few hours earlier. "Have a seat. Fill me in. What do they know so far?"

Stu remained standing. "The detectives want to test her gun. She says she doesn't know where it is. They're getting a warrant. It shouldn't take long and they'll be wanting to search in the morning."

Evan's pale blue eyes looked thoughtful. "Any reason not to let them do that?" He took a swallow of his drink.

"Depends what outcome you have in mind." They heard a toilet flush and the bathroom door opened. Stu cut his eyes toward Vangie. "Christ." He turned away and pretended to be studying a print on the wall.

Vangie was wearing a short, deep red Frederick's of Hollywood number that gaped open in the front to reveal a thong and push up bra. The bra was a black-and-white tiger print, naturally. She sat down next to Evan on the couch and snuggled up against him. "I got ready for bed like you asked me to."

Evan didn't touch her. "I'll come tuck you in when we're done."

"No," Vangie pouted. "I want to stay. This concerns me."

Evan slammed his glass on the coffee table and pulled her up onto her feet. "You need to let me handle this."

"Oh Evan, I'm so glad you're here."

Vangie tried to kiss him but Evan held her at arm's length. "Then show me you're glad and do what I asked."

"You gave me that pill so I don't know how long I'll be awake."

"I'll be right in."

She made a high-pitched whiny sound but left.

Evan watched her walk away, the skimpy robe not quite covering her fleshy butt cheeks. He'd consider fixing those if he wasn't done with her. He turned back to Stu. "It's safe. You can turn around." Evan sat back down on the couch, put his head back, and closed his eyes for a moment. When he looked up again Stu was still standing by the wall. "Sit down for Christ's sake. You're making me nervous."

"If it's all right with you I'll stand. I don't plan on staying long anyway."

"Actually, you're staying all night." Evan took another sip of his drink.

"What? No."

"I need you to keep an eye on her. If you don't want to do it, then sub it out to someone you trust. But I'm not leaving her on her own."

"Since when am I a babysitter?"

"Your bill rate's higher than any other fucking babysitter I know of. Especially when I pay you overtime."

"Shit." Stu pulled out his cell phone and made a call.

"Where's the gun?" Evan asked, after Stu finished making arrangements.

"Damned if I know." Stu looked toward the bedroom and lowered his voice. "What if she did it?"

"Two birds with one stone."

Stu looked back at Evan and hesitated for a moment. "What if you did it?"

"I didn't."

"Then we've got nothing to hide," Stu said.

Evan's index finger absentmindedly tapped against the rim of the glass. He repeated what he'd said to his mother-in-law earlier: "I think we should cooperate with the police."

"You're sure?"

"See what else you can find out. You have discovery, right? You'll find out what they have on her. I think that'll be very helpful." Evan stood. "I need to get back home. I didn't want to come out in the first place. You got this?"

"Aren't you going to tuck her in?"

"I don't pay for sarcasm."

"She's not going to come after me, is she?"

The thought of Vangie throwing herself at Stu made Evan smile. "She's very obedient. And I've taught her to do some interesting things."

"No thanks."

"Don't worry. I gave her something to help her sleep. Cops won't think it's strange she's meeting with her lawyer but I'm leaving out the back, same way I came in. Screen her calls and keep her away from a computer. Let me know as soon as they show up in the morning."

CHAPTER TEN

Corie didn't need to fake the exhaustion she used as an excuse to leave her mother and retreat to the master bedroom. Vi volunteered to spend the night in one of their guest rooms, allegedly to comfort Corie but really because she was too drunk to drive. Whatever. Vi and Evan could console each other or kill each other. The second option was infinitely preferable.

Corie rolled onto her side, punched one of the pillows into a more desirable shape, and tried to get comfortable. She badly wanted a drink herself, but last night her descent into oblivion had proved literally fatal. Tonight she'd keep her wits about her. She even had the windows open so she could hear anything that happened on the property. Too little, too late.

Now that she was lying down she wasn't sleepy at all. Evan's hands on her shoulders and in her hair earlier had woken up a feeling she'd hoped was long buried. She groaned, rolled onto her back again, and stretched her leg to the side seeking a cool stretch of sheet.

Dark desire. A ready kiss. Her body, so eager, arching towards him only to be told to lie still. "Discipline," Evan had said, "is the way to ecstasy." Love, in their case, was all about denial. Her denial.

In the beginning it felt good to let Evan take charge. It was exciting. They'd play sexual mind games. He'd give her instructions, rules to follow while she went about her day. Out in public, at work or around other people, there were things he would say to her, code phrases that sounded perfectly normal to everyone else but had a secret, sordid meaning. She had to obey him. Sit up straight. Don't cross your legs. Have three glasses of wine with dinner. Have nothing to drink. Don't wear underwear. Don't move. Say please. It turned her on. Until it didn't.

When the sex stopped being exciting it started making her sick. Literally. It was easy to hide the vomiting because Evan left her right after. From the very beginning he slept alone. So he wouldn't disturb her, he said. He didn't sleep well and he got up so early.

There was nothing wrong with her. Everyone experimented, didn't they? That's why she started taking the psychology courses, to figure herself out. Ironically, it was Evan who hit the nail on the head. "I was your walk on the wild side," he said one night, "but it's not really who you are."

Vivid images of Brice's body flashed through her mind like a demonic slide show. Had it hurt? He must have been so scared. The killer must have woken him because he'd gotten out of bed. *Had Brice's secret killed him?* Corie stared at the ceiling seeking answers. She hadn't told Jack. She knew she looked guilty, but it was because she was a really bad liar and she didn't know what else to do. Corie needed someone to help her and she had no one.

She almost wished Jack had arrested her. At least that would have gotten her away from Evan. It wasn't fair. She'd finally gotten up the courage to ask him for a divorce and then this had to happen. *Christ, I'm selfish.* But it was true. Evan might use the murder as an excuse to stay together. *Unless he did it.* The thought made her tremble—what if she'd had a killer's hands on her body? A killer's hands making her come? A killer making her beg?

A choking sob escaped but Corie was sick of crying. She rolled restlessly back onto her other side, seeking another cool spot in the bed. Although sleep was out of the question.

The bedroom door opened quietly. Corie saw a shadow play on the wall before she closed her eyes. With effort she steadied her breathing. Surely he would be able to tell that her heart was pounding.

"Corie?"

"Mm." Corie hugged a pillow and rubbed at her eyes; a sleep pantomime.

Evan sat down on the edge of the bed. An odd aroma followed him, a mildly sweet, floral smell. Not his usual cologne. Her mother's perfume maybe?

"I'm sorry to wake you." He put his hand on her shoulder and started rubbing her upper arm.

Oh God. Corie subtly rolled onto her back and pulled her arm away, pretending to stretch. She was surprised when he lay down on the bed next to her. Evan? Cuddling? Corie turned her head and looked at him curiously, their faces inches apart now.

"I thought you might be having a rough time. I'm sorry I had to leave earlier."

"'S okay." Corie slurred her words and forced her eyes to drift closed again. Maybe he would think she took another sleeping pill. That would be best.

His hand moved down her arm and then sideways until it rested on her stomach. She focused on her breathing, pretended to sleep, pretended that all her husband wanted was to offer a few moments of comfort.

She knew better. Eventually his hand moved lower and found the hem of the long t-shirt she slept in. Why couldn't she wear pajamas? Or a chastity belt for that matter? Why couldn't she have her period? Would any of that stop him? His trespassing hand quickly found its target.

Was she wet? Her thoughts about their former sex life still had the power to arouse as well as repulse her. He spread the soft lips he found uncovered between her legs with his fingers, and it took self-control for Corie not to gasp when he found exactly the right spot and pressed gently but firmly with his fingertip.

His continued touching her expertly, knowing from long experience what got her off. Even with her eyes closed she felt him watching her. When she didn't spread her legs for him he crawled under the covers and put one of his clothed legs over her naked one, moving her thigh to the side. His fingers probed deeper, dipping into her for moisture before resuming their agonizing caress.

In her mind Corie pictured the bookcases along the wall. Visualized the books lined up, tried to read the titles on the spines. She wanted to go home. What the hell did that mean? *Tell him to stop.* Maybe there was something wrong with her after all. Could she really be brought to orgasm against her will?

The ridiculous thought floated through her mind that this gave her new sympathy for men, the way they would have seemingly spontaneous erections. What did men do to keep themselves from premature ejaculation? *Think about root canals. Math. Calculus. Quadratic equations. Her mother.* Nothing worked.

She thought of her horse but that innocent image almost destroyed her fragile self-control. *Don't cry. He won't understand.* Or maybe he'll think it's because of Brice. That might work. A hot tear escaped and rolled down her cheek into her hair, but his disembodied hand didn't stop.

She bit her lip when she came to prevent herself from crying out. He still knew. Evan stayed with her barely a minute longer, his index finger pressed into that soft, treacherous mound, exerting steady pressure the way he knew she liked. Quite the technician, wasn't he? And all done without a word. In spite of her resolve, after he left she wept in earnest.

What else was Evan going to want?

CHAPTER ELEVEN

Evan's plan backfired. The orgasm didn't sedate Corie, it disgusted her. Without realizing she'd made it, Corie acted on her decision. She glanced at her phone as she made the call just after six. He said "Hello" instead of "Fariel" the way she noticed he did yesterday. He sounded sleepy.

"Jack?" Well that was stupid. Of course it was Jack. "It's Corie. Markham." Jesus, was she thirteen? "I'm sorry to call you so early."

"Corie?" Jack sounded confused for a moment. "Corie. What's wrong?"

All night she'd rehearsed what she would say to him. In the light of morning, it all seemed melodramatic and unreal and she felt stupid. "I have some things to tell you."

"Where are you?"

"In my car. I'm going to the barn where I keep my horse. Can you meet me there?"

He didn't answer right away.

"I know it's a lot to ask and I know it's early. I didn't know any other way to get to talk to you." Now she really did sound dramatic. But it was true.

"Are you all right? Did something happen?"

"No. I'm fine. I just—" *Just what?* "Can you meet me? Please?"

"Sure. What's the address?"

She told him and he promised to be there as soon as he could. He really did sound sleepy which made her smile for some reason. She pictured him turning to someone in bed next to him, telling her that he had to leave. She almost wanted to say, "Tell your wife I'm sorry." He probably had a girlfriend or was married; a man as good looking as Jack, why wouldn't he be?

When a car pulled up she knew it was him without turning around. She was outside by then in the sunshine, brushing her gelding, Sierra, to keep her hands busy. She'd practiced on the horse, not quite sure why she was so afraid to talk to Jack. Her hands were shaking and brushing the horse soothed her; Sierra was warm, calm, innocent. She heard the metallic thunk as Jack closed his car door and felt him approaching. What did he see? What did he think? Corie kept her hands on the horse for an extra few seconds, feeling Sierra's warmth and breathing in his scent before turning to face the detective.

What she'd forgotten was Jack was afraid of horses. He stopped a safe distance away and Corie laughed. Couldn't help herself. Tough homicide detective afraid of horses. "Do people know your secret? I would say he's more afraid of you than you are of him but I don't think that's true."

"Nice. You call me out here at the crack of dawn and then you laugh at me?"

"I'm sorry."

Jack was wearing a suit, dark blue today, with a light blue shirt and a tie. His dark hair was still wet. "I've never been fond of anything big enough to eat me."

"Horses aren't carnivores."

"Sure. That's what you think." The last—and only—time he'd been on a horse had been with Corie and he'd almost died. Or at least that was how he remembered it.

She put the brush she was holding into a bucket and started to untie the rope holding Sierra to a railing.

Jack backed up another step. "What are you doing?"

"I'm going to put him back inside. You're in no danger." Corie patted Sierra's neck and walked the horse into the barn, pleased with the relaxed and easy way he moved. All of that muscle and strength and yet so gentle. What was wrong with a man who didn't love horses?

They talked in Jack's car.

"Evan doesn't usually get angry. But when he came over to Brice's for the drink, oh, he was mad. It was my fault. I was ready to end it." Corie didn't elaborate on what "it" meant. Jack could probably figure that out on his own. "I wanted moral support. Now, of course, I feel like we ambushed him. 'Hey Evan, come on over for a drink,' and then we pulled the rug out from under him. I'm not happy with—" She hesitated and bit the inside of her lip. "With my choice. I shouldn't have put Brice in the middle and I shouldn't have surprised Evan in front of someone else."

She forced herself to look at Jack, into those striking hazel eyes he had. She'd forgotten about those eyes. He was watching her with a neutral expression like a good detective.

"Brice asked me if I'd really tried to talk to Evan. He didn't realize how impossible that was. It's hard to explain. Evan's like Dr. Jekyll and Mr. Hyde. He can be so charming and then just . . . go away." *Not interesting, Corie. He's not your freaking marriage counselor.* Her arms broke out in goose bumps and she fiddled with one of the air conditioning vents.

She struggled to continue. "I don't know why Brice was willing to put himself in the middle like that. I wanted Brice there because I was afraid."

"Afraid?"

"Not like that."

The barest hint of frown passed quickly across Jack's forehead before he composed his features again. "Corie, why did you call me?"

She realized she wanted him to hold her. It would be so nice for someone to hold her without expectations, simply because they liked her. She immediately dismissed the thought as weak and pathetic. "It was strange. It was so strange that I wondered if I'd heard him right."

"Who?"

"Evan. I didn't say anything yesterday because I felt guilty and because I convinced myself it couldn't be connected. But I thought about it—in fact I thought about it all night—and I decided to tell you and let you decide. When Evan came over to the guesthouse, he quickly realized it was a setup. His face was awful. He looked at me and—okay, Christ, you don't give a shit about my feelings for Evan."

"It's all right. Tell me in your own words."

His voice was gentle and Corie snuck another look at him. "What I didn't tell you yesterday was that Evan did threaten Brice. He turned on his heel to leave the instant he realized what we were up to but Brice tried to stop him. Brice followed him to the door and he put his hand on Evan's arm. It was as if being touched set Evan off, like a switch had been flipped.

"Evan shoved Brice really hard, so hard that Brice slammed into the wall. A picture fell. And then Evan put his finger in Brice's face and said, 'You need to stop sticking your nose into my business. You don't know what you saw.'"

"What does that mean?"

"I don't know."

"Did you ask?"

"No. Because when we got home I told Evan I wanted a divorce. His outburst was enabling. I was all stoked on adrenaline or something. He'd acted like an animal so I felt justified." She stopped and tried to breathe. "I can tell you that Brice looked terrified. But instead of staying and talking to him I followed Evan. I wanted to get it over with. I didn't realize it was the last time I'd see Brice alive."

"Did Evan go back out and talk to Brice again?"

"Not that I know of." She met Jack's eyes with a level gaze. "I heard Evan leave but then I took the sleeping pill. I am, unfortunately, an unreliable witness. I wish I'd seen something. I wish I'd gone back out to talk to Brice. You have no idea how I wish I had."

"Did Evan hurt you?" Jack asked.

"No." *Not that night, anyway.* Corie hugged herself and looked out the window toward the stable. Several women were outside saddling their horses. Oh to ride fast and never come back. Maybe fall on her head and have amnesia. Bliss.

"You needed to tell me this yesterday."

"I know."

"What else haven't you told me?"

Corie looked at him, a little surprised. "It's probably not related."

Jack laughed. It was short, bitter, knowing. "My favorite words in an interview."

"I didn't tell you yet because I feel disloyal."

"For what?"

"Brice's sister was murdered."

"What? When?"

"Fifteen years ago. He made me swear not to tell anyone. And I didn't. Before you ask, Evan doesn't know. How awful that Brice's sister was killed that way and now he's dead. It's the first thing I thought of."

"But not the first thing you told me."

There was a forced stillness about Jack. But she could feel the tension, the anger, like an unseen wave. It hit her in the stomach and Corie started to shake. "I had to think about it. I'm sorry. I was convinced I was being dramatic and imagining connections where there were none."

"You need to let me decide that." Jack had been taking notes, and he gripped his pen so tightly the knuckles on his left hand were white. "How drunk were you?"

"What?"

"The night before the murder, how much did you have to drink?"

She gaped at him. "You think I'm making all this up?"

"Answer the question, please."

"I had a few glasses of wine."

"Exactly how many is 'a few?' And there was nothing else? No vodka? No drugs other than the Ambien?"

"Three glasses of white wine. Over about three hours. I wish it had been more. Do you think I'm lying?"

"It's a wonder you remember anything after three glasses of wine and a sleeping pill."

Corie felt suddenly foolish. She looked down at her hands and fiddled with her engagement ring, turning it around and around. What else had she expected? Jack was a detective. And she was an idiot. They weren't in high school anymore and this wasn't a game.

"Corie." Jack softened his voice. "I'm not accusing you of anything. I think it's easy to get confused."

"I wish I was confused. I've heard Ambien gives some people amnesia. I wish it worked that way on me." No amount of wine or Ambien would ever erase the look on Evan's face. Or the sight of Brice on the guesthouse floor. Or the memory of finding Jack with Hennessy, for that matter.

"Who visited Brice?"

"I don't know."

"You didn't seem surprised."

"I wasn't." Corie looked up at him. "Why should it be a surprise that Brice had a personal life?"

"Do you know where Evan went that night?"

"No. Do you?" She asked it as a reflex, but something in Jack's reaction made the bottom drop out of her stomach.

He turned in his seat, reached into the back for a manila folder, and pulled out a picture. "Do you know this woman?"

"Why do you have a picture of her?" Corie's voice rose in scorn.

"So you do know her."

"Sure, it's Vangie Perez. She's a business associate." It took restraint for Corie not to make quote marks with her hands. What on earth did that crazy, desperate slut have to do with this? "She does the same kind of consulting as Evan. We'd see her all the time at conferences and stuff. She's married and lives in Dallas."

"When was the last time you saw her?" Jack's fingertips played at the edges of the photo.

"A couple of years ago. We spent the weekend at their house. Why?" She and Evan made fun of Vangie. They read Vangie's emails together and laughed at them. Or, they used to.

"So you and Vangie are pretty close?"

"No. I don't know her well and, to be honest, I never thought she liked me."

"What's her husband's name?"

"Oh Christ, Jack, how long are you going to drag this out? I don't remember her damned husband's name."

"They're way more than business associates, Corie. They're lovers. We're sure." When he met her eyes he looked sad. "Vangie is Evan's alibi. They were together when Brice was killed."

Corie pressed her fist to her mouth, turned away, and looked out the passenger window. Evan ridiculed her. Vangie the stalker. But why the fuck else would Jack have her picture?

"Didn't you wonder where Evan went that night?"

And the World's Stupidest Woman Award goes to . . .

It struck Corie that on some level she'd known all along. It had to be when she stopped having sex with Evan, not before. *Oh God, please not before.*

"How long?" Corie finally managed.

"Don't know."

"Really? Because you seem to know everything. This is a test, right? You see how I react. I'm an experiment, like bacteria on a Petri dish you're watching through a microscope."

"There was no good way to tell you."

And Jack, of all people, got to tell her. Corie was sure she'd appreciate the irony. Someday. In about a hundred years.

"When do you think it started?" Jack asked.

She wouldn't speculate. Not with Jack. Surely sex with Evan, or the lack thereof, had nothing to do with Brice's murder.

But he persisted. "Did you know she moved here?"

"What? When?" Corie's voice rose.

"I don't know the time frame."

"Time frame? Fucking 'time frame?' Is that all you can say?" Somewhere in the back of her mind Corie realized it was a cop game. If she was pissed off at Evan she'd say things she shouldn't. Well, it worked. "I suppose you want to hear what Evan likes."

Jack tossed the folder onto the backseat again. "Do you think this is fun for me?"

"Oh no, you opened this door. Let's walk through it, shall we? How much detail would you like? Evan likes to tie women up. He likes S&M, blindfolds, games, whips, nipple clamps, hoods, you name it. Come on, Jack, don't look so shocked. You're a cop. You know all about this shit. Even *I* used to think it was fun. Does that surprise you?" Her voice caught, broke. "But then I didn't. So here we are."

On a sharp exhale of breath he said her name.

"I wanted it, Jack. I did. I wanted to experiment. I wanted to try those things. And I got everything I ever wanted in return. I got the big fancy house and a horse and jewelry." She held up the hand with the wedding ring and enormous emerald-cut diamond. "Evan gave me everything. I have it made. I'll bet that's what you were thinking when you drove up and saw where I lived. Wasn't it?"

"Corie, stop."

"I hope this clears everything up for you." She stared at him, breathing hard, and slowly the need to hurt Jack drained away. Anger was preferable to the sickness that followed.

"I'm worried about you."

"No. You don't get to be nice to me. You don't get to be the hero. Can I go now?" she said, forgetting she was the one who'd asked to see Jack. At least her husband wasn't a murderer. Small blessings.

Jack frowned at her with concern and moved his right hand as if he might touch her. Corie instinctively flinched and leaned away from him. Her hand groped for the door handle. She was shaking so badly she was surprised she could still speak intelligibly. "You know, I never wanted to see you again, Jack."

"I know."

"Whatever other sick shit is going on in my life, Brice didn't deserve to die. If I have to reveal all of my most sordid secrets in order to get at the truth, I'll do it. And then I mean it. I never do want to see you again."

He let her out of the car and she walked as fast as she could on unsteady legs back into the barn, where she was promptly sick all over the fresh, green-smelling hay.

CHAPTER TWELVE

When Evan came back from his run Corie's car was gone. He went to the kitchen for coffee and spotted Vi sitting outside on the deck reading the paper. She was wrapped in a fuchsia silk robe with the sash tied tightly around her waist. When he joined her she quickly stubbed out her cigarette, and he could see a bright pink stain on the end of it from the lipstick she wore even at this hour of the morning.

"Evan. How are you holding up? Did you sleep?"

"Enough." Evan leaned down and barely grazed her cheek with the idea of a kiss. He nodded toward the newspaper on the table. "Are we one of the headlines?"

Vi handed it to him and they sat in silence for a few minutes while he read.

Evan sighed, folded the paper, and slapped it back onto the table. "Where's Corie off to this morning? Not more interviews with the police, I hope."

"She left a note. She went to see her horse."

Evan ignored Vi's mocking tone. "I'm glad. Riding usually makes Corie feel better."

"Yes." Vi hesitated. "It's none of my concern, of course, and stop me if I'm overstepping my boundaries, but I noticed you slept in the guest room."

As if there was a way to keep Vi inside a boundary. "It was an unexpected surprise that you stayed here last night."

"I'm never sure what to do where Corie is concerned, as you pointed out so succinctly yesterday."

Evan refused to let her bait him. Instead he smiled. "I'm certain it meant something to Corie to have you here."

"That's very sweet." Vi, unable to rile him, seemed at a loss. She pressed her thin fuchsia lips together.

The doorbell rang and it was a relief to excuse himself. Evan signed for a FedEx package, curious because he wasn't expecting anything. Downstairs in his office he sliced one end open with a silver letter opener. A large blue binder slid out filled with plastic sleeves, the kind you'd use for photographs. Only this scrapbook contained newspaper clippings. Old articles from fifteen years ago from the *Charlotte Observer* about the murder of an aspiring young actress named Monique Lawson. Evan's first time.

It felt like a blow to the gut. He dropped the binder as if it had burned him and stared at it dumbly. What if Corie had been home? Who had the nerve to do something like this? He locked the office door, waited until his breathing returned to normal, and then used a tissue to carefully turn the pages:

Aspiring young actress brutally murdered...
Police have few clues in stabbing death...
Young woman's dreams of fame cut ruthlessly short...

The last article described her appearance in a dinner theatre production of *Guys and Dolls*. She'd played Sarah, the pretty, naïve missionary who falls for the smooth gangster, Sky Masterson. Good girls falling for bad men. Ironic for that to have been her last role in real life, too.

All of that felt like a lifetime ago, like it was done by a different person. Evan had stopped. It hadn't been easy and he wasn't perfect, but he was nothing if not disciplined. He'd done the best he could to take care of Corie and his widowed mother, Jessie. To build a business, to have a life. Even Vangie was only because Corie had pulled away.

But someone knew about his past. Evan turned the grimy FedEx envelope over and over, pointlessly searching for clues.

The sender paid cash and used one of those shipping centers—a busy one downtown. He could go in and ask around, see if they remembered a person sending a package overnight and paying cash. Most people had an account or used a credit card. Someone at the shipping center might remember. But why would they talk to him? He could hand out bribes but then that made him memorable. They might even call the police, suspicious after a strange man asked questions about a package. And the police were not going to find out about this particular delivery. Not if Evan had anything to say about it.

As if of their own volition Evan's fingers turned the pages. He'd forgotten her name and many of the details. For example, he remembered her as a singer, not an actress. Apparently she'd been both. Photographs in the album did confirm his memory of her as beautiful, dark-haired, and voluptuous. One of the newspaper articles included a studio portrait of Monique that could have been her senior picture. In it her head was turned slightly to the left and her smile was bright, her eyes gazing out at a future that would include Evan Markham.

So much pain in those days. So much self-loathing. He used to feel like he walked through the world with a bad smell that no amount of disinfectant could cover. Women were happy to go out with him at first—after all, he was handsome and rich—but they soured quickly.

When Evan met Monique he was twenty-eight. For their third date, he took the singer out to dinner. Actress. Whatever. He remembered it was Italian, in a nondescript little shopping center near Southpark Mall. The restaurant had wonderful macaroons. He knew the signs that he was about to be dumped. Hesitation, a reluctance to look him in the eye, a lack of spontaneity, lame excuses. She hadn't wanted to go out that night; he heard it in her voice when he called to confirm. Women were such cowards! They could never come right out and tell the truth. It was always their undoing, a reluctance to scream, to make a fuss, or to hurt someone's feelings. But something inside Evan had changed. This time when he saw the rejection coming, he didn't try to hide.

They were sitting in his car after dinner. It was raining. He reached over and touched her hair. "You're so beautiful. I don't deserve you."

She looked down at her hands folded in her lap and her discomfort was palpable. "I'm just not ready for a serious relationship."

"No, I appreciate the truth." And he did. In that miraculous moment he saw it all so clearly. People always talked about epiphanies and Evan thought they were full of shit until that moment in a dark, rainy strip mall parking lot in Charlotte.

"I'm sorry." She was afraid to look at him.

"Don't be. No hard feelings at all." For the first time that night she relaxed. He drove her home, like a gentleman, and soon he had Monique on his terms. It was all about motivation. She wanted to do things for him but he hadn't given her a reason yet. In fact, he'd done the opposite—he'd given her reasons to run away.

He would improve rapidly but, like all first times, that night he was clumsy. There was blood everywhere and he wasn't even 100% sure she was dead. The clippings confirmed his worst suspicions—she'd lived long enough to drag herself downstairs to the kitchen. They found the phone on the wall in the kitchen off of the hook, the handset dangling near her head. It was a mess, an absolute mess. Using kitchen knives. He shivered at the memory. So crude.

And he hadn't anticipated how loud she would be. Sure, he expected screaming, but Jesus. That shrill caterwauling would have made him want to kill her even if he hadn't already been so inclined. All he wanted was for her to shut the fuck up. It made it hard to enjoy himself with all of that screeching. It made him hurry, which was a shame. Plus there were logistical problems he hadn't considered, such as how to step off of the bed without tracking blood everywhere. He really hadn't thought things through. To top it all off, he passed another car on the road leading away from her house. How many more ways could the night have gone wrong?

And yet even with his screw-ups, there was no denying the euphoria. It was better than any drug. He felt positively glorious. His skin tingled. His senses were heightened. There was all of the endorphin glow of sex with none of the sluggishness. It was like an orgasm that went on and on and on. He didn't want to go home, he didn't want to go to sleep. He wanted to stand in the middle of some empty field somewhere and bellow at the top of his lungs. He wanted to raise his hands skyward, tempt fate, and call God out: *Take me on, you bastard, if you even exist.* He could do anything. As time went on he would learn that this euphoria was dangerous. It was when he was most likely to be careless. But that first night he was simply too intoxicated to be aware of risks. No matter how good he got, no matter how much he refined his technique, nothing would ever compare to that first time.

For ten years he murdered without even the threat of apprehension. Evan was restrained and his activity strictly measured, killing only when the self-hatred and pressure built to crippling levels. And never at home where there were too many connections and everyone was up everybody else's asshole. Evan read about serial killers and how they were typically active in a limited geographic area or territory. At least, the ones who were caught. Familiarity may not lead to contempt, as the old saying went, but it led to capture.

After Monique, Evan killed where he was a stranger. Each new place was like a blank canvas waiting for his signature. Business trips took on new meaning. He'd fly in and out, no one the wiser. He developed rituals. On the flight home, he'd sit in first class in a window seat. He'd order a Scotch—always the same drink, no matter the time of day—and toast his latest vanquished city, looking out the oval aircraft porthole as the patchwork landscape receded.

It gave him pleasure to visualize the cops on the ground scurrying, a bag on a metal gurney, detectives in their unmarked cars—plain, undistinguished men in cheap suits. Later, with their jackets off, he could see them hunkered down at their metal desks, tapping clumsily with thick fingers on their computer keyboards, following leads that would amount to nothing.

Once he figured out what he needed, Evan was able to focus on the other parts of his life and he became a success. He used his secret safety valve until the day he married Corie. At his wedding he made a secret vow to himself and, with difficulty, he'd kept it. Corie could never know what had happened before. No one could.

As Evan leafed through the scrapbook, he was so lost in his memories that it took a while before the name jumped out at him. Once it did, it might as well have been highlighted in neon:

The body was found by her mother, Helen, and her half-brother, Brice Shaughnessy. Brice, fifteen, placed the call to the police because, "his mother couldn't stop crying long enough to make the call."

Evan's mind whirled. Had Brice somehow figured it out? Was Brice on Evan's trail? And now Brice was dead. It couldn't be a coincidence. Was this why Brice befriended Corie and rented their guesthouse? If so, how did Brice trace the murder back to Evan when the police couldn't? And how on earth did someone else find out about Brice?

Evan didn't believe in coincidences. Stark reality said that he was being setup. Why else send him the scrapbook? Demands were sure to follow. In the meantime, the closer the police looked at Brice the more likely they were to follow the same thread that had led him to Evan. Unless Evan figured it out first.

Killing was an art and whoever dispatched Brice Shaughnessy was a common criminal. Three gunshot wounds, *bam, bam, bam*; no finesse at all. Crude and loud. Evan couldn't abide loud noises. Cowards used guns. Executioners. Bullies. Easy thing, wasn't it? To creep into a man's bedroom in the middle of the night, stand across the room, and pull a trigger? Whoever shot Brice was either inexperienced or didn't enjoy killing.

Not, however, a theory Evan was about to share with the police.

An inexperienced killer. Corie asked for a divorce the same night Brice was killed. But Corie was the one truly innocent person Evan knew.

Pushing emotion aside, he carefully reread the scrapbook from the beginning. He examined the grainy black-and-white newspaper photographs, including one of the gurney holding her body poised at the back of an ambulance. An old, Victorian-style farmhouse was clearly visible in the background. The house. *It couldn't be.* He stared a minute longer and then returned to his mother-in-law on the deck. Predictably, she'd lit up again and he wouldn't be surprised if there was a splash of vodka in her orange juice.

"What is that?" Vi wrinkled her nose in the direction of the glass he'd brought with him.

"A protein shake with added greens. Would you like one? It's very good for controlling cravings."

"Thanks, I'll take lung cancer."

Evan took a healthy swallow. "Did Corie talk to you about the murder when you were alone yesterday? She didn't say much in front of me and I worry that she bottles too much up inside."

"Of course not. She doesn't confide in me. I think it helps, though, that she knows the detective."

Evan took another thick swallow of his health drink; he tried to down them as quickly as possible. "She does? You mean Detective Fariel?"

Vi's blue eyes, more faded than Corie's, narrowed. "I guess you wouldn't have realized because you were much older, but he knew Hennessy, too."

Evan forced himself finish the drink with one final swig. "He did? How did they all know each other?"

"They went to high school together."

"That sounds innocent enough."

"There was some competition there between my Corie and your sister. Jack was a bit of a character in high school."

In Evan's experience, parents and old people used the word "character" to explain any young person who wasn't afraid of them. "He dated Corie?"

"Until Hennessy took him away from her."

The bitch actually seemed amused by her own daughter's pain. He didn't need to ask how Hennessy had prevailed over Corie; his sister's sexual precocity was well-known in the family. But he wanted to keep Vi talking. "What happened? Corie's never talked much about her high school years."

"Corie was quite smitten with the young Jack Fariel. She didn't want me to know but a mother has a way of intuiting these things. I know she was planning to go to the prom with him, and they went on a senior trip together to a dude ranch. Everything changed after that. I don't know the details but Corie was heartbroken. Her father and I were chaperones on that trip and Corie begged him to take her home early. I wouldn't have indulged her. Corie has always been too trusting for her own good. But Gus couldn't say no to his little girl, especially when she turned on the waterworks."

Too bad Vi wasn't his type. He'd love to see her under his knife and wipe that smug, heartless smirk off of her leathery face for good. Instead, he leaned closer, like a gossipy conspirator. "Did Jack do something to her?"

Vi relished her opportunity to talk. "Corie never told me exactly what he did but I could put two and two together. She caught him with Hennessy. Until then it was 'Jack this' and 'Jack that.' After she came home from that trip you couldn't mention his name in her presence. She's too sensitive. I hoped the experience would toughen her up but instead she announced that she had no intention of going to the prom. I couldn't have that. She wasn't going to hide in her room licking her wounds. Not on my watch. I told her that she was going to that prom and she was going to hold her head up high, if I had to march her onto the dance floor myself."

Evan's smile felt frozen on his face. Poor Corie. Between his sister and her mother she didn't stand a chance.

"Corie went off to college and put that trash behind her. Until yesterday. Do you want to know what I said to the esteemed detective when he tried to interview me?"

Evan allowed his expression to relax into one of genuine amazement. "Violet, that was a long time ago. In the present I think we should cooperate with the police. That includes Detective Fariel."

"You're pretty understanding about everything."

"The only thing I won't be understanding about is if you light that cigarette." He nodded his head towards her hand. "The police were asking me questions yesterday about Brice. I felt somewhat at a loss."

"What did the police ask you?"

"Perfectly ordinary questions: How long had we known Brice—or Mr. Shaughnessy as they persisted in calling him. How had he come to rent our guesthouse? Did he have any visitors? What did we know about his background? So I was wondering, what did you know about him?"

"Me?"

Evan had a lot to do. There was no time to be subtle. "What did Corie tell you about Brice?"

Vi shrugged and shook her head.

"Did she mention anything about his family, for instance? Where he was from? Any problems he's had in the past?"

Another shake of her head. "No."

Evan bit back his frustration, kept his voice smooth. "The police asked about the obvious things—drugs, drinking, gambling—and the damnable thing is, I didn't know."

She patted his hand and Evan tolerated it.

"Violet, I need you to tell me anything you know about Brice. It could be a matter of life and death."

"That's a little dramatic, Evan, don't you think?" She fidgeted with the cigarette again.

"You remember that night you were here for dinner, in June I believe it was, and we were talking about the class Corie was in with Brice?"

Vi snorted. "Yeah. That crazy psychology class. Where they made the model, right? The toy house filled with symbols? Evan, what's wrong?"

Evan exhaled, realized he'd clenched his hand into a fist, and forced himself to relax it. "Yes, that's the night I'm referring to. I thought the house was charming. As I recall, Corie stored the model in your basement. Do you still have it?"

CHAPTER THIRTEEN

Later that morning in Vangie Perez's disorderly bedroom, an officer gingerly picked up a dildo with his gloved hand. "What exactly are we looking for?"

Jack looked over at him. "Gun. Nine millimeter." Serena and several uniforms were helping him execute the warrant.

Tubes of lubricant squeezed from the middle, as if someone were in hurry, lay uncapped and oozing onto the maple nightstand. Discarded pieces of lingerie were scattered on the floor. Handcuffs sat next to a partially finished glass of wine and some plastic things that looked like jumper cables. Pretty much Jack's memory of the place from yesterday.

In the living room another officer whistled. "Quite the collection of porn."

"Don't go slipping anything into your pocket, Nunnally." Jack walked to the bedroom doorway and watched the uniformed officer rifling through the DVDs stored in the entertainment center.

"What are you doing? That's none of your business. Do they get to go through my things like this?" Vangie's voice rose in hysteria.

Jack looked at her. "You could make this a whole lot easier if you tell us where it is."

"I don't know where the gun is! I told you twenty times." She was wearing a hot pink Juicy Couture sweatsuit with yet another stretchy animal print top underneath. There were dark circles under her eyes.

"Vangie, come on." Stu Graber tried, unsuccessfully, to get her to sit quietly with him in the kitchen. "Let's go have some coffee."

The lawyer's presence precluded Jack from asking any questions. For example, whose glass of Scotch was that on the coffee table? It wasn't there yesterday and Vangie didn't seem the Scotch drinking type. Maybe it was the lawyer's. And what happened to the men's razor and other toiletries Jack saw? Had Evan come by and cleaned up? Jack could argue those items were in plain view yesterday but he was on thin ice; at the time, he didn't have a warrant and most people had an expectation of privacy for their bathroom and their medicine cabinet. It made Jack wonder what else was missing. Or what might have been added.

The search moved outside to Vangie's minivan and she followed. Three officers made quick work of the van's interior and then cranked the spare down from underneath the car.

"Got something." Officer Nunnally pulled a Ziploc bag from under the driver's seat.

"What is that? I don't know how that got there." Vangie lunged for the bag and Stu grabbed her arm.

"It's so nice when it's gift wrapped for us." Jack took the gallon-sized bag from the officer and smiled. "A gun and a cell phone. It's like Christmas. Vangie, can you tell me why you have a dead man's cell phone in your van?"

"I don't know where that came from."

"Uh-huh." Jack guessed Evan Markham had a key to her van. Proving something was planted, though, was even more difficult than proving something was taken. The same thought crossed his mind as when he first interviewed her: *This was too easy.* It was almost like someone was leaving them a trail of breadcrumbs.

"She's not making any statement, Detective. Come on, Vangie." Stu tried to steer her away from the van.

"No!" She broke free of his grip walked up to Jack. "That's not mine. You have to believe me."

Stu was next to her in an instant. "Vangie, what the hell are you doing? Don't make my life more difficult than it already is."

"Wow, Vangie, great hiding place," Jack said.

"It's not a great hiding place." There was an imploring look in her brown eyes. "I don't have anything to hide. What's happening?"

Stu fought to get her attention. "Vangie, you have nothing to worry about as long as you keep your mouth shut."

"Vangie, help yourself here," Jack said. "He's Evan's lawyer. You think he's really working for you? You think he's got *your* best interests at heart?"

At the mention of Evan's name Vangie seemed to go limp. "Why didn't he stay last night? If he cares about me so much?"

Jack was becoming very fond of Vangie. So Evan *was* here. Unfortunately for the lawyer she couldn't keep her mouth shut. An admirable quality in a suspect. "Vangie, you need to think about what's best for *you*, not Evan. Maybe there is an explanation for why the gun's in your van. My job is to figure this all out. You can help me get it right."

Stu was having none of it. He put his arm possessively around her shoulders. "*Your* job? Let me explain what his job is, Vangie. His job is to be a nice guy and get you to like him."

"I am a nice guy."

"You trust him and you tell him things—about the weather, it doesn't matter what. Every word out of your mouth, no matter how innocent you think it sounds, becomes a nail in your coffin," Stu said.

"Thanks, Graber. I had no idea I was that clever."

"It wasn't me." Vangie's voice was small.

"That's enough. Detective, if you're arresting her you need to make her aware of her rights." Stu turned to Vangie. "You don't say another word. They're going to explain things to you. They're going to hand you a card with your legal rights printed on it. You read and sign that you understand. That's it. You don't say anything else."

One of the uniforms took her by the arm and started to lead her to a marked car. Vangie stiffened and looked at Stu, her eyes wide with panic. "Wait! Can't I go with you? Why can't you take me?"

"Because you're under arrest, honey," Stu said. "Think about Evan and I'll be right there when they set bail."

Vangie looked at Jack. "Can I ride with you?"

"That's not how this works. Don't worry. You'll get lots of chances to talk to me, if you want them." Stu made more indignant comments about how that would happen right after hell froze and pigs orbited the Earth but Jack didn't wait to hear them all.

CHAPTER FOURTEEN

"Hey, good work." Mike Delgado looked up from his computer and gave Jack and Serena a thumbs-up.

Back at the station it was congratulations all around. The two detectives headed for Dani's office and it seemed like everyone they passed had something encouraging to say.

"What is the big fucking deal?" Jack grumbled under his breath. He was in a sour mood. It felt like Vangie was being handed to him on a silver platter. And Corie's face before she slammed the car door stayed with him, as well as her last words: *I never want to see you again.*

"You don't take compliments well," Serena said.

"I take compliments okay when I feel like I deserve them."

"You got Vangie to talk and even show you where she kept the gun before she lawyered up. That's impressive."

Jack gave a noncommittal shrug. "You're sure this isn't because now I'm the sick guy and everyone's amazed I haven't keeled over dead yet?"

Serena hesitated in Dani's doorway. "Now I'm really impressed."

Jack followed her gaze and saw Paul Diamond, the chief of police. It took willpower to suppress an eye roll.

"Brilliant first week back, I'd say." Paul clapped Jack on the shoulder. Paul was in his late fifties, heavyset, with dark hair gone almost completely gray, especially in his neatly trimmed beard. Born in England, Paul still spoke in the clipped, elegant tones of his homeland.

Dani was actually smiling. "Good work, Jack. Your first case back and you got 'er done in less than twenty-four."

"The thing is—" Jack hesitated. What was the thing? Why was he so irritated?

"No false modesty. Great job. We'll be giving a press conference later this afternoon to announce our progress," Paul said.

"But we've only gotten started," Jack said.

"Agreed," Paul said. "But I don't see any reason to withhold what we've got so far. Do you?"

"I don't," Dani said. "We'll announce we've made progress and have a suspect in custody. Nice to have some good news to report."

Jack was being trotted out to give everyone a warm, fuzzy feeling. Cancer cop makes good. A lot of things had happened to give DPD a black eye the past few years and he got to be the competence poster boy. It made his blood boil.

"Before you broadcast to the world, I'd like a chance to actually do some police work." Jack fought to keep his voice even. "Evan Markham had assault charges filed against him a few years back and he was overheard threatening the vic."

Serena sounded surprised. "He was? When?"

Jack didn't look at her. "And the vic's sister was murdered. The case was never solved. There's a lot more here than meets the eye."

"I'm acquainted with Evan Markham," Paul said. "He's on the board of several charities. I've been on some fundraising committees with him."

Jack raised his eyebrows. "You know Markham?"

"I've been a guest in his home for dinner and I've worked with him on some events. What makes you believe he's not on the up-and-up?"

Paul was usually a straight shooter—as straight, narrow, and squeaky clean as they come. Who the hell was Markham? Jack couldn't forget Corie's eyes or the things she'd told him. "So you knew that your upstanding citizen and charity buddy was cheating on his wife."

Paul's practiced composure didn't slip. "I was not aware of that."

"Conveniently, his girlfriend's also his alibi. He was banging her before, during, and after the murder."

"Roger D'Ambrose is also part of Evan's alibi."

Jack had no evidence yet that it was Evan, but he wanted to puncture their smug certainty. "Time of death creates a window of opportunity. Markham could have swung by his house on the way to play golf. D'Ambrose said he was a few minutes late."

Paul continued in the same composed, elegant tone. "This is a high-profile case, Jack. But I don't have to tell you that."

"What are you telling me? Because it's sounding an awful lot like my direction should be the girlfriend and hands off the rich guys."

"No one is saying anything of the kind." Dani's irritated voice sliced the air.

Paul calmly held Jack's gaze. They could have been discussing the weather. "I stopped by to congratulate you on the progress you've made and see what else you need. I know it's not over but I, for one, am encouraged by the developments."

"The girlfriend feels too easy," Jack said. "If I find it's someone on the Denver A-list, you okay with that?"

Dani sounded disgusted. "Damn it, Jack—"

Paul held up a hand to stop her. "Jack. No one is telling you to stop investigating any avenue that looks promising. Quite the contrary. I'd like to think you know me better than that." He held

Jack's gaze for one long moment, then turned on his polished boot heel and left the office.

Silence for a minute after Paul left, which Dani broke first. "What was that about?"

Jack shrugged. He wished he knew. Everything just felt wrong.

"So it's a gift horse, finding the gun and cell phone in Vangie's possession?" Dani asked.

"In her *van*," Jack emphasized the word. "Which unlocked. Anyone could have planted it. Evan probably has a key. And we don't even know yet that it *is* the murder weapon."

"You sound hung up on Evan," Dani said. "Is that instinct or something else?"

Jack stared at her. "It's doing my job."

"Humor me," Dani said. "Let's look at Vangie. What's her motive?"

Jack considered for a moment. "Vangie wants Evan. Who knows what he promised her. Then Brice saw the two of them together. Maybe he threatened to tell Cor—Evan's wife and Vangie was afraid that would mess up their plans."

Dani nodded, then looked at Serena. "What about you, Detective?"

"The gun is our first good, solid piece of physical evidence," Serena said. "I think we wait and see what it tells us."

"Of course," Jack said. "I wasn't suggesting otherwise. But I don't think we know enough yet to gift wrap it for the media."

"All we're announcing is that we've made progress." Dani picked up a piece of paper from her desk and looked at it.

"But—"

"Jack, let me and Paul worry about the media. It sounds to me like you've got plenty of work to do." Dani turned back toward her computer, effectively dismissing them.

Serena walked back to Jack's desk with him. "What's the part about Brice's sister being murdered? And the threat?"

"It isn't like I've had a lot of leisure time to fill you in." Jack sat down, rummaged through a drawer in his metal desk, found some antacid, and popped two of the tablets in his mouth.

Mike Delgado walked up looking like he was ready to burst. "I was going through the vic's phone records, and I made the call that's going to break this case wide open."

"Oh, brother." Serena rolled her eyes.

"No, he's good for comic relief," Jack said. "I could use a laugh."

"When you hear my news you're gonna change your tune." Mike had a wide, shit-eating grin on his face. "Your vic? Brice Shaughnessy?"

"I know his name, Mike." Jack smiled, too.

"One of his last calls was to a homicide detective." Mike waited expectantly, hoping to build drama, but Jack didn't react. "Don't you want to know why?"

"Does it have anything to do with Brice's sister being murdered?" Jack said.

"The vic's sister was—wait. You knew? Son of a bitch. How do you do that?"

Jack's smile grew. "Corie Markham told me this morning. It's called police work, buddy."

Mike started to say something rude but Serena got there first. "What the hell? You talked to Corie without me? When?"

Mike slapped a manila folder down on Jack's desk. "Phone records are in there. Brice called the detective Thursday evening at sixteen forty-five. One of his last calls, in fact. Number goes to a detective named Lassiter on the Charlotte Mecklenburg Cold Case squad."

"Sister's murder is fifteen years stale," Jack said. "That's why it's with the cold case squad."

"Detective Lassiter didn't speak with Brice," Mike said. "It went to voice mail. All Brice said in his message was to call him, didn't leave any details. Lassiter tried to call Brice back but didn't get him, of course, because he was already dead. He's gonna send you his files."

Serena was watching Jack. "When did you talk to Corie? Why didn't you call me?"

"It was early. I stopped on my way here." Jack's focus was on Mike. "This Lassiter have any idea why Brice was calling him now?"

"Nope. Although he said it wasn't unusual for Brice to check in from time to time. Brice was only a kid, fifteen, when it happened. He found her—Brice and his mother. Lassiter says the scene was a mess. Bad news for a kid to have to see his sister like that. When Brice got older he started looking into it himself, couldn't seem to let it go. Lassiter felt really bad when I told him what happened to Brice. Asked to be kept in the loop."

"If Corie knew about the sister, why didn't she tell us yesterday?" Serena asked.

Jack answered too sharply. "I don't know, Serena. Jesus. Could you let it go for a minute? I'm much more interested in why Brice was in contact with a homicide detective hours before he was killed."

CHAPTER FIFTEEN

Evan stared at the model house Corie and Brice had built. After he retrieved it from Vi's basement he brought it to his mother's. He told Jessie he wanted to work on a secret project in her garage—a surprise for Corie, he said, something to cheer her up. Not that he had to worry about Jessie spying on him. She wasn't interested in what Evan was doing. Jessie's attention was focused on her new young protégée, a male sculptor named Lennon, ridiculously enough. His mother was forever taking in strays— mostly men, but sometimes women—artists who were young, ambitious, and trying to make their way in the world via Jessie's bed.

But he didn't have time for the luxury of censorious disgust. As he compared the model house to the real one in the newspaper photos, Evan realized he had a much bigger problem than his mother's sex life.

He circled the model lost in thought, unconsciously shaking his head. *Son of a bitch.* His innocent wife and her new friend had recreated the scene exactly. His crime scene. And they'd done it right under Evan's nose. He didn't know which bothered him more: Corie's betrayal or his own stupidity.

A Victorian house in miniature sat before him, complete with dormers and eaves and delicate gingerbread trim. A peaked roof made of real shingles was topped with a tiny metal weathervane. The front door was painted a dark, glossy green, and adorned with a tiny brass knocker and doorknob. The amount of detail the conspirators had put into their project was amazing. Even under the circumstances it was hard not to admire it.

On the rainy night Evan killed the singer, he hadn't paid much attention to the exterior of her house. The layout of the interior, the logistics of getting her to the bedroom, how far the house was from the nearest neighbor, choosing a murder weapon—those were his chief concerns, not architecture. Whether the house was indeed yellow and whether the trim was painted in a contrasting shade hadn't concerned him at all.

How did Brice explain this choice to Corie? When she talked about the project she said the house was meant to be symbolic. It didn't look symbolic. It looked pretty damned real. Had Brice meant it to be some kind of warning? But without the scrapbook Evan wouldn't have even recognized the house. It didn't make sense.

The model kitchen contained a table, four chairs, and appliances. A tiny phone adorned the wall with the receiver dangling off the hook, exactly as the Charlotte police had found it in reality. The table was loaded with fake food. His wife had talked about that. She said it represented bounty: "Sharing bounty with the people you love." Evan wished he remembered more of what Corie had told him about the class. He hadn't known there was a reason to be interested.

The centerpiece of the table was a miniature plastic turkey surrounded by side dishes. It hadn't been near Thanksgiving, had it? Evan's brow creased. It *was* November. That's why the weather had been so cold and rainy. He'd cut Monique from her loved ones right before the holidays. No pun intended.

The newspaper clippings said the house belonged to Monique's grandparents—Monique's and Brice's. They were away on vacation and called home to find their snug home had been turned into a bloody crime scene. Where did the victim's family have Thanksgiving dinner that year? Did they even celebrate the holidays? Was the holiday season ruined for them for years afterward? So many lives impacted by his actions. He felt a pleasant thrill deep in his lower abdomen.

How was he going to find out what Brice told Corie? Why did she let him touch her last night? Evan had wanted to regain control but his efforts backfired. He couldn't stop thinking about Corie and the way she felt under his hands. The way she throbbed. Her scent, her warmth, her softness.

Evan groaned and shook his head sharply to clear the images. So he longed for things after all: to keep the model as a souvenir, to make love to his wife. Instead, he forced himself to raise the axe. What took weeks of painstaking effort was destroyed in seconds. It made him inexplicably sad, and once the house was reduced to splinters and stuffed into a black trash bag, Evan felt desolate. No one knew him. Only in their final moments did anyone see who he really was, and for those carefully selected few, the knowledge brought no comfort.

CHAPTER SIXTEEN

Jessie Markham seemed thrilled to see Jack and Serena. She had to be at least sixty but looked years younger with smooth, creamy skin, long, curly blond hair, and wide, green eyes. She'd kept her figure and her deep purple silk blouse was cut low, drawing the eye to the shadow between her prominent breasts. A broomstick skirt skimmed her knees and a wide, silver concha belt was draped low on her hips. She spoke in a breathy, excited manner, asked them all sorts of questions about their job, and told them she adored—that was her word, not liked or loved but "utterly adored"—*Law & Order.*

When they asked if she would provide fingerprints for elimination she practically clapped her hands. "How exciting. Isn't this exciting, Len?"

Jessie turned to her houseguest, a man named Lennon Funderburk, who didn't seem quite as enthusiastic about the detectives' appearance.

"It's not as exciting in real life as it is on TV, ma'am," Serena said.

Jessie led them into a large, airy kitchen and prattled on happily about TV shows, books, and movies.

Jack showed her a picture of the ring they found under Brice's bed.

"I wondered what happened to that!" Jessie excitedly reached for the photo.

"Is the ring yours?"

Jessie nodded. "Mm-hmm. I must have lost it in the guesthouse."

Jack glanced at Serena but his partner was watching Len, who had slumped onto a barstool.

Jack turned his attention back to Jessie. "When was that, ma'am?"

Jessie made a playful motion, as if she was slapping Jack on the wrist. "Oh, don't call me ma'am; it makes me sound so old. Jessie will be fine."

"All right. Jessie. When were you in the guesthouse?"

"Early June, not long after Corie and Evan moved there. Such a gorgeous setting right on the Highline Canal, and it was so nice out. We had a decent amount of wine with dinner—Evan has such a lovely collection—and he decided it was best I didn't drive. I slept in the guesthouse."

"What about you, Mr. Funderburk?" Jack asked.

"Huh?" Len sat up straight. "What about me? What?"

Jessie looked at her friend and laughed. "Len, don't be such a ninny." She turned back to Jack. "He has authority issues. And he's never been to Evan's."

"We'd like to hear it from him, ma'am," Serena said.

"I haven't," Len said. "Never. Although I'd like to."

"And you're sure, ma'am, that the last time you were in the guesthouse was early June?" Serena asked.

Jessie scowled at her. "As I've said." Her voice was crisp.

"Jessie," Jack said, "don't mind my partner. She's new to homicide. If you don't mind indulging us, we need to hear about what you did Thursday night and then we'll let you get on with your day."

Jessie favored him with a brilliant smile and her voice turned breathy and excited again. "Oh, I don't mind at all. What time should I start with? Are you sure you don't want more iced tea?"

Jack smiled back. "Sure. That'd be great."

"We stayed in for dinner." Jessie reached for a pitcher on the counter and leaned in close when she refilled Jack's glass. "I made a frittata. In the Spanish style with potatoes and goat cheese and roasted red peppers."

"Sounds delicious," Jack said.

"And then what?" Serena asked.

"After dinner we watched one of my favorite movies, *Cinema Paradiso*, and then turned in early. Can you imagine? He'd never seen it! I thought everyone had seen that film." Jessie reached across the counter and touched Len's cheek indulgently. "All of that yearning and longing. Mmph." She made a kind of strangled sound and put her hand to her chest.

"Bit of a drama queen," Serena said when she and Jack were back in the car. She shed her jacket revealing athletic arms with toned biceps and cranked the AC up to high; it was another unseasonably warm fall day.

"What? You didn't like the organic, free-range, hibiscus iced tea she offered us?"

"I thought everyone had seen *Cinema Paradiso*!" Serena did a creditable imitation of Jessie's breathy voice and Jack laughed. "And what about her clothes? I was especially taken with the sandals and all the jewelry."

"And what about the fact that Evan's not here anymore?" Jack said.

"What?" Serena looked around.

"His car was here when we arrived. Jessie said he was working on something in the garage."

"I hadn't noticed. Crap." Serena's buoyant mood deflated a little.

"That's okay. She was very distracting. All of the Markhams are quite entertaining in their own way."

"*All* of the Markhams?"

"She's not a Markham," Jack said, too quickly.

"Speaking of Corie, did you ask her about Jennifer Suarez?"

"I wasn't speaking of Corie." *Shit.* How could he forget to do that? Jack answered his partner with forced casualness. "I hit her with the girlfriend and it seemed like too much at once. Judgment call. I'm sure we'll be talking to Corie again."

" *We'll* be talking to Corie?" Serena watched him but he didn't take the bait. "You still think this is all worthwhile? Following up with D'Ambrose's private investigator and talking to Jennifer? I mean, after finding Vangie with the murder weapon?"

"You too? If you want I can drop you off at headquarters. There's still time for you to join the press conference."

"No, Jack." Serena sounded angry. "I don't want to join the press conference. Trying to prioritize is all."

They fell silent for a minute and then Jack asked, "Any news on DNA?"

"They said by the end of the day."

"We may look really stupid a few hours from now."

Serena shrugged. Jack wished he could let it go that easily. He glanced at his phone, illogically hoping for, but not really expecting, a call from Corie. She'd made it pretty clear she wanted nothing to do with him. He couldn't blame her, but he'd hated leaving her that way at the stables and hoped he'd have a chance to make amends. How the hell he'd do that, he had no idea.

Their next stop was an Einstein Bagels near the University of Denver where Leigh-Anne Hough, Brice's former landlady, worked as an assistant manager. The store was crowded with students and Jack could feel the customers standing in line glare at him as he walked up to the cash register and asked for her. After a couple of minutes, a young woman walked out from the back wiping her hands on an apron. Jack showed her a picture of Brice's face taken when they performed the autopsy.

Leigh-Anne frowned at it. "I don't recognize him. Who is he?" She handed the picture back.

"His name is Brice Shaughnessy," Serena said. "He rented an apartment from you."

"No, he didn't." Leigh-Anne's frown deepened.

"Are you sure? He listed you as his previous landlord on a rental application." Jack said.

"He never rented from me. I don't know why he would say he did."

"Maybe he had a friend that rented from you. Can you think of any other way he would get your name?" Serena asked.

"What did you say his name was?" Leigh-Anne asked.

"Brice Shaughnessy," Serena said.

"Oh. Brice. I couldn't tell from the picture. What happened to him?" Leigh-Anne asked.

"So you do know him?" Jack asked.

"I was in a class with him at DU. I must have mentioned that I own rental property or something. I wouldn't have minded if he used me as a reference. Is he okay?"

"I'm afraid he's dead," Jack said.

"Oh my God. What happened?" Leigh-Anne's eyes grew wide.

"That's what we're trying to figure out," Jack said.

"We need to talk to his friends, his partners. We're hoping you can give us some names," Serena said.

Leigh-Anne shook her head. "Sorry, I don't know who he hung out with. He hadn't been around very long but he was really nice. Oh, wait. You know who you should talk to? His partner in the class. This woman named Corie something."

"That's who he was renting from," Jack said. "That's how we got your name."

"How weird. I'm sure it's all just some kind of misunderstanding." Leigh-Anne glanced at the line growing at the cash register. "I should get back to work."

"If you think of anything, I'd really appreciate it if you'd give me a call." Jack handed her a card.

"Sure. Sorry I didn't know anything."

"Gee, Brice lied." Jack held the door for Serena on the way out. "You could knock me over with a feather."

"It seems pointless. Corie liked him," Serena said.

Jack unlocked the car. "I've come to the conclusion that lying is an irresistible human reflex."

"Brice manufactured a housing emergency so Corie would invite him to stay in their guesthouse. But if Corie and Brice were friends, wouldn't she have offered anyway? Did he need an elaborate ruse?"

"There was a reason he wanted to be close to the Markhams. It's usually sex, drugs, or money, but in this case it's none of those."

"How can you say that? He was having sex with someone."

"Brice was investigating his sister's murder. I'd stake my career on it. And I'm also willing to bet Vangie Perez knew nothing about it."

Jack and Serena visited briefly with D'Ambrose's private investigator, then drove to Jennifer Suarez's neat, brick ranch house in Lakewood, one of Denver's western suburbs. An overhang provided a small shaded area outside the front door, which was decorated with a bench on one side and a grouping of several pumpkins on the other. A pair of muddy gardening clogs rested under the bench, along with a couple pairs of small children's shoes.

The investigator had been cooperative but unable to offer much in the way of information. D'Ambrose had really tried to take an interest according to the investigator, even going so far as offering to help her find new employment. But Jennifer made herself scarce abruptly and decisively, firmly rebuffing any offers of assistance or inquiries into her well-being. Just like Aranda Sheffield had told them.

Jack knew Jennifer wouldn't be happy to find them on her cozy doorstep either. The woman who answered the door was around thirty, with dark hair and a child on her hip. Her smile faded quickly when they introduced themselves and she didn't invite them in. Instead, she disappeared inside the house for a couple of minutes closing the door behind her. When she reappeared, she was alone.

"I don't understand why you're here." Jennifer's voice was cold. "How did you find me?"

"We need to ask you a few questions about a man named Evan Markham," Serena said. "We know you used to work for him. And that you filed assault charges against him."

"Those charges were dropped. Now if there's nothing else—"

"I read the report. It sounded like he really hurt you," Serena said.

Jennifer folded her arms across her chest. "I'm fine. I need to get back inside."

"We're investigating a homicide, Ms. Suarez," Jack said. "We could really use your help."

"It's Hoffman now. I'm married."

"Mrs. Hoffman," Jack said. "When individuals exhibit violent behavior, it's been my experience that they escalate. You were sexually assaulted and beaten. What if he's escalated to murder?"

No response. Jennifer's face remained stony.

"We'd like to know why you dropped the charges. Can you tell us why you didn't allow the police to proceed?" Serena asked.

Jennifer exhaled and her features softened slightly. "He seemed really sorry. I've moved on. I have a family now and I don't want to live this all over again."

"I understand," Serena said. "But someone is dead and we need to find the person responsible. Evan doesn't have to know we talked to you."

Jennifer glanced back over her shoulder toward the house and lowered her voice to a whisper. "My husband doesn't know. We have a child together and one more on the way." Instinctively she put a protective hand on her stomach. "I don't know that there's much I can say that would help anyway. What I can tell you is that he's got two faces—like, what's that story? Dr. Somebody? He was scary. And before that he'd been so nice.

"He had a knife. He acted like I should find that sexy or something. It was so weird. He said it was a fun game. Said he knew all along I'd be fun—he kept using that word. Said he could tell what I wanted. When I said no—and I did say no—was when he changed. At first he acted like he didn't believe me, but when it became clear to him that I meant it, he became enraged. I felt lucky to get away."

Jack was quiet until they were back in the car. "You know, Corie used almost those same words. That Evan was Dr. Jekyll and Mr. Hyde. That he could be charming one minute and then completely different the next. Although personally, I missed the charming part." Jack's eyes flicked to his partner. "Corie also said he liked to play games. Sex games."

"He convinces them that he's only playing and they're wrong for making a big deal out of it. Poor misunderstood guy."

Jack snorted. "It's hard to misunderstand being threatened with a knife."

"Was that in the report? Why wasn't this written up as felony menacing if there was a weapon?" Serena read for a minute. "Huh. Jennifer didn't mention the knife. All she told the police was that he knocked her around. And there was no sexual penetration, although she believed he'd meant to rape her."

"Maybe because she didn't let him act out his fantasy. Apparently Markham needs props or he can't play. I mean, look at what we found in Vangie's place."

"Poor Corie."

"Read my mind."

CHAPTER SEVENTEEN

Evan knew from personal experience that getting rid of a person wasn't easy. The Vangie problem had grown in his mind until the need to get rid of her blotted out all other concerns. The need to regain control was visceral. What did she know? Who was she working for? How was he going to neutralize the threat without backsliding into his old behavior? His vow might be self-imposed but he took it seriously.

He needed Vangie where he could keep an eye on her and, until he came up with a better plan, the Westin downtown was going to have to do. He found Vangie in the room he'd reserved, pacing and barely coherent.

Vangie glared at him. "Where the hell have you been? How could you all do that to me? Why'd you have Stu bring me here? They took my fingerprints and they locked me in a room and I didn't think I'd ever get out again."

Perpetual makeup smudged around her eyes, like a white-trash raccoon. She was rabid and unpredictable like a raccoon, too.

Evan walked to the window and, from force of habit, closed the drapes. "I need you to tell me everything. Would you like some wine? Tell me exactly what happened."

She rolled her eyes. "I already told your lawyer."

"Don't roll your eyes at me. This is important." A quick step across the room and his hand rose of its own volition to smack her before he sternly checked himself. A vision of Vangie's lifeless body flashed through his mind.

But she seemed oblivious to Evan's mood and flopped down on the bed with a whiny whimper. "I'm tired. I need to sleep." She glanced up at him flirtatiously. "Why don't you join me?"

"Sleep is for the weak. I need to know why. Don't you understand how much this is impacting my life?" He quickly corrected. "*Our* life. Why would you take a risk like that? Why would you kill him?"

"What?" She bolted upright in the bed.

"Vangie, the gun and his cell phone were in your van." Evan spoke as if to a child.

"I don't know how they got there. I told the detectives."

"That's it? That's what you're going to stick with? You don't know? Who believes that, Vangie?"

Brown raccoon eyes stared up at him.

Evan paced, his feet silent on the carpet. "Don't forget you were alone for three hours that morning. I'm not your alibi and, as far as I'm aware, you don't have another one."

Vangie tossed her hair back and sat up straighter. "How do you know it wasn't your wife?"

Evan sat down on the bed next to her. "I can help you, Vangie. I can say that I left you restrained while I was gone to play golf, that it was impossible for you to move. But only if you're completely honest."

"I didn't kill anyone!"

Evan tried to put his hand on her shoulder but she flinched away from his touch. "You're not giving Stu and me anything to work with. I have to know why and I have to know who else you told."

She slid away from him toward the head of the bed, as subtle as a snake. "No one. I told you first."

"First?" The word lingered like poison on Evan's tongue.

"I mean, I told you right away and I haven't told anyone else."

"You told the handsome detective quite a lot, so it's only fair that you tell me." The fact that this was his own fault didn't make anything better.

Vangie plumped a pillow and then slouched back against it. "I didn't tell the detective. I didn't know the gun was in my van. All I did was show him where I usually keep it, in the nightstand."

Evan stared at her throat. Felt his hands circle, felt her Adam's apple bulge under his thumb. But his voice was soft, almost sensuous. "Why would you do that?"

Vangie's voice was whiny. "Because he asked. And he was so rude. Before that, he asked to use the bathroom and he snooped around and looked at my things."

"Did he? Before he had a warrant?" Still in the soft voice. Evan stood, walked to the mirrored closet door, and smoothed his hair. "If so, that was very foolish of him."

"What about your wife?"

"What about her?" He turned back toward Vangie.

"Maybe she killed that man. And planted the gun in my van."

"Vangie, she didn't even know you were here. As far as she's concerned, you're happily married and living in Texas."

She rose up onto her knees on the bed. "I was right. You're never going to leave her."

"You *did* kill him." In two quick strides he was standing over her. He wrapped a hank of her hair around his hand and jerked Vangie's head back.

"Stop it."

She tried to pull away from him but he tightened his grip. Wearing one of her usual tight, low-cut tops he could see the mounds of her breasts. He imagined the point of a blade scoring that olive skin.

Abruptly, Evan let go of her hair and took a step back. "I understand. Our future was in danger. If Brice had told Corie about us, then I'd lose the advantage. Do you think my wife would have been agreeable about a divorce if she'd found out about you?"

Vangie looked wary. "When you said to tell the truth, I thought it meant we were finally going to be together. Was I wrong?"

He watched the pulse beat in her throat. "No. You weren't wrong. You're going to be mine. Forever."

Vangie gasped. "What do you mean?"

"You killed him," Evan said, "and then you found the scrapbook and sent it to me. To protect me."

"Scrapbook? What scrapbook? Evan, what are you talking about?"

If he was going to get the truth he couldn't do it here in the hotel. "I have a few more things to do and then I'll be back for you. We'll spend the whole weekend together. Would you like that?"

Her excitement was pitiful. With a happy shriek Vangie jumped up and threw her arms around his neck. Evan tolerated the embrace.

CHAPTER EIGHTEEN

Corie sat in her car in the driveway staring at her house. She needed to do something, pack a bag, get out of there; any action at all. But the more she tried to goad herself into moving, the more relentless the images became. She'd been ignoring her instincts for so long they'd atrophied. For example, Corie's instincts hadn't told her to be tied up, flogged, or have a needle inserted into—*stop it.* Ever since she'd told Jack about the S&M, the memories wouldn't quit.

She especially didn't want to remember the last time she had sex with Evan. No, that wasn't right. She didn't *have* sex; she didn't have any say at all. Evan had forced her. Corie screwed her eyes shut but the memory kept playing in her mind. Maybe it was some kind of weird penance, reliving everything.

One night six months ago, right after they'd moved into the new house, Evan said, "I'm beat. Let's get in the hot tub for a little while before dinner. We haven't tried it yet."

He acted casual, but for some reason he frightened her. *Run,* a voice said in Corie's head. As usual, she didn't listen.

Instead, she met Evan in the hot tub room like he suggested. She wore a robe. He was naked and snuggled up against her from behind. As was his habit, he picked out a few strands of her hair and gave them a tug.

"Evan, quit it."

"You don't tell me no, remember?"

"I'm not doing that anymore." She tried to pull away and his grip tightened.

"Here's what you are going to do, Corie." He was holding her so close his lips grazed her ear when he spoke. "You are going to take that robe off for me now. Or I will cut it off."

"Have you lost your mind?"

Suddenly Evan started laughing. The sound was shocking. It bounced off the hard tile floor and Corie froze with confusion. He stopped laughing as abruptly as he started, and she felt as much as she heard his silky whisper. "I bought you a million-dollar house. I thought it would make you happy."

"You wanted the house, Evan. Not me." Corie pulled away and took a step back.

His face changed and he looked hurt. "Why do you hate me?"

She took a second careful step backward. "I don't hate you. Don't do anything to change that."

"I only wanted to try out the hot tub. I'm sorry I grabbed you like that."

"You scared me." A third step.

"I thought you liked it when I was rough with you."

"I'll go get dinner ready." The door was ten feet away. Then the hallway, then freedom.

"If you don't love me anymore, why did you move here with me?"

And he had her. "I do love you." She longed to explain, to tell him how confused and frightened she felt. What were the words that could get through to Evan?

"Get in the water with me for a couple of minutes. I want to try it out and make sure it works. You'll be too full after dinner."

Why didn't she keep walking out of the room, out of the house, out of his life?

"This is nice, huh?" Evan watched as she timidly shed the robe, hung it up on a hook, and then sat down cautiously on the edge of the tub.

"Just for a minute." Corie slipped into the water slowly and took a seat across from him. Evan's demeanor had completely changed to warm and friendly. This was the face he presented to the world when he wanted to seduce a new client or reassure a jury—or manipulate his wife.

Her handsome husband grinned at her. "We can have a lot of fun in here, baby. No one will be allowed to wear clothes in our hot tub. It will be a rule. You get naked or you don't go in. Remember Cabo?"

"Of course I do." It was a reference to their honeymoon. They'd stayed in a cottage at a luxurious beach resort and had their own private hot tub. Evan had made love to her—if you could call it that—in the water.

"We could do that all the time." Still smiling, Evan slithered across the tub and positioned himself behind her. His hands cupped her breasts and he pinched her nipples between his fingers.

Corie tried to turn around and face him but he wouldn't let her. "What are you doing?"

"What do you think?" Before she could react, Evan bent her over the side of the tub and took her roughly from behind. Pain seared through her, made worse by the lack of any kind of lubrication and the hot water. She struggled, but he had her pinned against the side of the tub. Her knees banged against the fiberglass seats and her elbows slammed onto the tile floor. Her hands scrabbled but there was nothing to grab onto for leverage. She screamed, but there was no one close enough on the two-acre lots to hear.

When he was finished, she fought her way up out of the tub and onto the cold floor where she lay sobbing. Evan got out too, picked up his clothes, and looked down at her. "Corie, you're too uptight." Then he walked out of the room. And he never touched her again. Until last night.

Corie loathed herself. Not only didn't she report the attack, she never so much as mentioned it again. Could she tell Jack? Did she have the nerve? Would he believe her? Would anyone? Six months later she discovers a body in the guesthouse and all of a sudden she cries rape? Evan's attorney would tear her apart.

Maybe Vangie liked all of that sick shit. Well, she was welcome to Evan. Were there others? Had he given them all money? Corie used to do all of the books for the business when they were first starting out, but she had no idea where things stood now. She gritted her teeth and opened the car door.

Vi was in the kitchen making lunch. Corie began to congratulate her for making the effort but choked back the sarcasm. She needed someone and her mother was better than nothing. Maybe.

"That was a long ride," Vi said. "Evan and I were wondering where you were."

"Oh? Where is Evan?"

"I would imagine working. Although how he can concentrate with everything that's going on is beyond me."

Corie plunged in, deciding it was like entering a cold swimming pool—best to jump in and not prolong the inevitable. "Did you know Evan was having an affair?"

Vi, at the kitchen counter, scraped a butter knife around the bottom of a nearly empty jar of Miracle Whip. It made a clanking sound. "Your police buddy tell you that?"

Police buddy? "A woman named Vangie Perez. You ever hear of her?"

Vi kept on making sandwiches.

"Did you hear me?" Corie asked.

"I heard you. Do you want mustard, too? You really need to go to the store, Corie. There's almost nothing to eat in this house."

"I hate mayonnaise. But why would you remember that? I don't want a sandwich. I want you to acknowledge what I said."

Vi folded slices of deli ham and placed them neatly on the bread as she talked. "The police will tell you anything. They want to get you to talk to them. They're looking to railroad your husband. It's what they always do." Vi placed slices of Swiss cheese on top of the ham, placed the second slice of bread on top, and sliced the sandwiches into neat triangles.

"Mom, he's sleeping with someone. Her name is Vangie." Corie ignored the plate Vi tried to hand her. "I don't want a sandwich. Jesus."

"Suit yourself."

"Don't you care? My husband is cheating on me. And I know who she is. She's someone we work with. She's even kind of fat." Corie hated herself for saying that. It was so beside the point. She just wanted some reaction from her mother. But Vi sat down calmly at the kitchen table, ate her ham and cheese, and leisurely turned the pages of a magazine.

Corie fought back a frustrated sob. "I'm going to go pack."

That did it. "What the hell is wrong with you?"

"What's wrong with *me*?"

"You're in the catbird seat here and you don't realize it."

"Excuse me?"

"Now that the affair has been revealed, he'll treat you like gold. You can write your own ticket."

"That's repulsive."

"Men stray, it's what they do. What we do is use it to our advantage."

"*We?*" Corie stared. Her mother could still astonish her. "Is there some kind of sliding scale I should know about—$10,000 for a flirtation, $100,000 if there's actual penetration, a million if there's livestock involved?"

"Are you really going to throw all this away because he had a fling with some chubby little tramp? I wouldn't be surprised if the cops made that up. It's all a game to them."

Corie pointed in the general direction of the guesthouse. "What about my dead friend? What part does he play in this game?"

"I've expressed as much sympathy about that as I'm going to."

"Yes. Wouldn't want you to strain yourself. After all, your compassion muscles are pretty out of shape."

"What you need to do now is think about your future."

"I don't have a future."

Vi let out a heavy sigh. "What did the police tell you?"

"That he was having an affair. They weren't sure for how long. She's his alibi. Oh, and they have some inkling of his sexual proclivities. Let's just say Evan 'thinks outside the box' in the bedroom."

Corie wanted to shock her mother but Vi didn't react. "It could have been a onetime thing."

"And conveniently that one time is the night of the murder."

"I know it hurts."

"From personal experience?"

Vi narrowed her eyes. "Have you told Evan?"

"Why?"

"I recommend that you wait awhile before you confront him. Give yourself a chance to calm down."

If Corie had her way she'd never see Evan again. She stared into her mother's watery blue eyes searching for some sign of compassion, empathy, or connection.

There was none. "I'm sick and tired of watching you throw everything away," Vi said. "You have what everyone wants. Do you even know what it's like to have to set an alarm and get up out of bed while it's still dark out, or it's snowing, or you're sick and feel like crap, but you've got no choice and you have to drag yourself to some demeaning job? Do you even know what you have?"

"I know it was hard for you after Dad left. This is different."

"Oh, different." Vi mocked her. "You're the same spoiled brat you always were. It's all your little heartaches and your little hurt feelings and your need to feel good. Meanwhile, everyone around you is slaving away to give it to you. And then the moment it doesn't suit anymore, you throw it away and expect to be given something new."

"That's not true."

"Isn't it? Who paid for your first car? And your prom dress? And all the getups you needed for the rodeo?"

"I never even wanted to compete in the rodeo. That was all about you. I hated it." Her mother did the same thing as Evan, blame Corie for making them fulfill desires Corie never even had.

"Of course you did." Vi spat the words. "I said you were spoiled and I stand by it. You'll say anything to get your way, even accuse a good man of dreadful things. A man who has given you everything."

"A good man. That's funny. You wouldn't recognize a good man if you tripped over one. And up until now, neither would I. I'm going to go take a shower and then start packing. When I come back out of the bedroom, I want you gone."

"Or what? You don't tell me what to do, you silly little bitch." Her mother's voice, raised in a scream, followed Corie out of the room. "You're nothing without Evan. Nothing."

CHAPTER NINETEEN

Jack saw Aranda in line at Starbucks wearing another well-cut suit with a pair of high-heeled boots, her dark hair pinned up in a loose knot. He joined her as she was getting to the cashier and extended a twenty. "Let me get that." He added a large drip to the order for himself.

"Most cops don't look like you," she said while they waited for her drink.

"Yeah? What do they look like?"

She laughed. "They don't wear Armani, for one thing."

"You have a good eye. Just out of curiosity, what are cops supposed to wear?"

"Something from the Men's Wearhouse maybe. With a higher synthetic fiber count."

"I'm surprised you go out for Starbucks when you make a wicked espresso right there in your office."

"I'm glad you liked it."

"Nice perk having an espresso machine in your office. I'll have to see if I can get one for the station."

"Well maybe if you didn't spend all of your money on suits."

"Good point." Jack led her to one of the small round tables.

Aranda crossed her long legs and leaned back in the chair. "So, I got the files you asked for." She hesitated and poked at her frozen coffee drink with a straw. "I think Roger's finally had it with Evan. This Utah deal they're about to close is going to be the last one. There's also a golf course we're developing in the foothills, but Evan's consulting work on that is pretty much done."

"Has he told Evan that?"

"'Course not." She took a sip of her drink through the straw. "I told you Roger's careful, but when we ran a background check on Evan nothing showed up. This is his first marriage, he has no record." She gave a little shake of her head. "I know a lot about you, too."

"Yeah? I'm pretty boring."

"Your grandfather was a diplomat, which maybe explains the Armani, and your father was killed."

"Hey." Jack tried to sound outraged.

"Nothing personal. Like I told you, we have everybody checked out." She leaned forward and looked up at him. Aranda had a beautiful mouth and the smile grew slowly, languorously, forming dimples at either end. The temperature in the room simultaneously rose about ten degrees. Her voice dropped to a conspiratorial whisper. "So, what'd you find out about me?"

"I don't know what you're talking about." Jack shifted in his chair. He was out of practice; he was actually getting flustered.

"Oh, come on. It's not fair that only cops get to have all the information." She sat back again, slipped off her jacket, and draped it over the back of the chair. Jack watched, as she knew he would. The sleeveless silk shell she wore underneath was deep fuchsia and fit nicely. She caught his eye and a smile still played at those full lips. "I can't believe this weather. It's not still supposed to be this hot."

"I personally like cooler weather."

"So, busy detective, you drove all the way down here to talk about the weather? I could have had the files sent by messenger."

"You wanted to talk somewhere other than your office, which means you don't want your boss to know even though you said he wouldn't mind."

"I really wanted one of these." She indicated her drink.

"I don't know how you can drink that. It's a milkshake, not coffee."

She leaned forward and took another sip through the straw. "Mmm. Yummy." But she looked at Jack.

He unconsciously reached a hand up to fidget with his tie.

"You didn't tell me if you had me checked out," Aranda said. "I thought you guys did background checks on everyone you contacted."

"You're not a person of interest in a homicide."

She smiled. "Oh. That sounds exciting."

"It's really not." He changed the tone of the conversation. "How long have D'Ambrose and Markham been friends?"

"They're not friends."

"Okay. How long have they been working together?"

"Roger first hired Evan for a case about five years ago." Aranda took another sip of her drink and watched him expectantly.

Jack knew she was waiting for him to make a connection. "That's about the same length of time Corie and Evan have been married. Corie influenced Evan."

Aranda had pretty hands with short, neatly manicured nails bare of color. She made a circular motion with her index finger.

Jack thought about it. "Other way around. Corie influenced Roger."

"Roger usually only lets himself be influenced by two things: God and money. Not necessarily in that order, although you didn't hear that from me."

"How does he know Corie?"

"I'm not sure."

"Is he aware of the—" Jack decided to rephrase but there was no graceful way to ask what he wanted to ask. "Do you think she confides in him? Would Roger know if she was having marital difficulties?"

"I think he helps her out as much as she allows, in an advisory capacity of course." Pieces of hair had come loose and she reached up to fix the way it was pinned on her head. "Roger's sweet on Corie. But you probably figured that out already."

"Thought he was married."

She gave him a look.

"Right. And my point would be . . .?"

"Roger would never act on it. But he was pissed at you yesterday."

"Really?"

Aranda finished fixing her hair. "Apparently you offended her honor."

"I barely said anything."

"Don't get me wrong. I like Corie. She's smart, she's fun, she's got a wicked sense of humor. I used to think she was kind of boring. But lately she's been coming out of her shell. If circumstances were different, I'd be friends with her."

"Why can't you be?"

"The shell, as if I have to tell you, is the size and shape of Evan Markham's thumb. It's one of the reasons I don't like him. Is this the picture you wanted me to paint?"

"Pretty much."

"I never saw bruises. I never heard the 'oh I walked into the door, I'm such a klutz' routine. She also never confided in me. I was glad she finally had someone around to support her."

"You mean Brice."

"I hope you catch whoever it was."

"I will."

Her eyes met his. "I really don't think he hits her. Evan treats Corie well but like a prized possession he keeps up on a high shelf. Not like a flesh-and-blood woman. Now Jennifer on the other hand, or even Vangie . . ." Aranda wrinkled her nose.

"You don't like his new assistant?"

"What does she assist him with, the handcuffs?"

Jack arched a dark eyebrow. "Maybe Evan didn't like his wife coming out of her shell."

"Maybe. To be honest, it's hard to tell what Evan likes. Other than money and influence."

"He ever hit on you?"

She gave a snort of derision. "As if. I'd cut his balls off."

Jack couldn't help smiling at that. "Tell me a little more about the services Markham provides. What makes him so valuable?"

"Part of the consulting he does is helping developers avoid litigious situations *a priori*. Evan's brilliant at advising on risk. Or the potential for it. He can give a resort the once-over and point out vulnerabilities, if that's the right word. He's been trying to move into the development side for a while. He actually hates to be referred to as an expert witness. I'd consider it a personal favor if you managed to work that phrase into your conversations with him as often as possible."

Jack grinned back at her. "I'll keep that in mind. Is he that good?"

"Evan's smart enough to know where the big money is and he's managed to leverage his particular skill set quite nicely." She reached into a sleek leather portfolio and pulled out a folder. "I went back through our files like you asked and I talked to Roger to see if he could remember anyone particularly upset. Brice's name didn't ring a bell with either of us. You really think Brice was killed because of a lawsuit?"

"Stranger things have happened."

"Killed the wrong man, if you ask me. Sorry. I know that's a terrible thing to say."

"You really don't like Evan."

"I feel like I need to take a shower after I've been around him."

Jack walked her back, and before she went inside her building, she looked up at him with serious brown eyes and a shy smile. "I know you're in the middle of an investigation and I'm a shameless flirt. But I'm serious about the offer to help, and I'm equally serious about the offer to have a cup of coffee—or something stronger—with you sometime when you're off the clock."

He returned the smile. "Best offer I've had all day."

CHAPTER TWENTY

Corie pulled a photo off of a shelf in the living room and stared at it. Herself and Hennessy from their rodeo queen days, with full makeup and big hair like they were competing to be Miss America or something. Big smiles, too. Their arms around each other's shoulders and ridiculously embellished, oversized cowboy hats on their heads. Her fingertips traced patterns on the glass. "How could you?"

Hennessy's exotic green eyes smiled back from the photo. Corie wanted to remember Hennessy as the fearless, smart, funny, talented girl she idolized. But it was all a lie. Hennessy's life had always looked so charmed and impossibly glamorous, and yet she wound up starving herself.

During high school the Markham home was a refuge. After Corie's father left her mother, she brought home a string of men Corie was supposed to call "Uncle." Such a cliché. Vi drank and smoked and ran off with one man after another. Jessie Markham, on the other hand, was warm, artistic, and easy to talk to. Corie used to confide in Jessie about her fights with her mother and Jessie listened to her without judgment. Jessie gave the two girls a lot of freedom and she treated them like adults. Corie had her first tastes of champagne and pâté at the Markham's. She and

Hennessy, allowed to do pretty much what they pleased, were inseparable. Until Corie fell for Jack.

At first, Hennessy made fun of Jack, called him a geek and a nerd. Corie smiled remembering the funny, awkward boy Jack used to be. *Of all the people to wind up being a homicide detective . . .*

Long before she had a crush on him, Jack made Corie laugh and he was her friend. But then Hennessy made it her mission to take him away from Corie and Jack succumbed. All too easily, it seemed.

When she reached her twenties, Corie looked for older men, powerful men, men she thought would protect her. Men who could pay the bills. Corie wasn't going to wind up like her mother, struggling to get by and growing bitter. The irony was that Corie wound up with a man who didn't protect her at all.

From the dusty, abandoned books on the bottom shelf, Corie pulled out her high school yearbook. *Why am I doing this to myself?* Her fingers found the page with their senior photos. Farantino, Fariel. Scrawled in blue ink across his photo, it read: 'To the prettiest girl in the entire school, Love Jack.' At the time, Corie never gave Jack a chance to explain. Her pride was wounded, her trust was shattered, and it just plain hurt too much.

What had she written in his yearbook? Did he still have it? *Stop it.* This was no time for a trip down memory lane. She slammed the book closed but she took it, along with the photo and her overnight bag, and put them in the trunk of her car. Then she put Murphy in his run with water and dry dog food. That worried her, but surely Evan could manage to take care of the dog.

While she was looking through the photo albums, an envelope addressed from Vangie fell out. Inside were photos taken of her and Evan at the pool party in Dallas she told Jack about. Corie and Evan in bathing suits, smiling, with their arms around each other. In one photo Evan clowned for the camera, putting his head on Corie's shoulder. Vangie had written little notes on the back in her loopy girlish handwriting. Corie took them to the office and fed them, one by one, into the shredder. Then she wondered if that was a good idea. It was proof of a connection between Evan and Vangie. *What if they were evidence?* But the cops already knew about the "connection" between Evan and Vangie.

Corie surveyed their office. What she needed was some proof of money going to other women or some evidence that he'd been hiding assets from her. How could she know so little about their finances? *Idiot, idiot, idiot.*

Evan's desk seemed like a good place to start. She opened each drawer in turn but the large drawer for files was locked. Corie walked to one of the bookshelves, reached up, and retrieved a small, carved wooden box off the top shelf. A souvenir from a trip to Bali, it was where she kept all of their office keys. Corie was itching to go online and look at their bank accounts but the police still had the computers. What if he'd changed the passwords? When was the last time she'd even checked?

She tried every key in the souvenir box but none worked. *Prick.* Anger overtook reason. Corie ran upstairs and out to the garage. She came back with a long flat-edge screwdriver and attacked the edge of the drawer savagely. So much for stealth. When the drawer cracked open she stared in dismay at the empty hanging folders. *Fuck.* She worked on the side rails with the screwdriver until the whole drawer pulled free with a loud squeal. A lone piece of paper was wedged between the back of the drawer and the inside of the desk.

"Corie?" Evan's voice.

She snatched at the paper. A bank statement with a check stapled to the upper left-hand corner. She saw "Perez and

Associates" on the check before she crammed the paper into her pocket.

"Corie, are you down there?"

The drawer lay on its side on the floor. She briefly considered trying to put it back but knew she didn't have time. She heard Evan's feet on the stairs.

"What are you doing, Corie?"

She walked to the foot of the stairs and glared up at him. "The fuck you think I'm doing? It's my office."

"*Our* office." He stopped on the second step from the top. "What's gotten into you?"

Her heart hammered in her chest. *Get out of here. Don't say anything, just leave.* He stared down at her, a phony concerned look on his face. He was dressed in a suit. Had he been to a meeting? Had he been in bed with Vangie? Had he been fucking someone new? Corie started up the stairs.

"Where's Violet?"

And it just came out. "Oh, your other lover left."

"What the fuck?"

"Don't you realize? She has a massive crush on you. She wants you for herself. You could have her along with all of the others. She wouldn't care. She told me I was silly to care."

"Don't be vile. What did they tell you?" He didn't even sound surprised.

"One thing, asshole. If you've given me any kind of disease, I'm going to sue your ass."

"Corie, you need to tell me what has happened."

She recognized the stiff, formal way he talked when he was mad. But she didn't care. It felt freeing not to care about Evan. "Oh yeah? You need to tell me what's been happening with Vangie."

"Vangie? Vangie Perez?"

"That would be the one, unless you're fucking another Vangie too." She faced him near the top of the staircase.

"What have you heard?"

"Get out of my way."

"Is it your detective friend who told you?" His face was close to hers. "I know all about the two of you. Or I should say, the three of you."

"Please let me by."

"I had Detective Fariel checked out. You know how thorough I am. You all went to high school together. Did he fuck my sister, too? Oh yes. I know. And he has a record. Sealed because he was a juvenile."

"Evan, do you make this shit up?" Her heart pounded so hard she felt dizzy. If he knew Jack slept with Hennessy there was no telling what he might do. She had to warn Jack. But first she had to get by Evan. Her left hand gripped the banister.

He smiled. "Corie, as you well know from our business experience, it is rarely necessary to make shit up to hang people with; they provide enough rope all on their own. That is, you would know that if you had been paying the least bit of attention."

"Now you sound like my mother. Who really does adore you by the way. And none of this changes the fact that you've been screwing around on me. How long has it been going on, huh? How much money have you been giving your whores?"

"My private life is none of your business." He leaned even closer and his voice was a low growl. "What did you tell him? Please do not lie. You were alone with him all day. I know you betrayed me. What did you tell him?"

"Fuck you, Evan. Or rather, fuck Vangie. She's about your speed."

"You were here all alone with him and now you are spewing accusations at me? Did you enjoy fucking the detective? I want to know if it was good. Was it like old times? I want to know if he was able to please you, because God knows I can't."

She was blind with rage and, in that moment, didn't care what happened to her. Fear of Evan was replaced by hatred so intense she could taste it. "You son of a bitch. Go live with your fat slut Vangie. Get the fuck out of my way." She hit him with both hands, tried to push him away, but he was far stronger. She felt his hands on her shoulders as he shoved her, hard. She tried to grab the banister again with her left hand, but that only succeeded in slowing her fall and wrenching her wrist. Completely off balance, she tumbled and landed in a heap at the bottom of the stairs, not quite sure how she got there.

Evan stood where he was and watched as Corie slowly pushed herself up to a seated position. "You're okay." He made no move to approach her.

Not "are you okay?" Not a question of concern but a statement of fact, with disappointment in his voice.

She stared up at him and felt like she was in one of those dreams where you try desperately to run but can't.

Evan's voice and eyes were ice cold. "I do not know why you always have to make things so hard."

CHAPTER TWENTY-ONE

"Maybe it was part of some kind of weird S&M shit," Mike said.

Jack looked up from his reading. He, Mike, and Serena were hunkered down in a conference room reading through the files Detective Lassiter had sent from Charlotte. Monique's grandfather owned a furniture manufacturing company and the Charlotte police interviewed all of his employees. All fifty-six of them. Then there were neighbors, family members, and friends.

"I can believe Vangie would do a lot of things for Evan," Serena said.

"Maybe he was with her," Jack said.

"Kind of a test. Prove you love me," Mike said.

"No one would have found it suspicious Evan was at home." Serena nodded slowly, thinking. "We could have a conspiracy, or Evan could be an accomplice. We'd have to find evidence Evan orchestrated Brice's death."

"*If* the shooter is Vangie," Jack said.

"You still don't buy it," Mike said.

Jack waved a hand toward their laptops. "What about all of this? I don't believe in coincidences. Not one this big. What brought Brice here to Denver? To Evan Markham's house? Brice made it his business to get close to Corie."

"When I talked further to Brice's family they said he wanted a fresh start," Mike said. "Monique's murder had become a bit of an obsession—their word. His father was happy when Brice decided to move away."

"That poor family," Serena said.

The three of them read for a while in silence after that.

There were several suspects the Charlotte cops had honed in on: a black gardener with a record—mostly petty theft and misdemeanors—but it was November and the gardener hadn't done any work at the grandparents' house in over a month; a business partner of the grandfather's with a grudge, but it turned out he'd been in Florida at the time of the attack; and an ex-boyfriend of Monique's who still worked at the furniture factory, but the police were eventually able to confirm his alibi.

Monique's murder was brutal and heartbreaking. Mike pulled up crime scene photos on his laptop. "Lassiter said it made him think of an abattoir. I see why."

"What's that?" Serena asked.

"A slaughterhouse." Jack stared at the pictures.

"It was Lassiter's first case as a detective," Mike said. "Told me it always bugged him that they never closed it."

Monique was raped and sexually mutilated; there were deep, gaping incisions to her chest, abdomen, and genitalia. Twenty-four stab wounds in all. The perpetrator used a knife with a serrated blade, possibly a kitchen carving knife—they'd found a wooden block of knives next to the stove with one slot empty—although they never found the murder weapon. There was blood everywhere, starting in the upstairs bedroom where the attack occurred, smeared down the hallway, on the staircase, across the dining room floor, and finally in the kitchen where she was found.

"Personal," Mike said.

"A lot of rage," Jack said.

"Did we find anything of Brice's that connects him to this?" Mike asked.

"Nothing." Serena shook her head. "But his computer's still missing."

"Your killer was looking for any evidence Brice had in his possession," Mike said.

"Everyone's convinced my killer is Vangie," Jack said. "Who else knew about Brice's past and about Monique's murder?"

Jack got up and wrote "Vangie" on the whiteboard, with an arrow pointing to the name "Monique." Under that he wrote "Evan," with a similar arrow.

"There's no mention of Evan Markham in the case materials from Charlotte." Serena frowned.

"Doesn't mean there isn't a connection," Jack said. "Someone figured out who Brice was, found out he was getting too close to solving his sister's murder, and killed him."

"We don't know that for sure yet, Jack." Serena spoke carefully.

Jack shrugged and went back to reading. After a few minutes he said, "Holy shit," and felt himself grinning.

Mike looked up. "Something good?"

They watched as Jack stood and wrote "Len Funderburk" on the whiteboard, with a big red arrow pointing to Monique. Jack tapped on the board with the marker. "Lennon Funderburk? Jessie's friend? There was a *Leonard* Funderburk who worked for Monique's grandfather. What are the odds?"

At the time, Len's alibi had checked out: he'd been drinking in a bar at the time of Monique's murder. The police had talked to several people in the bar who all said they saw Len. As a result, they eliminated him as a suspect and never compared Len's DNA to the sample taken from the scene.

"That would mean Len followed Brice to Colorado." Serena's frown deepened. "And it's a coincidence he's friends with Jessie? What's going on?"

"What could Brice have found out after fifteen years?" Mike asked. "How the hell does all of this tie together?"

"Let's find out." Jack directed Mike to keep going through the case files and follow up with Detective Lassiter. He told Serena to work on a more thorough background check on Len Funderburk. Jack called Len himself and arranged an interview for the next morning.

After that, Jack only stopped working to refill his coffee. Five o'clock came and went. *No radiation today.* Which was okay, because he could do with a night off from nausea. He felt relief and then a twinge of doubt, which he ignored.

Back at his desk, Jack thumbed through the notes Aranda had compiled. He couldn't explain it. A hunch maybe, or something more, but he needed to get a picture of Evan Markham's world. It didn't feel like a waste of time; patterns emerged from the darnedest places if you were thorough, and Jack was all about patterns. An early professor of his in college had coined the expression "organize, don't agonize," and it had saved Jack's mental health numerous times when he felt buried by information overload on a case.

On his computer Jack organized a spreadsheet:

Plaintiff(s)
Type of Injury
Defendant
Type of Entity (Corporation, LLC, Individual)
Date Filed
Jurisdiction
Court Date (if any)
Judge's Name
Outcome
Award (if any)
Settlement (if any)
Settlement Date

He added a column for Evan's fee, calculating ten percent of the settlement amount as an estimate.

Many of the cases didn't wind up going to trial. Jack wondered if Evan was still paid in those situations. He made a note on the second tab of the worksheet where he kept track of his list of questions. Maybe Corie could answer them. If she ever spoke to him again.

He made quick work of the files once he had a system in place, and by the time he was finished, Jack had a pretty good picture of Evan Markham's work life for the last ten years, not to mention his cash flow. Many, many times higher than a homicide detective's salary. Even with overtime.

How important was the money to Corie? Jack sipped coffee and stared at the subtotals at the bottom of the columns for Award and Settlement. They were already in the tens of millions. Aranda said Evan also did consulting performing risk analysis. How much did he get paid for that? Jack jotted another question on the second tab.

What he didn't have was a connection between any of these consulting jobs and Brice Shaughnessy. Which made Len look even better. So why the feeling of disappointment? He was on the verge of closing not only his own case, but an unsolved, fifteen-year-old cold case. That should feel really good.

Jack was so absorbed that his cell phone startled him when it rang around six thirty. Afraid it would be Dani, he was relieved for a moment when he heard the patrol officer's voice. Until the man said, "Corie Markham. Hospital. Assault."

"Say again? Which hospital?"

"The husband got away," the officer continued. "We're looking for him."

"Got away? How?" Jack shrugged into his jacket and headed for the door. They were supposed to be watching Markham. Couldn't they even do that right?

"He took off in his car while the reporting party was waiting for the responders to the 911 call."

"Son of bitch."

"We've put it out," the officer said.

"Consider him armed and dangerous." Jack thought of Serena as he drove through the Denver streets, lights flashing, breaking every speed limit known to mankind. At least this was a real emergency. Had Corie confronted Evan? *Shit.* Maybe he shouldn't have told her about Vangie after all.

He braced himself for what he was going to find but Corie was awake. She looked up when he walked into the examination room and she seemed glad to see him.

The detective tried to smile. "You look like you're in one piece."

"Yeah." A tremor in her voice.

"What happened?" Jack bit back his own sense of urgency. "I talked to the officers who responded, but I'd like to hear it from you, if you're up for it."

Sitting on the examination table with her legs swinging over the edge, Corie nodded. But when she tried to speak, all that came out was a choking sob.

"Corie." He took a step toward her and then stopped, uncertain.

"Jack—I–I'm sorry." She grabbed for his arm and the tears started in earnest.

What the hell was she sorry about? Tentatively, he sat on the edge of the table next to her. He looked at her hands still holding onto his arm, and the next thing he knew she was leaning into him, really crying. He watched her shoulders heave for a few seconds and then his arms found their way around her, as if it was the most natural thing to do. She was thin and warm and wretched. She pressed her face against his chest and sobbed uncontrollably, and he let her. He tightened his grip and really held her, not some bullshit pat on the arm.

"Corie, shh. You're safe now."

Jack's experience with cancer had made him feel very human. He'd rejected the knowledge. Being human meant you were weak, you made mistakes, you fell in love. His entire life, the most important thing—the only thing that ever brought any relief—was finding out the truth. It wasn't that Jack refused to take the easy way out on principle. If the truth happened to come easy, great. Except it never did. And that was okay with him.

As he held Corie, it was as if he could feel her despair leach into him through his pores.

"It's all so awful." Her voice came in choking fragments, muffled against his chest. "He forced me . . . can't believe I let him . . . awful things . . . needles . . . I can't . . . in the water . . . his face . . . he made me . . . wasn't proud . . . not proud . . ."

"It'll be okay. You have to believe me." Her hair felt silky under his hand, the bones of her back fragile. How could she tumble down a flight of stairs and still be in one piece?

She sat back a little, although she didn't let go of him. "I think I got makeup on your shirt."

He looked down into her puffy eyes, the lashes spiky from the tears. "Oh no. Now the other cops are gonna make fun of me."

She wiped at her eyes and pushed her hair back behind her ears. He noticed a box of tissues on a cabinet next to some medical supplies, gently extricated himself, and got it for her.

"I'm not going to let him hurt you anymore." He felt calm. It wasn't forced anymore. It was as if something had shifted.

"You can't promise something like that."

"I can. But you have to tell me what happened."

She nodded. "I will . . ."

"Corie, I know you're scared."

She looked down at her hands and then back up at him. "It's not that. Evan seemed to know about . . . us. He said awful things."

"Like what?"

"'Did he fuck my sister, too?'"

Jack froze.

She held his gaze. "Hit a little close to home, to tell you the truth. And he said you had a record. He said he had you checked out."

First D'Ambrose, now Markham. Didn't anyone trust anyone else anymore? He started to give her a stock answer, to say that Evan was talking trash, and then changed his mind. "What were his exact words?"

"He demanded to know what I told you. And then he said that his private life was none of my business, which would be funny if it wasn't insane."

"What did you tell him?"

"Nothing. I told him to fuck himself. And then I asked him how much money he'd given his whores. In response, he asked if I enjoyed fucking you and then he pushed me down the stairs."

Jack turned away from her and stared at the cabinet where he'd gotten the tissues, his mind racing. The work Jack had done that afternoon formed a picture of a man who was under control; cautious, calculating. Evan lost control with Corie, but why? He didn't strike Jack as someone easily goaded.

"Are you good at your job?" Corie asked.

He turned and faced her. "You can ask for another detective. Maybe you should."

"I don't want another detective. But I need to know. Have you changed?"

He knew what she meant. Had he?

"I'm not making this about the past," Corie said. "But I need to know you're not going to let me down."

"Yes. I'm good at my job."

Corie took a deep breath, then gave an almost imperceptible nod. "I don't think Evan was trying to kill me."

"Neither do I." Jack sat back down on the table next to her, although he didn't touch her.

"I think if he meant to kill me he would have." She wasn't asking for reassurance and he didn't offer any. "It struck me that it was exactly like that night with Brice. I touched Evan first. You don't do that." She laughed a short bitter laugh and exhaled sharply.

"Not even me. Not ever." She snuck a shy glance at him and thought about how to say it. "Not even during intimate moments. You don't touch Evan."

"I believe you."

"He was so goddamned smug. He acted like he was the wronged party. I hit him and he pushed back. Do you want to know what he did after I fell?

"Nothing. He didn't rush down the stairs. He didn't try to help me. He stood at the top watching. I was so scared that he was going to come after me. I tried to get up as fast as possible so I could get away. He said, 'You're okay.' Like he was disappointed. Then he left."

Jack's throat felt tight and he wanted to hold her again. "You need to let them check you out. You're safe here. I have an officer posted right outside."

She nodded. "You know that's Evan's style, finding out about you. He's probably run a background check on the mail carrier and our house cleaners."

"But he didn't run a background check on Brice?"

"Oh hell." She shook her head in disgust. "Of course he did."

Jack smiled. "I'll come check on you later."

Corie leaned back on the table, frowned, and then sat bolt upright again. "Shit. I almost forgot." She pulled a crumpled piece of paper out of the pocket of her jeans.

"What is this?" Jack smoothed out the piece of paper and looked at it curiously. He already knew the meaning of the Perez and Associates check.

She jabbed her finger at the paper. "From a Swiss bank, no less, for an account I know nothing about. The asshole's been hiding money from me."

"You don't know that."

"The hell I don't. Three million dollars? And it's current. Where the hell did Evan get three million dollars?"

"That's a lot of money." Jack thought about his spreadsheet. It was also a lot of motive. But for what?

"That's it? That's all you have to say?"

"Until I know more? Yep. I'll get this into evidence and look into the bank account first thing in the morning. Now you stop playing detective and get some rest."

Corie's eyes narrowed appraisingly. "You're going after Evan, aren't you?"

"I'm going back to work."

"Same thing, isn't it?"

CHAPTER TWENTY-TWO

As Evan drove west from Denver into the mountains, Vangie fished in her handbag for some pressed powder and worked on her face in the dim light of the visor mirror. He couldn't think with her around. Not like Corie. Corie made him feel better. Except not today. Why had she said those things? What had that cop told her? Why did she have to shove him?

He had to get away. Had to think. Vangie's whining had long ago past the point of annoyance and he entertained fantasies of shoving her out of the car at seventy. In his mind, he saw her body grind and skid to a pulp on the pavement. In the passenger seat, adding insult to injury, she started to hum.

She caught him watching her and giggled. "I can't get this song out of my head. Do you know it?"

She started to sing it for him and he shoved a plastic trash bag at her. He would have rather put it over her head. "Take everything out of the glove compartment and put it in this bag. Clean the car. Go through all the other storage areas. Don't miss anything."

"Why?"

Evan reached across her for the door handle.

Vangie swatted at his hand. "What are you doing? I never understand you." She cleared out the glove compartment and the storage bins on the doors. Then, with many huffs and sighs, she climbed into the back seat.

Evan glanced at her in the rearview mirror. "Make sure you check the very back, too."

"Seriously?" Another whine. But she did it. "I don't see anything. There's probably just the spare tire and stuff."

Bent over the backseat, her skirt rode up and he could see her thong. "Come on back up here. That's giving me an idea." At least there was one way to shut her up for a while. He put his hand on the back of her head and pushed it down towards his lap. "Take your time, it's a long drive."

Expertly using her tongue and her hands, Vangie brought him to the brink of climax and then paused, letting him relax before she worked him up to the edge again.

"At least there's one way you're useful." Evan shifted in his seat.

"I like doing this." Vangie scraped her acrylic nails lightly on the underside of his cock.

Evan groaned. "Well, you're very good at it."

Vangie giggled, as if she were very clever. "Practice makes perfect."

About forty miles later, Vangie fixed her lipstick in the light from the back of the visor. "Do you think we can stop somewhere and get a soda or something?"

"Can't. I should have let you bring something from the hotel." Some of the edge had gone out of his voice.

Vangie shook her head. "I think it's sad how your wife doesn't appreciate you. If I was married to you, I'd want to spend as much time with you as possible. I'd never let you out of my sight."

"Really." Evan thought about Corie and the scene on the stairs. His wife wanted nothing more than to get as far away from him as she could. Permanently.

"Do you think it's going to be okay?"

"Is what going to be okay?"

"The murder charges."

"Well it would have been much better if you hadn't gotten chatty with the detectives, but Stu and I can still fix it."

"It's not fair. I was only trying to help."

Evan frowned. "What do you mean?"

"Nothing." She looked down and pushed at a cuticle with one of her nails. "I was scared and I haven't been able to sleep right. I'm not thinking straight."

"You didn't have that excuse yesterday, though, did you?"

"From now on I'll do exactly what you say, Evan."

"I can't always be telling you what to do."

"You're so much smarter than me. Sometimes you tell me things and I don't understand why at first, but then later on I see how you knew what you were doing all along. You're amazing."

"Vangie, no more talking."

"Oh. Sorry. Okay."

Finally, some blissful silence. Evan drove west through the town of Fairplay and then through an even smaller town that was really only a collection of shacks. He turned off onto a dirt road that deteriorated quickly after about a mile.

Vangie stared out the window into the darkness. "Now I know why you couldn't take the Mercedes. This is more like a trail than a street."

Evan stopped and got out to unlock a padlock from one end of a heavy chain.

An old pickup was parked by the side of the road. Vangie hadn't noticed it in the darkness until it roared to life and the headlights suddenly flashed on. A man got out and approached the Cadillac.

"Get out," Evan said.

"What?" Vangie sounded panicked.

"Do as I say."

"Evan, please don't leave me here. I'm so sorry. I'll do anything. Don't leave me out here all alone."

"Vangie, you are such an idiot. We're trading cars."

"We are? Why?"

Evan slapped her hard and the man outside pretended not to notice. "Enough. Do as I say or stay in the car and go back into town with him."

Evan got out and she scrambled to follow him. "Wait. I want to go with you. Of course I do. I'm sorry. I don't understand what's happening."

"The bag." Evan pointed.

"Oh. Of course." She retrieved the plastic bag from the backseat and picked her way to the pickup, stepping carefully in the brush with her high heels.

Evan put the truck into gear and drove through the makeshift gate. Behind them the other man replaced the chain. He noticed she was shaking. *Good.* Evan hadn't been here in a long time but he knew the road well and navigated confidently, avoiding ruts and boulders. In the dusty yellow glow of the headlights, the road deteriorated even further and became increasingly steep.

"Not that much further." Evan spoke as if to himself and, for once, she didn't answer.

The old pickup had no shocks, and when Vangie put out a hand to brace herself, the glint of a chunky gold bracelet caught his eye. She must have snatched the jewelry from the hotel. He'd have to make sure he got all of it back.

When Evan ground to a stop in front of an old building, Vangie took in the weathered siding, the sagging front porch, the rusting propane tank, and practically sobbed with disappointment. "Where are we?"

Evan stared at the cabin, lost in thought. "It's a place I use to get away."

"Why did we come here? Why couldn't we stay at the hotel? The hotel was much nicer."

It was as if she was insulting an old friend. Evan snapped out of his reverie. "God, I am sick of your whining." The truck door squealed as he jerked it open.

Uneven, weathered floorboards creaked under his weight as he strode to the front door. He didn't really care if she followed or not. A wave of sadness washed over him as he pulled on the metal hasp of the padlock securing the front door.

"Evan, I'm scared."

The unmistakable cabin smell hit him: mustiness, cedar, mothballs.

Her voice rose to a high-pitched, childish whine. "I can't shoot Bambi. I can't."

He turned and looked at her. She clung to the newel post at the bottom of the front porch steps, standing on her tiptoes, as if she didn't trust the ground to support her. "What the hell are you talking about?"

"I know you came up here to go hunting."

Evan gave a bark of laughter.

Inside he lit the pilot on a gas fireplace in the corner that served as a heater. Then he opened cabinets and checked the refrigerator in the small kitchen. "Good. They did what I asked."

"Who?" Vangie stood on her toes at the front door now. "The man who met us?"

"Let me show you around." Evan pulled her inside. "There's a small wine refrigerator under the counter. Help yourself to whatever you want. And the water's great. It's from a well. Very clean. Only tap water I'll drink. Bathroom's through there and the bedroom is over here." He indicated the rooms. "There's satellite TV, lots of channels but no pay-per-view because there's no phone service. But there should be enough on to entertain you."

"Okay." Vangie sounded uncertain. "I don't have any clothes."

He looked at her short skirt and heels. "Rummage through the dresser in the bedroom. There are probably some sweaters. I have to go into town for a while. You have everything you need: plenty of food, the propane tank is full, there's a backup generator in case the electricity goes out, the—"

"Town?" She cut him off. "What are you talking about? I can't stay here by myself."

"Of course you can."

"Why did you bring me here if you're going to leave? I didn't mean to say so much. I didn't. I'll do anything you ask. I'll tell you all about the gun. Please don't leave me here. I hate to be alone. Especially when I don't know where I am."

He grabbed her wrist and yanked her toward him. His voice was a low growl. "You're right. You will tell me everything. But not now. I have to leave and I have no qualms about tying you up while I'm gone. Would you like that?"

Vangie pulled away with a shriek. "No! Don't tie me up when I don't know where I am."

Evan watched her curiously. "While I'm gone, why don't you try to work up some gratitude. You are the reason I'm doing all of this."

"I'm grateful." Tears made shiny streaks in the powder she'd applied earlier in the car. "What if I need something? How do I get in touch with you?"

"What do you need?"

"I don't know. What if there's an emergency?"

He fished in his pocket and then set a bottle of pills on the counter. "There won't be. Here. This is what I gave you last night. Drink some wine. Watch TV. Think of it as a vacation."

And then he was out the door. He heard her call his name and try to follow but she wasn't quick enough, and as he drove away, he didn't look back. There was no landline at the cabin and no cell service. When he passed back through the makeshift gate, he saw the small orange dot of a cigarette as the man nodded to him. Evan's prey wouldn't get far, even if she had the sense to try.

One problem taken care of, at least temporarily.

CHAPTER TWENTY-THREE

Jack nodded and the hotel manager opened the door.

Yelling "Police!" with guns drawn, Jack and Serena burst into the empty room.

Serena checked the bathroom and called "Clear."

Jack re-holstered his .45 and surveyed the room: the ropes hanging from the lights on the wall, the rumpled sheets, and the half-eaten cheeseburger on the room service tray. Amidst a sea of melting ice and water in a silver bucket sat two unopened bottles of wine. "They left in a hurry."

"All of her makeup and toiletries are still in there." Serena nodded toward the bathroom.

"And her clothes are in the closet."

"Maybe they're planning on coming back." Serena pointed to a plate holding an untouched fruit and cheese assortment.

Jack felt a chill of certainty. "I don't think so."

He took one last look around the room. Evan had parked his mistress in a downtown hotel. He'd brought his sex paraphernalia. Evan's intention appeared to be staying here with Vangie, which confirmed Jack's suspicion that the attack on Corie was unplanned. Why had Evan gone back to his house? What set him off?

"Let's go check out the car." Jack walked out and headed down the hall.

"I talked to the hotel manager." Serena followed him onto the elevator. "The reservation was open ended. Markham told them when he made it that he wasn't sure how long they would need the room, but he thought maybe a couple of weeks."

"Really."

"They put a sizable hold on Evan's credit card. He was planning a romantic stay with his girlfriend." Serena's tone was ironic.

Jack told her about the bank statement and the check Corie had given him.

Serena frowned. "If he's hiding money from his wife, maybe he was getting ready to leave her, even before all this."

"The money can mean a lot of different things."

"Know a lot of other reasons rich guys have bank accounts they keep secret from their wives?"

In the garage, two police cruisers were parked behind Evan's shiny silver Mercedes, their lights circling.

Hotel security cameras had caught Evan and Vangie emerging from the elevator into the garage at 5:47. Corie's 911 call had come in a little after five. Evan must have rushed straight here from the house. In the video, he had Vangie by the hand and was pulling her along.

"Why do you think he took Vangie? He that horny?" Serena sounded disgusted but one of the uniforms laughed.

"Maybe he's babysitting his bail." Jack watched the grainy footage where Vangie struggled to keep up in her high heels. "Show that again. Right there. Freeze that."

"What do you see?" Serena asked.

"No jewelry. When I talked to her she was all decked out in long necklaces, earrings, rings—she doesn't strike me as the kind of woman who forgets to put on her bling."

"Wherever they're going, it's a surprise to her."

"Lot of surprises tonight."

"You think Vangie's in danger?" Serena asked.

Jack stared at the surveillance footage. "He's out a quarter mil if she fails to appear in court. Even for Evan that's a big chunk of change."

Evan and Vangie were off camera when they got into their vehicle, but seconds later another camera picked up a black Cadillac Escalade exiting the garage. As the car pulled away there was a nice shot of the license plate.

"Let's see whose car that is," Jack said.

The officer who'd found Evan's car typed the information into the console in his cruiser. "The car is registered to a Stuart Graber. No warrants. Here's his address and phone number."

Jack looked at Serena. "Well, well. Full-service lawyer, isn't he?"

"D o you have a reservation?"

By way of answer, Jack flashed his badge at the tall, thin blonde in head-to-toe black behind the hostess desk at the fancy steakhouse.

Stu Graber was seated in a booth near the front, eating alone. He'd rolled the sleeves up on a rumpled, blue button-down shirt which was open at the throat revealing a patch of sparse, gray chest hair. His paunch draped over the waistband of charcoal gray dress slacks. His cheeks were ruddy in an unhealthy way, which suggested he could be on a poster warning about the dangers of hypertension. And he'd doused his filet in A1 sauce, which Jack considered a crime against humanity.

"How's that steak, Stu? Cooked the way you like it?" Jack pulled out a chair and sat down.

Stu didn't stop cutting his meat. He glanced up for the merest second, dismissing Jack with flat gray eyes before turning his attention back to his meal. Everything about the man seemed gray except for the unhealthy spots of color highlighting his flaccid cheeks. He forked a piece of steak into his mouth, chewed, and then picked up the glass of red wine to the right of his plate. "You're wasting your time, Detective. I'm not at liberty to discuss anything concerning any of my clients." Stu cut off another bite of steak and dragged the edge through a puddle of A1.

Jack picked up the bottle of steak sauce and grimaced. "Sure. I understand. And I hate to interrupt your dinner. But I'm curious why you loaned your car to an individual wanted for attempted murder. I know there's probably a very good reason. Lot of sodium in that steak sauce, by the way."

Stu kept his expression neutral and forced himself to take the next bite before he answered. "I don't understand. Have the charges changed?"

"Which ones?" Jack set the bottle down.

"My client was charged and released on bond, which means they're free to go wherever they please as long as they don't leave the state." Stu's hand reached for the wine again.

"Which one?"

Stu blinked. His tongue worked a piece of gristle from between his teeth. "I assume you're referencing Ms. Perez."

"I didn't say that. Who borrowed your car?"

"I don't see how that's any of your concern."

"It is when the individual is wanted for attempted murder."

"Are we playing a game here, Detective? Ms. Perez was charged and released on bond. I can loan my vehicle to whomever I please. Now if we're done, I'd like to finish my dinner in peace."

Jack leaned back and watched him. "I'm talking about your other client who, at approximately five o'clock this evening, pushed his wife down a flight of stairs and tried to kill her. There's a warrant issued for Evan Markham on counts of aggravated assault and attempted murder. Imagine our surprise when we located his vehicle and found he'd switched cars with you. Can you explain why you loaned your car to an individual fleeing a felony? I believe that is considered harboring a fugitive. But then my legal expertise isn't as sophisticated as yours."

There was a long pause. "It would be if I'd known he was wanted on criminal charges, which I didn't. Still don't. Unless that's why you're here. To inform me. Nice of you to bring counsel up to speed. Usually law enforcement's not this collaborative."

"No? Can't imagine why when you're such an agreeable guy. Want to be really agreeable and tell me where Evan's going?"

Stu's stomach rumbled ominously, belying his calm exterior. "I'm sorry I can't be of any help, Detective."

"Yeah, you look sad." He looked like he was going to have a stroke. "And you're being very helpful. Or rather your Cadillac is, as I'm sure you're aware it's equipped with OnStar. And luckily for us it's brand new." Since 2009, OnStar had provided the capability to cut engine power in cars if the police requested it.

Jack smiled. "When we determine you knew that Evan was wanted for an attempt on his wife's life at the time you loaned him your car, we'll be charging you. Enjoy your dinner."

At the hostess stand on his way out, Jack asked to see a menu. While he waited for his takeout order, he thought about how they'd most likely find the Cadillac abandoned in a parking lot or empty field somewhere. If it was even still in one piece. Markham was smart, ruthless, and he knew his way around the law. Jack was concerned about Vangie, but his first priority was Corie.

CHAPTER TWENTY-FOUR

Corie sat cross-legged on the hospital bed with a psychology textbook open in front of her. One more chapter and she'd rest. But she kept reading:

> *The whole purpose of the endeavor is to communicate to the submissive that their body is not their own. Even basic bodily functions, such as bowel movements and orgasm, are under the control of the dominant.*

Corie stared at the text written by a psychology professor at a major European university. The academic writer had gone to great lengths to avoid judgment. Some of us are neurologically wired to enjoy pain, endowed by nature with a higher tolerance. Out of our hands. Merely a choice—like red or white, what kind of dressing, for here or to go. BDSM was a subject of mass fascination, and it seemed, at least from her research, that the things Evan had done to her were only the tip of the sadomasochistic iceberg.

Maybe the memories would fade with time. No lasting harm. Maybe.

"Hey."

Jack appeared as if she'd conjured him, a dour island of normalcy in the midst of her fucked-up life. Corie slammed the book closed.

"How are you feeling?"

"Not bad enough to be admitted to a hospital, although I must be in a weakened state because I'm not even mad at you." She watched him set a plastic carrier bag on the table, along with his computer case. "What's in the bag?"

"My last stop was at Del Friscos. I got some takeout."

"Pretty high-end takeout. Did Evan go out to eat? Did trying to kill me work up an appetite?" She slid the book under the covers.

"He wasn't there. His lawyer was."

"Stu? That figures. Evan's lapdog. But why were you talking to Stu? I don't understand."

"I got something for you, too. You don't have to eat if you don't want. I just thought—"

"Are you kidding? I'm starving."

"What were you reading?"

So much for thinking he hadn't noticed. "Nothing. Some old psychology stuff from a class."

"You in school right now?"

"No." She changed the topic back to Evan. "So what happened? Did you find my husband?"

Jack unpacked the food—cheeseburgers and thin, crisp, shoestring potatoes—and he didn't answer right away.

"Well?" Corie grabbed a handful of the fancy French fries. "Where is he?"

Jack shrugged. "No major developments."

"I see." She took a bite of her burger and closed her eyes. "Oh, yum."

Jack looked pleased. "I'm glad you like it."

"So are you going to tell me where Evan is or not?"

But Jack was guarded. He took off his suit jacket, rolled up his sleeves, and took a bite of his own burger before he said anything. And then he digressed. "I wasn't sure what you liked. Maybe you were a vegetarian now or something."

"This is so good, I'm not even going to give you crap for holding out on me."

"You need to rest and let me do my job."

"I wasn't aware I was impeding. But whatever. I like the shifts back and forth from warm concern to gloomy and withholding. Very unnerving."

"I've already told you too much." He tried to maintain his stern demeanor but she saw a smile play at the edges of his handsome features.

"Funny, I feel the same way about you." He could never know. She remembered her earlier resolve to tell him about the rape. *Alleged rape.* Her eyes flicked down to where she'd hidden the book and she suddenly felt sick. Corie set down her burger.

"You can't be finished already."

She couldn't sit here and wait, passive, a quarry. "I wish there was something I could do to help."

He told her about the files he'd gotten from Aranda, about some of his theories, and his conclusions from the spreadsheet.

As he talked she found herself noticing his hands. Jack's were square and strong, with long slim fingers. Beautiful hands. "Have you ever—" She stopped. What the hell was she doing? *Never. Never talk about it.*

"Have I ever what?"

She toyed with a French fry and was saved from answering by a nurse, who came in and looked at them and the food with disapproval. She spoke directly to Jack and slammed an ice pack down on the table. Corie was to apply the pack, fifteen minutes at a time, to the lump on her head.

"Wow, I'm glad I'm not really sick," Corie said.

"You have a lump on your head?"

"It's nothing. And I love how everyone talks to you as if I'm not competent enough to understand spoken words."

"It's my natural air of authority." Jack handed her the ice pack. "Did they say you have a concussion?"

"I have a goose egg. It's no big deal." Corie shivered as the cold ice touched the tender spot. "They had me follow lights with my eyes and answer questions like what day is it and what planet do we live on, and I'm fine. I don't have a concussion. Nothing's broken. The vehemence and wonder with which everyone insists I'm lucky is downright heartwarming."

"Wow, I thought *I* was cynical." He looked at the display on his phone.

"You're going to time the fifteen minutes? Were you always this anal?"

"I might get distracted by your sparkling conversational abilities and lose track."

"Touché." Corie slumped in the bed feeling thoroughly defeated. "Ask me questions if you want. It's not like I've got anything better to do."

Jack apparently decided her sanity was intact because, in between bites of his burger, he asked a question about Evan's compensation.

"He charges straight consulting fees for some things, but sometimes it works out better to take a percentage. Like if someone is being sued for ten million dollars and Evan helps them defend successfully, he might work out a bonus arrangement."

Corie watched Jack wipe at his mouth with a napkin, then make a note in the ubiquitous pad.

"You said he makes a good witness."

She nodded, lost in thought. "Evan seduces juries." Over the years her husband's performances on the stand had gotten better and better. Confident. Charming. She tipped her head to the side and looked at Jack. "You haven't seen that side of him. He has a knack for making people trust him."

Jack's eyes were dark and serious. "Do you usually go to court with him?"

"No. Not anymore. At first I used to go all the time. But then like everything else . . ." Her voice trailed off. Like everything else what? Got old? Got nauseating? "I suspect he was happy to replace me with more docile assistants."

"Speaking of that, do you know a woman named Jennifer Suarez? Hoffman now."

"Smooth, Jack. Yes, I remember her. Jennifer worked for us about two years ago. Evan told me he fired her because she wasn't willing to work the hours needed for the job. I think that was crap, but as usual I didn't press him. Why? Is she okay?"

"Tell me about when she worked for you."

"Do you ever actually answer a question?"

He smiled and took another bite of his burger.

Corie in fact remembered Jennifer fondly. The young woman had been nice and eager to please. Unthreatening. Maybe not so bright but more than willing to make up for her lack of experience with enthusiasm. Like Vangie.

Jack noticed her frown. "What?"

"I just realized that Jennifer reminds me of Vangie in some ways."

Jack looked like she'd surprised him. "I hadn't thought of that but you're right. About the same age, a little on the heavy side, long dark hair."

"Apparently I'm not Evan's type." The corner of her mouth turned up in a bitter smile. "Cynical, huh?"

"It's a defense mechanism."

"Speaking from personal experience?"

"I have another question. It might be rough."

"Here we go. Was Jennifer sleeping with him, too?"

Jack held her gaze and he didn't blink. "No, I think that's the problem Evan had with her. That wasn't my question, though. Did Evan ever threaten you with a knife?"

She'd steeled herself to do this, to be done with self-pity, and the sudden tears pissed her off. "You didn't sneak in a bottle of wine with the food, did you?"

"Sorry."

"I'm in a hospital. You'd think the least they could do is give me some good drugs. Augh. You're going to think I'm so stupid."

"It doesn't matter what I think."

Corie wished that were true. "There was this one time I let him blindfold me. Years ago, back when we were first married. That really scared me, not being able to see. But he told me I was uptight. Evan loves telling me I'm uptight." The scene in the hot tub flashed through her mind and she shoved it away.

"Anyway. We were in bed and I felt him touching me with something." Corie could hear the hum of the air conditioner in that long-ago room, feel the silk sheets against her skin.

"It's okay," Jack said.

She made a motion with her hand. "No. I can do this." Then she spoke quickly, afraid if she hesitated she wouldn't get it all out.

"Evan was running this thing lightly up and down my leg, on the inside of my thigh. It felt weird. Cold. I asked what it was and he said, 'Don't you trust me?' At least I wasn't tied up that time. I pulled the blindfold off and he had a knife, a fancy stainless steel kind of thing, almost like a scalpel. I couldn't believe it. I jumped up out of the bed and all I could think about was covering myself. I pulled the sheet off and I screamed at him and I told him that he was a sick son of a bitch.

"He acted as if nothing out of the ordinary had happened. He wasn't concerned or upset or angry—nothing. I left. For real. I moved out and I was going to divorce him. But Evan made it his business to win me back. He apologized and swore he'd change.

He promised to go to counseling. You know the drill, I'm sure. This is where the stupid part comes in." She nodded toward his notebook. "You're not writing."

Jack shook his head, as if trying to wake himself up from a bad dream. "Jesus."

"Yeah. You want to know the really weird thing?"

"I'm afraid to ask."

Corie felt as if a knot in her stomach had suddenly unraveled. "I feel better having told someone. That surprises me."

"Corie . . ." Jack cleared his throat.

"I thought homicide detectives were tough. Surely you've heard worse stories than this?"

"Ice time again. Let me hold it for you."

"You don't have to do that." She thought of the yearbook. *To the prettiest girl in the entire school.* Not so pretty now, was she?

Then Brice's face flashed through her mind. This wasn't about her. This was for him. She said she'd do whatever it took to help find her friend's killer and she meant it.

Jack pressed the ice gently against the sore spot and, when he did, his fingertips brushed her hair. He misinterpreted her shiver. "You really don't like having the ice on your face, do you?"

"You notice everything, don't you?"

The corners of his mouth twitched. "Occupational hazard."

"It's very annoying."

"So I've been told."

She wanted to ask by whom, but she didn't. He probably wouldn't answer anyway. "I hate him, Jack."

"Don't think about it right now."

"I don't know why I tried to protect Evan. I think I was just trying to hold everything together. God knows why. I don't want any of it. Do you know what my mother told me earlier today?"

"What's that?" Jack, with those slim, graceful fingers, held the pack carefully, as if her head were an eggshell.

"That I don't realize how lucky I am."

CHAPTER TWENTY-FIVE

"Evan?" The word was a question, her voice soft, no panic yet. Corie had dozed off and, for a confused moment, thought she was back in her own house, back in time, and Evan had come into their bedroom. His presence was so familiar that, for a split second, it felt perfectly ordinary. Then she remembered she was in the hospital and Evan wasn't supposed to be there.

Jack heard. Faster than she thought possible he was out of the chair. The two dark forms merged, blended, and their feet squeaked on the linoleum floor as they fought. Corie heard grunting. Something metallic crashed to the floor. She groped for the light.

Jack had a look on his face that scared her. His first punch backed Evan up away from the bed and he followed quickly with a second to the gut. As Evan doubled over, Jack grabbed Evan's right arm and twisted it back in a way that looked like it must hurt a lot. With his left hand behind Evan's head. Jack slammed him into the wall. Jack seemed to be enjoying himself. "Scrubs, Evan? Really?"

Evan had worn a disguise. He didn't come to the hospital as her husband but as something else entirely. Corie wasn't fighting but she still was breathing hard.

"I'm allowed to see my wife. Corie, are you all right?"

"The fuck you care." Jack reached for Evan's left arm and yanked it back brutally for the handcuffs. Then he spun him so roughly towards the door that Evan's face smashed into the jamb. Jack didn't have a mark on him and he wasn't even out of breath.

Evan laughed. "Keep it up, Detective. The worse I look, the more it will cost you." Blood appeared under his nose.

Unconcerned, Jack looked over at her. "If you'll excuse me, Corie, I have to take out the trash."

Corie held Jack's gaze for a long moment. *Who was this man? Who were either of them?*

The look was not lost on her husband and Evan spoke as if he were the wronged party. "Very touching. But the real question, Jack, is what are you doing in my wife's hospital room? Because she is still my wife. You have overstepped your bounds and I will make you pay."

Jack opened the door.

Evan froze on the threshold. "I insist on speaking to Corie. I need to know that she's all right. Corie, tell him. Tell him you understand."

Jack was having none of it. "Visiting hours are over." He shoved Evan ahead of him into the hall.

And they were gone, just like that. It hadn't taken five minutes. Other than Evan's name, Corie hadn't said a word. *Tell Jack she understood? Understood what?* She sat for a long time, her mouth hanging open, staring at the door.

CHAPTER TWENTY-SIX

Jack's phone woke him from a sound sleep at seven thirty the next morning.

"There's someone here who says he has information about the Shaughnessy murder," the dispatcher said.

Jack felt like crap and fought to clear the cobwebs. He couldn't seem to get enough sleep lately. "Be there in forty."

He dragged himself under a hot shower, leaned his forehead against the cold tile, and tried his best not to feel sorry for himself. He had to get it together. He shaved and dressed and started to feel a little more human. A large coffee from a drive-through helped.

At headquarters, a nervous young man waited in the reception area. Alex Cantrell was clean-shaven, twenty-one years old, and a senior at the University of Denver. The same school where Brice and Corie took their class. He jumped up when Jack introduced himself and stuck out his hand. The young man wore flip-flops, baggy khaki shorts, and a black t-shirt.

Jack led him upstairs into an interview room. "I really appreciate you coming in."

Alex nodded, then sat down and leaned forward, elbows on his knees. "I couldn't believe it when I saw it on the news. Couldn't sleep after that. I was up all night deciding what to do. I checked it out on the web to make sure I heard right, and it was the same dude."

"Brice's body was discovered early Thursday morning. It's Saturday. Why the delay in going to the police?"

"I was up in the mountains with some friends so I didn't see it on the news until last night. It—I had no reason to think anything would happen to Brice. I don't talk to him that often."

"How did you know Brice?"

"I met him at school, at DU. Nothing like this has ever happened to me before." Alex kept leaning back, then sitting bolt upright again; he didn't seem to know what to do with his hands.

Jack had run a quick background check before retrieving him from reception. Alex had no record and was a straight A student. He tried to put the young man at ease. "What I need you to do is answer my questions the best you can. If you're truthful we can get you cleared pretty quickly. Sound good?"

"Whatever you need."

"Appreciate it. How long had you known Brice?"

"Couple of months. We went for a beer a few times." Alex named a bar near the school.

"You ever go over his house before?"

Alex looked down, clasped and reclasped his hands. "That was the first time."

"How did you wind up going to visit Brice Wednesday night?" Jack asked.

"He wanted to know if I could help him get some stuff." Alex hesitated, then reluctantly met Jack's eyes. "Am I going to be in trouble?"

"For what?"

"We smoked some weed."

Jack almost smiled. "I'm homicide, Alex. Not my department."

Alex nodded. "Yeah. Okay. I uh, found some of what Brice was interested in, so I texted and he said come on over. He didn't pay me or anything. We were gonna party."

"What time was that?"

"Around ten. Wait, I can tell you exactly." Alex checked his phone, then looked up proudly. "Ten thirteen."

"Tell me about what happened when you went over to Brice's house."

Alex shrugged. "We hung out. Brice smoked. Is it okay to tell you that? I was mostly interested in the wine."

Now Jack allowed himself a smile. "I saw the glass by the bed."

More nodding. "Yeah. I drank a bunch of wine. He snatched a bottle of some really good stuff."

"The Petrus." They'd found the bottle on the kitchen counter. The set of prints lifted from it might now have an owner.

"That stuff's like a thousand a bottle." Alex appeared excited, then crestfallen again. "Brice said the people he rented from were really rich. But nice. He said they wouldn't mind, that he was tight with the wife. And then, you know, you saw the bed. I hung for a while. Brice was cool. It's lousy what happened to him."

"You see anyone else while you were over there?"

A shake of the head. "Uh-uh."

"What time did you leave?"

"I was home by around two thirty."

"Can anyone corroborate that?"

"Yeah. Yeah, totally. My roommates. I share a house with three other people. One of them was still up studying." He gave Jack an address on South Gilpin Street, a couple of blocks from the university.

After he left, Jack thought about what this did to the timeline. If Alex did indeed leave Brice alive at two a.m.—and Jack would get a detective working on confirming Alex's story—then it fit with the theory that Brice was killed around dawn. Alex had willingly agreed to give DNA and fingerprints. But then so had Evan. Jack would get Tiffany on this ASAP and, in the meantime, see what he could shake loose from Len.

CHAPTER TWENTY-SEVEN

Evan spoke to a judge's image on a TV screen, playing his best, contrite self. Video advisement got him out of jail bright and early Saturday morning; judges didn't like their weekends ruined any more than anyone else. Stu stood by his side, a slouching, gray lump, and let Evan do most of the talking.

Evan wasn't, as Jack had threatened, charged with attempted murder. Evan's record was spotless and his family well-known in the community. The charge was reduced over the prosecutor's strenuous objections to simple domestic violence. For the moment, Evan wasn't allowed near Corie and he required a police escort to go home and get his things, but he was free. Imagining Jack's reaction to the news made Evan happy.

"What are you smiling about?" Stu looked over at Evan as they walked outside. "How was it? Did you manage to get some sleep?"

Stu sounded worried and Evan was impatient. People dwelt far too much on the past and their feelings and what may or may not happen. "Did you bring my car?"

Stu proceeded to nag as he trailed behind Evan like a lost puppy dog. There was a lot to go over. They needed to review the case. What did Evan want to do about Vangie? Was Corie serious about the divorce? Did the business need to be restructured?

They reached Evan's Mercedes, which Stu had braved the police to fetch from the underground garage at the hotel. Evan opened the door. "Did you get gas?"

But Stu wouldn't let it go. "We really need to talk, Evan."

"You really sound like my wife, Stu. Only I don't want to fuck you."

"We should go over Ms. Perez's defense, too."

"Why?"

"Why?" Stu blinked at Evan as if the question had stumped him.

"The further away I stay from Ms. Perez the better."

"You mean you're not going to see her now?"

Evan made an impatient motion with his hand. "Move on. I let her use my cabin last night to get out of the spotlight. But I made it clear it was for one night only. She should be gone by now."

"What do you mean, gone?" Stu's voice rose in alarm. "In my car?"

"Have you reported it stolen yet?"

"Yes."

"So you can follow instructions. You're not out one red cent and filing the police report covers your ass. I can't believe I paid a hundred grand for a car. An American car no less. Eww." Evan shuddered. "That price better include quite a few hours of your time as well."

"I liked that car. And I still don't think—"

"You told me to stay away from her. I'm away. Let it go." Evan's hand gripped the top of the car door. "I was trying to help her, and she repaid me by stealing your car and taking flight. I'm out a quarter mil, let's not forget."

Stu squinted against the bright morning sunshine. "That detective has you in his crosshairs. You need to be careful, Evan."

"I'm done with this conversation. I'm done with the accusations. Assault? I was visiting my wife in the hospital. Murder? I didn't even know Brice Shaughnessy. If you don't want to work for me anymore I'll get a lawyer who inspires confidence."

"Evan, you had to know visiting hours were over."

Evan slipped on sunglasses and tipped his head from side to side. "They always allow immediate family. Even if you're in intensive care, or what do they call it? Even in recovery. Fariel roughed me up pretty good. Let's initiate a suit against the department."

"Evan—"

"You have your marching orders, or are you confused?"

"No, I'm not confused." Disgust, or resignation, tinged Stu's voice.

"If you want to see me later, you know where I'll be."

Stu stood and watched as Evan conscientiously put on his seat belt and backed out of the parking space. Speeding west toward the mountains, Evan made a quick call. "I need to borrow your truck again."

The man on the other end of the line didn't need to ask who it was. "What time?"

"Two hours." Evan's radar detector chirped as he turned it on. "Maybe a little less. Don't keep me waiting."

Evan circled his shoulders and flinched. His neck really did hurt. Maybe he'd have Vangie give him a massage. She'd like that. Evan wondered if anyone had paid her a visit last night or if everyone had stayed where he left them. Evan knew he couldn't usually count on people to follow orders.

Other than my wife.

But he'd been foolish to trust Corie. He'd let his guard down. He'd let her new friend stay in their guesthouse and what had they done? His wife and Brice had recreated Evan's first crime scene.

Not Corie.

Her sapphire eyes were frightened when she propped herself up at the bottom of the stairs. Evan knew that look. He never expected to get it from his wife. Contrast that with the look she gave Detective Fariel at the hospital. That trusting look sat in Evan's gut like a sour, indigestible meal. Apparently those old feelings from high school weren't dead and buried, at least not on Corie's side. The detective was harder to read.

Wincing, testing, Evan worked his jaw back and forth. He still felt Jack's fist, still tasted blood. He'd outsmarted cops before. But this time Corie was involved. You didn't kill your wife. Everyone looked at the husband when that happened. He'd succumbed yesterday afternoon on the stairs to a fit of disorganized emotion and he couldn't let that happen again. You didn't kill a cop either. Evan's split lip curled into a snarl imagining Jack's gray, lifeless body. Who would Corie gaze at fondly then?

Not Corie.

But why not Corie? Maybe he was blinded to who Corie really was due to long association, in the same way that he counted on for himself. Why did she say those things? Why did she leave his bed? Why did she push him on the stairs? If only she hadn't done that. He'd changed. He'd stopped. He'd fought his demons and won and found himself capable of love. He'd become a fool like everyone else.

Evan laughed bitterly. He finally knew what it was to love a woman, and it was going to destroy him.

CHAPTER TWENTY-EIGHT

Vi put her hand on Corie's back and guided her into the BMW like Corie was an invalid.

"How are you feeling? Do you need me to adjust the seat for you?"

Vi's car had the sickly sweet smell of someone trying to mask a worse one. Probably didn't want her real estate clients knowing she smoked. Better they should gag on vanilla air freshener, like the jar-shaped piece of cardboard hanging from the rearview mirror.

"It stinks in here." Corie hadn't slept in what seemed like days and felt churlish and out of sorts.

Vi sighed. "I know we had words, but I'm glad you called me to take you home. I'm still your mother, Corie."

And that was the closest she'd get to an apology.

"I can't believe Evan would do something like this," Vi said softly after a while.

"Sorry about your perfect son-in-law." Corie shifted in her seat so she faced the door.

"I'm sure he feels bad. I think when you're ready, you should give him a chance to explain." Vi actually sounded sincere.

"What the fuck is there to explain about pushing me down the stairs?"

"It makes me sad to see things turn out this way. Up until now he's been so good to you."

"You're right. On the way home can we stop at a card store? I want to see if they have a special thank you category for situations like this. Homicidal Expressions: When you want to let them know you really don't care."

"Ha ha."

Then Vi took a call from a client and was blessedly, mercifully quiet until she pulled into Corie's driveway. "I know what happened. You confronted him. About that woman. Even after I told you not to."

"Yes, of course, this all happened because I didn't listen to you." Corie got out of the car and, unfortunately, Vi followed.

"I'm right, aren't I? Corie, I know you better than anyone."

Corie wondered if her cringe was visible. "You don't need to come in with me."

But she did. Vi looked around the empty house and shook her head slowly. "Such a shame. Everything changed so quickly."

"Don't worry about me. I'll be fine, thanks." Corie walked into the backyard and let an excited Murphy out of his pen. She talked to the dog for a few minutes and played with him. Murphy cheered her up. She also hoped if she stalled long enough her mother would leave.

No such luck. Vi followed Corie into the kitchen. "Of course I'm worried about you. How could you think otherwise? How exactly did it happen?"

Corie started a pot of coffee and thought about the phrasing of the question. How did *it* happen? As if it was a spontaneous event that occurred without warning.

"What are you going to do now?" Vi asked.

"I didn't get much sleep. I might take a nap." Corie decided not to tell her mother about Evan's midnight visit.

Vi wasn't budging. She settled in on a barstool. "I meant, what are you going to do about your marriage?"

"Oh, is that up to me?"

"Corie, you've let everything that's happened go to your head. It's understandable. Finding a dead body . . . Ugh. But not everyone is trying to kill everyone else."

Corie turned away and got one mug out of a cabinet.

"Evan made a mistake." Vi sounded like it pained her to admit fault in her son-in-law.

"You can say that. Several." Several million.

"Yes. That's true. But he's still a human being."

Corie let that incongruous thought hang in the air between them. She fixed her coffee and didn't offer Vi anything.

"Well then. I guess your chauffeur service will be leaving." Although she didn't move.

Corie sighed and got out a second cup. "Cream? Sugar? Vodka?"

"You have your father's sense of humor."

Corie watched Vi take a sip. "I have one simple request. And please, I beg of you, don't make any smartass comments or I won't be responsible for my actions. Since it's one of the last things he worked on, I thought Brice's family might like to have the model we made together. Can I come by and get it later?"

"For a couple who can't stand each other, you and Evan certainly think alike."

Sleepiness fled. A jolt of adrenaline set Corie's heart pounding. "What?"

Vi beamed as if conveying good news. "Evan came and got it. I believe he's already sent it to them. See? You have more in common than you give him credit for."

"What? When?" Corie's voice rose.

"Yesterday morning."

"Why didn't you tell me?"

"You've had a lot going on. What difference does it make?"

"What . . . diff–difference?" Corie was so surprised she stuttered. "Are you insane? Evan doesn't want the model to do something nice."

"He's a good man, Corie, if only you'd give him—"

"Cut the good man bullshit and tell me exactly what happened."

"Tell? What's to tell? Are you sure you don't have a head injury?" Something about the look on Corie's face made Vi reconsider her cavalier attitude. "Evan asked if I still had the thing in my basement. He came and got it the morning after the murder."

"Goddamn you." Corie had stored the model at her mother's so it would be safe. Tears pricked her eyes and her voice was a low hiss. "Get out of my house. Get out now or, I swear to God, I will drag you out."

"You and Evan deserve each other. You're both insane."

CHAPTER TWENTY-NINE

Len Funderburk showed up for his ten o'clock interview fashionably late at ten fifteen.

Jack examined him more closely. Len was thirty-nine although he looked older. Deep wrinkles were already setting in around the corners of his eyes and he had a receding hairline. He wore his sandy blond hair on the long side but at least it wasn't in a ponytail. He was dressed in a long-sleeved, denim button-down shirt and jeans. Around his neck was a striking necklace—large, irregularly shaped hunks of turquoise strung on a leather string.

Len took a sip of the water Jack had provided, then folded his hands in his lap and sat back.

"I appreciate you coming in and talking to me," Jack said. "I'd like to review what you told us about your whereabouts the night before and the morning of Brice Shaughnessy's murder."

Like the first time Jack talked to him, Len said he and Jessie watched a movie and then went to bed. They were both sound asleep at six the next morning and didn't get up until after eight.

Jack thought about Jessie's dramatic flourishes when she talked. "Mrs. Markham seemed very fond of that movie. What was the name again?"

"*Cinema Paradiso*—it's one of her favorites."

"So you watched the movie, had some wine, and went to bed around . . . what time did you say?"

"I'd say we were asleep by midnight."

"Great, thanks." Jack remembered Jessie had said it was earlier. "There's one more thing I'd like to go over. We've been looking into the victim's background and we found out that Brice's sister was murdered. It was a long time ago and we don't think it's related, but your name came up in that investigation. What can you tell me about that?"

Len didn't startle but his smile faded. "Monique." He said her name the way a lover would and then seemed to go into a kind of reverie.

Jack settled back into his chair and let the silence stretch out. He watched Len take another sip of water.

Len broke the silence first. "I've cleaned up my life since then."

"How did you know Monique Lawson?" Jack asked.

"I worked for her grandfather."

"Pretty girl," Jack said, still friendly. "Did you date her? I know I would have wanted to."

"No. She was out of my league." A hint of a smile touched the crevices at the corners of his eyes. "I'm not sure Monique knew I was alive."

"Sounds like you had a crush on her."

"Everyone did, Detective. Monique was wonderful. I think half of the men that worked for her grandfather were in love with her. She was friendly to everyone, not a snob. That was one of the great things about her. Her death messed us all up."

Len's face was open and his memories of Monique seemed fond. Jack almost felt bad asking the next question. Almost.

"Maybe you wanted to do something to get her attention?"

"Like what?"

"You tried to see her, you wanted to talk to her, to get her to notice you, and it backfired?"

"Oh, I see where you're going. Oh no. No, no, no. I could never hurt Monique. I could never hurt anyone. I know that about myself." Len spoke softly but adamantly. His deep-set blue eyes looked right at Jack, darting neither right nor left.

"You said you've cleaned up your act. What did you mean?"

"I used to drink. A lot. I lost my license, I went through jobs. I let people down, most of all myself. I assumed that was why I was here. Because you found out about my record."

"When we talked to you and Mrs. Markham yesterday you both said you didn't know Brice."

For the first time, Len seemed uncertain.

"Len?"

"Jessie doesn't know." Len's voice grew even softer.

"That you know Brice?"

"About my past."

"Or your connection to Brice."

"About any of it. And I didn't know Brice then. He was only a kid when—at the time of the—" Len seemed unable to use the word "murder."

Jack did. "At the time of his sister's murder, Brice was only fifteen."

"Awful." Len shook his head. "That poor kid. But he never came around to the factory. I had no reason to talk to him. I didn't even know what he looked like until I saw his pictures in the paper."

"How did you meet Jessie Markham?" Jack asked.

"At an artist's colony in North Carolina. She was there taking a workshop. We hit it off."

"So you still live in North Carolina?"

"I'm what you could call a citizen of the world."

What a load of crap. "It seems quite a coincidence that you were a person of interest in Monique's murder, and now you're right nearby when her brother's killed."

"It struck me that way, too. I've been wondering what it means," Len said with no trace of irony.

"You have?" Jack was used to dealing with combative suspects, withholding suspects, or, as in Evan's case, arrogant suspects. But there was nothing about Len's demeanor that suggested anything other than a man being forced to relive a painful memory.

"I've wondered if it's some kind of opportunity."

"How so?"

"I know it sounds hokey, but I wonder if the universe put me in Jessie's life to give me a chance to atone." As he spoke, Len's hand went to the necklace he wore. He fingered the rough chunks of turquoise.

Interesting choice of words. Jack nodded at the necklace. "Does that have significance? The turquoise?"

Len smiled.

"Something funny?" Jack asked.

"The Native Americans believed turquoise brought peace to the dead."

I should buy that in bulk. Jack said, "You haven't told me what you need to atone for."

"I wasn't as helpful to the family as I could have been. At the time. I was too impaired and dysfunctional. I've always felt bad about that. So if there's anything I can do now, perhaps that's my opportunity."

"Good to know." After Len left, Jack picked up his empty cup and put it in an evidence bag, which he personally delivered to Tiffany in the lab.

She huffed out an aggrieved sigh when she saw him. "You gonna have any more extra, special rush DNA samples for me today? Just wonderin'. You're wearing out all of your favors at once, you know." Tiffany took the bag containing Len's cup and regarded Jack with a wry expression. "It *is* Saturday."

"Got a hot date?"

"Just 'cause some of you don't have a social life is no reason to ruin it for the rest of us."

Jack leaned against a counter. "Who's the lucky guy? Please tell me it's not that rookie Rodriguez who's been sniffing around you lately. I hear he still lives at home."

"Get out of here and let me do my job. I'll call you as soon as I'm finished. Which I plan to be by six, just FYI. You look like crap, by the way."

"You sure know how to brighten a guy's day."

Tiffany smiled. "You're welcome. Seriously. This'll take a while. Maybe you should go home and take a nap."

"Can't. But I appreciate your concern."

CHAPTER THIRTY

Jack stopped in the men's room and splashed cold water on his face. He dried off with a rough, brown paper towel and regarded himself critically in the mirror. A nap sounded like a stellar idea but was unfortunately out of the question. His concession to well-being consisted of a relatively healthy lunch—a Cobb salad from a nearby restaurant—that he didn't eat in his car.

Serena found him later in his office slumped tiredly in his chair, staring at the whiteboard on his wall. A list of open items extended down the left side written in black marker. Answers, when they had them, were written in blue. Next to "3 unknown prints," "Vi Bellenger" and "maid" were scrawled. The third had now been identified as belonging to Alex Cantrell. DNA results were also back from the various glasses. Three samples from Brice, Corie, and Evan. The fourth unknown would most likely belong to Alex, and Jack expected they'd also find his DNA on the second condom. Jessie owned the ring. All of the usable shoe impressions were accounted for. No trace of Vangie.

"You were right." Serena followed his gaze.

"'bout what?"

"The maid was there the day before the murder. I talked to her boss at the cleaning company who was extremely cooperative, to the level of paranoia. Probably afraid we were gonna call INS, lose them some of their Mexican employees." Serena grinned. "Cleaning lady left shoe impressions in the dirt outside. Apparently the Markham's cleaners do windows."

Jack didn't laugh.

"What's more interesting is the bank account." Serena handed him a piece of paper.

Why did he feel reluctant? "You've been busy this morning."

Serena watched him read. "Before you ask, I had them double-check."

Corie Markham was the beneficiary. Jack's head snapped up and he stared at his partner.

"Why wouldn't she know about it?" Serena asked.

"I have no idea." His mouth formed a grim line. He added the paper to the piles on his desk.

"I have something else to show you." Serena pushed a pile of papers out of the way and turned on a computer.

"Corie's laptop?"

"Uh-huh. Found a folder for her school project, the one she was working on with Brice." Serena double-clicked an icon and a picture of a model house displayed on the screen. "Look familiar?"

Jack stared. "It's the crime scene. From Charlotte."

"Yep. Right down to the paint color and the little knocker on the front door."

Serena folded her arms across her chest. "Corie told us she was in a class. She told you about the sister's murder. She ever tell either one of us she built a scale model of the crime scene?"

Jack scrolled through the pictures on Corie's computer, his frown deepening. "They even have the phone off the hook in the kitchen."

"And a bedroom full of blood. Seriously creepy. Maybe Corie should go into forensics."

"Where's the model now?"

Serena shrugged. "Didn't find it."

"Maybe the killer took it that night, along with the computer. Or maybe that's what Evan went back for."

Serena nodded. "Find the model, find the murderer."

CHAPTER THIRTY-ONE

Corie placed her hand on the guesthouse door. Her heart was pounding. *Would it smell? What would it look like?* There was powder on the door from where the police dusted for fingerprints and still the strip of yellow crime scene tape, which she pulled down, angrily. Inside she took a tentative breath but the smell wasn't bad. A little funky, and she could easily talk herself into it being worse, but definitely manageable.

In her mind she saw the model on the coffee table in the living room. *Was that only a few months ago?* In her memory Brice looked up with a smile, glad to see her. It was so good to have a friend. Corie forced herself to take another step.

She remembered exactly when Brice told her about his sister. It was a rainy April night and she'd found the right color paint for the exterior of the model house. Rain was unusual for Colorado and Corie had prattled on excitedly about how much she loved the rain, how green it would make everything, how she hoped it would continue all night. It took her a few minutes before she noticed her friend's subdued mood. The coffee table was covered in newspaper and the model sat on top. Brice was seated on the floor staring at it, lost in thought.

"Brice? Hello?"

"Sorry." Brice got up, walked into the kitchen, and poured her a glass of Chardonnay. She used to joke that he was turning her into an alcoholic.

They worked on the model in the guesthouse because they didn't want Evan to see it. Which of course was stupid. If she wanted to hide something from her husband, she shouldn't have worked on it at home. Or stored it at her mother's house.

Corie returned in her mind to that April night. Brice had told her that the rain reminded him of home and his dead sister. And then he explained why. Monique was housesitting for their grandparents and Brice and his mother had gone to visit her. When he and his Mom pulled up, they saw Monique's car in the garage. All the lights in the house were blazing and they didn't suspect a thing.

"When Monique didn't answer the door," Brice said, "Mom thought maybe she'd fallen asleep. It was raining like crazy and we were getting soaked, so Mom let herself in. We walked into a nightmare."

Brice's voice faded and Corie had waited for him to continue.

"The first thing we saw was the blood," Brice said. "It was hard to make sense of it at first. Mom yelled, 'Monique!' I said, 'Maybe she cut herself.' But why would there be so much blood? It didn't sink in. We walked through the house looking for her. In the kitchen, the phone was off the hook and my Mom, without thinking, automatically replaced it. It was as if we couldn't acknowledge for a second what we saw. My sister was sitting up, slumped against the wall, as if she'd leaned against it and then slid down when she . . .

"Her eyes were open. I didn't know that happened. I remember I waved my hand in front of her face. I didn't want to touch her. My Mom was behind me and she yelled, 'Brice. Don't do that.'

"I said, 'We have to call the police.' I picked up that same phone and dialed. When I hung up, my mother stared at me and she started to scream. That was scarier than anything. She kept screaming and screaming and I yelled at her to stop. Later, I realized I'd gotten blood on my face from the phone. Monique's blood."

Corie's heart had been pounding, and when she picked up her glass to take a hefty swallow, her hand shook. "Oh God, Brice." Then she set down her glass and held him. He hung onto her and cried and—the memory hit Corie with such stunning force she gasped. How in the world could she have forgotten? Evan had walked in on them. He'd caught her holding Brice and she'd jumped up in a panic. Her friend forgotten, she ran to catch her husband who'd immediately turned on his heel and stalked back to the main house. Corie had tried desperately to explain, although she hadn't told him about the murder, only that Brice was upset. Evan had pretended he didn't care. But Evan cared about everything.

Her cell phone rang, interrupting the reverie; a second call from Jack. This time she answered.

"Corie, we've got some information about the bank account."

Corie dragged herself back to the present. "Okay."

"There's a couple of other things we'd like to ask you. Can you come down to the station?"

She hesitated and he grew concerned. "Where are you? Are you all right? Did you get a call about Evan's release?"

"I'm in the guesthouse." Her tone was flat. She was neither shocked to learn of Evan's release nor, to her own amazement, scared.

"Why?" Jack asked.

"I live here," Corie said.

"Well I don't think you should be in there."

"Right. You don't." Corie walked to the bedroom doorway and stared at the brown stain on the floor. What was left of her friend. Her vision blurred.

"Corie, are you sure you're all right?"

Just sick of everyone telling me what the fuck to do. Corie saw Brice's clothes hanging in the closet. She should take them to Goodwill. But she couldn't think about that now.

"Corie, what's happening? Talk to me. Is Evan there?" Alarm tinged Jack's deep voice.

"No." Corie turned away from the bedroom and walked back outside into the sunshine. "No. I'm fine. I can come to the station."

Her feet dragged up the stone steps. *So beautiful here. So sad. What a waste.*

God, she was starting to think like her mother. And what, exactly, was being wasted? Corie remembered the way Evan watched her when they used to engage in the BDSM stuff, the way his eyes glittered when she was in pain. This house was contaminated by those memories.

Evan's technique was so well calibrated. Ratcheting up the sensations a little more each time, knowing exactly how long to let it continue and when to back off. Evan had a sixth sense when it came to sadism. Corie remembered one time when he dripped hot wax onto her. Carefully, slowly, drawing out the suspense in between each small infliction of pain. The effect was cumulative. The point wasn't to hurry and get it over with, he told her. Evan was her guide through the experience and he used to talk to her during their sessions—she couldn't call it lovemaking. He would hurt her and then reassure her, his voice soft and soothing. He said the point was to anticipate the pain and then embrace it, like a lover. She used to think Evan had monumental self-discipline. He could torture her for hours before obtaining release himself; it seemed a source of pride for him.

Corie's stomach hurt. It felt like she'd been resisting the urge to vomit for days. Why had she allowed it? Why had she liked it? Would she ever feel clean again? Would a normal, healthy man's lovemaking arouse her anymore, or had that simple pleasure been taken away, too?

A car pulled up. Corie heard the door slam. Instead of going into her house she crept around the side, flattened herself against the paneling, and waited. Someone rang the doorbell. Once, twice, three times. She crept closer to the front until she could make out an unfamiliar car in the driveway. Stu Graber walked back to the car and put his hand on the door handle.

Corie stepped out and confronted him. "What the hell do you want?"

The lawyer jumped and put a pudgy hand to his chest.

"Are you alone?" Corie looked beyond Stu into his car, searching for any sign of Evan. She wished for the first time in her life that she had a gun.

"I'm alone," Stu said. "Can I talk to you for a minute? I have a proposal to run by you."

You had to give the dirtbag lawyer credit for one thing: he cut to the chase.

"I only need five minutes," Stu said. "Can we talk inside?"

"No." So this was what it took to finally drop her good-girl manners.

Stu looked like an owl the way he blinked at her. His eyes bulged like he had Graves' disease or something, only he was fat instead of thin.

"Stu, if you have something to say, please say it. I'm not going to stand here playing guessing games."

"There are a lot of ties between you and Evan," Stu said. "Both business, as well as the obvious personal."

"What on earth are you talking about? You charge that high bill rate for this shit?"

"Evan did not wish for the dissolution of either the personal or the business partnership. He's sad you want to go that route."

"Did not wish or does not wish?"

Stu blinked at her in that owl-like way again. "What?"

"Stu, why the hell are you here?" Corie didn't want him to see she was rattled, but it was hard to keep her voice level.

"I'm trying to explain. Evan doesn't want a divorce, but—"

"Too goddamn bad." Corie turned away from him and started walking.

"Wait."

Corie stopped and turned. "I know Evan didn't pay for you to drive all the way out here to feed me bullshit platitudes about the heartache of divorce."

"Evan would like you to do something for him. It's something you want to do anyway."

"I'll bet."

"The benefit tonight. It's very important to Evan, I know to both of you. Go to the benefit. That's it. That's all he's asking for."

"I'm sorry you wasted your time. Now get the hell off my property."

"Hear me out," Stu said. "I know this is a rough time. But if you do this one thing for Evan, he'll treat you well."

"He should have treated me well in the first place."

"Agreed. I can't argue. But I think we both know what Evan's like."

"Stu, you're not really going to try and act like we're in this together, are you? I know you work for Evan, not me. I'm getting my own attorney to represent my interests in the divorce. You're off the hook. You don't have to pretend you like me any longer." It was a relief really, finally speaking her mind.

"About that."

"Liking me?"

"No, the divorce. Don't you even want to hear the bargain I have to propose?"

"You can take your bargain and shove it up your ass."

"I think it's something you'll be interested in."

Corie hesitated. "What in the world could you have to bargain with?"

"Your freedom."

Now it was Corie's turn to blink. "I'm not sure what that means. But you have my attention."

"You go to the benefit, you do this one thing—and it's really such a simple thing—and Evan won't contest the divorce. It's not what he wants, let me be clear about that, but he'll give you your freedom, an even split of the business assets, and his equity in this house."

"The business is half mine anyway. I don't want the house. And I'm in no mood to go to a party."

"Corie, you and I both know how difficult Evan can be. You do this one thing and he's prepared to let you get on with your life—no games, no roadblocks. You want your freedom? Here's your chance to have it on a silver platter. He had me draw up a statement. No bullshit."

A statement? When the hell had Evan done that? "If I don't?"

"Do I have to spell it out for you?" Stu looked at her.

They both knew full well the range of Evan's vindictiveness. This had to be a trick. And it stung Evan was ready to let her go so easily. He'd used her like he used everyone. "It won't just be this one thing. I know him. There will be something after that, then something else, then one other detail."

"No. It won't be like that. Here, look at what he had me draw up. Have your lawyer look at it." He reached into his briefcase and pulled out a piece of paper which he held out to her. "I don't think I have to tell you how much easier it will be if you give Evan what he wants."

Corie took the paper from his outstretched hand but didn't look at it. She wouldn't give the lawyer the satisfaction. He wasn't going to have any tales of her emotional reaction to take back to Evan. She'd have lots of time once she was free to nurse her hurt feelings. "You must get in a lot of billable hours because I'm sure you don't sleep soundly at night. Now if there's nothing else, you really need to get the fuck out of here."

CHAPTER THIRTY-TWO

This was his plan: start with something innocuous, something he would do anyway. Once Vangie let her guard down he'd ask the real questions.

When Evan got back to the cabin and told her an edited version of his night in jail and the circumstances leading up to it, Vangie was, predictably, outraged. "How could they treat you like that? Why are they doing this to us?"

She looked like a crazy woman, naked except for a thick pair of wool rag socks. She told him there was nothing to wear, that the clothes in the dresser smelled of mouse droppings and mothballs. She'd even seen a mouse, which seemed shocking to her.

Evan liked her naked but demanded she take off the socks and put the high heels back on. He needed to think clearly, so he sat back on the couch and let her kneel in front of him. Not one complaint about the hard wooden floor. He assumed from her excited and happy demeanor that she hadn't had a visitor.

Then he got everything ready. He unlocked the second bedroom, the one that had been his sister's. He made sure the bed was prepared. Most importantly, he made sure there were plenty of towels. Evan wasn't ever going to make that mistake again.

He told her they were going to try something new.

When he covered Vangie's head with the hood he noticed that she was trembling. "Are you cold?"

She shook her head and he fastened the strap around her neck, pulling it snug but not tight enough to choke her. The hood allowed her to hear and openings left her nostrils and mouth unobstructed. It was a strange effect and something he'd never tried before. The sleek, black leather made her head look smaller and her breasts more pronounced. As long as she didn't speak he could almost forget it was Vangie. A definite plus.

Evan explained that she was going to taste wine and answer questions about it. "Wearing this, your senses will be focused on taste and smell." And touch, of course, although he didn't say that. He'd never wanted to cover Corie's face because he liked watching her reactions, but now Evan pushed away any thoughts of Corie or his own failure.

Vangie had been a tedious student so when he selected a bottle of wine he chose something tricky: a Rhone blend. Hardly anyone could guess all of the grapes in a Châteauneuf-du-Pape, which could contain up to thirteen different varieties in varying proportions, including obscure varietals like Mourvedre and Cinsault. Certainly not Vangie.

"You're not chewing gum or anything like that, are you?"

"Mm-mm." Vangie shook her head.

"Take this." Evan placed a white tablet on her tongue.

She was still trembling but obediently swallowed without question. Maybe he'd made some progress with her after all. *Too little, too late.*

"Eat a piece of bread to neutralize your palette." Evan fed Vangie a thin baguette slice. "Can you swallow all right?"

The black leather bobbed up and down as she nodded.

"I want you to smell the wine and identify five legitimate aromas. That's the first game."

"Five? That's hard."

"I don't believe I asked you a question."

"Sorry."

"Excuse me?"

"I'm sorry, sir."

Evan stroked the side of her left breast with one hand and Vangie flinched. Really marvelous large breasts, hard, much better than nature intended. Evan couldn't help but admire the plastic surgeon's work. Shame it was going to go to waste.

With a sigh he attached a clamp to each perfect nipple.

Vangie gasped. "Evan, no. I don't want to do this."

"You don't tell me no, remember?" He carefully added a small weight, similar to a fishing line sinker, to the chain strung between the clamps.

Vangie gasped again and whimpered, but didn't say anything. Her trembling intensified.

Along with the hood, the clamps were new. It was really an ingenious design. Any weight or tugging on the chain caused the clamps to tighten. He watched his index finger circle each insulted nipple, fascinated with the way they reacted. Then he poured a little of the lovely Rhone red into a stemmed crystal glass and put it in her right hand. "The way you're shaking you're going to spill the wine."

"Sorry." But she couldn't seem to stop.

Evan balanced another small weight in his palm. It had been so long he'd almost forgotten how it felt. The nerves, the electricity that hummed along his veins, the longing for it to end, the longing to make it last. "I want you to smell the wine—don't spill it—and tell me one aroma."

He'd ask questions. She'd answer them. A knife waited on the nightstand. Evan's heart thudded in his chest. There wasn't another house within two miles so it didn't matter how loud she screamed.

CHAPTER THIRTY-THREE

Park County Sheriff's Deputy Christopher O'Dwyer pulled his cruiser up to the old-fashioned gas pumps in front of a former service station on the outskirts of Fairplay. The pumps, which still displayed a price of 36.9 cents a gallon, hadn't worked in decades and paint peeled off of the old building. A hand-lettered sign read "Chicks Auto Repair," but you could still make out the remains of a green dinosaur, the old Sinclair logo, on the side of the small building.

A man was at work in one of the two service bays and Chris walked toward him, calling "Shaun." When the man didn't respond he pounded on the hood of the car. Shaun O'Dwyer, Chris's older brother, wheeled himself out from under the faded blue Grand Cherokee. His torn, grease-stained jeans rode low on his narrow hips. In a concession to the cold, Shaun wore a flannel shirt with the sleeves cut off. Tattoos covered his arms and, as Chris knew, Shaun's entire lean torso, the most prominent being a large skull in the middle of his sunken, hairless chest.

Shaun squinted up into the slanting afternoon sunlight, taking in the uniform and his brother's serious face. "This an official visit, carnal?"

Did he think using that Mexican slang made him tough? "I got a call to do a wellness check on someone at the old Markham place," Chris said. "A woman. Know anything about that?"

"A whatness check?"

Shaun got up, wiped his hands on a rag, and shrugged into a leather jacket. Chris watched his brother leisurely light a cigarette, which he held between his grease-stained thumb and forefinger. What a douche. "You been up there in the last day or two or what?"

"Road sucks."

"You seen Markham?"

"See him regular, bro. He brings lots of work my way. Says no one fixes cars like your big brother."

By fix he probably meant chop. "When was the last 'regular' time you saw him?"

"Can't say for certain." Shaun rubbed at a pimple on his chin, leaving a black smear.

Chris shifted his weight. "He's a person of interest in a homicide. I got a call from a detective down in Denver. You know what that means?"

"Don't know nothin' about that."

"What are you involved in now? Cars are one thing, Shaun, but if you know anything about a homicide you better tell me."

"Or what, little guy? You gonna take me into custody?" Shaun jumped into a fighting stance pumping his fists, his cigarette hanging from his mouth. Chris took a step back and Shaun laughed. "You gonna call for backup? You gonna shoot me?"

"You're an idiot."

"She's fine. I saw the bitch myself. She's hot, though." He grinned at his brother, the gap in his front teeth showing. "Maybe I should do that fitness check myself."

"It's *wellness* check, you moron. And I don't want you anywhere near her."

"Who put the stick up your ass?"

"I mean it, Shaun. This is my job we're talkin' about here."

"Big important man with a gun. Well guess what? I got guns too, Chris. How much they payin' deputies these days? Forty grand? I make more than that in a bad quarter."

"Yeah, and between all the smoke you blow up your nose and out your ass, all you got to show for it is this shithole."

"Why're you all high and mighty all of a sudden? You been known to party."

"Fuck you." Chris turned on his heel and headed back toward his car.

Shaun followed him. "Wouldn't try makin' it to the Markham place in that thing. Road's shit. You won't make it halfway." He nodded toward the cruiser.

"We got SUVs."

"See here's the thing." Shaun dropped the cigarette butt and ground it with the toe of his work boot. "Evan was very specific about the lady not being disturbed. Paid extra. A lot extra. Enough to share."

"Are you bribing a police officer?"

"You on some kinda power trip, Chris?"

"I should've known better than to expect you to cooperate. I don't have time for this shit." Chris opened the cruiser door.

"I seen her."

Chris paused. "I don't believe you."

"No?" Shaun tried to light another cigarette. With the wind it took several attempts. "I can give you a complete report. Even tell you what she was wearing."

" *Was* wearing?"

Shaun grinned. "Well maybe she's wearing nothing by now, you know what I mean? Big tits, you shoulda seen her. They were goin' up for a romantic weekend. Evan don't want his wife finding out about it, that's all."

"Then why would a detective be calling? I have to report back," Chris said.

"I don't know anything 'bout that but our families have known each other forever. I think we know the Markhams better than almost anyone."

That was true. Their families had known each other for years. "Yeah, and we always do their dirty work."

"And they always treat us well. Think about it. When have the Markhams ever not done right by us?" Shaun paused to take another drag and examine a filthy thumbnail. "I got the information you need. I saw her. She's fine, bro, perfectly healthy, not a mark on her. You can report back, do your job, and save yourself trashing your manifold or high centering your cop ride on that piece of shit road. Unless the county's springin' for Hummers now."

"A homicide, Shaun. I have to investigate."

Shaun shrugged. "Up to you. Told you what I know." He tossed his cigarette into the weeds, turned, and walked back inside.

Chris was torn. Shaun's bad behavior was limited to smoking dope and processing the occasional stolen car. He'd never hurt anyone. And they had known the Markhams their entire lives. Hell, the Markham and O'Dwyer kids grew up together. It seemed that did warrant at least giving Evan the benefit of the doubt, even if the idea had originated from his dumbass brother. Besides, it was already after three. By the time Chris rounded up an SUV, filled out the paperwork, swung by the service center for gas, and started up it would be getting dark. It wasn't like the department would spring for overtime and Shaun was right about the road. From what he remembered, it was terrible and Chris hadn't been up to the Markham place in years. How goddamn embarrassing would it be if he got a department vehicle stuck going to do a wellness check? Or worse, if he got lost? He could always drive up in the morning if he had to.

Chris followed his brother inside. "Wait. When exactly did you see her?"

CHAPTER THIRTY-FOUR

Jack led Corie into a small interview room. Just him, not Serena. He seemed serious but she didn't pay much attention; she was preoccupied with Evan's prepared dismissal and all of her confused feelings.

He pulled up a chair and sat next to her instead of across the table, then handed Corie a piece of paper.

"Everyone's gotta fucking stop handing me pieces of paper." Corie stared at the sheet in his outstretched hand for a few seconds before she took it.

Jack raised his eyebrows but he didn't ask what she meant. He waited while she read.

"So?" Corie shrugged and tried to hand the paper back.

"You're the beneficiary on the Swiss bank account. What can you tell me about that?"

"There's nothing the fuck to tell." Wow, her language had really deteriorated over the last two days.

Jack acted like he was picking his words carefully, and while he didn't avoid her gaze, he didn't really look at her. "It seems odd that you're the beneficiary, and yet you said you knew nothing about this bank account. Maybe the other night you were confused. You were shaken up and scared. You had fallen down the stairs."

"It was last night and I hadn't *fallen*, I was pushed. Which you seemed concerned about at the time."

Jack leaned forward with his arms on his knees. "Corie, three million dollars is a lot of money. Help me understand how you could not know about this account."

This was like déjà vu. Hadn't she just been telling *him* how it was a lot of money and must mean something?

"Evan does a lot of shit without telling me. And I'm sick of everyone treating me like I'm some kind of—I don't know—fucking ornament or something. Like I'm dispensable and can be bought off."

"What the fuck does that mean?"

Was he mocking her? And what was with the big concerned act last night? Bringing her dinner and holding her and helping with the ice pack?

"Here. While we're on the subject of payoffs, I have something for you to read." Corie pulled the offer from Stu out of her purse and handed it to Jack. She would have thrown it but that seemed childish.

"I want to hear more about the Swiss bank account."

"Then you're going to have to talk to the person who opened it." Corie pointed instead at the settlement. "In the meantime, since you're so interested in our finances, read that. It's all there. Evan's buying me out. Like our marriage is a corporation. He had that all ready to go, even before Brice was killed. He was done with me."

That shut Jack up.

"My compensation." Corie practically snarled. "For being abused, raped, and having him fuck other women practically on my doorstep. I sign on the dotted line and I'm free. It pays well, apparently."

Jack's head jerked up. "Raped? What do you mean?"

"Oh no. Don't even. I'm the stupid rich bitch who's got it made, remember? I know you hadn't seen me for twenty years and then when you did, I was standing over a dead body. I know you've got to do your job. Before I leave, I just need to know one more thing."

"I'm afraid to ask."

"Was Hennessy good?"

"Aw Jesus, Corie. Now? You have to bring that up *now?*" He stood and waved the pieces of paper at her. "Don't you have enough to worry about in the present without bringing up ancient history?"

She stood too. She was seething. "I guess I'm a glutton for punishment."

There was a knock on the door and Serena walked in.

Jack recovered first. He sat back down and indicated the other chair with his hand. "Corie, please sit down. We have a couple more questions for you. It won't take long. I promise."

"That's encouraging, you promising something." But she sat.

"Everything okay in here?" Serena asked.

Corie felt a twinge of embarrassment, although she still glared at Jack. "What're your other questions?"

"We were looking at your computer," Serena said, "and we saw the pictures of the project you worked on with Brice. We were wondering where the model house was because we'd like to take a look at it."

The twinge of embarrassment turned into a wave of heat. Corie turned her face away from their eyes. The one thing she had to remember Brice by and she couldn't keep it safe. "I don't know where the model is. I lost it."

"Lost it?" Jack's voice was a mixture of disbelief, anger, outrage.

Corie looked at Serena. "I asked my mother if she would keep it for me in her basement. Which was a big mistake because my mother never gave a fuck about anything I cared about."

"What do you mean?" Serena asked.

Jack made an impatient motion with his hand. "Corie, you're not making any sense."

She turned on him. "Oh, Jack, shut up. You don't know every fucking thing. I know you're a cop and you're probably a good cop, but you think you know everything there is to know about human behavior and you don't. I don't know where the model is because my mother gave it to Evan without telling me. It's something I cared about and she gave it away."

"When did she do that?" Jack asked.

"The morning after the murder." Had she really just told a detective to shut up? It was kind of exhilarating.

Jack and Serena spoke almost in unison. He said, "Why didn't you tell me?" and Serena said, "When did you find out?"

Corie felt a fresh flash of anger at Jack. He was acting as if she was doling out information on purpose when she was the most in the dark of anyone. But before she could answer, he made it even worse.

"You expect me to believe you're so clueless you didn't miss three million dollars? And then you lose the model? The very thing that might have gotten Brice killed?"

"I told you. I made a mistake. I told you everything, which is apparently another mistake."

"Not everything," Jack said.

"You want the blow by blow? My mother drove me home from the hospital. I told her I was going to ask Brice's family if they wanted the model. Too late! Evan had already gotten it from her. She then made some crack about how Evan and I sure think alike, which I hope to God isn't true."

"Do you think he still has it?" Serena's voice was the only calm one.

Corie looked at her and deflated. "My fear is it's splinters by now."

"We'll have to re-interview the charming Mrs. Bellenger." Jack made yet another note.

Corie stood as calmly as possible despite warring feelings of rage, confusion, and grief. "If there's nothing else, I'm going to go now. I know you can't hold me. I'm not that stupid."

"I never said you were stupid," Jack said.

"No, you said 'clueless.' Big difference. You know, I'm not some dumb seventeen-year-old anymore."

Jack ignored the dig. "Where are you going? I'll get an officer to drive you. You shouldn't—"

Corie held up a hand, palm out, cutting him off. "Don't try to sound concerned. I'm not buying it anymore. I'm going to go spend my three million dollars and I'd rather do that alone," she spat it at him. And then she was gone.

S erena trailed behind Jack as he stalked back to his office and slammed his notebook down on the desk. "Where do you think she'll go?"

"No fucking clue."

Mike Delgado walked up, said "Ballistics," and then stopped dead when he saw Jack's face. He looked questioningly at Serena who shook her head slightly. *Don't ask.*

"Ballistics, what?" Jack asked.

"Confirms the gun we retrieved from Vangie's minivan is the murder weapon."

"Great." Jack slumped in his chair and rubbed the bridge of his nose between his thumb and forefinger.

"We just talked to Corie Markham," Serena said. "She had no idea she was the beneficiary on the Swiss bank account."

"And there's this." Jack handed Mike the settlement agreement between Corie and Evan.

"How much money do these people have?" Mike's tone was ironic.

Jack snorted. "Right?"

"Remember when we were at Jessie's?" Serena asked. "Evan's project in the garage?"

Jack looked at her and nodded, disgust still palpable in his voice. "Yeah. Maybe he was working"—Jack made quote marks with his hands— "on the model. Why would he bring it to Jessie's house? Who the hell knows. Nothing about this case makes any fucking sense, so why not? Let's get some uniforms going through the trash in Jessie's neighborhood. And we'll need a search warrant for her garage."

"We'll get it right," Mike said. "You have a tendency to overreact but then you always figure it out."

Jack cut him off. "Overreact? Really? I've got a person of interest in a fifteen-year-old cold case in here spouting New Age aphorisms about opportunities for atonement; I've got a murder victim who may have gotten himself shot over a toy house; I've got another suspect with a murder weapon in her unlocked van who's too stupid to come in out of the rain; I've got an arrogant son of a bitch who threatens women with knives and pushes his own wife down the stairs, but he fundraises with the chief so he must be okay; and I've got Corie, who sleeps through gun shots and finds and loses evidence so fast, it makes my fucking head spin.

"Not to mention the fact that she didn't notice three million dollars was missing? Or that her husband had a mistress? Or that he disappeared for long stretches at a time? She goes and rides her horse and sticks her head in the sand and pretends everything's fine."

"Good to see you're not personally engaged with her or anything." Mike looked like he was fighting a smile.

"Fuck you."

"You kind of chewed her head off, Jack," Serena said.

"I thought my summation was pretty goddamned good. Did I miss anything?" Jack wound down and slumped back in his chair again.

"We gonna go interview Vi Bellenger?" Serena asked.

"Mike, you do it."

Serena started to say something and Jack cut her off. "Before you ask, Vi Bellenger remembers me as the eighteen-year-old punk who screwed her daughter over. She's got the mayor on speed dial. I don't need any more aggravation than the raft I've already got."

"I wasn't going to ask. I was going to tell you that I got a call from a sheriff's deputy in Park County. He checked on Vangie like you asked and apparently she's fine."

"Maybe she does know enough to come in out of the rain after all," Jack said. "Although I don't have high hopes."

CHAPTER THIRTY-FIVE

Vangie shouted out the name as if it would be her salvation, the name of the person who borrowed her gun. Evan stood next to the bed frozen. And then she wouldn't stop. She kept shouting the name over and over until Evan thought he would go insane.

"Shut up!"

In the silence that followed, he could hear her sobs and her choking gasps for air. He hesitated so long her head turned slowly from side to side, as if trying to see what was happening. Perhaps she felt hope. Evan watched her and his mind raced; he hadn't seen it coming. But then, betrayal never comes from where you expect.

It was no longer fun. No longer optional. Evan forced himself to move. He worked on her breasts first, making quick, jagged tears. In the opening of the hood, her mouth worked and snot from her nose made shiny streaks on the leather. The screaming annoyed him even more than usual.

Her body writhed and flexed, instinctively pulling away from the weapon. She screamed and choked and gasped. "Stop! No! I don't understand!"

She moved around quite a bit, almost as much trouble in death as she'd been in life. Evan would like to find the woman who could lie still. Could his wife do it? He thought about bringing her to orgasm while she pretended to be asleep. She didn't move or make a sound.

But he couldn't think about Corie. Couldn't.

He thrust with himself and the knife. Vangie's body bucked beneath him. She screamed in earnest.

It was true that they went through stages. First anger: cursing, yelling, and fighting. Next, fear. Then sadness and tears. It was such a cliché. Finally she bargained, like they all did. She wouldn't say anything, she'd do whatever he wanted, she'd forget all about it. He wondered if they ever reached acceptance. Maybe right before the end.

He remembered that he had to act fast. Blood changed once they died. It didn't flow. It didn't spurt. Even the color was different. While they bled out was the sweet spot. Nirvana. A sacrifice of the life force for his pleasure.

"Don't." Vangie's voice grew faint. "Not too late."

Evan, still hard, had to finish before it was indeed too late.

She grew quiet; maybe she was hallucinating. That wasn't good. He wanted her to be fully present. "Say my name," he demanded. "Say my name."

A hoarse croak. "Evan."

She didn't deserve an expedient death. She deserved to be tortured for all the trouble she'd caused him. He hadn't chosen her, she'd pursued him. And then she'd ruined him.

Her words slurred. "Did . . . ev'thing . . . you wanted . . ."

Slowly, her movements weakened and then ceased entirely. Time stood still. Evan shuddered, experiencing release, although he didn't make a sound.

It was bad to linger. Carefully, he raised himself up and wiped off with a towel, paying special attention to the soles of his feet so as not to track blood everywhere. When he cut her ankles free her legs landed awkwardly on the bed. He put them together, then unzipped the mattress cover and pulled it up over the lifeless form. When he zipped the cover again it made a makeshift, waterproof container. Evan put that into a second, heavier bag, to be on the safe side. He gathered up the tarp from the floor and put it in with her.

Still naked, he carried the double-bagged package outside and loaded it into the back of the pickup. Savoring a moment of relief, Evan stood naked in the cold mountain air, spread his arms wide, and threw his head back. A bird cried—something big, maybe a hawk or a golden eagle. Another predator. Evan let out a loud yell, answering with his own primal shout of despair, rage, satisfaction.

Back inside he showered thoroughly, the hot water scalding. When he was finished, he sprayed the shower down with bleach and poured some down the drain. He dried himself off carefully and replaced the towel on the rod, folding it neatly. Attention to detail was critical. Evan inspected the bathroom and then looked at his reflection. Ordinarily, he had no problem looking at himself in the mirror. He never understood where that expression came from. But the man that stared back at him was haunted and Evan turned away.

In his usual methodical way, he'd stopped by the dry cleaners on the way up and picked up his tuxedo. Evan dressed and then checked the time again. He poured himself a glass of the Châteauneuf-du-Pape—only one, although he wanted more—before he headed back down to Denver. It wouldn't do to get pulled over for a DUI. He closed his eyes and sniffed, picked up the acrid smell of the Mourvedre which instantly dried the surface of his tongue, the soft round notes of the Grenache, the spice of the Syrah, the crispness and structure from the Cinsault. It wasn't that hard if you paid attention.

Shaun was waiting at the old Sinclair station with Evan's car.

"I thought you said you were going to get it detailed?" Evan got out and left the pickup running. The exterior of the Mercedes was still dusty from the dirt roads. "I can't show up with my car looking that way."

"You said it was more important to focus on the interior."

"That's the best you could do? For five grand?"

"Short notice, bro."

"One more thing and then you can go spend that money."

Shaun waited, working his tongue around his teeth.

"I need you to make a dump run. There's a bag in the back."

Shaun smiled. "Hunting out of season again?"

Evan smiled back. "Something like that."

"My brother came sniffing around. A detective called from Denver. Something about a wellness check."

"Really." Evan shot a starched, white cuff and examined his hand.

"Told him I seen the bitch and she was fine." Shaun's eyes flicked to the bag. "I do the right thing?"

Evan reached into his pocket and peeled off a few thousand from a thick roll of cash. "You performed adequately. For your extra trouble." He extended his hand, the money folded neatly between his index and middle finger.

Shaun licked his lips. "See, that's what I told Chris. The Markhams always take care of us. That's what I said."

"As long as you do the right thing, we always will. Your mother is going up to clean in the morning, right? Make sure she gets something extra for her trouble. Tell her not to come until after ten." Evan spoke slowly making sure the words sunk in, although Shaun was so stupid he couldn't be sure. "My friend is staying there tonight. All by herself. She likes to sleep in."

Shaun shoved the money into his greasy jeans. "You look nice. You goin' to a party?"

"One must keep up appearances."

CHAPTER THIRTY-SIX

"Jack." Aranda had seen him arrive from inside the art museum. She approached him wearing a form-fitting evening gown.

"Aranda, hey." Jack tried his best to keep a lid on his urgency. "Thanks for your call."

She gave him a rueful smile. "I wasn't sure if I should call you or not."

"You did the right thing. Where is she?"

"She said she was stopping at her place for a minute."

Jack frowned. "But that's—"

Aranda pointed toward the modern condos across the plaza from the museum. "Fifth floor."

"And Evan?"

"Last I saw him he was inside the museum chatting up the luminaries."

Aranda herself was pretty luminous. Like everything else she wore, the dress was well cut, expensive, sexy, and tasteful all at the same time. The top half of the dress was white and the bottom half a mocha close to her skin color. In the back the dress plunged, displaying what seemed like acres of flawless skin. Her makeup was subtle, lips tinted a deep rose color that was somehow exotic against her light brown skin.

"I like your handiwork," Aranda said.

"My what?"

She touched her cheek under her eye. "His face is swollen and he's got a cut."

"Let's just say he didn't take kindly to my pointing out visiting hours at the hospital were over."

"I'll bet."

"You look very nice, by the way," Jack said.

"Now you're humoring me."

"It's true." Jack smiled. "I would much rather be here to taste wine with you."

Aranda tilted her head to the side and looked at him with velvety brown eyes. "Well, if you have time when you're finished you should stop in. The benefit tickets were five hundred but I'll vouch for you."

"Rain check."

Aranda's flirtatious smile made those eyes sparkle. "You always say that." Then her expression grew serious and she lightly touched his arm. "I hope Corie's all right."

"Me too."

The woman who opened the door of the condo was Corie, but Corie as if she were on the cover of a magazine. Glamorous makeup highlighted her full lips and made her eyes look even more enormous. Long lashes, pale skin, a waterfall of luxurious golden-red curls.

"What are you doing here?" She sounded indignant.

Jack had his hand on his gun and his eyes swept the room behind her. He slid past her, and it wasn't until he was satisfied the condo was clear and she was alone that he turned on her. "Corie, what the hell are you doing?"

Her answer was to glide across the living room on her strappy stilettos and walk out onto a small balcony. He gritted his teeth and watched as she casually picked up a champagne glass and leaned on the brushed chrome railing, looking down at the well-dressed people milling around on the plaza five stories below. Corie looked amazing. Her dress was silvery blue, with enough shimmer to be eye-catching but still on the classy side of Las Vegas showgirl. It was low cut, short, and tight, Jack's three favorite attributes in a dress.

Behind her across the plaza, the Libeskind addition to the Denver Art Museum subtly gleamed. Its unique architecture looked like an intricate work of origami, only fabricated from aluminum and glass instead of paper. The condo was also sleek and modern, with floor-to-ceiling windows and cement-clad pillars. A counter intersecting the living area and kitchen was wrapped in stainless steel. The overall effect was cold, dizzying, and impersonal. The opposite of cozy. The opposite of Corie.

He walked outside and stood next to her. Music, talk, and laughter floated up to them.

"Look at them," Corie said. "They look like they don't have a care in the world. I guess I do, too. It's all a lie."

Jack's eyes swept the crowd below looking for Evan. "Whose place is this?"

"Ours. Evan thought it would be fun to buy one of these." She took a delicate sip of the sparkling wine.

Fun. The place cost half a mil, probably more. "Why would you go to a party with Evan? He's not supposed to come anywhere near you."

"I'm not with Evan. Do you see him?"

"Are you sure you aren't suffering from a head injury? One of the symptoms is impaired judgment." He was so worried about her, it was all he could do not to scoop her up in his arms, load her in his car, and lock her up somewhere safe. For a brief moment he searched his mind for a reason to arrest her.

"This party"—she mimicked his sarcastic tone—"has been planned for a long time and it's for a very worthy cause. Or don't you care about children with cancer?" She walked back inside, picked up her cell phone off the sleek kitchen counter, glanced at it, and slipped it into a small, sparkly evening bag.

He trailed behind. "I read the agreement. You have every right to feel used. Which makes your presence here all the more inexplicable."

She looked him up and down, took in his dark blue suit. "The invitation said black tie."

Jack's eyes narrowed. "So have you seen him?"

"Who?"

"Prince Charles. I heard he was flying in special from England. Who the hell you think I mean?"

"You're not in a very good mood."

Jack followed her down the short hall to the elevator and fought to get a handle on his temper. "I was abrupt earlier and I shouldn't have been. My main concern is for your safety."

"Abrupt?" He could see a quick flash of anger before she turned away.

"I don't understand why you're here."

"It's not all about you." In her spindly stilettos she was almost his height. Even so, she didn't make eye contact.

Inside the museum Corie swapped her champagne glass for a larger, more rounded one, filled with liquid the color of a ruby. "Don't follow me around all night."

Jack's eyes sought Evan. "Why would you go to a wine tasting with someone who raped you? What kind of hold does he have on you?"

Corie froze for a second but recovered quickly. "Am I supposed to introduce you? As what exactly?"

She took a healthy swallow of the wine and he noticed, despite her defiance, that her hand was trembling. "I know you don't want to be here."

"Ah, but I always do the things I don't want to do. It's a bad habit."

"What do you mean? What have you done?"

214

"Detective." Evan's silky voice came from behind Jack.

Corie's eyes skimmed over Jack's shoulder toward her husband. "In answer to your question . . ." Then she turned adroitly on one of those impossibly fragile heels and slipped away.

"Goddamn it, Evan. I don't have a tape measure handy but I'm sure you're within five hundred feet."

Evan glanced at Corie's retreating back. "You're absolutely right. I'm going to get some more wine. Why don't you join me?"

Without waiting for an answer, Evan walked away too.

Jack hesitated and then followed Evan, who walked to a bar set up on one side of the gallery. A bartender appeared instantly with two large, stemmed glasses.

"Surprise us," Evan said. His tuxedo was impeccable. Not a blond hair out of place. Other than the cut on his cheek and the bruising around his eye, he looked bland and harmless.

"I'm on duty." Jack watched the bartender pour.

"What marvelous self-restraint." Evan swirled the contents of his glass a few moments and then lifted the rim to his nose. "That really is remarkable. Brown from age yet there's still some ripe fruit. Cassis. Plum. Maybe even a hint of cherry." He sniffed again. "Am I getting chocolate?"

Jack let the bartender see his badge. "It'd be a shame to shut this down while I make sure all of the permits are in order."

The bartender slid away. Evan watched Jack placidly. "I didn't take you for a common bully, Jack. It appears I was mistaken. I tell you what. Let's play a game."

"I don't play games."

"No? You can have me subpoenaed but that will take some time. Or, you can talk to me right now and find out whatever you want to know."

"Go fuck yourself." It took significant restraint not to grab Evan and throw him through one of the plate glass windows. Anything to break through that glib exterior.

Evan had the gall to glance at his watch. "In that case, I have important people I really should talk to."

"How'd you get her to come tonight?"

"It's the other way around. Corie wanted to come. She's been looking forward to this for months."

"That's crap. I know about the settlement. Tell me what you have on Corie."

Evan held his glass up to the light. "Good legs. That means the streaking down the side of the glass. When a wine does that it's an indication of—"

"High alcohol content. Let's go." Jack had Evan by the arm.

"You really have no questions? It's all right with me, I found jail rather fascinating."

Jack noticed that Evan's eyes, even when he was staring right at you, seemed to be looking somewhere else. "I'll take your little quiz if you tell me what's going on with you and Corie."

"You waited too long. You guess correctly, you get Vangie. Corie's off the table."

"You don't own her, Evan."

"Humor me. What do you smell?" Evan swirled his wine and took another sip.

Jack moved the base of his wineglass on the bar in a violent circular motion, sending the liquid inside into a mahogany-colored whirlpool.

"Ah. I see you're going to play. I'll make it really easy. All you have to do is guess the vintage. It's a Burgundy," Evan added helpfully.

Jack picked the glass up by the stem and took a whiff. He was struck by the earthiness of the wine, combined with a distinctive spiciness: clove, anise. "1990."

Evan watched him with those vacant, icy blue eyes. "Very good guess."

"I don't guess. Where is she?"

"At my cabin." Evan stared at his glass for a long moment. "I'm heading up after this to join her. I won't be anywhere near Corie. What about you?"

"Call her."

"There's no cell phone service at the cabin and we don't have a landline."

"Convenient. Why'd you trade cars with your lawyer?"

"The road to the cabin has deteriorated. My Mercedes wouldn't make it."

Jack watched Evan through narrowed eyes. "Bonus points: You tell me how you got Corie to come tonight if I tell you the estate."

Evan arched a pale eyebrow. He looked amused. "All right. I'll play."

For a moment, Jack was back in his grandparents' dining room at their house in Paris. He'd sit terrified and transfixed while his grandfather held up a glass and lectured Jack on the proper way to evaluate and consume wine. Almost nothing was taken more seriously in his grandfather's elegant home. Servants slipped in and out unobtrusively, while at the other end of the long, linen-draped table his mother chatted amiably in French with his grandmother.

"Terroir, Jacques. The life of each man that touched those grapes, that tilled the soil, is in that glass. It must be treated with respect."

His grandfather's voice quavered as he pronounced names for ten-year-old Jack to repeat: d'Yquem, Lafaurie-Payraguey, Lynch-Bages. The names sounded like music. Jack sat patiently while the old man lectured—as if he had the nerve to do anything else.

Jack thought about answering Evan in French but figured that would be overkill. He knew he shouldn't let a suspect bait him, but he couldn't resist showing off a little.

Jack swirled the glass again, closed his eyes, took a sip, and swallowed. Took a second sip. Thought about it for a minute while Evan watched with that insufferable smile. Jack drew the moment out with a third sip and then reluctantly set his glass down. "Since you go for flash instead of class, I'm gonna guess a La Tache and not a Richebourg." The names rolled off Jack's tongue as if that lesson in his grandfather's dining room had been yesterday. He called the bartender over and asked to see the bottle. Took it, grinned, and set it back down on the bar.

Evan's smile faded as he stared at the words "Annee1990" on the distinctive white label of the Domaine de la Romanée-Conti La Tache. "I told her I wouldn't contest the divorce if she'd put in this one last appearance for me."

"Right."

"If you really saw the settlement offer, then you'd know it's the truth."

"What'd you go back to your house for yesterday?"

"Checking on Corie. I won't bother expressing outrage at how quickly she resumed your relationship. Not very ethical, though, is it? How is it you have such little regard for your career?"

It was Jack's turn to smile. "How is it I've had both your sister and your wife?"

Glass shattered. Red wine spread on the counter and dripped onto the floor; the spatter pattern reminded Jack of blood. So satisfying to jolt Evan out of his smug certainty. He'd worry about his ethics later.

"Was Corie going to end up like Monique?"

"Who?" Evan looked confused.

Two bartenders rushed over with rags to clean up the mess. Ruby drops oozed, glittering along the gash outlining Evan's thumb.

"You'd better get that looked at, sir," a bartender said.

With delicate precision, Jack set down his own intact glass. "Two things Evan, pay very close attention: One, Vangie better show up at her arraignment all bright-eyed and bushy-tailed. Two, you and Corie are done. Take your settlement and shove it up your ass. If I catch you 499 feet away from Corie I'll personally haul you off to jail. And I won't be as gentle the second time."

Jack found Corie talking to an older couple. They looked up when he approached and Corie started to make introductions, but he took her by the arm and pulled her toward an exit.

"Hey. That's very rude."

"Call a cop."

"Cute. What the hell is wrong with you?" She tried to pull away but he held tight.

"You want to nurse a grudge, fine, but I'm going to keep you alive. Although you're safe for the moment. Evan's going up to the cabin to be with Vangie."

"Nurse a grudge?" Her voice rose. "I think you're enjoying this."

Jack walked her across the plaza toward her condo. "That was a cheap shot, I'm sorry."

"Oh, *finally* that word escapes your lips. It doesn't look like it was fatal."

"All that matters is keeping you safe."

She made a sound like an outraged snort and pulled her arm free. "You think you have all the answers. You think you have everything under control. You're as bad as Evan."

The comparison stung. "You can't stay here. I'm going to take you someplace where you'll be safe and then—"

"Like hell."

"What did you mean before when you said doing bad things had become a habit?"

"I didn't say 'bad things.' I said doing things I don't want to do."

"Like what?" Jack's strong, slim fingers closed around her upper arm again. "What does he have on you? Tell me."

Corie glared at him. "Get your hands off me. I told you everything I know and you didn't believe me. I'm going inside now. Away from Evan. That's what you want, isn't it? And Jack always gets everything he wants."

"What the hell does that mean?"

"You're an arrogant prick, Jack. And trust me, I'm rather an expert." Her voice dropped, became low and malevolent. "Did you even know?"

He wasn't sure at first he heard her right. "Know what?"

"About the baby."

"Oh God, Corie—"

"No, don't worry about me. I get it. Your little it-didn't-mean-anything got pregnant. And then she asked me to go with her when she got rid of it. And I went!"

Jack stepped back as if she'd shot him. "Corie, what the hell?"

"Please. Spare me the surprised act." She stalked into her building.

After a moment of hesitation, Jack followed and caught up to her as she stepped into the elevator. They were alone and she turned on him as the doors closed.

"I'm sick and tired of covering for everybody. That was the start, back then, covering for Hennessy. And it's a bad habit I've continued to this day. I mean what the hell is wrong with me, huh? I go with her and hold her hand after she's fucked the guy I was in love with. I must be a complete and utter moron."

"What did you say?" He would get answers. With one hand he reached out and pressed the stop button on the elevator. An alarm sounded.

Corie's eyes got wide. "What are you doing? Are you insane?"

"I'm only going to ask you one more time what you're talking about."

"She had an abortion. Are you slow?" Corie's voice dripped with twenty years of pent-up pain and scorn. She didn't care if she hurt him. She didn't even see him. "Nice of you to pay for it, though."

"No. That's not—"

"You paid for it and I held her hand and she used both of us. I stood there in that awful room with those sounds and all of these women in the waiting room, half of them angry and defensive and the other half crying—guess which group Hennessy belonged to? She lay there on the table while they sucked it out of her and tried to make jokes. I was crying and she was cracking jokes."

"Stop it!" Jack couldn't bear to hear anymore. "You're lying."

"No, I'm not. Why the hell would I lie about this?"

He backed her up against the wall, his grip hard on her arms.

"You son of a bitch. Let me go!" She broke free and groped for the stop button. The elevator lurched upward. Corie lost her balance in her heels and fell against Jack but straightened up instantly. "You know, they have security cameras in these elevators."

When the doors opened on the fifth floor, Jack didn't move. Corie took a few steps and then turned in time to get a good look at Jack's anguished face before the panels slid closed again.

CHAPTER THIRTY-SEVEN

His mother was home but she wasn't alone. Evan had forgotten she had company, and now he felt like he'd caught Jessie and her new friend in the act. They were both fully clothed but looked at him with sheepish smiles.

Jessie was wearing a kind of long tunic, white, over a longer skirt in a deep red color. On her bare feet were sandals in a strappy gladiator style. For some reason it was sexy.

Evan felt slightly ill and abruptly looked away from his mother's feet toward her younger man. Maybe not so young after all. He had a wrinkled, weather-beaten face going ruddy. What was this new one's name?

"Evan, you remember Lennon."

Ah. That was it.

"Len, this is my son Evan. You met the other day when he brought the—"

"When I worked on the project in Jessie's garage. I'm not sure we were formally introduced at the time." Evan interrupted his mother and belatedly stuck out his hand, although he was loathe to actually touch the other man.

Len reached for Evan's outstretched hand and Jessie noticed the bandage.

"What happened to your hand, darling?"

Evan yanked his hand back and shoved it in his pocket. He wanted to turn around and bolt. Instead, as if drawn by an irresistible force, he allowed Jessie to take him by the arm and lead him into the kitchen. There was a six-burner Wolf stove on one side and a wall of windows opposite. Two sets of atrium doors opened onto a deck. The large island and kitchen counters were covered with colorful tiles and the floor was paved with large terracotta squares. Brightly colored, high-backed wooden chairs pulled up to the island; they'd been painted by another young artist friend of his mother's. A previous, female incarnation of Lennon.

"Have you been to a party?" Jessie asked.

"The benefit at the museum." She tried again to examine his cut but Evan resisted.

"At least let me make you something to eat. They never have much except snacky things at those wine tastings."

Evan stood and watched Jessie pull food out the refrigerator.

"I wasn't sure if you would go with everything else you have on your plate." Jessie took the lid off of a small round container, sniffed it, and placed it on a wooden board. "Mmm. I got this from the farmer's market. Artisanal goat cheese."

She added paper-thin slices of prosciutto, hard salami, and wedges of cheese to the board.

"Was Corie there?" Jessie added it offhandedly, as she scooped a mound of quince paste into a small square dish.

"Yes," Evan said.

"That must have been awkward for you." Jessie reached into a cabinet and pulled out a jar of Marcona almonds. "For both of you. Would you mind if I called Corie?"

"Of course not." Evan watched Len slice a large, round loaf of bread into thin slices for the cheese. At the sight of the knife Evan's hand tingled. "I'm sure Corie would like to hear from you."

Jessie's eyes glittered with tears and she blinked them back. "I can't imagine what it's like for her. Losing her friend and then all of your other difficulties." Her voice trailed off.

Len opened the refrigerator and retrieved a jar of mustard. "J, where did you put the olives we bought?"

"Look on the bottom shelf."

J? "Mom, I should go."

Jessie dabbed at her eyes and tried to smile. She knew better than to try and hug Evan. In fact, Jessie understood him better than anybody.

"Don't be silly. Here. You can carry this for me." She handed Evan the large board with the cheese and meat. "Let's eat over in front of the fire."

While Len got the fire going, Jessie poured each of them a glass of wine from a bottle of Sancerre. "It's a shame it's gotten too cold sit outside in the evening. I've thought about putting gas heaters out on the veranda." She raised her glass. "What shall we drink to?"

"I'm not feeling very festive, Mother."

"How about drinking to all of this bounty?" Len suggested.

"Bounty. I like that." Jessie touched each of their glasses with hers.

Corie's voice floated through Evan's mind, describing the project with Brice: 'I put a dining room table in the model loaded with food, a symbol of bounty and sharing with those you love.' Corie told Evan Brice's contribution to the house was scenes from his childhood in North Carolina. *Scenes. Was that a slip? Had she meant to say "crime scenes?"*

"A symbol of bounty," Evan said. Len and his mother stared at him curiously so he motioned with his glass toward the fruit and cheese. Where was Corie now? With Jack? Evan drained his glass in one swallow.

"I didn't think you liked Sancerre." Jessie refilled her son's glass with the straw-colored liquid and then sat down next to Len on the loveseat facing the fire. Evan remained standing.

"It's one of the few white wines I can abide." Evan watched his mother cut herself a sliver of manchego and top it with a dab of quince paste. He'd hoped for a chance to talk to Jessie alone.

Len attempted conversation. "Evan, tell us about the benefit you attended. Did you get to taste some interesting wines?"

"I didn't stay long."

"My son is rather shy." Jessie's green eyes lingered on Evan, then she turned toward Len and leaned close. A white hand rested on Len's knee. "Unlike his mother."

Evan stood transfixed, as if watching a slow-motion accident.

"Evan, what *are* the latest developments in your little mystery?" Jessie asked. "Tell us: What do the police know so far?"

"It hardly seems relevant, with all this bounty before us."

She sat up straight. "Are you mocking me?"

"Not at all. You were planning an intimate evening and I've spoiled it."

Jessie held Evan's cold gaze. "Yes. I suppose I'm being terribly selfish but I really don't want to talk about it. This is what I want to focus on. Now. This moment. I think the Buddhists are right. Don't you, Len?"

Len didn't answer and Evan watched them curiously. "Everything all right?"

Jessie sighed. "Those dreadful police interrogated Len."

"Jessie, he doesn't want to hear this," Len said.

"Hear what?" Evan felt a surge of energy. The evening was suddenly very interesting.

"They dragged him down there." Jessie's green eyes blazed. "He didn't even tell me he was going because he didn't want me to worry. Terribly brave but terribly foolish. I told him you have the best lawyers on retainer. Tell him, Evan. You know how to handle these things. Len doesn't realize it but the Markham name means something around here. They can't treat him that way."

"It was no big deal," Len said.

"You see?" Jessie looked at Evan as if requesting his assistance with a dull child.

"I'm sure they're only doing their jobs, Mother." Evan's lips twitched from the effort of resisting a smile. "Len doesn't seem to be upset."

"I told him you'd help." Jessie glared at Evan.

"I'm hurt, Mother, that you're more worried about your friend than about Corie and me. If Len has any information that can help solve this awful crime, I should think he'd be happy to cooperate. Isn't that right, Len?"

"How dare you!" Jessie stood and brushed crumbs off her skirt. "How dare you insinuate that Len could have anything to do with this? How dare you take the cops' side!"

"But I do support the police, Mother."

"I don't know what's gotten into you. I don't know you at all anymore." With as much dignity as she could muster Jessie turned and stalked from the room. As she passed the tile counter in the kitchen she set down her wineglass with a sharp clink.

The smile escaped. Evan couldn't help it. He grinned at Len. "Sorry about that. My mother has never been able to tolerate conflict of any kind."

"I should go to her." Len stayed seated on the couch looking down at his hands.

"I can see you're very fond of my mother, but I know her much better than you do. Let her go off by herself for a little while and then she'll come back out and be her old self again. You'll see."

"Do you really think so?"

"Absolutely." Evan picked up the bottle. "Here, let me top off your glass."

"Thanks." Len relaxed and unclasped his hands.

"How long have you known my mother?"

"A couple of months."

"I can find out, Len." Evan said it conversationally.

Len's hand reflexively reached up and fidgeted with his necklace. "We met in North Carolina. I'm not sure exactly how long ago, a couple of years maybe. I don't think it's very nice of you to accuse me of lying."

"I've never heard her mention you before." For the first time all night Evan was enjoying himself.

Len took a long drink. "Do you know all the people your mother dates?"

"Are you originally from North Carolina?"

"I've already had one interrogation today."

"And Lennon's your real name?"

Len looked away again. "It's going to sound silly."

"I have an excellent sense of humor."

"The name on my birth certificate says Leonard, but I always felt a spiritual bond with John Lennon. It's no crime changing your name."

Evan laughed. "Of course not. When you were at the station, which detective did you talk to?"

Len seemed surprised by the question. He retrieved a card from his wallet and handed it to Evan, who stared at Jack's card.

"Why do you want to know?" Len asked.

"No reason." Evan took the card and tossed it into the fire. "Len, I think it's time for you and me to have a nice, long chat."

CHAPTER THIRTY-EIGHT

"Hi."

Jack opened his door and found Corie on his doorstep with a sheepish smile on her face. She seemed tentative, shy, uncertain.

He'd removed his jacket and tie but was still wearing a white dress shirt with the top buttons open and slacks. "What are you doing here?" He didn't say hello. He didn't invite her in. He wasn't going to make it easy for her.

She held up a bottle of La Tache. "I brought a peace offering."

"I'm not sure that's a good idea."

"I know. I just can't leave it like . . . I just want to talk to you. I won't stay long."

Her eyes were imploring. *Bad idea!* a voice shouted in his head. Jack ignored the voice. He stepped back and opened the door wider. Her eyes swept his living room, the Craftsman furniture, the Oriental rug on the floor, the stained glass panels at the top of the old windows. Was she surprised?

"No beer can pyramid. Sorry to disappoint you." God, he sounded bitter.

"I'm not—what? Sorry, I'll keep my eyes averted. I should have asked if there was someone else here."

"I'm alone." There was something in her eyes he couldn't read—fear, hope, longing?

She leaned against the back of the couch, almost as if for protection. "Do you want to open that?"

"Not really." He was still angry.

"Well can you give me a glass of something? I need all the help I can get."

He walked toward the kitchen and she followed. Eighteen years. His child would have been a teenager, practically grown. Bile rose in his throat and Jack realized he wanted the wine. Needed the wine. He wouldn't look at Corie; instead he examined the label. "This should really be decanted. Surprised I know a word like decanted?"

Why was he mad at her? It was Hennessy who'd done it. No. He and Hennessy.

"Let me see your hand," Corie said.

Without warning, she grabbed his free hand and he looked at her, surprised.

Just as quickly she dropped it again. "Nope, no scrape marks. Now that we've determined you're not a Neanderthal can we move on to a new topic?"

He turned away and reached for a decanter on the top shelf of a cabinet, his thoughts racing. She should have tried to stop Hennessy. They were best friends. She should have done something. Corie was always so goddamned passive. Jack carefully emptied the bottle, noticed the color of the wine—a brownish tinge, as Evan had observed—and marveled at the amount of sediment at the bottom of the bottle.

"What should we drink to?" He handed her a glass and forced himself to look at her.

She met his eyes, not hiding, not scared. "Confession is good for the soul. Or so they say."

"I think they lie."

"I thought your job was extracting confessions."

"Apparently I suck at it."

"I don't know. It worked on me. I confessed far more than I ever meant to." She swirled her glass for barely a second before she took a sip. "I don't get it. I'd still rather have a glass of Chardonnay."

"My grandfather is rolling in his grave."

"What? Why?"

"Never mind. You realize this is like a three- or four-thousand-dollar bottle of wine?"

"At least. I've got another one in my purse. Just in case."

"In case what?" It wasn't bile that rose in his throat this time. But why? He didn't even like her.

"In case one doesn't give me enough nerve."

She'd changed clothes into a cranberry-colored sweater and jeans, and she'd wiped off most of the showgirl makeup. She looked like Corie again. He found himself wanting to touch the sweater, to see if it was as soft as it looked. His voice lost some of its angry edge. "What do you need nerve for?"

"Jack." She looked at him with that even, confident look. "It's so weird. It's like I know you but I don't. There were moments when you felt familiar, but right now you seem like a complete stranger."

He turned away from her and walked back into the living room. Purposely, he sat in one of the armchairs so she couldn't sit next to him. He hated himself for desiring her. He stared into the translucent surface of the overpriced wine and tried to sort out his emotions. It was impossible.

Corie took another sip of the wine, almost as if she was forcing herself to take cough syrup, and set her glass on the coffee table.

"You really don't like it."

"It was more for you anyway. Evan donated a case for the auction."

"How nice of him."

"I'm so sorry."

He knew she wasn't talking about Evan's donation. He waited.

"I was never going to tell you. Of course I never thought I'd see you again. I prayed I would never see you again. But if I ever did, I wasn't going to talk about it. And I sure as hell was never going to tell you like that. I don't know. I was mad. I am mad. I feel like I've been manipulated my whole life by everyone who supposedly cared about me. I've been a fool. I've let everyone use me and I've had it. I was determined not to take any crap from anyone anymore and you happened to cross my path first."

She reached for the glass, took a gulp, and shivered. "It broke my heart—I—oh hell, I came over to tell you the truth so I'm just going to say this: She had everything I wanted, which included you. And she was throwing it away. It wasn't fair. I hated both of you. My first thought when I heard that she'd died was . . . let's just say, uncharitable."

Jack didn't know what showed in his face but he wouldn't let himself look away.

"I couldn't stop her," Corie said, as if she'd read his mind. "You know how she was."

"She told me that she lost it."

"Well then that makes both of us stupid."

"I can't argue with that." He swirled his glass, grateful he could finally take a real drink.

"I should go." She stood, found her purse, pulled out the second bottle, and set it on the coffee table.

Jack felt caught off guard. "I have Chardonnay."

"I shouldn't stay."

"No, you shouldn't." He stood too.

She had her purse over her shoulder but didn't make a move toward the front door. "Your house is nice."

"Thank you."

"What I've seen of it. Oh God, that sounds like I'm flirting. I'm not flirting. I don't know what made me say that. I don't know what makes me say anything. I better go because there's no telling what might come out of my mouth. I'm an idiot. I hope you enjoy the wine."

Jack's face relaxed. "You're not an idiot."

"No? I feel like one."

"Well maybe for liking Chardonnay better than the La Tache, but not otherwise. Although if you continue to let Evan anywhere near you, I'll change my opinion."

"No worries."

Her boldness shifted into something else. She didn't hold his gaze but for a different reason, one that had nothing to do with courage. Jack took a step toward her and she looked down and fidgeted with the clasp on her bag. When she looked up again he'd closed the gap. He took her handbag off her shoulder and tossed it onto the couch, then rested his hand where the strap had been. He wondered what she would do, if she would pull away. The sweater was soft.

"I can't do this," Jack said.

"I know."

His hand moved up over her collarbone and then along her jaw, under her chin. He tipped her face up to his. Corie seemed to melt at his touch. "But I think I have to."

Her mouth was soft, welcoming, delicious.

She read his mind again. "The wine tastes much better on you."

"I won't push you. We both know you shouldn't stay. Although I want you to."

"Being a good girl hasn't worked out so well for me."

She reached for him and Jack leaned into her, breathed her in, before his mouth found hers again. This time more insistently, more thoroughly, exploring, teasing, devouring. Soon there was no mistaking the fact that she was kissing him back.

His hands moved over the soft sweater, down to her lower back. He drew her in until she was pressed tight against him, no longer worried about what she saw in his face or what she could feel in his desire for her. Corie didn't resist. She responded as if she wanted him as much as he wanted her, which was a lot—twenty years' worth of pent up anger, desire, frustration, curiosity, loss.

In the bedroom he gently lowered her onto the bed. She reached for him and he debated for a moment. "I should tell you something."

She put her fingers on his lips and shook her head.

He kissed the palm of her hand. "No. There's something—" Jack sat up and cleared his throat.

"That's a very serious look."

"It's kind of embarrassing. I have testicular cancer. Well, had. I've had surgery, and treatment, and I haven't . . . been with anyone . . . since all of that."

"Are you okay?"

Great. Now she looked scared. "Yep. I'm fine. Or so they tell me. I just thought you should know."

Corie smiled and brushed his hair off his forehead. "I'm honored."

"I've, um, had some trial runs on my own and everything seems to work okay."

She tipped her head back and laughed. "Thanks for sharing."

"Have I totally killed the mood?"

Her beautiful blue eyes moved over his face, taking his measure. She shook her head. "It's like a miracle being here with you."

He smiled and let himself go; the moment his lips touched hers he forgot about everything else anyway. He'd never had the chance when they were teenagers to kiss her, not like this.

He undressed her slowly, purposefully, taking his time until Corie lay back on the bed naked. His eyes traveled as slowly and methodically over her body as his hands. Her breathing was ragged but she didn't shy away from him. She watched as he removed his own clothes and he could see the desire on her face.

"You're so beautiful." Jack trailed a line of kisses down her neck, along her collarbone. His fingertips brushed over her breasts, softly, tracing slow circles around her nipples that grew hard at his touch. He lowered his head and kissed them, traced smaller circles with his tongue.

"Jack." She said his name on a sigh of pleasure. "Oh."

It felt so good to be fully engaged—his body, his mind, and his heart—not wanting to be anywhere or with anyone else. Astounding to be able to graze her nipples with his lips and to hear her say his name like that. Jack didn't know exactly what she'd been through, but his mind was pretty good at filling in the blanks. He wanted to somehow make up for all of the times she'd been mistreated and abused. He wanted her to know what it felt like to be adored. He took his time with her breasts before letting his hands continue their thorough exploration. He watched her face when his fingers eventually slipped between her legs and reveled in the way she responded to his touch.

"Corie."

"Oh God." Her voice was a hoarse whisper.

"You like that?" His own voice a ragged whisper, too. He knew she did but he longed to hear her say it.

"Oh. God. Yes."

He leaned up and kissed her while still touching her. She kissed him back with such ferocity it took his breath away. She pressed herself against his hand. He wasn't sure what he was expecting, but Corie's passion surprised him.

He rolled on top of her but held himself still for a moment. She seemed impatient but he didn't want to hurry. He could still stop. If he had to. Maybe.

"Corie, are you sure?"

She reached for him, curved her hand around him, pulled him down, and pulled him in until he was lost.

Then there was only ravenous need.

Any fear he had about how things would function or how things would feel was gone, replaced by a new fear that this would go too fast. It had been a while, and maybe he'd forgotten, but had sex ever felt this good? This was like a whole new universe of sensation. And she was so damned gorgeous.

"Corie." He captured both of her wrists in one of his hands and held them over her head. He was trying to get her to slow down. "If this is over in like, five seconds, I promise I'll do it again soon."

Her entire body seemed to rise up off the bed to meet him. She was taking what she wanted and the only answer was to take back, to answer her greed with his own. He kept closing his eyes and then opening them again, as if he couldn't really believe it was Corie there underneath him, all around him, making those sounds, saying his name.

She held him while he pounded into her, shuddered, and eventually stilled. In the lull that followed, she seemed to luxuriate in being trapped underneath him and the pressure of his body. Jack felt all of the tension go out of his shoulders and slid off just enough to not crush her.

Her lips grazed his shoulder and her voice was soft. "It seems everything works fine."

He lifted his head and grinned down at her. He'd no doubt pay for it later, but right at that moment, all he felt was pure happiness. "Mmm." He buried his hands in her hair, kissed her, and made a sound like she was the most delicious thing in the world.

When he rolled off and got up to deal with the condom, Corie let out a disappointed whimper.

Jack laughed. "You know what would make this night perfect?"

Corie gave a long, satisfied sigh and stretched leisurely. "What?"

"More of that wine."

"That's what would make it perfect, huh?" But she didn't sound annoyed. She hugged a pillow and smiled at him.

Jack padded into the kitchen naked and came back with two glasses, white for her.

Corie sat up and took the Chardonnay from his outstretched hand. "Aw. Thank you."

"Leaves more of the Bordeaux for me." He climbed back into bed and she settled herself comfortably against him. He watched her take a sip of wine. "What are you thinking?"

"You really want to know?"

"Uh-huh."

"I had the right idea when I was seventeen."

CHAPTER THIRTY-NINE

Later, Corie sat at the granite counter and watched Jack cook. Neither of them had eaten anything at the benefit and they were ravenous. He stood in front of the stove in a t-shirt and jeans, barefoot, his hair messy, looking very cute. Murphy, who she had brought in the car with her, now drank happily from a plastic bowl Jack filled with water and put on the floor. When he was finished, the dog curled up in the middle of the kitchen and went to sleep.

On his way to the refrigerator Jack nudged the collie with his foot. "Dog, you're right in the way."

"He has a knack. Murphy!" Corie pointed toward the corner. Murphy gave her an insulted look and walked over to have his head scratched. Then he lay down on the floor by her feet and rolled over onto his back. Corie got down on the floor with him and rubbed his belly.

"Lucky dog," Jack said.

"It seems to me that you've gotten some attention yourself recently." It was like some miracle of normalcy. Just a couple cooking dinner late on a Saturday night in the middle of a murder investigation. Corie looked up at him. "You sure you don't mind about the dog?"

"If I have to take the dog to get you, it's more than a fair deal."

"Thanks. I think." She poured herself more Chardonnay.

The pasta he made turned out to be simple but delicious, angel hair with garlic, a little fresh parsley, good quality olive oil, and shaved Parmesan.

"Who knew? You're not only a wine connoisseur, you can cook." Corie twirled a healthy portion of pasta around her fork.

Jack smiled and then he looked thoughtful. "Do you remember the last time we saw each other?"

"At the convenience store. That was awful. You looked so angry."

"I was miserable," Jack said. "You practically jumped out of my way when you saw me as if you'd been scalded. It was clear you couldn't stand me."

"I thought . . . You know what I thought."

"That I had knocked up Hennessy without a second thought and cavalierly handed her a few hundred bucks to take care of it."

"No, that's not—" She hesitated. "Okay, yes, that's exactly what I thought."

"Want to know the real story?" Jack's eyes were serious. "I asked her to marry me."

Corie set down her fork. "You did?"

"She laughed in my face. Told me I was 'sweet but stupid.' I'll never forget those words. She said she didn't want to get married and, if she ever did, it wouldn't be to me. I was convinced that you and Hennessy were having a great laugh at my expense."

"If anyone was having a laugh, it sure wasn't me."

"It's amazing how it stayed with me, though. I vowed no one would ever be able to accuse me of being 'sweet and stupid' ever again."

"Well that's too bad. Not the stupid part, but you were sweet."

"Coming from you that doesn't sound like quite as bad an insult."

Corie laughed. "I know it's something men hate to hear. But I mean it in a good way. So catch me up on what you've done since the summer after high school. It's very lopsided. You know all about me."

"What would you like to know?"

"Do you ever actually answer a question?"

"Like what?"

Corie gave an aggrieved sigh and then thought about it. "How'd you become a cop?"

"You really want to know?"

Corie swatted at him with her napkin and Jack held his hands up in a motion of surrender.

"All right. I'll tell you." There was a pause while he took another leisurely sip of the La Tache.

"I went off the rails in college. My father died when I was a junior and after that my grades suffered and I experienced a lack of focus."

"Oh, Jack. I'm sorry."

He shrugged. "Long story short I fell in with a bad crowd. I didn't give a shit. It felt like . . . I don't know what it felt like. It felt like nothing. I didn't care anymore. I was on the verge of flunking out, bailing on the degree, and someone intervened.

"This man, a friend of my father's, took an interest in me. I don't know where I would be if it wasn't for him. He was an attorney. I got into some trouble. I did some things I'm not proud of." Jack frowned. "That may be what your charming husband was referring to on the stairs, although how the hell he could have found out is beyond me."

"Jack, be careful. Evan has a way of finding out—" She paused and shook her head helplessly. "Everything."

"You let me worry about Evan. Anyway, to answer your question, my father's friend had some contacts in the district attorney's office and he somehow convinced them that I had potential." Jack laughed shortly. "Why he thought that I'll never know. He made me a deal: I could go into the Academy or he'd throw me to the sharks. I didn't really want to go to jail, so I guess you could say I was blackmailed into my current profession. Do you want to hear the real cliché?"

"Sure."

"My Dad was murdered."

Back in his bedroom she said, "You know, I had forgotten all about you."

She was wearing one of his shirts. He started unbuttoning it. "I know. Me too. Completely."

Corie closed her eyes for a moment when he slid the shirt off her shoulders. "I certainly worked hard enough at it."

"Me too."

"If we'd gotten together when we were teenagers, it never would have lasted."

"Never." He pulled his t-shirt off over his head.

"Even now I wonder if it's a curiosity thing."

"The one that got away."

"What would it have been like? When we were teenagers?"

"We'll never know. Because of me." He stepped out of his jeans and kicked them away.

She leaned back on her hands on the bed, naked, looking up at him. "Let's just say you disabused me of my girlish notions about fidelity early on. I should thank you."

"Ouch."

"It's true."

"What about now?"

"What *about* now?" Her eyes traveled over his body, down his chest, and over his flat stomach to what lay beyond. She broke out in goose bumps.

"You still want me."

"I do. Nice of you to notice."

He smiled. "Still curious?"

"You're a very handsome man, Jack. Hard. Funny. Smart. The hardness didn't used to be there."

"You like that about me?"

"Part of what makes me curious."

He leaned down and grazed her lips with his, then let his mouth wander until it found a nipple.

"Mmm." Corie sighed.

"What are you curious about?"

"What made you that way. I don't flatter myself that I had that big an impact."

"You were the start. Things going wrong with you was the beginning of a long string of disasters."

"Things don't just go wrong," Corie said.

"No. They don't, do they?"

"Well, sometimes they do. But this wasn't a typhoon. It wasn't a natural disaster out of your control."

"Are you kidding? Being an eighteen-year-old boy is the definition of an out of control natural disaster."

Corie laughed. "Fair enough. I'll give you that one."

"You will? What else will you give me?" He leaned into her and kissed her. When he stopped he said, "For the record, I am sorry."

"Apology accepted."

Her hand slid down his stomach but he grabbed her wrist and stopped her. "No. I want to make you come."

Corie's eyes grew wide.

"I want to touch you and I want to see your reaction. I want to watch your face when you come." He looked very serious.

"Jesus, Jack."

Without taking his eyes off her face he touched her between her legs, lightly so that his index finger barely grazed her softness. Corie gasped. "You do like that." His voice was low and soft and sexy.

Corie couldn't answer. She could breathe but that was about it, and even that was becoming more difficult.

"Lay back."

She found it hard to endure that dark, hazel gaze. His eyes bore right through her and he felt again like a stranger. Corie leaned against the pillows, propped up in the bed while he spread her legs wider and touched her, carefully, softly, teasing, exploring; her breath came in stuttered gasps. "Jack."

"No. Don't think." Still with his eyes on her face.

She closed her eyes. She couldn't hold his gaze. His light touch was agony. Did he know what he was doing? What was he doing? "Jack."

She opened her eyes for a moment and he was looking down, looking at her, there, watching what his fingers were doing. It was unbearably sexy. She said his name again but he didn't stop. So Corie surrendered. She lay back against the pillows and let him do what he wanted. Gradually he increased the pressure, no longer teasing, until it was the most perfect thing she'd ever felt. She didn't care if he was watching her. Soon she didn't care about anything.

"Is that what you like?" He changed the stroke. "Or like that?"

"Oh God, Jack."

"Tell me."

Corie whimpered.

"Tell me. Do you want me to stop?"

"No." Corie's voice was hoarse with agony, longing, frustration, desire, lust. "No. Please."

If he stopped she would die, but he didn't. His fingers moved on her more firmly again until she couldn't even think anymore. She was incoherent with pleasure and, for a few blissful minutes, didn't care about anything but Jack, how he felt, how he tasted, how he sounded. When he finally moved on top of her Corie clung to him, the only real thing in the world.

"Yeah." A rough whisper, his lips in her hair. "That's what I wanted."

After she'd sufficiently recovered Corie rolled onto her side, holding her head up with her hand, and watched him. Jack looked supremely satisfied, even with his eyes closed. Suddenly everything about him was endearing. The charcoal shadow of a beard on his face, the way his thick, unruly dark hair sprouted in several different directions, his amazing long eyelashes. Corie touched his face. "I should go." She didn't sound sure.

"But then how will I do that again?"

"Again?" Corie's voice rose an octave. "I think if you do that again you might kill me."

"Stay. I've waited almost twenty years."

"This is insane." But Corie found it too much of an effort to sit up and sank back onto her side facing him. With a finger, she traced a line down his jaw and then dragged it across his lower lip. His wonderful, sexy, full lips.

He turned his head and kissed her palm. "You have to admit, we do have a lot of time to make up for."

Her eyelids felt heavy and Jack was so warm, the bed so comfortable. His voice was soothing and his touch was magic. She let her head drop onto his shoulder for a moment. All she wanted was to curl up against him and finally, really sleep. She felt safe. Corie realized with shock she couldn't remember the last time she felt safe. If ever. Even her dog sleeping on the floor shifted position, stretched, and let out a satisfied sigh.

But Corie couldn't quite trust comfort. "What if I'm the killer?"

"You're not."

"But what if I was?"

"Then I'd send you to jail." He sounded like he was falling asleep.

"Just like that?"

"It's only 'just like that' on TV."

"You know what I mean."

Jack roused himself enough to look at her. "I know that you don't really want to leave. I know that I love having you in my bed. I know that the attraction between us is very, very mutual."

"And that's enough?"

"It just is. Nothing makes up for anything else."

"That's very simple."

"I'm a simple guy."

Corie shook her head slowly from side to side. "Oh no. You're not."

He tried and failed to keep his eyes open and to sound tough. "You don't know me."

"I'm not sure I want to know you." Still. Corie considered for another moment and then switched off the light. She turned so that her back was toward him, slid down in the bed, and fitted herself against him. His arm closed around her. She pulled the covers up over her shoulder and gave in to the luxurious sleepiness. "And you might not want to know me."

CHAPTER FORTY

Shaun let the door of the bar slam behind him as he stormed out into the cold night. Last call his ass. Who was around to give them a hard time? Who gave a fuck? The mountain town was closed down and silent. Who the hell did that tight-assed bitch think she was, throwing him out? Stupid uptight bartender had her nerve telling him it was the law, they had to close at two. Had to get home, she said. Had to go to bed.

"It's the law." Shaun sang in a high-pitched falsetto, followed by, "Law, my ass!" His breath fogged the night air. He dropped his pants and showed the sleeping town his own white ass and then laughed hysterically. Almost hoped his uptight little brother would drive by. Chris deserved a frigid, shriveled-up cunt like the bartender. Maybe Shaun'd fix them up. He laughed harder.

Shaun pulled up his pants and climbed into the pickup. Her loss, missing out on the party he had to offer. He could fix her up good but she'd never know it now, stupid bitch. He reached into his jacket pocket and weighed the baggie of crystals in his hand.

"Go fuck yourself you ugly, dried-up cunt." Shaun beat the steering wheel and let out an excited whoop. The crystals in the bag were the real deal. Clear white shit, high quality, thanks to Evan and his roll of cash. Shaun pulled a ragged U-turn in the empty street, driving up onto the sidewalk on the other side to complete the maneuver. The pickup's gears whined in complaint as he shifted.

As Shaun drove, his tongue worked its way habitually around his teeth. Maybe he'd get them fixed with some of the money. His ex told him he looked like a hillbilly. Not that he gave a shit what she thought, but maybe with his teeth fixed he'd get more women. High-class women. Maybe someone with big tits like the one he saw Evan take to the cabin.

Was Evan dropping a hint earlier? He'd clearly let Shaun know that she was there by herself. That she liked to sleep in. A feral grin spread across his face. Hell yeah. He let out another loud whoop. She could sleep in with him anytime.

What the hell time was it anyway? Shaun blew on his hands. The night had turned cold, bitter, well below freezing. He cranked the heat lever to high in the old truck. He was wide awake.

He remembered Vangie picking her way through the brush in her high heels. She was fine. Maybe she was like a tip or something. Shaun tapped a ragged rhythm on the steering wheel, sang aloud to a nonexistent radio, and reached over to touch the empty passenger seat. She'd been right there. In his truck. With that round ass and those long legs and those tits. He imagined he could smell her, that musky, rank female smell. He cast an occasional glance at the road but it was deserted this time of night. He'd been one of only two people left in the bar when Tara or Tina or whatever the fuck her name was threw them out into the cold. Well fuck her. Shaun had a much better woman waiting for him at the cabin. Evan had as much as said so.

Shaun's erection made him impatient, and out on the highway he ground gears and pushed the old pickup to go faster. He rehearsed what he was going to tell her. He'd say, 'Evan wanted me to check up on you.' He'd say, 'It's such a cold night, I wanted to make sure the stove was working.' He'd say, 'I thought you might be scared out here all alone, a pretty girl like you.'

Shaun eyes darted back to the passenger seat. His fingers raked the tattered old upholstery. Right there. Her ass had been right there. He pictured her naked, bent over the arm of the couch while he stroked his fingertips fast, back and forth, back and forth, back and forth on the greasy ridges of the upholstery. The sensation was enervating but he couldn't stop. He steered with his knee, raised up in the seat, and used his other hand to unzip his jeans. A motion stabbed at the corner of his eye and he glanced up in time to see a big buck in the road. Shaun yanked the wheel but the fucking pickup had the maneuverability of a cinderblock. He overcompensated back the other way and felt a grinding collision. Glass shattered and the scenery spun through the patchwork maze of the windshield like one of those scenes in a cartoon where the characters are fighting but it looks like a big spinning blur. His foot pumped the brake pedal but he felt only air.

A squealing, grinding metal sound, and then silence. The buck thrashed once, twice, tried to stand and fell back. Shaun cut himself on glass groping in the upside-down pickup for the baggie. The truck shifted position, settled, and a searing pain shot up his leg. *Had to find the fucking baggie.* It must have fallen out of his jacket. All his hard work, gone, because of some fucking stupid deer. Because some mean, ugly bitch threw him out. Because things never went his way no matter how hard he worked or how hard he tried.

Shaun's breathing was ragged. The cops would come, maybe even his brother. Was Chris on graveyard? That bag had cost thousands. Practically the entire payment from Evan. Cops couldn't find it, couldn't find him, not like this, not when his little brother worked for them. *Fuck.*

A car was coming and Shaun thought about running. He crawled out through a window but his legs wouldn't hold him. He looked down and the bone in his right leg didn't look right. He tried to haul himself up against the truck and failed. *Where's the fucking baggie?* He felt in his pocket for it but he couldn't think straight with the pain. A woman got out of a car, ran to him, then stopped and stared.

Why was the bitch screaming? It wasn't that bad. Hadn't she ever seen anyone hit a deer? But she wasn't looking at the buck or at him. Shaun followed her frightened gaze. He'd completely forgotten about the big bag in the back of the pickup. Evan's bag. It must have fallen out and ripped open when the pickup flipped. It lay now near the shoulder of the road, clearly illuminated in the car's headlights. Something was wrong. Something was sticking out of the bag that wasn't a hoof or an antler or a piece of trash. A hand stuck out, a girl's hand, white and ominous. Shaun gave up on hauling himself to his feet, gave up on the idea of flight, and sank to the pavement. The woman backed away from him in terror, toward her car. He couldn't take his eyes off the bag and the woman wouldn't stop screaming. High-pitched screaming, scary and loud. Even louder than the wind that blew cold and relentless down from the unseen black mountains, wind that whipped and sliced at the bag, making the torn edge flap and snap like a canvas sail. *Fuck.*

CHAPTER FORTY-ONE

Jack instinctively grabbed past Corie for the phone. *Past Corie.* His hand stopped mid-reach and he stared. Corie. In his bed. Naked. With that hair spread out on his pillow. The memory of being inside her was fresh, with those long legs wrapped around him and her hands clawing at his back. The insistent, vibrating electronic thing on the nightstand irritated him beyond belief.

"What?" Jack barked into the phone.

She looked at him with sleepy blue eyes, stretched, and then sat up, pulling the sheet over her breasts. "What is it?"

"I have to go. You don't have to get up, though." Jack swung his legs over the side of the bed with a beleaguered groan. He ran a hand through his hair.

"What time is it?"

"A little after nine." Not how he wanted the morning to go.

"It has to do with the case, doesn't it?"

"It has to do with *a* case. Stay as long as you like." He got up and headed for the bathroom.

"Please don't lie to me."

But he did. "Got some results back. I have to meet Serena at the station. Shouldn't take too long." He wasn't sure whether to be relieved or disappointed that he could lie so easily and convincingly.

"They woke you up for that?"

"It's after nine. Not unusual at all. When they get results in they call me. No big deal." He shrugged and smiled. The smile felt false but she looked like she believed him.

While he was in the shower Corie made coffee and brought two cups back to the bedroom. She watched him dress. "You have to wear a suit? Even on Sunday?"

"Even if massive earthquakes and tidal waves are consuming the Earth and hell's freezing over."

"What a great job."

"I like it."

"I hope the coffee's okay. I made it really strong."

"I knew there was a reason I liked you." Jack finished knotting his tie and gave her a quick kiss.

"I'll get dressed and leave with you," Corie said.

"No reason. You'll be safer if you stay here and I'll have one less thing to worry about." What he'd really like was to find her naked and waiting in his bed when he got home. Nice fantasy. Jack checked his gun and his phone and then walked into the kitchen where he picked up his keys off the counter.

Corie followed. "I have to start looking for a place to stay sometime. Might as well be today. I'll be fine."

"Yeah. Where have I heard that before?"

She gave him a wry, tight-lipped smile. "This isn't—" She stopped and watched while Jack got something out of a drawer. "This whole night didn't turn out to be what I expected."

"What did you expect?"

"Hmm. When I let my lying, deceitful husband manipulate me into going to the benefit? Good times. I don't know. If I planned ahead I suspect I wouldn't be here right now."

Jack walked over to her and kissed her more thoroughly. His hand slid down her back and she tasted like coffee, which wasn't a bad thing at all. "Well I, for one, am very glad about how last night turned out."

She gave him a real smile that lit her whole face.

"Spare key." He handed it to her.

"Seriously? You're very trusting for a homicide detective."

"What're you gonna do? Steal my television?"

CHAPTER FORTY-TWO

"How could you!" Jessie's voice shrieked out of the speakers in Evan's Mercedes.

"Mother, calm down."

It was Sunday morning and Evan was driving toward Fairplay after a breakfast meeting with Stu. Evan intended to stay close to the investigation into Vangie's death and keep tabs on things to the best of his abilities. He wondered how soon the police would let him back into the cabin. Evan had some pull with the locals, but he had no doubt Jack Fariel would be involved.

"Don't tell me to calm down. How dare you? How. Dare. You!" In stuttering, high-pitched shouts articulated by sobs, the story came out. Jessie woke up to find her bed, and her house, empty. "Len left me. And it's your fault. What did you say to him?"

"When did he leave, exactly?" He really wanted to ask if she'd inventoried the silver. So the loser had taken Evan's not-so-subtle hint. And right before Jessie called, Evan had gotten the news that Shaun had been found with both a bag of meth and a bag full of dead Vangie. From Evan's perspective, the morning was going extremely well.

"I wasn't timing him with a damned stopwatch. I was asleep, Evan."

"It's important." Jessie liked to sleep late. She was a night person, plus she usually took an Ambien. Practically the whole world aside from Evan was addicted to pills.

"Oh, shove your importance up your tight ass. He's gone. What difference does the time make? He took all his things. He didn't leave so much as a toothbrush. Do you even care how that makes me feel?"

Evan was glad she couldn't see his face. "I am terribly sorry."

"No, you're not."

"All right. I can't say that I am. But I am sorry you're having such a hard time. You must have been scared."

He let her cry for a while, and when she spoke again, her voice was shaky but calm. "He wasn't strong. I don't need to be with a man who will abandon me at the first sign of discomfort."

"He was unsavory."

"You have always been jealous of my relationships."

In his mind's eye, Evan could see Jessie stiffen. It was healthier, he decided, for her to be angry at him rather than waste tears on a loser like Leonard Funderburk. "I know you're upset, but that's beneath you."

"It's not that easy finding companionship at my age."

"You don't seem to have much trouble. You're a beautiful woman."

Jessie's voice quavered. "Wh–where do you think he went?"

"How would I know?"

"You talked to him at length last night. I wouldn't be surprised if you suggested a destination. What was it?"

CHAPTER FORTY-THREE

"What was it, Shaun? A murder for hire?"

Jack dropped the baggie with Shaun's meth on the table. They were in an interview room at the Park County sheriff's office.

"Man. What is that?" Shaun licked his lips.

Shaun's leg, his good one, bobbed up and down about a thousand beats a minute. Crutches leaned against the cinderblock wall of the interview room and his broken leg, in a temporary cast, stuck out awkwardly in front of him. He was still coming down from his last tweak right before he left the bar.

Jack watched him. "Can you tell me why your knife was found in the bag with her?"

Shaun O'Dwyer was irritating almost beyond endurance. His bouncing and fidgeting and tapping made Jack want to hit him. Even though it was cold he wore a flannel shirt with the sleeves cut off. Better to impress the ladies with his tats, no doubt. He was sweating, his pimply skin had a greenish cast, and his teeth were awful. Jack was dragged away from a warm bed and Corie for this.

"The duct tape you used on her? We found tape like it at your service station."

Shaun started coughing and couldn't stop. Finally he said, "Tape? Tape? What tape?"

"You realize how this looks for you, Shaun? You need to help yourself here."

"I didn't do it, man." Shaun's bloodshot eyes darted around the room, up to the fluorescent lights, down to the dingy industrial carpeting, back to Jack, and away again.

Jack suppressed a deep, disgusted sigh. "Shaun. Help me understand what happened."

"I was working. And Markham came back with my pickup. I have several cars. I loaned it to Evan because the road to his place sucks."

"You had loaned your truck to Mr. Markham? When did you do that?"

"To Evan. Yeah. Me and Evan go back a long ways."

"And?"

"What?"

Jack could be patient when it was warranted, when he sensed a payoff at the end. In this case he wasn't sure any amount of tolerance was going to achieve results. "Evan borrowed your truck. And when he brought it back there was a bag in the back?"

"That's right. In the back. Back. Back."

"What did you do with the bag?" If this messed up piece of shit kept rhyming Jack wouldn't be responsible for his actions.

"I didn't do nothin'! I told you. I told my brother. Shit."

"Deputy O'Dwyer?"

"Who?"

"Your brother."

"Right. Christopher. He's my little brother. Three years younger than me. We overlapped two years in high school because I had to repeat a grade. Not because I'm dumb. I scored really high on all of those IQ tests they give you. But because of the ADD. I told you about that, right?"

"Shaun. Try to focus. What'd you tell your brother?"

"I told him Markham asked me to make a dump run. I didn't do it because I had things to do. And by the time I got to the transfer station it was closed."

The things Shaun had to do involved controlled substances. Jack noticed the hem of his shirt was stained black, probably from wiping off the edge of a pipe. "What time did Evan Markham ask you to make the dump run?"

"Who? I'm messin' with you, man. Don't look at me like that. Around six. He came by my garage. I repair cars. Been doing that all my life. Forever. I mean, not forever but since I was a kid . . . well not a kid but maybe around sixteen. No, fourteen. Took shop in school. Only class I liked. My teacher, Mr. Farnsworth, wore this bad toupée and we made fun of him and he always wore these sport coats or whatever the fuck they're called. Polyester. Youevernotice whatafunnywordthatis, polyester?"

"Shaun, how much of that did you smoke?"

"No man, it's not that. I got that . . . whaddya call it? ADD. And I'm in pain." His good knee continued to bob up and down.

"The rate you're going that baggie wouldn't have lasted long."

Shaun licked his lips again. "What're you gonna do with it?"

"You're kidding, right?" Jack stood. "I'm gonna give you some time to think."

"What? You leaving? It's Markham, I'm telling you. He had me wash his car. The Mercedes. Fine car that Mercedes. Said he was going to some big party."

"Speaking of parties, I hope you enjoy our hospitality." Jack brandished the baggie and enjoyed the look of desperation that flashed across Shaun's face. Finally. Some sign of recognition.

Jack talked to the deputies on his way out. "Call me when he's had a chance to sleep more of that shit off and says something intelligible."

Chris O'Dwyer kept his voice neutral. "He lawyer up?"

Jack studied Chris for a moment. "You're his brother, right? We should talk."

Chris followed Jack miserably into the sergeant's office. Busting Shaun had seemed like a good idea at the time. Satisfying, even. But now he felt guilty.

The sergeant closed the door behind them. Never a good sign, although Jack seemed understanding. He used Chris's name and he smiled. "Can you tell me again what your brother said?"

"Markham switched cars," Chris said. "Came up in a Cadillac but didn't think it would make it all the way to the cabin. That's why it took me so long to go up there. I, uh, needed to round up an SUV to do the wellness check."

"What happened to the Cadillac?"

Chris froze.

"I know your brother's record," Jack said.

"I don't know what his intentions were for the car, sir." That was true. "Did you find it?"

"It's still at your brother's shop," Jack said. Luckily for the police, drugs made criminals inefficient. "Tell me the rest, Chris."

Chris nodded. "Markham drove up in the Cadillac on Friday and Shaun met him on the road to the cabin by the gate. Not really a gate, just a chain. Then later—the next day—Markham brought the pickup back and swapped again for his Mercedes, which Shaun had been doing some work on. The bag was in the back and Evan asked Shaun if he would make a dump run."

"Why would he do that?" Jack asked.

"Um, we do odd jobs for the Markhams."

"We?"

"Well, our family." Chris twisted a school ring on his right hand. "The O'Dwyers and the Markhams have known each other for a really long time. Evan's grandfather and my grandfather were friends. They leave the cabin empty a lot and we'll check on it, make sure a pipe doesn't burst, things like that. My mom cleans the cabin every week even though they don't use it that much. Evan knows she can use the money. Same with Shaun. Evan brings his cars up here for Shaun to work on even though he could have it done in Denver. Evan's a good guy."

"Your families are close then?" Jack asked.

"For generations."

"It sounds like the O'Dwyers work for the Markhams. They're a rich family after all and your family's not."

"It's not like that." Chris sounded defensive. "They're not snobs."

"No? That's nice. It doesn't always work that way."

"Evan's a good guy." Chris repeated himself.

"How'd his Mercedes get up here if he had the pickup?" Jack frowned. "Can't drive two cars at once."

"What?" Chris looked back and forth between his sergeant and Jack.

Jack spoke reasonably, as if he was thinking it through for the first time. "You said that Markham drove the Cadillac up Friday night and switched cars with Shaun. Then he returned to Denver and went to the hospital to see his wife. How'd he get there?"

Chris stared.

"Markham was in custody Friday night. The next morning when he made bail, he drove his Mercedes back. So he either got a ride to Denver Friday night or someone else rode with him and then drove the pickup back, because it didn't get back up here by magic."

"You think Shaun?"

"You tell me." Jack watched Chris for a minute and then spelled it out. "Markham was arrested for assault Friday night. Whoever helped him is an accomplice."

Chris's sergeant finally spoke up. "I think this would be a good time to take a couple of days off, Chris."

"But—"

"You've done nothing wrong but it's a conflict of interest, son. You have some personal time coming. Why don't you take it?"

CHAPTER FORTY-FOUR

While Jack interviewed Shaun—or tried to—Serena talked to the deputy in charge of the Park County motor pool. She explained who she was, that she had authorization from the sheriff, and asked to see the vehicle log for yesterday.

"Afraid I can't help you there," the deputy said. He was a big man, thick through the middle, with a buzz cut and a face gone to jowls.

"You keep track of the vehicles being checked in and out, right?" Serena asked.

"'Course we do. Our policy is to record the check-in and checkout times in fifteen-minute increments. I maintain the usage logs myself. If you come back tomorrow I'll have everything for Saturday entered into the system. We're short-staffed, budget cuts and all. I do everything myself."

Serena knew it wouldn't help to jump all over the man, but still. "You're telling me that the vehicle logs are updated after the fact?"

The deputy stiffened. "Well you don't know how long a vehicle's gone until it's back now, do you? We're more informal up here than you guys down in the city. All someone has to do is call up and ask and one of us knows where the cars are at."

As he spoke, the deputy's eyes roamed all over Serena, although they rarely strayed to her face. She fought the urge to grab his chin and force his gaze upward. "Who was working here on Saturday?"

"Let me check." He pretended to read a schedule on a clipboard, then leaned toward her and grinned. "I was. Now sugar, if you were to ask me nicely, I could tell you whatever you need to know."

Serena barely managed to suppress an eye roll. "All right. Which of your deputies checked out an SUV Saturday afternoon, say between noon and six?"

"Well see, there you go. That's a question I can answer. Deputies Quinn and Zirklow."

She glanced to her right at the lot surrounded by a chain-link fence. "That's it? All these cars and only two of them got used?"

The deputy scowled. "Even folks who don't wear a suit can count."

"Of course." Serena's voice was sweet. She pulled out her notebook and wrote. "Want to make sure I get the names right. You said Quinn and Zirklow? No one else? Maybe when you were on a break?"

He snorted. "Break. What's that?"

CHAPTER FORTY-FIVE

Corie rapped on the doorframe and called through the screen door. Someone was inside the cabin. "Hello?" she called again and then tentatively took a step inside. The door slapped behind her. She didn't recognize the car parked by the gate. It wasn't one of Evan's. At least not one that she recognized. Was it Vangie's? The car had Colorado plates.

Corie's life was like the aftermath of a giant party; it was hard to know where to start picking up the pieces. She'd driven up here to get the few things she wanted: ribbons from old horse shows, photos, maybe find her gun. No. That was a lie. She wanted to confront Vangie. She wanted to find out for herself if Jack's taunt last night at the museum had been merely spiteful or had a grain of truth to it. Now her heart thudded until she felt sick; had she made another blunder and put herself in harm's way again?

A thin woman with gray hair pulled back in a greasy braid appeared in the doorway of the second bedroom. Hennessy's room. The one that was never open.

Corie let out a startled "Oh," surprised and relieved at the same time.

Erin O'Dwyer had been cleaning and held a dust rag in her hand. She glared at Corie.

"Erin, hi. How are you? Are you alone?" There was no spark of friendliness or recognition from the old woman. Corie started to reintroduce herself and stopped.

Erin seemed defensive. "I clean every week. For Mr. Markham."

"That's great." Corie spoke lightly. "I don't mean to interrupt. I just came to get a few things."

Erin didn't move from the doorway, forcing Corie to squeeze past her into the room.

"Does Mr. Markham know?" The way Erin asked, it sounded like an accusation.

Corie squared her shoulders. "It's my house, too."

Erin turned back to her dusting without a word. She'd already stripped the bed, revealing a stained mattress and sagging box spring. The bed itself was Hennessy's old four poster with a canopy Corie had so envied when she was twelve. It was Evan who salvaged some of his sister's furniture and mementos and moved them here. Jessie couldn't bear to have any reminders of Hennessy around. What a bitter irony that by marrying Evan, Corie had become what she'd always wanted to be growing up: Jessie's daughter.

Lost in memories, Corie put her hand on one of the posts for a moment and felt something sticky under her hand, like the residue from tape. She frowned at it and picked at it idly with her fingernail. The canopy was gone and there used to be a rug covering the scarred, wooden floor, but that was gone now, too. Corie felt an oppressive sadness and shook herself out of her reverie. The sooner she got out of here the better.

In Hennessy's old dressing table Corie found some faded blue ribbons and a gold locket. Erin's beady, suspicious eyes bore a hole into her back as she slipped the necklace into the pocket of her jeans.

In the master bedroom Corie's gun was where she thought it might be, in the metal cabinet in the corner. She checked the clip on the Smith and Wesson, which was full, then put the gun and the ribbons in her purse along with some extra bullets. Erin apparently hadn't gotten to this room yet. Corie looked around but saw no sign of Vangie. Was Jack lying? Or had Vangie been here and left? Impulsively, she pulled back the comforter on the bed and sniffed the sheets. The result was inconclusive.

Corie listened to Erin's mop move rhythmically across the floor. It made a *thwip* sound when it hit the baseboard. *Thwip, thwip, rinse.* The smell of bleach burned the air. Erin must be almost seventy now and still cleaning houses.

With a sigh, Corie picked up a broom and swept the living room floor. Erin didn't stop what she was doing or say thank you, but she didn't object either. Corie emptied the dustpan in the kitchen trash and saw two wineglasses sitting by the sink. A flash of anger flared and she picked one up, her fingers curving around the cool glass. *Is it really that much of a surprise?* Instead of hurling the glass against the wall, she ran the water until it was hot and found rubber gloves under the sink. Not sure why she was cleaning, not sure why she was doing anything anymore.

At the door, Murphy barked and Corie jumped. She looked outside saw several police SUVs. There were heavy footsteps on the front porch and someone rapped loudly on the door.

A male voice yelled, "Police!"

She moved to open the door and came face-to-face through the screen with Jack. Shock registered on his face before he wiped it clean. Corie didn't know what to say or if she should say anything at all. Three uniformed deputies poured into the room behind Jack and the space suddenly felt very small.

Erin stopped mopping the bedroom floor and watched from the doorway. It occurred to Corie that there was only one way out, the front door, and that was hopeless. Why did she want to run? It must be some kind of instinctive reaction. Erin looked like she felt the same way.

"We have a warrant to search the premises, ma'am," an officer said. He handed her a paper.

"Please wait outside," Jack said, as if to a stranger. He looked curiously at Erin who in turn looked beseechingly at Corie.

Corie nodded. In fact, her head was bobbing up and down like a frightened rabbit. What did she have to feel guilty about? Corie tried to catch Jack's eye but he wouldn't look at her, so she picked up her purse and walked outside onto the porch. No one objected to her taking the purse.

Erin walked outside too, and without a word to Corie, got in her car and drove off. A deputy looked out through the screen door.

"Is she allowed to do that?" Corie asked.

"The detective would like to talk to you, ma'am. Please wait there on the porch."

Jack took his sweet time before he came out, though. When he did, he didn't sit down with her on the porch steps but instead said, "Let's take a walk," and led her away from the cabin toward the cars, where he turned on her.

"What the hell are you doing here? Do you have a death wish?"

Corie opened her mouth but couldn't find words. He was so angry and his eyes so hard that she found herself a little afraid of him. She managed a feeble, "What?"

Jack jammed his hands onto his hips and fixed her with that icy stare. "Corie. Vangie's dead."

"What?" A second time.

He did nothing to sugarcoat it and he didn't give her a chance to process the shock. He watched her reaction to the news. "You were cleaning a possible crime scene. Want to tell me why you were doing that?"

"I didn't know it was a crime scene. She was killed here? When?" Corie felt like she was choking. She blinked at him and her mouth hung open in confusion.

Jack didn't seem to register her horrified response. "Did you move anything? Touch anything?"

Corie swallowed. "There were two wineglasses by the sink. I washed them." She felt her face contort into a grimace and resisted it. "I swept the floor, then emptied the dustbin. Erin mopped."

"Very thorough."

"Jack, what happened?" Then she remembered. "That's the phone call you got this morning."

"You should have stayed at my place." He broke eye contact and she saw his mouth twist. He looked bitter, as if it were a foregone conclusion she was guilty and had let him down.

"I wanted to start getting my affairs in order. I couldn't just sit around and wait for you. I had to do something."

"That's bullshit."

"What?" She hated how weak and strangled her voice sounded.

"You wanted to come up here and confront Vangie. After all of your assurances last night that you'd stay far away from Evan." Jack tipped his head back and let out an angry groan. "Goddamn it. I shouldn't have told you he was bringing her here."

"I'm sorry I washed the glasses. I wanted to smash them to bits."

"Don't fucking lie to me. What did you really come up here for?"

Corie decided on the truth. As unconvincing as it was. "Personal things. Photos, ribbons from horse shows. Sentimental stuff. Jack, I didn't know, I—"

He cut her off. "Where is it?"

"The ribbons?"

"The gun."

Corie hugged herself and looked off toward the distant mountains. "In my purse. Do you need it?"

"*You* don't need it. What the hell were you going to do?" Without waiting for an answer, Jack paced a few strides away and she wasn't sure she heard him right. "I can't find you. I can't."

Eventually he turned and walked back toward her and he seemed calmer.

She wanted to touch him but knew that would be wrong.

He paused, as if deciding. "What else did you take?"

She pulled the locket out of her jeans. "I thought this was Hennessy's but the monogram is wrong."

Jack turned the gold heart over and saw the letters "YH" engraved on the back in a fancy scroll.

Corie bit her lip. "Does this . . . I mean, did she die here?"

"Here's what you're going to do." His hand closed around her wrist. "You're going to drive back down to Denver to my house and wait for me."

She spoke without thinking. "You're not going to give me the speech about leaving town or anything, are you?"

His eyes were serious. "Promise me. You'll drive straight there."

"I promise."

CHAPTER FORTY-SIX

Later that afternoon, back at the Office of the Medical Examiner in Denver, Jack looked down at what was left of Vangie—after being hacked at with a serrated hunting knife and then bouncing off the pavement at sixty miles an hour—and listened to Frank Yannelli describe his findings. Jack wondered not for the first time how he ever got used to this. He usually found autopsies fascinating. But this time, he couldn't help wondering what he would do if it were Corie. And what he could do to make her listen. And then he reminded himself for the nine-hundredth time that day that he couldn't control everything. It wasn't a satisfying conclusion.

Vangie's body on the metal table. Evidence. Corie waking up in his bed that morning, sleepy and beautiful. She couldn't exist in the same universe with the sight in front of him. But try telling that to his brain.

Frank was asking him a question. "Got a primary crime scene?"

Jack snapped back to the present. "I don't even have a secondary crime scene."

"Signs of vaginal penetration. No semen. Whoever it was wore a condom. You guys find that?" Frank asked.

Jack shook his head. He noticed the blood smeared on the inside of Vangie's thighs. "Did he have sex with her while she was bleeding out?"

"Sick son of a bitch," Serena muttered under her breath.

Jack glanced at his partner. Was it possible for a black woman to be green?

"I can't tell you exactly *when* in this process she had intercourse," Frank said. "Only that she did and by all appearances it was rough."

"Understatement," Serena said.

Frank picked up one of Vangie's arms with a gloved hand and the forearm moved at a funny angle, as if it wasn't still attached at the elbow.

"He do that?" Jack asked.

Frank shook head. "I don't think so. She was in full rigor, not to mention it was below freezing. This presents as a postmortem defect. Could have happened from the force of hitting the pavement."

Jack looked warily at Serena again. "If you're going to be sick . . ."

"I know, I know."

"Just aim it away from me."

Frank showed them a hand. Vangie's reverse French manicure was in good condition. "Scraped her nails but didn't get much. It doesn't appear she scratched her attacker. Her wrists were bound together with duct tape. Found traces of adhesive on her ankles, too. Hard to say for certain but it appears she was restrained without a struggle."

"Tied up willingly," Jack said.

Frank arched a bushy eyebrow. "Taped, to be specific. And yes, it looks that way. No apparent defensive wounds."

Serena stepped closer. "What's that abrasion around her neck?"

"Doesn't look like a ligature," Frank said. "Too straight and defined to have come from a human hand. Something was around her neck, possibly her head. I'm guessing she fought against whatever it was when she was being cut."

"She would have been in pain for sure," Serena said.

Frank directed their attention to her genitals, or what was left of them, and allowed himself a rare editorial comment. "Butchered her pretty good."

Jack's eyes flicked to Serena again but she held her ground.

"When did the genital mutilation occur?" Serena asked.

"Perimortem. She was still alive."

"So we're looking at sexual sadism."

"It's consistent with that," Frank said. "Combined with the injuries to her breasts."

"Almost like he was trying to take the implants back," Jack said.

Frank's expression was somber. "This has the hallmarks of an extreme S&M session gone incredibly wrong."

"Maybe Markham has a disciple," Serena said.

"Or he wants us to think that." Jack stared at Vangie. "Any useful trace?"

Frank grunted. "Road rash from hitting the pavement. She was wrapped in a sheet and then double bagged. Probably why she's not in worse shape."

"Would Shaun think to do that?" Jack asked.

Serena shook her head. "No. But the way he slashed at her—"

"And a condom? Shaun's gonna wear a condom?"

"Based on lividity patterns she was moved not too long after death," Frank said. "Then she bounced around in a pickup and spent hours in the cold. Then hit the pavement at sixty miles an hour. It's a miracle she's in one piece."

"Sort of," Serena said.

"Time of death?" Jack asked.

"Between eight and eleven Saturday night."

"You sure?"

Frank favored Jack with a dry look. "Makes my job more difficult when they've been on road trips, Fariel. I'm running tox screens. I'll let you know if I find anything that changes my estimate."

"I was with Evan between eight and eleven." Jack vented his anger on the swinging door on his way out of the autopsy suite. It slammed open and banged into the opposite wall. "I'm Evan's fucking alibi. All of us—Corie, Aranda, Roger; everyone at the benefit. Evan could call any of us to testify on his behalf."

Serena followed him outside into the harsh, late afternoon mountain sunshine.

"And I made him memorable. With his banged-up face I'm sure Evan made quite an impression. I feel like we're playing a demented chess game and Evan's three moves ahead of me. It's like he wanted me to mess up his face at the hospital. He wanted me to show up at the museum and drag Corie out of there."

Serena frowned, thinking about it for a minute. "So Evan leaves Vangie at the cabin and goes to a party."

Jack laughed bitterly. "Where he fed me precisely the information he wanted me to have."

"What isn't he telling you?"

"Was she alive when he left? He didn't tell me that. But with that time of death? Shit. Best case with that road, it's a two-hour drive from the cabin to the western edge of Denver. Evan would have had to have time to kill her, bag her, get cleaned up himself, switch cars with Shaun—she would have had to have been dead by five and that's way outside the window the ME gave us."

"Hard to believe even Vangie would have partied with Shaun," Serena said. "All he has to offer is crystal. And that handsome smile of his. They searched his apartment, his service station, and the trash and didn't find any bloody clothes."

Disgust and frustration were palpable in Jack's voice. "And not a mark on him. But if she was tied—taped—up that could explain it."

"We know Shaun's truck has been to the cabin." Serena hesitated. Considering his mood she was reluctant to even mention the next thing. "Why do you think Corie was there right afterward, cleaning?"

Jack acted as if he hadn't heard her. "Another killing at another home of Evan's. Another place he had every reason to be. If we determine he had sex with Vangie, so what? She was his girlfriend. We have to put that knife in Evan's hand at exactly the right time and he has me for a fucking alibi." Jack looked at his partner but didn't really see her. "I don't know how he did it, but I sure as hell am going to figure it out."

CHAPTER FORTY-SEVEN

"Corie?" Jack let himself into his house through the back door, threw his keys on the kitchen counter with one hand, and loosened his tie with the other. It was after ten and he'd brought work home: crime scene photos, interview transcripts, police reports, 911 calls, lab results.

Murphy appeared in the kitchen doorway and broke into frenzied barking.

"Murphy!" Corie called.

Jack approached the dog and crouched down to his level. "It's okay, boy." He scratched Murphy behind the ears. Corie appeared in the kitchen doorway and Jack looked up at her. "Good watchdog. Bit of a delayed reaction, though."

Murphy flopped down on the floor and rolled onto his back so Jack could give him a belly rub.

"He's a whore," Corie said. "What time is it? I must have fallen asleep."

"Late." She was wearing a t-shirt, a gray, wool hoodie sweater, and jeans. Her hair was mussed and Jack's first instinct was to reach and smooth it down. He didn't. "I'm surprised you're really here. Relieved. But surprised."

She bit her lip. "I left your key on the counter."

"Might as well keep it until . . . things settle down."

"It felt really weird being in your house without you here." She walked over to the refrigerator. "I got a pizza. Are you hungry? There's a lot left."

He looked appreciatively at Corie's ass in the jeans. "Starving." She reached into the refrigerator for the pizza box. When she turned back toward him, he took the box from her with one hand and set it on the table; his other hand reached for her.

"Jack."

"How sleepy are you?" He took her arm and pulled her close.

"Haven't you had a very long day?" Her eyes looked amused.

"No day's that long."

CHAPTER FORTY-EIGHT

Evan sat gingerly on the bed in Jessie's guest room and pushed a quilted, green satin camel out of his way. Plush velvet throws and pillows adorned the bed in deep shades of purple with beaded and jeweled trim. An elaborate brass lamp sat on the nightstand, its light obscured with an artfully draped scarf. It was an effect that made Evan think of a harem or an opium den. Or a whorehouse.

What made him think it would be tolerable to spend even one night at his mother's? From a young age all Evan ever wanted to do was leave home. But Jessie had begged and wept and finally he succumbed. She said the house felt sinister with Len gone. She was out of her mind with terror and, besides, it was all Evan's fault.

Evan thought his mother was dramatic, brittle, and unreliable. Jessie's coping mechanism, if you could call it that, was to pretend everything was glorious. And it would be as soon as she found a Len replacement, which she would with alacrity. Zen, Jessie called it. Live in the moment. Stay centered. Evan called it garden variety denial, if he chose to think about it at all.

Corie looked up to Jessie for some unknown reason. Found her charming instead of ridiculous, creative instead of unstable, affectionate instead of wildly inappropriate. Evan refused to consider what had gone on downstairs in the master suite, in the massive, carved mahogany bed Jessie had once shared with Evan's father.

Had Len used the guest room before he moved downstairs? Slept in this bed? Evan imagined the other man's scent was still on the lime green silk sheets. It felt unclean. It was also hard to be in this room and not think of Hennessy—it used to be hers. That was another reason Evan stayed out of this house as much as possible. Usually he could push the memories away, but tonight he failed.

It must be the timing. The scrapbook, the model, his recent play bringing it all back.

Fifteen years ago Hennessy had been brought home for hospice care. Jessie begged Evan for help and he flew to Denver from North Carolina. Jessie opened the door for him barefoot, her face devoid of makeup or emotion, her hair wild. He was twenty-eight and hadn't met the singer yet.

Jessie had hired a nurse who urged Evan into Hennessy's darkened room. "Come say hello."

"Isn't she in a coma?" Evan asked.

"No. She can hear you."

The nurse told him that Hennessy's heart had grown too weak to adequately pump blood through her body. Her organs were failing. Her weight had fallen below eighty-seven pounds, her previous low-water mark.

"Maybe you can get her to eat," the nurse said. "There's still a chance. She's young."

"She might survive?" Evan had been surprised.

"She's young," the nurse repeated. "Only twenty. The effects of anorexia are reversible. But there's no time to lose. She's already lost heart muscle. When your body starts consuming muscle to survive it attacks the organs, too."

Evan hadn't known his sister well but she'd always seemed like a selfish girl. Not someone who would deny herself. "I don't think she'll listen to me."

"You have to try."

Did he? Evan sat in a chair next to the bed and tried to find his sister's hand in the bedclothes.

When the nurse was gone Evan said, "Hennessy." Then he repeated it a second time, louder. Did he imagine it, or did he see a slight flickering of her eyelids? Hennessy's eyelashes were somehow still lush and dark, incongruous against her gaunt, bluish-white face. Evan raised her hand to his lips and kissed it.

In those days the room was painted a pale rosy color, the color of dawn. Fashion magazines littered the floor. Hennessy's ribbons—all blue—from horseback riding events were proudly displayed, stuck around the edge of the mirror over her makeup table and tacked to the walls. A photo of her with her friend Corie was on the dresser. When Hennessy left for college Jessie left the room alone.

Various pictures of movie stars and fashion models were taped up on the walls. Was that why? Did she want to look like one of them? To be perfect? Evan understood the drive to be perfect. Machines whirred quietly. Hennessy's chest barely moved the blanket up and down. The nurse said the disease ate her heart. Not that his sister had a big heart to begin with.

"Hennessy, it's me. Evan." They were far enough apart in age to be strangers. "I know I haven't been around much, but I'm here now."

Get her to eat, the nurse had said. And keep her eating for the rest of her life. The fatality rate from anorexia was higher than almost any other mental disorder. He looked it up. Constant vigilance was required, and even then, the odds of her ever being really healthy were bad. What if she ate just enough to drag this out? That would be torture for everyone.

"Hennessy, I want to help you. I know we haven't been close, but I will do whatever it takes if you choose to live." Did he feel her hand move? He looked down. She was so weak that even if she tried to squeeze his hand, he wasn't sure he'd be able to feel it. "You have to choose." He found himself speaking loudly, as if she were deaf, and lowered his voice to a more conversational tone. "You have to choose, Hennessy, and you have to let me know. You have to let all of us know."

Jessie used Evan's homecoming as an excuse to cook. She busied herself for hours in the kitchen, her hair pinned up haphazardly, still barefoot, with cooking magazines open on the counters and pots simmering on the stove. His mother insisted on taking all of their meals together, on eating in the dining room even though it was only the two of them, and on using all of the fine china and crystal and silver.

So the two of them sat in the elegant, formal dining room, gorging themselves and making small talk, ignoring the irony of the young woman starving herself to death right above their heads.

You could smell the food upstairs which seemed cruel. Evan sat with Hennessy for hours each day while Jessie rarely made an appearance. His mother said that she preferred to remember Hennessy the way she used to be—beautiful, vibrant, and full of life. The specter in the bed was not her daughter. That was the word Jessie used: specter.

"Hennessy, none of us are mad at you," Evan said the second day. "None of us can bear to see you suffer. Mom and I can't bear it." Was she suffering? It was hard to tell.

No sound other than the machines. Her shallow breathing was silent.

"If you want to live, I will help you." Evan glanced over his shoulder. As usual, the nurse had left them alone. Still, she might be right outside the door. Evan lowered his voice to a whisper.

"And if you don't want to live, I will still help you. Do you understand?"

He gently set her hand down on the sheet and walked around her room. He picked up the photo of the two young rodeo queens from the dresser. Hennessy and Corie stared back, in heavy makeup and ridiculously large cowboy hats. Corie was Hennessy's best friend. In the photo his sister looked happy, but looks, as he well knew, were most often used for deceit.

He set the framed picture down and walked to her makeup table. Fingered the ribbons stuck around the edge of the mirror. Trailed his fingers in some spilled powder. The closet was open. He straightened the garments on the hangars and made sure they were spaced evenly before he closed the door. This wouldn't do at all. He aligned the edges of the magazines into neat piles and noted that the wastebasket needed to be emptied. He'd tell the nurse. When he was done straightening up he saw that his sister's eyes were open. Terrible, shadowed eyes, as if already looking into an abyss somewhere beyond this room.

"Hennessy?" She didn't turn her head. Her eyes, which he knew to be green, looked black, like a raven's. He touched her forehead. A vein throbbed beneath the pale skin under his fingertips. "You've been brave all along, haven't you? I know that about you, Hennessy. I haven't been around but I do know that. It's not cowardly to die. In fact, I think that takes the most courage of all."

She didn't answer, but a single tear slid out of her left eye and ran down her temple, into her hair. Her dark hair used to be long, lush, and lustrous. Now it was dull, matted, and provided such a thin covering that he could clearly make out the shape of her skull. She was so frail that his hands looked huge as he gently stroked her face. It would be so easy to twist her neck, cover her mouth, and stop her heart. If only he knew what she wanted.

Evan spent the next few days taking long runs past the elegant houses on Seventh Avenue Parkway and through the familiar streets of his childhood. It was Evan who washed Hennessy's hair and gently cleaned the crust that built up around her eyes. The nurse, teary-eyed, patted his arm and told him that she'd never seen a brother so attentive. He was sickened by the nurse and glad they wouldn't need her much longer.

In the dining room each evening Jessie sat at the head of the table with him to her right. There were always three courses: a soup or salad, a main course, and dessert. For the first time in his life Jessie seemed to relish conversation with him. She took a genuine interest and asked Evan about his life back east. When he talked she watched him rapt, her eyes wide, almost breathless with delight. In return, he let her take comfort from the things she loved and he didn't judge her. He never forced topics on Jessie that caused her distress until the time came, after sitting with his sister for four long days, that he had his answer.

Evan waited until after the dishes from the main course had been cleared and they were having their coffee. "How did you know when it was time with Dad?"

"Oh, that was a terrible thing." Jessie twisted her napkin, a heavy, cream-colored linen with a scalloped detail around the edge. She blinked at him, afraid.

"You were very brave. Hennessy's more like you than you realize, you know. She's brave, too."

"Do you really think so?"

Did he imagine it or was there an edge to her voice? "This could go on for a long while. I've done some research."

Jessie nodded.

He chose his words carefully. "I know you will do whatever this demands of you and that's the difficulty. How do we know what needs to be done and what's merely a result of longing?"

His mother seemed to relax and let out a deep breath, as if she'd been holding it for a very long time. "Yes. That's it exactly. I knew you would understand. We all long for things." She took a sip of her after-dinner cordial, a delicate stemmed glass of honey-colored Sauternes.

"Longing is treacherous." He watched her.

"It is the most treacherous thing. No one can be held accountable for their longing."

"They can't, can they?"

"No." She lifted her napkin from her lap and folded it neatly before setting it on the table—Jessie's signal that dinner was finished. She picked up her glass and stood. "It's so cold out. I think I'll finish this in front of the fire."

Evan looked up at her. "Do you need to know that I forgive you?"

She shook her head slightly. "Let's not speak of it. It is enough to know that you understand. That you truly do understand."

"I truly do."

"I'm glad you're here, Evan." Jessie placed her hand on his shoulder and left it there for a long minute, the pressure firm. Evan could still remember how warm her hand felt, like a benediction. He liked to imagine the experience created a bond between the two of them, mother and son, although they never mentioned that night again.

How had everything unraveled? Evan fingered the tassel on a bolster pillow. It started with Brice. No, with the sister; what was her name again? Monica? No, that wasn't it. He tried to get comfortable on the overly embellished bed. Undressing and slipping between the sheets was unthinkable. He'd just nap a little until it was time for his run.

It had all started someplace before memory, before Corie or the singer–actress or even Hennessy. He was born into a situation of such longing and tension, it was unbearable. An ordinary man would have broken under the pressure long ago. But Evan was no ordinary man. He would begin again. He would rebuild, and what he created would be even better than what he had before. He'd been looking at it all wrong. This was an opportunity for a new beginning and he'd almost been too blind to see it. Evan reached for the glass of wine on the nightstand and drained it. Then he twisted the brass knob on the lamp, plunging the room into darkness. Evan found it comforting. He dozed and his sleep was dreamless.

CHAPTER FORTY-NINE

The next morning, Jack was in Dani's office at eight. He was joined by Mike, Serena, and two other detectives, Scalamandre and Warren. Serena took one of the chairs facing the lieutenant's desk and Jack habitually stood.

Scalamandre and Warren had talked to Alex Cantrell's roommates who confirmed the young man was home by two thirty a.m.

"They seem credible?" Jack asked.

Warren shrugged. "They don't have to be. We have Cantrell's car caught on not one but two security cameras near the university. At 2:17 and 2:23 to be exact."

"Kid's got no record," Jack said. "No gun registrations. Came in voluntarily, gave us prints, DNA, whatever we asked for."

Dani had reading glasses perched on the end of her nose and she looked at Jack over the rim. "So now we've got two murderers? What else do we know about Vangie Perez?"

Mike looked at Jack, who leaned against a beige, metal filing cabinet along one wall. "I talked to her husband in Texas, like you asked."

Jack nodded. "And?"

"When she first started spending time with Evan last spring, she used the excuse of business trips. She flew back and forth for a while, and then in May, she left for good. Left a four-year-old daughter, too."

Mike paused to let that sink in before continuing. "When I made the death notification her husband didn't sound surprised. He told me she was determined to claw herself out of the trailer park, no matter who she hurt in the process. His exact words. Husband hasn't set foot out of Texas in years, though. And has tons of alibis."

"I collected a DNA sample from Len Funderburk," Jack said. "That and the sample Evan provided are being compared to the unknown from Monique Lawson's murder. Tiffany ran it Saturday. The reports should be on my desk by now."

Dani nodded. "If one of them killed the sister, that could give them motive to get rid of Brice. What about Vangie? Who has motive to kill her?"

"Evan," Jack said.

"Corie," Serena said. Jack kept leaning, but he tensed. She continued quickly. "But the way Vangie was killed suggests a man. Although, she was cleaning the crime scene."

"Doesn't matter," Mike said. "Corie and Evan share the same alibi. They were both at the wine tasting at the time Vangie was murdered. What about the guy in custody? Shaun O'Dwyer? He had her body in his truck. His knife was the murder weapon. The tape she was restrained with came from his service station."

"May have," Serena said.

"There was nothing under her nails," Jack said. "She was restrained without a struggle. That points to Evan."

"Who couldn't be in two places at one time," Dani said.

Jack shoved his hands into the pockets of his gray dress slacks. "Evan told me at the wine tasting that he'd left Vangie alone at the cabin. He didn't specify how he'd left her." The concession pained him. He wanted responsibility squarely where he felt it belonged: on Evan.

"So it's possible Evan left her restrained and alive while he went to the tasting." Mike looked at Jack. "You said yourself Evan's a selfish son of a bitch, that you called him on it, leaving her there helpless at his beck and call."

"Maybe this O'Dwyer guy goes by the cabin, finds her lying there helpless and naked, and can't help himself," Detective Scalamandre said.

"Corie told me Evan had a vasectomy," Jack said. "Whoever had sex with Vangie wore a condom." He hoped Serena wouldn't ask when exactly Corie told him about the vasectomy. At least not in front of the lieutenant.

"Did we get skin cells or DNA from the condom?" Scalamandre asked.

"We didn't recover the condom," Serena said.

"This Shaun O'Dwyer's got a sheet?" Dani asked.

Jack answered. "Laundry list of offenses but nothing violent. Car theft, possession, larceny."

"This a step up?" Dani asked.

Jack shrugged. "Shaun saw Evan take Vangie to the cabin Friday night. Then Evan stopped by Shaun's station to get the Mercedes Saturday afternoon on his way to Denver. Shaun knew she was gonna be there alone."

Detective Warren spoke. "You're suggesting Evan left a trail of breadcrumbs for Shaun to find Vangie, knowing he wouldn't be able to resist?"

"Evan also got him high," Jack said. "We all know what meth does to a guy's sex drive, and there was a sizable baggie of the shit in Shaun's possession."

"If this is all true, Evan's a pretty brilliant manipulator," Mike said.

"Manipulation's not a crime," Dani said.

"Providing drugs is," Jack said. "Conspiracy to commit murder is. Assault is."

Dani took off her glasses, sat back in her chair, and looked at Jack. "Evan's creating a lot of static. He plans to sue the department. His girlfriend was persecuted and we stood around picking our noses while the real killer ran free. Now she's dead. If we go after him we better have our ducks in a row. Your assumption is that the two murders are connected. Prove it. Find the link."

"The link is Evan. I'm sure of it. I just need some time."

Dani rubbed the bridge of her nose between her thumb and forefinger. "Jack, if we're going to successfully go after someone as high profile as Evan we need a lot more than your hunches."

At the mention of Evan's status Jack's pulse escalated. He couldn't keep the sarcastic edge out of his voice. "It's not a *hunch* that he pushed his wife down the stairs. Corie heard Evan threaten Brice. If Vangie died because of what she knew about Brice's murder, how do we know Evan's not going to try to go after Corie again?"

Dani wasn't impressed. "Stay away from Evan Markham until you have something real."

Jack gave up on being reasonable. "Right. Of course. Let the wife get killed while we bend over backward to preserve Evan's reputation."

Dani's smile was mean. "I'm concerned you're developing a blind spot here, Jack. You sure your old *friendship* with Corie isn't influencing you? Maybe you should recuse yourself."

An awkward silence descended. Jack could feel the other detectives' eyes on him. He wouldn't give in, although he felt himself deflate a little. The lieutenant was bluffing. She had to be. "I'm not making up the fact that Evan assaulted a woman with a knife."

"Dropped and useless." Dani bit off the words.

"Corie told me that Evan tried to use a knife on her during sex play, too. Now his girlfriend's cut up? That seem like a big coincidence to anyone else?"

"Jack, you have got to be the most stubborn detective I've ever worked with. And that's saying something." Dani put her glasses back on and picked up a piece of paper from her desk. She was obviously ready for this conversation to be over. "This is all speculation. Give me something real I can use against Evan and, trust me, I'll use it."

"You sure?" Jack asked.

"You got a death wish?" Mike asked Jack after they left Dani's office. "Or a new career lined up?"

"I'm beginning to wonder." Jack hesitated. "You think I have a blind spot?"

"I think it's about five-foot-seven with a really nice head of blond hair." There was a pause before Mike added, "I've been there. We all have."

"Why's it they have to turn everything into a soap opera? Serena, Tiffany, all the women. How about you? You think I'm doing my job?"

"Tiffany's not a reliable source. She has the hots for you herself."

"Nah. We're just friends. And you didn't answer my question."

"Buddy, as a detective you're one of the best. But when it comes to women you're pretty dumb."

That got a smile. "*You're* giving me advice about women?"

"Yeah. Pretty weird, huh?"

"I'm thinking I should go buy a lottery ticket, because winning the Powerball wouldn't be any stranger than taking romantic advice from you."

Mike lowered his voice. "Speak of the devil . . ."

Jack followed Mike's gaze. Tiffany was sitting in the visitor chair opposite his desk. She looked up at Jack when they walked in.

"How come you don't answer your phone?" Tiffany asked.

"I was busy committing career suicide. What've you got for me?"

"In this hand," she held up a paper, "the DNA from the second condom in Brice Shaughnessy's house. In the other, the comparison to the unknown from Charlotte." She brandished that in her right hand and smiled.

"Am I going to like any of this?" Jack asked.

"You tell me. Which one do you want first?"

"Left hand," Mike said.

Tiffany glanced at Mike for the first time. "That's not the interesting one."

"Tiff. Seriously," Jack said. "I've worked eight straight days. I'm not in the mood to play games."

She looked back at Jack. "DNA from the second condom is a match for Alex Cantrell. No surprise, huh?" She shrugged, wrinkled her nose, and set the report on Jack's desk.

"And the second?" Jack prompted, his teeth clenched.

"You have a match."

"Seriously?" Mike took a step forward but Tiffany snatched the paper away out of his reach.

"Hold on. At least let me have one tiny moment of drama. The unknown sample, taken from vomit at the scene of Monique Lawson's murder, is a match to Leonard Funderburk."

Mike gave an excited whistle and reached for the report. Tiffany looked pleased. Jack felt an overwhelming surge of frustration. "Fuck." With one sweeping motion he knocked a pile of manila folders off his desk.

Their surprised looks only pissed him off more.

"I'm not cleaning that up," Mike said.

CHAPTER FIFTY

"What did you want to talk about that you had to drag me to this place for breakfast?" Evan had made his escape from Jessie's before it was light and now sat in a coffee shop across from Deputy Christopher O'Dwyer. The restaurant in Fairplay was called the Bear Paw, but as far as Evan was concerned, it should have been called the Bear Scat based on the quality of their offerings.

Chris's eyes darted to his left, scanning the crowded dining room. "The county put me on leave. That's why I'm not in uniform. In case you were wondering."

Evan hadn't been. He leaned back with his arm extended along the top of the cracked vinyl booth. He drummed his fingers. "And?"

"These detectives came up from Denver." Chris lowered his voice. "They interviewed Shaun. Well, the man did. His partner went snooping around the motor pool, asking to see their records. What if they find out I didn't do the wellness check? I'm screwed."

"What did the detectives find out?"

The waitress came with Evan's coffee. She set a bowl of small plastic tubs containing something that wasn't half-and-half in the center of the table.

All Chris seemed to care about was his brother. "Shaun needs help."

"Yes, he certainly does." Evan pushed his coffee away.

"I mean he needs a lawyer. They found Shaun with all those drugs and his knife was used to kill her." Chris scrubbed his face with his hands. "I still can't believe it. He must have been high out of his mind. Shaun would never hurt anyone."

"It's my fault." Evan shrugged. "I shouldn't have mentioned that my friend was staying there by herself. Shaun knew I would be gone."

"I can't lose my job, Evan."

"Ah. It's not brotherly love after all. What a shock."

"I've—we've done a lot for you."

Evan started to slide out of the booth.

"Wait. That's it? You're not going to help?" Chris sounded like a whiny little boy.

"I thought you had information. Since you don't—"

"They know I helped you the other night."

Evan sat back again. "How do they know that?"

"That detective—Fariel—he figured it out. He listed the chronology of events like someone had given him a fucking program."

"Do you think I killed her?"

"No." Chris threw up his hands in a defeated gesture and then dropped them in his lap. "But I can't believe Shaun would do it either."

"Belief is tiresome, Chris. It takes much less energy to simply acknowledge reality."

"So I'm supposed to throw my brother under the bus?"

The waitress came for their order. Chris asked for something called a skillet, with various over-salted, chemically enhanced breakfast meats, cheese, eggs, and potatoes. Evan declined.

After she left Evan asked, "Why would I do it?" He was curious to hear what Chris would say.

"I didn't mean to offend you."

For the second time in as many days, Evan felt sad. He noted the feeling and filed it away. "I'm getting a divorce."

"Oh. That's too bad. I didn't know."

Evan took a deep breath through his nose and slowly let it out. Smelled grease, onions, and burnt coffee. "Why would you? Here's the thing: dead, Vangie became public knowledge. I didn't want Corie to find out ever, and certainly not like this."

Chris started to say "I can't believe" again and Evan held up a hand to stop him.

"We're at a stalemate. You can't see what Shaun is capable of. Although you have no trouble *believing*"—Evan emphasized the word sarcastically—"that I'm capable."

"My mom saw the blood when she went up to clean. She thought she was doing you a favor."

Evan's eyes widened and his mouth hung open, a pantomime of wounded pride. "Unbelievable. Does your whole family think I'm a killer?"

Chris couldn't meet Evan's eyes. He looked down and unrolled the napkin that was wrapped around his silverware. He scraped at something on the knife with his thumbnail. "I don't know what to bel—think."

"The detective seemed smart, didn't he? You think it took some kind of brilliance to figure things out the way he did? You've been around small-town losers too long. Those big city homicide detectives don't screw around. You'd best figure out how to be professional and offer him all of the cooperation that you can muster. Now if there's nothing else—"

"Corie was there."

"What the hell are you talking about?" Evan's stomach lurched. He thought about all of the blood and he tried to remember exactly how he left the cabin.

"She was there with my mom cleaning when the deputies showed up to serve the warrant."

"Cleaning? What the fuck?"

Chris shook his head helplessly. "I don't know why she was there. She told my mom she came to get some of her things."

With an effort, Evan kept his breathing even. "Tell me exactly when Corie got there and how much your mom had gotten done. And why, in God's name, she let my wife clean."

Chris licked his lips. "I don't know. Mom said Corie didn't seem to notice anything was wrong. So I guess she'd had enough time to get the place straightened up. Now it looks like she was cleaning up after her son. Is she going to be in trouble, too?"

"You're in a better position to know that than me. No wonder they placed you on leave. They don't want you too close to the investigation." Jack was smart taking Chris out of play. Emotions warred within Evan. A surge of adrenaline at having an intelligent adversary. Amusement that his plan appeared to be working. Insane worry about Corie. "What did they find when they searched?"

"Not much. Mom had started mopping the floor. They used luminol and found blood spatter that Mom had wiped off the walls. There was some tape residue on the bed and her—Vangie's—purse is missing. So they figure Shaun robbed her in addition to cutting her up."

"That's what you consider 'not much?' What did they do with Corie? Did the police detain her?"

"No. Detective Fariel talked to her for a few minutes and then let her go."

Evan remembered Jack's words at the wine tasting. Everything else Jack had done so far was smart; that was stupid. He had to get out of there. "Let me know what else you find out." He stood and threw a twenty down to pay for Chris's breakfast.

Chris looked up at him, panicked. "What should I do now?"

Evan thought for a disgusted second that Chris might cry. "Your job. As well as you're able. For as long as you have it."

Evan wished he could call Corie. He felt weak thinking about her almost finding that mess at the cabin. He didn't want her to know. More than anything, he didn't want her to know. Why in hell would Corie go up there? She hated the place. Was she running and telling everything to the detective? Was she fucking Jack? Evan hadn't believed it when he'd said it to her on the stairs; still didn't want to believe it. *Believe*. Christ. He was losing it.

Getting rid of Vangie was supposed to remove risk, not add it. He thought he'd found the leak. He'd found out who borrowed Vangie's gun. He'd dealt with everyone who was causing him trouble and everything was going his way. But suddenly, the carefully constructed barriers between the different parts of his life were coming down. And that couldn't happen.

CHAPTER FIFTY-ONE

Jack called Corie while he waited for the apprehension team to assemble to go with him to pick up Len. He heard traffic noise in the background and was instantly on alert.

"Where the hell are you?"

"I went out for coffee. Why? Am I a prisoner?"

"No. Of course not." His nerves were raw; he'd been overreacting to everything and everyone today. Sleep deprivation was part of it, but that wasn't a novelty and certainly no excuse. He couldn't expect her to stay holed up in his house indefinitely.

He softened his voice. "What are you up to today?"

"I'm going to continue getting my affairs in order. I asked for a password reset on our business bank account. Now that I've got my computer back, I'm going to look and see what's been going on in my life for the last couple of years." Her tone was ironic.

"I don't have to say it, right?"

"Jack, I have no idea where Evan is, and if I had my way, I'd never see him again." She was quiet for a moment and then added, "What about you?"

"I don't want to see Evan either."

"You know what I mean."

"I have two active homicides. I'll be lucky if I ever sleep again."

"What about your radiation? You only have a couple left."

"No way. No time."

"Jack."

"Corie."

"I'll make you a deal."

Inwardly, Jack groaned.

"I'll be very careful and give you hourly updates if you promise you'll go to your radiation this afternoon."

Serena walked up to his desk and looked at him expectantly. Jack stood and grabbed his jacket off the back of his chair, juggling the phone from one hand to the other as he put it on.

"Can't possibly."

"Well then, I can't possibly remember to call you," Corie said.

"You're comparing two things that can't be compared." Jack consciously filtered his conversation now that Serena was within earshot.

"Really?"

"Yes, really. I can't promise something like that." He and Serena reached his car.

"Neither can I."

Serena got in the car and Jack stood outside a moment longer. "Corie, you don't understand. I'm buried in work. Everyone needs something from me and it would be helpful if I could be in, like, twenty places at one time."

"You don't understand how tedious it is to have you for a babysitter."

"I'm trying to keep you alive, you stubborn, beautiful woman."

"Right back at you, minus the woman part."

This time Jack's groan was audible. "I don't have time for this. Serena's here with me and we're on our way to make a—to go check something out."

"Then stop wasting time arguing."

"Fine. But I expect to hear from you every hour on the hour."

Jessie opened the door and stared at the cruisers angled in at the curb and the officers swarming the front yard wearing bulletproof vests and armed with assault rifles. Her right hand flew to her chest and her green eyes widened.

"My word," she managed.

"I have a warrant for the arrest of Leonard Funderburk," Jack said.

"Jessie, we need you to step aside." Serena took Jessie by the arm and led her towards the kitchen.

Jessie didn't resist. She wore an oversized gray shirt over black leggings, flats, no discernible makeup, and her hair was a little more unkempt than usual. Jack had come to think of Jessie's colorful clothes as costumes, which made it hard for him to take her seriously, but today she was subdued.

"It won't do you any good," Jessie said. "But you're welcome to look around."

Jack looked at Jessie's face more closely and could tell she'd been crying. "What do you mean?"

"He's gone," Jessie said.

They searched anyway but found no sign that Len had ever been there. Jessie had collapsed onto a loveseat in front of the fireplace in the kitchen. Jack crouched down in front of her, and she looked so sad, he was tempted to take her hand.

"Is it okay if we ask you a couple of questions?" Jack asked.

He thought of Evan's fleet of lawyers and fully expected her to invoke, but Jessie's face, full of misery and absent of guile, turned up to Jack's and she nodded.

Serena sat down on the loveseat next to her and set a recorder on the low coffee table. "Can you tell us where he went?"

Jessie shook her head. She tucked a hank of hair behind her ear and sniffled.

"All right," Jack said. "You don't know where Len went, but can you tell us when he left, Jessie?"

"We had a fight." Jessie bit her lip. "He packed up while I was asleep sometime Saturday night or early Sunday. He took everything."

"What did you fight about?" Serena asked.

"It was Evan. He's so overprotective. He positively grilled Len and then Len accused me of taking Evan's side."

Jack and Serena exchanged a look. "Does Len have any friends or relatives in the area? Anyone he could stay with?" Jack asked.

"No. He might try to go back to North Carolina." Jessie took a shaky breath. "I know I should think 'good riddance to poor rubbish.' That's what Evan says, but I can't."

Jack's pulse quickened. "Evan knew Len was gone?"

"Yes." The word broke into two syllables. Jessie blinked furiously but couldn't seem to stop the tears. "Evan stayed here last night because I was afraid to be alone. He's so kind. I'm grateful I have such a good son, but I miss Len dreadfully."

Once they were outside again, Jack blew out a deep breath. "Let's notify the airports, train stations, bus stations—that is, if he hasn't already left town." Unspoken in the air between them was the awareness that Len had had a thirty-six hour head start.

"What did Evan grill Len about, do you think?" Serena asked.

There was a connection. Jack knew it. Sometimes it felt like it was right there in front of him, and then, like a quicksilver fish, it darted away again, out of conscious reach. "Evan could have found out Len murdered Monique and was protecting his mother. God knows, Evan's not going to come to us with whatever he has."

"Why is it everyone seems to have figured out who the murderer is except us?"

"We'll figure it out."

"You sound like Mike. You think Len's alive?"

Before Jack could answer, his phone rang. It was Aranda and he answered abruptly. "Tell Roger I'll need the files a little bit longer."

"Nice to hear your voice, too."

Aranda's silky alto made Jack laugh. "Sorry. I'm always happy to hear from you. What's up?"

"Actually, it is a work call. I wanted to tell you Roger is planning to have a conversation with Evan."

"A conversation? Or handing him the billionaire version of a pink slip?"

"I told you Evan's consulting work is almost complete on the golf resort in the foothills. Roger doesn't see any point in waiting. I thought I should warn you."

That was funny. She was calling to warn *him*. "Can you get Roger to hold off?"

"As a favor to you? What's going on?"

"And you might want to steer clear of Evan yourself in the meantime."

She let out a derisive snort. "Hmph. I'm not afraid of Evan. Wait how long? Roger will want answers."

"I can't give you a definite. We're working some leads. We're very close."

"Now you sound like you're giving a press conference."

"A couple of days. Tell him to wait until the end of the week."

"That's four days. You're cute but you can't count." Aranda huffed out a breath. "I'll see what I can do, but Roger's very determined once he makes up his mind."

CHAPTER FIFTY-TWO

The office complex was located in an industrial area of Commerce City not far from the Denver airport. The building was U-shaped, with parking all around the outer edge and some token landscaping near the office entrances. The inner side of the building featured loading docks and large, corrugated metal doors for receiving deliveries.

Corie chose the left side of the U to start her search. There were six office suites on that side and she struck out at the first four. As she walked to the fifth, Corie stretched and circled her head in a vain attempt to work some of the tension out of her shoulders.

As she told Jack, she'd gone online and studied transactions in and out of the business bank account. She was surprised Evan hadn't removed her from the account yet. Was that an oversight? Or did he still trust her? Once she logged on and started reviewing the account activity, she knew for certain that she couldn't trust him. There were deposits she knew nothing about from names she didn't recognize. Transfers to Perez and Associates. And payments to a property management company. It had taken a few phone calls but Corie learned Evan had been renting an office. She'd gotten the building address but not the suite number.

What she hadn't told Jack was that Evan's older tax records, from before everything was computerized, were missing. She felt a grim certainty that wasn't an accident, and when she saw the office complex, her sense of dread only deepened. Warehouses in the back with office space in the front. Why the hell did Evan need warehouse space? What else was he into?

In the fifth office, Corie encountered a receptionist sitting at a desk inside the front door. The sign on the wall behind her read "Gorham Properties" in nondescript gold lettering. The payee from the business bank account. The young woman behind the desk had limp, mousy blond hair and was wearing a thin, black cotton cardigan over a dull gray t-shirt and polyester slacks.

Corie caught a glimpse of CNN on the computer screen to her left before the receptionist hit the combination of keys to invoke the screen saver: a photo montage of a baby, a Labrador Retriever, and a smiling couple—the receptionist and a young, dark-haired man—on vacation someplace tropical.

The young woman seemed resentful of the intrusion. "Can I help you?"

Her voice implied she could not. Corie didn't imagine there were a lot of visitors and wondered why Evan bothered with the expense of a receptionist. "Yes, hi, I'm looking for Evan Markham's office. I think he rents a space here. Do I have the right office? Are you Laura? He said to ask for Laura." Corie was getting better and better at lying as the day wore on.

"I'm Mallard, the office manager. Are you sure you have the right suite?"

"Oh, sorry, I must have gotten the name wrong." Mallard? Like the duck? Corie had heard of people resembling their pets, but this took it to a whole new level.

Mallard looked at Corie suspiciously. "I haven't seen you before. His assistant usually comes with him."

"You must mean Vangie. Dark hair, a little overweight, about this tall?" Corie put her hand out at waist level and immediately felt guilty for being a smartass. The woman was dead.

"I'm Evan's wife. Hi. Corie Markham." She extended her hand, which Mallard shook limply. Evidently Evan had kept his marital status to himself. Hell, maybe he'd fucked the receptionist too, although she really didn't look like his type.

Corie spoke too brightly. "Evan told me you could let me into the office. I hope that's okay. There're some papers I need to get. Taxes, ugh. The CPA gave me a checklist as long as your arm: 1099s, P&Ls, 10Ks, alphabet soup."

"No one let me know you were coming." Mallard didn't move from behind her desk.

"He said you had a key and could let me in." Corie was bluffing, of course. She folded her arms across her chest and tried to look stern and impatient.

Mallard didn't seem the least bit intimidated.

"Would you like to see some ID?" Without waiting for an answer, Corie opened her wallet, pulled out her license, and held it up several inches from Mallard's face. "See? I can show you our wedding pictures if you're still not convinced."

Corie shoved the wallet back in her bag. Why was she being such a bitch? Duck Girl was only doing her job. A job she probably wanted to keep.

Mallard bit her lip. "I'll have to call him."

"Okay." Corie tried not to sound excessively sarcastic. "Do you have his number handy? Or would you like me to call him? When I do, I'll tell him what a fabulous job you're doing. I mean, jeez, what's in there? The crown jewels?"

With a heavy sigh, Mallard opened her center desk drawer and pulled out a big ring of keys. Corie followed meekly down the hall and forced herself to bite back an apology.

"Damned accountant's got me crazy. We filed some kind of extension, and now the deadline's looming and the IRS is breathing down our necks. It's got me a bit frantic. I'll make sure and get a copy of the key from Evan so I don't have to bother you again." *Stop talking.* Corie realized she'd make a terrible criminal.

Mallard hesitated in the doorway, as if she was going to stay and supervise.

"I won't be long." As gently as possible, Corie closed the door in Mallard's face.

What Corie didn't know was whether or not Mallard was going to run right back to her desk and call Evan. Corie needed Evan's old appointment Day-Timers and, as tempting as it was to snoop, she figured she'd better hurry.

Two old-fashioned, wooden filing cabinets stood along one wall. Next to them sat a set of bookcases with glass doors that folded up and out of the way, the kind lawyers used to use. There was a massive, carved oak desk, a high-backed leather office chair, an Oriental rug on the floor, and in the corner by the window, a pedestal on which sat a bronze sculpture of an eagle taking flight.

For some reason, the place felt familiar. Then it hit Corie that Evan had copied Roger's office. She let out a disgusted laugh. Did Evan have no taste of his own? What a poser.

The Day-Timer calendars used to come in distinctive gray binders with slipcases so they could be neatly arranged on a bookshelf. Corie strode to the glass-fronted lawyer shelves and found they weren't locked.

Not wanting to make Mallard more suspicious than necessary, Corie decided to only take two sets of calendars: the year of Monique's death and the year after. Her fingers shook as she opened the metal binder rings, pulled out the loose-leaf pages, and shoved them into her purse. She expected Evan to storm in at any second. He had a kind of sixth sense, like the way he surprised her Friday in their home office.

Corie replaced the binders neatly on the shelf and stared at them for a moment. She would tell Jack about the office so he could write a proper warrant. Hopefully the duck wouldn't make a call and Evan wouldn't have a chance to destroy everything first.

Mallard was at her desk leafing through a magazine and Corie thanked her on the way out the door. It took restraint not to run for her car.

CHAPTER FIFTY-THREE

Jack and Serena were in their car on their way back to the station when Mike called. "Got a tip from Crime Stoppers that Leonard Funderburk's holed up at a motel down on Arapahoe Road."

Jack took down the address and exchanged a glance with Serena.

"That's right near Centennial airport," she said.

Jack executed a U-turn on Broadway and turned on his lights. "No commercial flights out of there. It's general aviation, corporate jets, and charters."

Serena frowned. "Len charter himself a plane? Or did someone do that for him?"

"Evan."

"Jessie as much as said he ran Len out of town on a rail. Maybe she meant flew him out."

It was another fucking chess game. What move had Evan executed this time? "Wherever Len's headed you can bet Evan is sending him there."

The motel was a dreary, three-story brick building with a parking lot on the west side. Len had a room on the second floor. The room's drapes were closed and there was a plastic "Do Not Disturb" placard hanging from the metal doorknob. The manager told them that Len was due to checkout by eleven.

They tried calling the room and then Len's cell phone but got no answer. Jack had requested backup, and he gave instructions to the officers on how he wanted them to position themselves.

"Is his car here?" one officer asked.

"He doesn't seem to have one," Jack said. "Apparently he transported himself here magically. He told me he didn't live in any one place like us mere mortals. He's a citizen of the world."

"World's about to get a lot smaller," Serena said.

"Let's do this," Jack said.

The motel manager swiped a plastic room key in the lock and then leapt out of the way. Len hadn't fastened the interior security bolt and the door swung open. Inside, the small room was empty and the bed unmade. Wordlessly, Serena pointed out the suitcases near the door. They heard the shower running. Jack nodded at Serena and then moved in that direction.

His right hand flat against the bathroom door, Jack eased it open as the water in the shower stopped running. Metal rings jangled against the shower rod as Len pulled the flimsy plastic curtain aside and came face-to-face with Jack's .45.

"Oh shit!" Len shouted, and his feet scrabbled on the slick porcelain as he instinctively tried to run away from the gun. Somehow he managed to remain standing. He tried vainly to cover himself with the curtain but his hands shook too badly to be effective. Yellow rivulets snaked down his leg and then toward the tub drain.

"Good thing for you you're already in the shower," Jack said.

"Jessie Markham isn't going to be thrilled to learn she let a murderer into her home." Jack slapped a manila folder down on the table in front of Len Funderburk in the interview room.

"I'm not a murderer. She knows that." But there was no defiance in Len's voice. His handcuffed hands were in his lap and he slumped in the metal chair.

"Really? Because she didn't seem all that thrilled with you when I talked to her earlier."

Len sat up straighter. "What did she say? Is she all right?"

Jack would let Len worry about Jessie's feelings. "In addition to being a person of interest in Brice Shaughnessy's homicide, your DNA is a match for a sample taken from the scene of Monique Lawson's butchering."

Len's eyes followed Jack as the detective pulled out a chair and sat down. He never questioned how Jack had obtained his DNA.

"Let's talk about Brice for a minute. I'm assuming he found out you killed Monique?"

Len spoke in a small voice. "No, I didn't. And Brice was my friend."

"Tell me about that. When we first talked, you said you didn't know Brice."

"I didn't know him back then."

"You need to stop playing games. It doesn't look good."

Len reached up awkwardly and scratched his head. His hair was still damp from the shower at the motel. "I came to Colorado with Brice but I didn't get to know him until recently. And I never hurt Monique. I couldn't. You have to believe me."

"What will help me do that is for you to tell me everything about your relationship with Brice, how you came to Colorado with him, how you met Jessie." Jack felt a strange calm settle in his belly. Not an unfamiliar feeling. He had to parse Len's lies and that was something he knew how to do.

Everything about Len's posture indicated defeat, from the way he slouched in the chair to the way he wouldn't make eye contact. He spoke to the table. "Years after—after that happened—I finally stopped drinking. That's when I connected with Brice. Would I have befriended Brice if I killed his sister?"

"Stranger things have happened."

Reluctantly, Len looked up and the story slowly came out. "Like I told you the first time we talked, I met Jessie in North Carolina. I was teaching a writing workshop she attended. It's a great way to pick up women. Mostly women go to those things and they look at you as some kind of guru.

"Last fall Brice came to one of my writing workshops, too. He thought it would be healthy to write about his memories and I agreed. That's how he met Jessie. They hit it off right away. Brice was young and handsome and artistic. Jessie seemed drawn to him because of the tragedy. She encouraged him to talk about Monique."

Len suddenly snapped out of his memories and terror was plain on his face. "You're not going to tell Evan about any of this, are you?"

"No. This stays between us." *Trust me, you piece of shit. And then I'll hang you.*

"Jessie likes to get high. Creative people, you know? But she doesn't want Evan to find out."

"I hear Brice liked that, too."

"Yeah, he did." Len hesitated, and then under Jack's benign, friendly guidance, warmed to his story and picked up steam.

"Jessie's older but she's cool. And she's still hot. One night during the workshop, the three of us sat up late talking and Jessie said, 'You know my son was living in Charlotte at that time.' I thought that was weird. She asked a lot of questions about Monique's murder. A lot. She seemed really bent about it. We were in the mountains and we had a fire going. She took Brice in her arms and held him like a baby, and both of them cried together. Of course, we were all pretty stoned. Then she said that Brice had to figure it out. That he'd never have any peace if he didn't. She said, 'I have money, I'll help you. Come to Colorado.'"

"It was Jessie's idea?"

"Yeah, the whole thing. She knew Evan's wife was taking these psychology classes. She thought it would be a good idea for

Brice to do that, too. She's all into facing your truth and figuring yourself out. She introduced Corie to Brice. It was really a big deal to her that we all be friends."

Jessie introduced Corie to Brice? *What the fuck?* Was Corie still lying to him? Or was Len? "Corie Markham told me she met Brice in the class."

"Well yeah, that's true, but Jessie engineered the whole thing. She made sure they met each other."

"Corie also never mentioned that Brice was friends with Jessie."

"Really? That's weird." Len shrugged. "Maybe she's afraid of Evan, too. God knows I am."

"So you do know who killed Brice?" Outwardly Jack was still calm, his voice soothing.

Len shook his head rapidly. "No, no, no. Neither of us had any idea. Jessie and I were so scared. I'm worried sick about her. I agreed to leave when Evan asked me to because I thought that would help Jessie. Oh man. What a mess."

"I don't like Evan much either." Another smile. "It would really help if you could remember exactly what Evan said to you."

"He told me he didn't want me around his mother anymore. That I was a bad influence. That she's very fragile and couldn't be dragged into something like this, and that my being questioned by the police was the final straw. He also asked me if I killed Brice, then he asked me about Monique."

"He knew about Monique?"

Len stared at Jack with wide, frightened eyes. "All about it. He asked me where I lived back then and I lied. He accused me of knowing more than I did. When he told me that he'd help me if I cooperated and left his mother alone, I agreed. Tell Jessie I'm sorry."

"How was Evan going to get you out of town?"

"He told me a friend of his had a plane and could fly me, but it would take a day or two to set up. He said it wouldn't be good for me to try and leave on my own. That you'd, you know, be watching cars and the regular airport and stuff. He told me it would upset Jessie too much if I got caught, and that he couldn't abide—that was his word—he couldn't abide his mother being upset any more than she already was."

"That sounds like Evan." Jack paused for effect and relished the spark of hope that leapt into Len's eyes when he said the next thing. "I'm inclined to believe you. But there's a detective headed out here from North Carolina who may not be so open-minded."

"I remember the detectives."

"They didn't like you very much, did they?"

Len gave a quick, sharp shake of his head. "No. They made me feel guilty, even when I wasn't."

"See, that's too bad. You don't get the truth that way." Jack leaned forward, arms on his knees, and rolled his chair closer. "While that plane's in the air, the one with the North Carolina detective in it, that's your window of opportunity to tell me exactly what happened the night Monique Lawson was killed. To help me understand."

Len nodded. "Anything."

"Here's the problem, Len." Jack pushed a piece of paper on the table closer so Len could read it. "That's a DNA report. I'm showing you this because it's one of the main reasons you were arrested. Your DNA is a match, a conclusive match, for what was found at the scene near Monique's body."

"Oh crap." Len looked away and wiped at his eyes.

"That plane's on its way here."

"I was there."

Jack wasn't sure he heard him right. "Excuse me?"

"I was there." Len's voice faded to a whisper and Jack had to strain to hear him. "I went over to her house. I found her like that."

"Why didn't you ever tell anyone?" Jack asked.

"I wasn't supposed to be driving. I didn't have a license—it was suspended. That's why I didn't tell the police. I didn't want to go to jail."

"You'd been drinking. And then she rejected you. You got angry, I can see that."

"No. I just wanted to see her. I sat outside her house staring at her windows, longing for a glimpse. Not like a stalker, but, oh hell I guess I was. I was in love with her. I used to go over and sit outside her house in my car. God, I was pathetic. That night, I sat there for a while and I didn't see any movement behind the drapes. I got worried and decided to see if she was okay."

For a minute Len couldn't continue. He buried his face in his hands again and Jack saw his shoulders heave. When he looked back at Jack his eyes were red.

"I was going to tell her that her granddad asked me to check on her. I don't know. But she didn't answer the door. I called for her and I tried the handle. The door was unlocked which was weird. I walked inside and she was there in the kitchen. I saw all the blood."

"Why didn't you call for help?" Jack asked.

"I told you. Because I didn't have a license and I'd been drinking. Her grandfather had already warned me that if I screwed up one more time, I was history. The phone was off the hook and I thought maybe she'd already called the cops, so I hightailed it out of there.

"But Monique . . . Jesus. Did you see what they did to her? I lost it. I puked." Tears streaked down Len's tanned face. "I got sick and I tried to clean it up. But I'm a different person now. You have to believe me."

Jack kept the excitement out of his voice. "You got sick and you took the time to try and clean it up, even with her lying there like that. You can see how that doesn't look good."

"She was already dead."

"Did you touch her? Did you check her pulse?"

Len shook his head.

"You tried to clean up your mess but you didn't do anything for her, a woman you say you loved?"

"Now do you understand why I said the other day I feel as if I need to atone?"

"Did you see anyone when you were watching the house?" Jack asked.

"No. I only saw one car and it was when I was driving away. I thought for sure they were going to bust me. I kept waiting for the call. But it never came. No one, not even Brice, ever found out I was there. Until now." Len sniffled and wiped at his eyes again. "I really did love her."

"Would you be willing to take a lie detector test?"

The look on Len's face was pathetically eager.

CHAPTER FIFTY-FOUR

At the hospital, Jack undressed and got into position on the metal table. He'd left his cell phone on the bench in the dressing room and he heard it buzzing. Dom had gotten him all arranged, including the clamshell thing clamped onto his groin, but Jack rolled onto his side to get up. He'd left messages for Jessie and the Charlotte detectives. "I have to get that."

"You know the drill." Dom's voice was firm. "We're all ready to go. You'll be done in five minutes and then you can get back to saving humanity."

With a disgusted sigh, Jack lay back again, the table ice cold against bare skin. Corie had kept her half of the bargain so here he was, against his better judgment, keeping his.

He stared at the white tiles on the ceiling, as he had a dozen times before, and counted the perforations in a square. He wondered if they were asbestos. He wondered if this was what an autopsy table felt like. He wondered a million irrelevant things, and then he closed his eyes and listened to the machines whir. As the unseen radiation hit its mark, Jack imagined he could see the cell destruction, healthy cells dying, his body revolting. How long before the nausea hit this time? How could this possibly be good for him?

As soon as Dom walked back into the room and released him, Jack jumped up and grabbed his phone. Aranda. He wondered if she'd heard from Evan and what Roger had decided to do. When Jack called her back it went to voice mail.

Outside, snow was falling and exhaustion hit Jack with such sudden weight his shoulders sagged. He walked slowly to his car while, in his mind, all of the players in the case arranged themselves like pieces on a chess board. Brice dead. Vangie dead. Len and Shaun in custody. Evan was somewhere. Corie was safe, at least for now.

He made her his excuse for going home first instead of directly back to the station. Traffic inched along, and a drive that ordinarily took fifteen minutes consumed almost forty. He called Jessie again and this time she answered on the second ring. She asked about Len.

"He's fine. He said to tell you he was sorry to cause you concern."

"Oh."

Jack could picture her wide green eyes and her hand pressed to her chest. "I was wondering if there was any way we could talk further."

Again, she surprised him. "Yes, of course. Anything I can do to help. When?"

He calculated additional time for the snow and the stop at home. "I can be there in an hour and a half, if that's not too late."

"No, of course not. Is Len . . . is he spending the night in jail?"

"I'm afraid so, Jessie." Jack debated and then decided against asking if she'd heard from Evan. She was still his mother after all, and would likely want to help her son. No need to make her any more suspicious than she already was.

When Jack got home, Corie's car wasn't there and all the lights were off. *Fuck.* But Jack didn't have time to process his reaction. He barely opened his back door before he had to run for the bathroom. *What the hell?* This was faster than usual. A wave of misery hit him after the nausea. Was this normal? Were they doing it right?

Goddamn Corie. Why had he listened to her? After several lurching trips to the bathroom, and sickness that felt like he was being scraped raw from the inside out, he collapsed onto the couch feeling thoroughly sorry for himself. His mind whirled, replaying the interview. Was Len telling the truth? Why had Jessie tried to help Brice, and why was she so willing to talk to Jack? On the coffee table, Jack's cell phone shuddered and he stared at it dumbly. He had too much to do to be sick. He had to find Corie. He had to get up, answer his goddamn phone, get to Jessie's. He ordered himself to toughen up but his body didn't listen. Jack had never been this sick before. Was it because he skipped an appointment? One second he felt leaden and exhausted, the next moment sickness was shooting up his throat like a geyser and he barely made it to the bathroom. It had to stop soon. Had to.

Didn't it?

CHAPTER FIFTY-FIVE

Aranda immediately regretted leaving her coat in the car and hugged her short cashmere sweater tighter around her. Her legs were bare and her heels were high, and she was freezing. Her skirt hiked up when she climbed down from Roger's Lincoln Navigator, and she tugged at it as she picked her way across the dirt parking lot toward the trailer that housed the temporary construction office. Another D'Ambrose resort under development in the foothills west of Denver with thirty-six PGA-worthy holes. The forecast called for snow, a lot of it, and Aranda's thin sweater was no shield against the stiff mountain wind.

Workers were already calling it a day, heading into the office to clock out. Aranda checked the time on her phone and scowled; not even four thirty. The project was behind schedule—thanks in no small part to Evan Markham—and there was a sense of urgency to get as much construction done as possible before winter. Was Evan dragging out the project on purpose? Did he know what Roger had in mind?

She tugged at her skirt again and did her best to ignore the stares from the construction workers. One of them held the trailer door for her, a young, skinny guy with a long, greasy ponytail wearing shorts and work boots. Inside the trailer, Jeff, the construction manager, had his coat on.

"Aranda, what are you doing here?"

"You knew I was coming up this afternoon. We talked about it yesterday."

"I thought you'd cancel. There's a front moving in. I had the guys wrap things up early. The high winds are a hazard. Evan says—"

"Yes. I know what Evan says." She looked around at the empty desks. "It's good that you're safety conscious. There's no wind in here, though, so we can still have our meeting."

"Can't. I have to pick up my daughter from band practice. They're ending early because of the weather."

"I guess if you have to pick up your daughter . . ."

"I'm sorry you wasted a trip but you should have called."

She didn't like the man's attitude, acting as if she worked for him. Everyone, it seemed, aside from her, was panicked about a little snow. She sat down at a computer and moved the mouse in abrupt, angry circles to wake up the monitor.

Jeff stood there uncertainly. "I can stay for a few minutes."

Aranda looked at him and saw his eyes were on the computer screen. He seemed reluctant to leave her alone. "No offense, Jeff, but accounting is drudgery and I'd like to get it over with as quickly as possible. If I have any questions I'll call you tomorrow."

"You sure?"

"Go get your daughter. I'll copy the files I need and then head out myself. I know how to lock up."

She tried to say it without rancor but Jeff let the flimsy trailer door slam shut behind him. There was a space heater under the desk and she turned it on high, then pulled a memory stick out of her purse and plugged it into a USB slot on the computer. His behavior made her curious; what didn't Jeff want her to see?

It was always good to know what was going on behind Roger's back. Roger said he could read people, that he hadn't gotten where he was without being a pretty good judge of human nature. Except for Evan Markham. Roger had really screwed up there.

In a desk drawer Aranda found a half-empty bottle of Jack Daniels. She wrinkled her nose. Jack Daniels was disgusting. She decided she'd take the bottle with her and smiled imagining Jeff's reaction when he found it missing. Apparently the diligent Evan didn't have any problem with drinking on the job. She couldn't wait to tell Roger. Or maybe she wouldn't. At least not right away.

Aranda lost track of time while she snooped and jumped when the door to the trailer burst open.

"Windy out there." Evan stood in the doorway and looked around. His eyes stopped on the bottle of whiskey. "I didn't take you for a Jack drinker."

She hadn't heard his car over the wind. Well, she wouldn't let him see she was startled. Very purposefully Aranda turned back to the computer. "What do you want, Evan? Making sure your little plan worked?"

"I don't know what you mean."

"Ha. Look out there. The site was shut down before five."

"High wind is a known cause of industrial accidents," Evan said. "Why, the cranes alone are deathtraps. Not to mention flying debris and poor visibility from dust."

"Oh, spare me." Aranda's tone was acid but Evan's placid demeanor didn't waver. He didn't take his coat or his gloves off and she hoped that meant he didn't plan on staying. In spite of her brave talk her heart was pounding.

"You don't have a very high opinion of me, do you Aranda?"

"I don't think anything about you one way or the other." She pulled the memory stick out of the computer, which gave a warning beep and displayed a message indicating she hadn't ejected it properly.

"No? You seem to have quite a lot to say about me to Roger."

Roger would never have betrayed her confidence. Evan was guessing. She turned and looked at him, her gaze cool. "Don't flatter yourself. We don't talk about you."

"No? I hear you were very cooperative with the detective, too."

"I don't have time for this." She shoved the memory stick in her purse and hated herself for the fact that her hand was shaking. She picked up her phone. Jack Fariel was in her recent call list. Easy to hit the entry and dial. And what exactly would she say? Evan was stressing her out at work?

"Has quite the way with women, doesn't he?"

"Who?" She stood. She didn't dial but she kept the phone ready in her hand.

"Go ahead. Call Jack. I'll wait."

"I wasn't." She took a hesitant step toward the door but Evan blocked her path. "I'm going to go now and I need to lock up."

Evan's voice grew soft, almost sensuous. "I won't keep you. I wanted to leave something for Roger. A present."

She frowned at him, confused. "Why would you bring something here? Roger never comes up here."

"I think he'll come for this."

Aranda's fingers curled around the phone. Her thumb tapped Jack's name. "What is it?"

"You."

His voice was so soft and low she didn't think she heard him right. She gave a little shake of her head and her heart hammered even harder. Before she could think or react Evan closed the distance between them. His fingers closed around her wrist like a vice and the phone skittered across the floor. She yelped in surprise and pain.

With an open hand, he hit her full in the face so hard that she fell to the floor, striking her head on the edge of a desk as she went down. The force of the blow was shocking. She pushed herself up on her hands and saw him leisurely pick her phone up off the floor. He looked at the display and slipped the phone into his pocket.

Aranda scrambled to her feet and ran for the door, shouting for help. Evan was right behind her. His hands closed around her upper arms. She struggled, but he easily lifted her off her feet and her legs bicycled in the air. She tried to kick him.

"How delightful. You're going to fight." He threw her against the door like a rag doll and Aranda crumpled to the floor. She sat there stupidly, momentarily stunned, and Evan's eyes traveled greedily up and down her body.

"That is a beautiful outfit," Evan said in that silky voice that made her skin crawl. "I admire the fact that you dress up, even to visit a construction site. Those breasts and those long legs probably get you further with the men than anything."

"You're disgusting." She propped herself up on her hands, although her movements were hesitant. "Don't come near me or I'll scream."

"Why do you always warn me that you're going to scream? Why don't you do it?"

"What?" That didn't make any sense.

"I tell you what. I'll give you a head start. I'll count to three. One, two—"

She scrambled to her feet and managed to open the door of the trailer. But the stairs were made out of a metal grating and one of her narrow heels slipped through. She fell awkwardly and helplessly onto the rough metal surface, letting out a cry of frustration and terror.

Evan watched her try to yank her foot free. "Those shoes are very sexy, but apparently they're a safety hazard at a construction site."

"Roger will destroy you."

"I doubt that." Evan yanked her arms behind her back and she felt the terrifying pinch of handcuffs. "I think you should keep the shoes on. They're lovely, if treacherous."

He pressed her face-down into the metal stairs. Tears streaked her cheeks and her knees were bloody. Still, she screamed and tried to kick him with her free leg.

"Really, Aranda, this is becoming quite tedious." He held her down with one hand and reached under her dress with the other. He felt the thong underneath and pulled it aside.

"Leave me alone. Roger will find out. He's on his way here now." Aranda practically choked on her fear.

"Is he? Even though you said he never comes up here. But it would be delightful for him to find you. You're the present, Aranda, in case you haven't already figured that out. You're so smart." Evan cupped her pubic bone with his right hand.

"Roger betrayed me, Aranda. That was wrong. He coveted my wife. Coveting another man's wife is a sin."

"You killed that man, didn't you?"

"I'm disappointed that you have such a low opinion of me." He yanked her roughly to her feet.

"Let me go!"

"Of course, my dear." Evan threw her down the stairs. Her right foot was still stuck and her hands were locked behind her. She couldn't defend against the fall. Aranda splayed face-first and full force onto the metal stairs. Her ankle twisted, sending a sharp burst of agony up her leg. For a minute she didn't move. Aranda had never been beaten. No man had ever laid a hand on her. This couldn't be happening.

Evan watched her. "Why do you always have to make things so hard?"

"Make what hard? What are you doing? They'll catch you. You won't get away with it." Aranda told herself to stay angry, not to be weak, not to cry.

"Detective Jack can't help you now. I always do exactly what I want. Always have and always will. And the police will never be able to stop me."

"What do you mean?" A million thoughts raced through Aranda's mind, things she'd heard about rape, about how to survive. Maybe if she could keep him talking. But what do you say to a madman?

"I'd hoped to use your mouth, but you're screaming so much I'm going to have to gag you."

"No. I'll do what you want. I–I'm good at blow jobs. Let me show you."

Evan stared at her for a few seconds and then he shook his head, amused. "Oh, Aranda."

"No one has to know." Her voice sounded hoarse. She had to try. "I'll do anything. I like it rough."

She fought the gag. Just like she fought being arranged spread-eagled on her back on the cold, rough stairs. She begged. She bargained. She made the most obscene offers she could think of.

Evan finally had enough. He grabbed a handful of her hair and banged her head against the edge of a step. The gag went in and Aranda nearly blacked out from panic. What happened if you hyperventilated while you were gagged? Would you die?

"You'll wear yourself out." Evan spoke gently now, softly. "It's going to be fun. You'll see. You may not believe me now, but you'll see."

He undressed and she saw his erection. Aranda tried to fight but she could barely move, scarcely breathe. The metal stairs were so cold. Perforations on the steps formed small stars with sharp edges. She flinched and strained and rubbed her skin raw.

"Doesn't that hurt?" Evan's voice was thick. He dragged a fingertip through the shiny streak on her cheek. And then he took her roughly, quickly, without preamble.

It happened so fast Aranda barely had time to process the pain. When he was finished he carried his clothes to his car. Aranda thought, *that was it?* Maybe it was just rape. Maybe he was done. Maybe—but then she saw he was getting something out of his car. He came right back to her, and when she saw what he had in his hand, she wished she was already dead.

CHAPTER FIFTY-SIX

Corie couldn't tell if Jack was home. Murphy was on a leash so he wouldn't go chasing anything, like the two baby squirrels who spiraled up the trunk of an elm tree in Jack's front yard.

It still didn't feel right letting herself in. She rang the bell but he didn't answer so she used her key. He was coming out of the bathroom and she started to blurt out her story, but the words died on her lips. He was dressed in a t-shirt and sweats and the dark circles under his eyes looked like bruises. His skin was waxy and he was sweating.

"Jack, what's wrong? Is it the radiation?"

"I'll be okay. Give me a minute." Jack didn't sit so much as fall onto the couch. He reached for his phone on the end table and looked at it with bloodshot eyes. "Crap."

"Two of them are from me. You can ignore those." She sat down next to him. "What do you need? Can I get you something?"

"I have to get up."

"Are you sure?"

"Yeah. Too much going on." Jack struggled to his feet, almost immediately veered right, and disappeared back into the bathroom muttering, "Goddamn it."

To distract herself from the sound of puking, Corie went into the kitchen, found a bowl, and gave Murphy some water. She left the water in the sink running until Jack, looking even grayer, came out of the bathroom again.

"I need to head back to work." He swayed in the kitchen doorway.

"That sounds like a swell idea." She took him by the arm and helped him back to the couch, then picked up the TV remote from the floor where he'd dropped it. She wanted to cry. He couldn't be sick. Not now. Not when she had so much to tell him. She thought of Evan's secret office, and the binders, and the tax records she'd found. Jack needed to know.

But not five minutes passed before he was lurching toward the bathroom again. When he came back she noticed his hair was plastered to his forehead. She got a damp washcloth and started wiping his face and neck.

"That feels nice, Mom." Jack tipped his head back so it rested against the couch.

Corie swallowed her feelings of desperation. Damn it. She needed Jack. "Don't they give you something for the nausea?"

"The drugs make me sleepy. I can't work."

"As opposed to projectile vomiting, which is conducive to accomplishment."

"Don't be mean to me."

"Where are your pills?"

"Never filled the prescription." He sounded reluctant to admit that.

"That's really smart. Do you still have it?"

"What're you gonna do?"

"What do you think I'm going to do? Go to the pharmacy. You're no good to anyone this way. You'd be more effective asleep. Or at least less offensive."

He fell over onto his side with a moan. "You're a real humanitarian, Corie."

CHAPTER FIFTY-SEVEN

Evan reminisced as he worked. Each time it was as if he was making love to all of them. It wasn't weakness that brought him here. This was his calling.

"This one is similar to a scalpel." There was a glint of silver in the fading light. "Very sharp. It will cut through your skin like butter." He touched the top of her breast, above the dress, and was gratified when she flinched and shied away. "Do you want to feel it now?" She shook her head desperately back and forth.

"I agree." Evan smiled at her. "No need to hurry."

He held the tools up one by one. There were a lot of them: curved blades, angled blades, a straight blade like a razor. Each one served a specific purpose. Over the years Evan had learned a lot, and he took his time patiently explaining everything so that she understood. Evan never minded the moment when a woman's face changed, the moment when she realized who he was and what he was about to do. In fact he relished it. That was the only time Evan ever felt seen, the only time he could be himself.

As he talked she fought with renewed vigor, and he worried that she was going to make herself sick. He had to watch out for that. With the gag in place she could die from choking on her own vomit. That would be terrible.

The temperature plunged as the sun disappeared and snow began to fall, but Evan was oblivious. For him this was the delicious part. He loved the moment of anticipation, when he knew it was going to happen but hadn't started yet. He smiled at her, like a little boy anticipating a thrill, and pressed his hands together in front of him. "Now we're going to play."

He began by cutting her clothes off, working in sections, taking his time. As he did so, the blades scored lightly into the gooseflesh underneath. Evan felt a bit sad as he cut through the cashmere sweater. It was so soft and it fit her so well. He checked the label as he tossed it aside and suppressed a sigh; Evan appreciated couture.

Once she was naked he stood back and looked at her. Where would he begin this work of art?

Gagged so she couldn't scream, he knew from her reactions that she felt everything all the same. She made sounds in her throat; sexy sounds that encouraged him. Steam rose from her wounds in the cold night air. She was warm inside, even warmer than the first time he took her. They needed to be opened up. They needed him to set them free.

He had been right about her. She made him work for it, she made him concentrate. He would revel in the memory. He loved her long, slim legs and the way they flexed and straightened. He loved her long, dark hair and her smooth skin, luminous in the fading light. It all came to him like inspiration, like music—the order in which to cut, the tools to use, the placement and timing of the wounds. He played a symphony with sharp metal and movement. The cutting was slow and purposeful, and the blood was luscious—all the more striking against the powdery, white snow. He loved the second orgasm, the glimpse of eternity that came so slowly, gradually gathered momentum, and left him shuddering and helpless in the vast silence of the night. Most of all, in that moment, he loved her.

As soon as he could Evan stood. The body that had been D'Ambrose's assistant lay a lifeless shell; her blood dripped through the open metal and soaked the ground below. Her head was turned to the right with her sightless eyes open. Snowflakes fell gently and caught on her still eyelashes. *So lovely now.* He'd already forgotten her name. It was of no use anymore and Evan never remembered useless information.

He took a deep breath and then slowly exhaled. He watched his breath fog. There was nothing like the calm—the peace—he felt after finishing. If only the feeling lasted longer. The animal that lived inside of him was sated for the moment. He inhaled more draughts of the cold air. Evan felt intense relief. No shame; not anymore, not for a long time.

He looked around. It was snowing heavily and more than an inch had already accumulated; the wind blew it in icy sheets across the still form on the stairs. Sulfur lights mounted on the exterior of the trailer gave everything a pinkish cast. He gazed for a moment into the trees at the edge of the clearing around the trailer, his breathing deep and even. It was a shame he had a long drive ahead of him because all he wanted to do was sleep; he always slept soundly after he played. Evan forced himself to move.

He walked to a spigot with a hose connected, lifted the lever, and turned it on. He held the nozzle above his head, cleansing and refreshing himself with the icy water. It occurred to him that most people would find it unpleasant and he wondered, as he often did, why people were so weak. They were cold, they were hungry, they were tired. People always sought comfort.

When he was finished washing he looked around, surveyed the scene, and put himself for a moment inside the mind of a criminal investigator. How would he sign this landscape? Each killing was a work of art and, like a painter, Evan signed each canvas. If only the police were smart enough to read it. So far they hadn't been.

Evan left the hose running and draped it over the railing at the top of the stairs so the frigid water ran down over the body. *Lovely*. He'd never used running water before. Why hadn't he thought of it? The water would run without freezing obliterating footprints, tire marks, diluting blood, degrading DNA; it would wash her clean.

He retrieved a large piece of cashmere from where it had snagged against the bottom step and held the soft remnant to his cheek. A souvenir. *Perfect*. He considered what to do with her cell phone and smiled when he had the answer. He propped the phone on one of her lifeless hands and used her finger to dial Jack one last time.

CHAPTER FIFTY-EIGHT

Corie came back from Safeway and it didn't look like Jack had moved, although there was now a beer bottle on the table next to the couch. Murphy had climbed up and was stretched out near Jack's feet.

"Aww," Corie said.

"I'm too sick to even care that I'm sharing the couch with a dog," Jack said.

"I'll put your wallet back on your dresser."

"I know how much money was in there."

She picked up the beer bottle. "Are you sure you should be drinking?"

"Beer settles my stomach."

"I bet that works real well. Here. Try and keep this down." She handed him a pill and swapped the beer for a glass of water.

"Didn't you have trouble filling that?"

"Nah. I said I was getting it for my husband." He stared at her blankly. "Wow, you really *are* sick."

Jack sat up long enough to take the pill, then fell back over onto his side. "I don't ever take these."

Apparently he hadn't listened to his messages. Corie watched him and chewed the inside of her lip, debating. God, she wanted to tell him; she was desperate to tell him. But Jack was in no shape to do anything and he would want to. Corie swallowed hard. What difference would a few more hours make?

Murphy, on the other end of the couch, shifted position and curled up into a ball. The sight made her impossibly sad. "That really is too cute." Neither one answered her.

Corie walked into the kitchen and stared out into the backyard. The snow fell and fell; the roads were slick and treacherous driving back from the store. Ordinarily she loved snow. But now it made her think of simpler times, innocent times, and the bright contrast of who she used to be with the darkness now was unbearable. Where was Evan? Corie exhaled, a deep shuddering breath. He wouldn't dare look for her here.

Tomorrow. Jack will fix it tomorrow.

She checked on her patient and then, back in the kitchen, found his wine supply. Sometime into the second bottle, Chardonnay both lubricating her descent into despair and unleashing a thorough bout of self-pity, cutting her hair seemed like the thing to do. Penance. Who was it that cut his hair off and lost all of his strength? Hercules? No, that wasn't right.

In the bathroom Corie looked at herself in the mirror, picked up thick section of hair, and ran her fingers through it. She thought of all the biblical, symbolic uses for hair: washing Jesus's feet, escape from the tower, drying tears. She pulled a long piece across her own cheek, touching her own tears. *Yes.*

She rummaged through Jack's kitchen looking for scissors. Should she be going through his things? *Fuck it.* Evan's voice from the night she asked for the divorce, the night Brice died, floated back to her: 'Things could have been so good.' Yeah. Right. Whatever. Was that just a few days ago? Corie topped off her glass, sloshing some wine on the counter. *Whoopsie.*

At some point she noticed Jack was no longer on the couch. She checked on him and found him sound asleep in bed, Murphy stretched out next to him. The dog looked up at her standing in the bedroom doorway. "Traitor," she whispered. Jack didn't stir.

Cutting her hair wasn't easy. Not that she cared what it was going to look like. The point—the whole point—was to do penance. But she had a lot of hair. And she was drunk. Her friend Anne told her once that you could gather your hair up as if to put it in a ponytail, cut straight across, and it would come out layered. Corie tried that, sawing with Jack's scissors, which were bad. "This is going to take forever," she told her reflection and then peeked into the bedroom again. "Great. Jack'll find me talking to myself and be convinced I'm a lunatic." But both he and the dog were sound asleep. The very pictures of contentment. Which made Corie cry harder.

Soon there was hair everywhere—in the sink, on the counter, on the floor. The scissors made a kind of grinding sound as she cut. *Squeak, squeak, squeak.* Was she making too much noise? Would he hear? But every time she checked he was in the same spot under the covers. He even started to snore.

Corie drank more wine and considered. *Christ, I've got a lot of hair.*

Her glory, her mother used to tell her: 'Other girls wish for hair like this.' Vi believed in that old hundred strokes thing. When she was young Corie used to dread their bedtime hair brushing ritual.

And then there was Evan. Corie felt a chill remembering his hands in her hair, the way he would lift it off of her neck, wrap it around his hand, or pull out a few strands and tug. And not a chill in a good way but one like you'd stepped onto an elevator only to find it wasn't really there and you were in free fall.

Her fucking hair hadn't done her any good. *Stupid hair. Annoying hair. Troublesome hair.*

"Goodbye, Vi," she said, as another big hank fell to the floor.

"Goodbye, Evan, you prick." Squeak went the scissors.

"Goodbye, Jack." *Where did that come from?*

She started weeping in earnest. Her life was never going to be any fucking good and no amount of Chardonnay was going to help. She picked up the glass anyway, drank, and set it back down precariously on the top of the toilet tank. Okay, maybe the wine helped a little. She scrubbed at her face with her hands and then stood in front of the sink and finished, cutting by feel until there was nothing left that was long enough to grab onto.

"Take that, Evan. See if you still like me now. See if I'm still your beautiful Corie." Being beautiful had done her no fucking good either. It had only hurt.

She sat on the toilet and drained her glass. Then she rummaged through Jack's kitchen again for a sponge and a trash bag, and forced herself to clean it all up. For some reason, when she was done cleaning the bathroom, the crying stopped on its own.

Feeling strangely calm, she let herself out through the security door, into the alley. Lifting a lid on a Dumpster, she tossed in the bag filled with her glory. The thought made her laugh. It was dark and quiet, not many people out and about because of the snow, lights off in the surrounding houses, sounds muted. A streetlight made a fizzy sound and flickered. She ran her fingers through what was left of her hair and savored the strangeness of it. She felt better. She had no idea why, but she did. Corie looked up at the stars and snow landed on her face; the cold felt good.

Back inside the house, she walked to the bathroom and looked in the mirror. A stranger's face stared back at her. *It was Samson.*

CHAPTER FIFTY-NINE

Panting woke him, warm breath on his face. Jack opened his eyes, blinked, closed them, and then blinked again. There was a Border Collie on the bed staring at him. It was morning. Jack turned his head and looked at the slim form hidden under the covers.

"Corie?" He put out a hand and touched her back. She moaned and pulled a pillow over her head.

In the kitchen he saw the two empty wine bottles and understood the moaning. Jack put on coffee and was surprised to find food when he looked in the refrigerator. The pill bottle sat on the counter. He picked it up and stared at it. Murphy's toenails clicked on the floor and Jack looked at him. "See? This is why I don't take pills." By way of answer, Murphy walked to a plastic bowl of water on the floor and drank.

In the bathroom Jack noticed bits of blond hair stuck to the grout between the tiles. He frowned at them but figured he'd find out soon enough. In the meantime, he had about a thousand phone calls to return, including two from Aranda and one from Frank Yannelli.

Jack called Frank first.

"There you are," Frank said. "Enjoying the snow? I have good news."

"I could certainly use some."

"The tox screen showed traces of ecstasy in Vangie Perez's blood."

"Okay."

"Don't you get it? She was overheated. A very particular designer strain, too, called PCA. Not very common. It causes whoever takes it to overheat dramatically without any compensating increase in pleasure, or so they say. I wouldn't know. There are documented cases of body temp still being elevated by as much as seven degrees hours after death."

Jack found it hard to breathe. "That changes the time of death?"

"Moves it up. By as much as five or six hours."

"That's fucking great."

He called Dani, Mike, and Serena in turn, and in between kept trying Aranda. Her last message had been weird. Aranda didn't speak and it sounded like there was running water in the background. It filled the two minutes allowed on his voice mail, as if she'd accidentally hit redial without realizing. It wasn't like Aranda not to call him back. He thought about calling Roger but decided there was no good reason to alarm the man yet. Almost two feet of snow had fallen; she was probably taking a snow day.

He also talked to Jessie who still sounded friendly and accommodating. She said she assumed his plans had changed because of the snow. Jack tried to swallow his frustration at not talking to her last night. Jessie told him she would be available later that afternoon, and they signed off with him agreeing to call her when he had a definite time. That is, if Jessie didn't lawyer up by then.

Couldn't be helped. The new information about Vangie changed everything.

He tried to burn off nervous energy by shoveling snow. When he came back inside he heard the shower running. Finally, Corie was up. When she came out of the bathroom, Jack was glad he had years of practice keeping his face neutral in extreme situations because she looked like she'd used a lawn mower on her hair. She didn't say anything, just slumped into a chair at the kitchen counter and put her head down on her arms so that he couldn't see her face. She was wearing his robe. He put on a fresh pot of coffee. When it was ready he put a mug on the counter in front of her. She didn't raise her head.

"Hungry?" Jack asked.

It looked like her head moved from side to side.

"When you're ready to talk about your messages, let me know."

Something was really wrong. In her voice mails she'd sounded frantic to see him. What else had he missed yesterday? *Goddamn it. Goddamned cancer, goddamned radiation.*

But it wouldn't have mattered how much warning he had, because nothing could have prepared Jack for what Corie was about to show him.

When she came into the living room she had a pile of what looked like loose-leaf pages in her arms. She sat on the opposite end of the couch and dumped the papers between them. Jack looked at the pages and realized they were old calendars. He gave her a puzzled look, but didn't say anything.

"Evan's tax records." She explained which two years they were for and her rationale for taking them. "I'll give you the complete address of the office so you can write a warrant. Hopefully everything will still be there." Her eyes held on his for a short second and then skittered away before continuing.

"This is what I wanted to tell you yesterday," Corie said. "Evan was in Charlotte when Monique was killed."

Jack frowned, mentally reviewing Len's statement. "Corie, we have a suspect in custody."

"Wait, please. Let me tell you." Her voice faltered and she looked down for a few moments, her hands nervously rearranging the pages.

Jack badly wanted to reach across the papers and touch her, but he didn't.

Corie looked up again and took a deep breath. "Evan had a receipt from an Italian restaurant for the night she was killed—the night Brice found her. That's meaningful, I think, because Brice told me Monique had a date that night. She didn't tell anyone who her date was, but she did say he was taking her to this new Italian restaurant. That's why it stuck out in Brice's memory. The restaurant was the hot new place in town."

Corie cleared her throat and reached into an envelope pocket with the old calendars. She came out with a receipt and showed it to Jack. "Marchianos. They opened a couple of weeks before Monique was killed. I found an old restaurant review online. The critic raved about the place. And I know this is, like, not something you'd use in court, but the reviewer specifically commented on the restaurant's macaroons."

"Macaroons?"

"Evan isn't big on desserts, but one of the few things he likes is a good macaroon. He loves almonds, marzipan, anything with that kind of flavor. I know that sounds silly."

She looked impossibly fragile. Without the hair her head looked tiny, her features delicate, giving her the appearance of a child. It struck Jack how much of a prop the hair had been.

"A few months after Monique was killed," Corie squeezed her eyes shut and seemed to will herself to continue, "a young woman in Philadelphia named Yvonne Harris was murdered. Evan was there at the time. I have all the receipts."

Corie handed Jack an article about the murder she'd printed from the internet, which included a photo of the victim. It was a studio shot for a high school or college graduation, a hopeful young face. Yvonne's smile was wide. Her dark hair was pulled back and Jack could tell from the ample curve of her breasts and her upper arms that she was slightly plump.

"Look." Corie pointed at the photo. "Twenty-five. Long, dark hair. Slightly overweight. The killer cut her up pretty bad and had sex with her. The case was never solved."

Corie showed him a receipt from the Philadelphia International Airport dated February 12th, probably for a bottle of water or a magazine from a newsstand. "Thank you, come again" on the check from the Madison Restaurant in downtown Philadelphia where Evan had lunch on February 13th. And the night of Yvonne Harris's murder, Evan parked in a garage on Latimer Street.

"Evan was there when she was killed. The bastard was there."

"You know how many people were in Philadelphia on that date?" Jack hoped to protect Corie for a little while longer. Until he was sure.

Corie ignored his protest. Her gaze and her voice were steady. "After Philadelphia Evan had a trip to New York. On March 15th he drove into Manhattan. There's a receipt from the Triboro Bridge. I wonder if any dark-haired young women were killed in New York that March? I know you can find out. And this is only two years."

Jack looked down at Yvonne Harris's picture again. She was wearing a heart-shaped locket. YH. The monogram on the necklace Jack had recently checked into evidence, that Corie had found in the cabin. He answered carefully. "Corie, you realize what you're implying?"

"Implying? Hell. I've been sleeping with a sociopath, at the very least. And this isn't even the worst part."

The hairs stood up on Jack's arms. What could be worse than realizing your husband was a murderer?

"Once when we were in Atlanta we stayed at a Motel 6. Horrible place. Completely out of character for Evan. I had my period too, and that usually repulses guys, but Evan seemed to like it. We had sex and Evan got crazy."

"Crazy how?"

"No knives, but we trashed that hotel room. I know, it's disgusting. But the worst part? A woman named Alicia Stavros had been murdered there. Unsolved like the rest."

She handed him another printout and, with tremendous reluctance, Jack dragged his eyes away from Corie and looked at it. The grainy photo showed a young woman, Caucasian, with long, dark hair. From what he could see in the photo she was a little overweight with full breasts. *Shit.*

Corie's eyes filled. "I think Evan had sex with me at the very same place where he killed someone. I've read about serial killers. Some of them do that, it turns them on. You know the weirdest thing? After a while, Evan didn't want me to go on trips with him anymore."

A rock landed in Jack's stomach.

"I asked him why," Corie continued, "and he said it was important to keep business and pleasure separate. I thought that was strange because I was part of the business, too. And then it hit me yesterday when I was looking all this up: I was *only* the business part."

Jack felt utterly at a loss for words. "What?"

"I was business and murder was pleasure. That's what he meant on the stairs."

"Corie."

He reached for her but she leaned back, away from him. "Evan loved my hair. He used to run his fingers through it and tug at it. He'll never do that again. He'll never touch me again. He'll never lay a hand on anyone. Either you lock him up or, I swear to God, the next time I lay eyes on him I'll kill him."

CHAPTER SIXTY

Jack hated leaving Corie alone. They made the same agreement as yesterday—hourly phone calls—and when she walked him to the door, Jack gave her a soft, careful kiss, as if she were made out of spun glass. He wrapped her gently in his arms, rested his cheek on the top of her head for a moment, and breathed in her scent. He didn't want to let go of her but what choice did he have?

She said, "Do what you need to do. I'll be fine."

He said, "Yeah, where have I heard that before?" But he smiled at her fondly, drew a line with his index finger along her jaw, and touched the short, spiky hair. "Be careful."

"Funny. I was going to say the same thing to you."

She closed the door behind him and he waited until he heard the reassuring click of the deadbolt sliding home.

On his way to the station Jack stopped at Aranda's condo, but there was no sign of her. Now seriously worried, he decided to issue a BOLO. He could be overreacting, and if it turned out she was fine he'd apologize. If she wasn't . . . He couldn't think about it. Not now.

In Dani's office Jack presented everything he had, including Vangie's updated autopsy results, to Assistant District Attorney Hayden Tafro. It was hard to keep the excitement out of his voice. As usual, he stood while he presented, and today he also paced.

It was unusual to see Hayden in jeans and boots. Usually she wore expensive suits and high heels. Hayden was young and she was ambitious.

"Three murders is the threshold for a serial killer," Dani said. "If he's killed in multiple states it goes federal."

Hayden sat back in one of Dani's visitor chairs and stretched her long legs out in front of her. "Yep. I've already given Special Agent Rogers in the Denver FBI field office a heads up."

Jack ran a hand through his hair and blew out a sharp breath. He looked at Hayden. "Do we have enough to make an arrest? Or do you want to wait on the Feds to tie up all the loose ends for you?" He didn't intend to antagonize her, but he felt an almost unbearable sense of urgency.

"I want a conviction." Hayden picked up a coffee container off of Dani's desk and took a drink. She didn't seem the least bit excited or irritated. "Your main witness is a meth addict who I don't want to put on the stand. Everything else is circumstantial."

"Time of death isn't." Attempting to mirror her calm demeanor, Jack forced himself to stop pacing and took a sip of his own coffee.

"Ugh." Hayden made a dismissive sound. "It was below freezing outside. After Vangie was killed, her body was riding around in the back of a pickup exposed to the elements for an undetermined amount of time. It'll be dueling experts and Markham has the money to hire the very best. Any idea where Evan is? Considering his status in the community, it'd be better for everyone to work this out quietly."

"Let's send him an engraved invitation. If he hears jail is black tie, he'll present himself with alacrity."

Hayden answered coolly. "Sarcasm doesn't help anything, Jack. I know you're frustrated but we'll only have one chance at this guy. I want to have enough that he's denied bail. You know

I'm right. It wouldn't matter if the judge said ten million dollars, Evan would pay it."

"What about the necklace?" Jack had written a list of evidence on the whiteboard in Dani's office. He walked over and tapped it for emphasis. "A necklace engraved with the letters YH—the initials of one of the murdered victims. Come on, Hayden, do you want me to gift wrap this for you?"

Hayden glanced at the detective's room through the window in Dani's office. "Let's see what they have."

Mike and Serena were back from executing the search warrant at Evan's mystery office, accompanied by a uniform pushing a hand truck loaded with boxes. Dani and Jack followed Hayden. Detectives Scalamandre and Warren joined them.

Warren looked at the boxes and whistled. "We're not going anywhere for a while."

"Finding a judge to sign a warrant in a blizzard was no easy task," Serena said.

"Blizzard's over," Jack said. "What a bunch of wimps. You find all the tax records?"

Serena unwound a burgundy wool scarf from around her neck. "Uh-huh. Had to persuade the property manager of the office complex to brave the roads and open the outer office door for us. Apparently Evan's receptionist took a snow day."

"Everything was still there." Mike wore a parka over his suit and a fur-lined hat with ear flaps that fastened under his chin.

"Nice hat," Jack said. "I don't understand why you can't get a date."

"Hey, it's cold out there," Mike said.

Serena watched Mike pull off the hat and run his hand over his bald head. "Lucky you don't have to worry about hat hair."

"You oughta try it," Mike said. "Helps if you have a pretty head."

Jack stared at the boxes and thought about what they implied. "I think we're lucky it snowed. Maybe that deterred Markham from clearing the office out."

"Do you think Evan knows Corie was there?" Serena asked.

"Corie's sense was that the receptionist was gonna call him," Jack said.

"We know where Corie is?" Mike asked. "She could be in danger."

"She's someplace safe." The other detectives didn't ask Jack to elaborate, just like they hadn't mentioned his being AWOL the night before.

"So what's our plan?" Mike asked.

"Hayden here thinks he's going to come to us all polite and contrite, hat in hand, tail between his legs, and issue a formal apology," Jack said. "All we have to do is wait."

Hayden pulled a binder out of a box and riffled the pages. "I said it would be best. I didn't say we were going to sit around on our asses. Hopefully you'll find something useful in here for me."

Jack knew getting excited wouldn't get him anywhere with her. "Look, Hayden, I understand your caution. I respect it. But while Evan's out there, women are at risk. I'm worried about his wife. I'm worried about his mother. I haven't been able to get a hold of Aranda Sheffield since yesterday and—"

"Aranda's missing?" Hayden's voice sharpened, betraying emotion for the first time.

Jack told her about the strange voice mail, how he'd tried several times to call Aranda, and that she hadn't been seen at home or at work.

"I know Aranda," Hayden said. "We're in a women's wine tasting group together. Under ordinary circumstances I'd say she's most likely in Aspen with some hottie sipping Veuve Cliquot, but she fits the profile. You convinced me, Jack. Do it. Bring Evan in. We have someone in imminent danger and, besides, why should the Feebs have all the fun?"

CHAPTER SIXTY-ONE

Serena watched Jack with narrowed eyes. "You look like you feel better."

"I finally have a mission. I'm going to arrest this psychotic son of a bitch before anyone else and, more importantly, before he gets *to* anybody else." Jack turned to Dani. "I'm heading back to the jail. I have to clarify a few things with Len Funderburk."

"Want me to go with you?" Serena asked.

"No. I need all of you to start going through these." Jack indicated the boxes. "Corie's already found receipts that put Evan in Charlotte the day of Monique Lawson's murder, and in Philadelphia for a second. She's got suspicions about a third in Atlanta."

"How's Corie holding up, knowing all that?" Scalamandre asked.

"About how you'd think." Jack remembered her white face watching him leave through the glass panes in his back door. "Start with those three victims. Put together a timeline of Evan's travel and compare it to unsolved murders fitting the same pattern in VICAP. So far this is all circumstantial. As I pointed out to Corie, a lot of men were in Philadelphia the day Yvonne Harris was killed. We need physical evidence. *If*," Jack was careful to emphasize the word, "Evan is responsible for these killings, they're messy, violent, personal. The victims fight. They might not have gotten his DNA from the scene in Charlotte, but if he's done this more than once, he's bound to have screwed up somewhere. I'm getting his DNA run through CODIS, see if anything else pops."

"Doesn't make sense that Evan gave us his DNA so willingly," Serena said.

"It wasn't willing," Dani said. "We had a warrant. Not giving it to us would have raised a red flag and Evan's too smart for that."

"I think he took a calculated risk," Jack said. "I'll be back from the jail as soon as I can."

"How good a witness is Len?" Mike asked. "You think he's telling the truth?"

"Let's just say Len didn't do anything to increase my suspicions," Jack said. "And his story checks out. He did have his license suspended. He had DUIs. He worked for her grandfather. Everything I can check out checks out.

"I called Lassiter in Charlotte. It's a long shot, but he's going to the restaurant where Monique went on her date, which is still in business. See if anyone's around who was working there fifteen years ago. Gonna show them Evan's pictures."

"And then there's Brice Shaughnessy," Dani said. "That doesn't fit Evan's profile."

"And then there's Brice." Jack weighed one of the Day-Timer binders in his hand and looked at the other detectives. "Killed, so far as we've been able to determine, by Vangie Perez, who I'm convinced did Evan's bidding. Markham thinks we can't touch him. Let's prove him wrong."

CHAPTER SIXTY-TWO

Corie slipped into her customary parking spot next to Jessie's garage. "Slipped" being the operative word. The side streets and alleys hadn't been touched by a snowplow and Corie was grateful for her car's all-wheel drive. She stood in the cold, hugging herself and admiring the Markham mansion for a minute. Evan thought the large, brick house was old-fashioned and way too big for Jessie, but his mother refused to consider moving. Corie admired Jessie for that. She admired Jessie for a lot of things.

Through a lot of troubled times in Corie's life—Vi's drinking, her parents' divorce, and all the assorted traumas of high school—Jessie had always been there. Jessie listened to her, even when Corie was a child. Jessie comforted her after Hennessy died, when Corie was torn up with guilt and confusion. Jessie even seemed to understand about Evan and how difficult he was to be married to. She was perceptive, warm, and generous. So opposite her son.

The information Corie had uncovered would destroy Jessie. So while Corie felt sick to her stomach about lying to Jack, when Jessie called and asked Corie to come over, she didn't hesitate. Besides, if she stayed holed up in his house with nothing to do but think, she'd go crazy.

Outside the kitchen Corie stamped her feet to warm them and knock off snow. Then she slid open one of the atrium doors and called for her mother-in-law.

"There you are." Jessie was wearing a fuzzy sweater the color of the sea. Her smile faltered for only a second when she saw Corie's hair. Corie walked into Jessie's arms and her mother-in-law touched the chopped off remnants tenderly.

"Good for you," Jessie said.

Corie hid her face against Jessie's soft shoulder. She'd promised herself she wouldn't cry. "It's hideous."

When Corie stepped back, Jessie was smiling. "Your other hair was too conservative. Change is always freeing. Always."

Corie tried to smile back. "You look nice and cozy."

"Are you cold? You're shivering." Jessie rubbed Corie's upper arms. "Come over by the fire."

"I'm fine. I'm worried about you." Wood-burning fireplaces were all but extinct in Denver and pollution laws dictated what and when you could burn. But Jessie said she was going for a "Tuscan farmhouse" effect and she got it.

Jessie walked to the counter, picked up some dishes, and placed them on the low, rough-hewn wooden table in front of the fire. "I thought we could have a late lunch. Nothing fancy. I figured you likely haven't been eating regularly with everything going on."

Corie detected no trace of irony in Jessie's voice. She seemed the same as always: warm, generous, nonjudgmental. How could Jessie be so nice to her after everything that had happened? How could Corie stand to lose her love?

"It's nothing much. Some soup and bread." Jessie poured two large glasses of white wine and handed one to Corie.

Corie took the glass gratefully. "You're a saint." She thought Jessie looked like a saint too, with that patient smile and her halo of golden curls.

Jessie set a bowl of soup in front of Corie.

"I'm glad you called. You know how I feel about you." Her stomach was sour from last night, but to cover her discomfort, Corie took a healthy swallow of the wine anyway. She was becoming a drunk as well as a liar.

"I don't want to lose you too, Corie." Jessie shook out a terracotta-colored napkin and draped it across her lap.

"Thank you." Corie felt utterly at a loss for words in the face of Jessie's incredible generosity. She took a second gulp of wine and tried a spoonful of soup, to be polite.

"It's gotten cold all of a sudden. But I like days like this. It makes it that much more warm and cozy to curl up by the fire. It's all about contrasts, don't you think?"

What an odd thing to say. And how strangely accurate. It was certainly a contrast being here in this beautiful house, drinking wine in front of a blazing fire, after what Corie had so recently discovered. It made no sense. But Corie couldn't think about it right now. Jessie was reaching out and that was like a miracle. It was one thing to marry a murderer. Imagine if you'd given birth to one?

Corie nibbled at a piece of bread and took another sip. "I think you're right."

Jessie topped off Corie's glass. "Are you sure you like this wine? It's Italian. I don't know much about Italian wines."

"I like it but maybe I shouldn't have any more." A wave of dizziness hit Corie and her face felt flushed. She squinted into the fire, trying to focus.

"What's happening?" Jessie watched her with concern.

"A little dizzy."

Jessie's voice was indulgent. "It's because you haven't been eating. Why don't you lie down after lunch?"

"How embarrassing." Corie put a hand on the table to feel something solid. She felt like she was crumbling.

"So much pain." Jessie's voice was soothing. "You've been incredibly wrong."

Corie closed her eyes and opened them again. She couldn't be drunk already. Jessie didn't say 'wrong.' She said 'strong.' Didn't she? "Maybe I should drink some water. Oh." Corie tried to stand and found she couldn't. She plopped back down in the chair.

Jessie laughed. "I'll get you some water, but first I think a little more wine."

Corie took the glass from her outstretched hand. Although it didn't make any sense, she drank. What could it hurt? She was already dizzy and Jessie was being so nice.

"That's good."

Jessie smiled and Corie suddenly realized it looked a lot like Evan's. Why hadn't Corie noticed it before? They had the same smile. The same even white teeth. Like the Cheshire Cat. No. Something far more evil. Corie tried to set the wineglass back on the table but she missed.

"Always making messes messes messes." But Jessie was still smiling.

The room was spinning. "Jessie, what was in that wine?"

". . . messes for someone else to clean up up up . . ."

Jessie stood and looking up at her made the room spin worse. Corie went to put her hand on the table again but it moved. Or maybe she moved.

"Corie. You're too emotional. As I tell Evan, it's best not to dwell. Best to be Zen about these things. It's all a journey."

Jessie had been speaking but Corie hadn't followed everything. What was wrong with her?

"Have you ever been in a labyrinth?" Jessie's voice echoed strangely.

"One now." Corie felt like she was in some kind of sick 'pin the tail on the donkey' game, all spun around. Someone ripped the blindfold off and she didn't know which way to go.

"It's all a journey, Corie, don't be afraid."

Jessie's voice was melodic, soothing, so beautiful. There was a golden haze behind her. The dining room light? Was she still at Jessie's house? What was happening? "Jessie?"

"I'm here."

Corie remembered her purse. Something was in it that she needed. But it was so far away. At the end of a tunnel.

Jessie's laugh was like silver. No, like a mirror, shattering into a million sparkling pieces. Corie's eyelids drooped. She had to stay awake. She had to make it to her purse.

"Where are you going?" The sound came from very far away. "What's wrong? It shouldn't hurt."

It was like being at the bottom of a barrel filled with water. Voices. Echoing. Laughter. The water tugged her down. Corie's last thought: *Is the entire family insane?*

CHAPTER SIXTY-THREE

"You ever hear of a restaurant named Marchianos?" Jack asked.

"Oh God, yes." Len sat up straight and his voice rose angrily. "This is like a bad dream. I told those damned detectives! I told them that Monique had been talking about going to that restaurant on a date. She was really excited about it because it was a new restaurant and really hard to get a reservation. She was bragging about it at work."

"To you?"

"To some of the other women. But I overheard. I told them this," Len repeated.

"I have all the files. If you're lying I'll find out."

"I told them." A third time. "But they didn't believe me."

"And you're sure you never saw her with Evan?" Jack asked.

Len looked down and shook his head.

"The car you passed when you drove up to the house, did you recognize it? Can you tell me anything about it—the make, the model, the color?"

Len's head snapped up. "I didn't tell you that. I said I saw a car when I was driving *away*."

"We're about to arrest Evan. He can't hurt you. He doesn't even have to know."

"He already knows." Len leaned forward, groaned, and raked his hands through his greasy blond hair.

Jack held himself perfectly still. In the silence that stretched out, he felt as much as heard the jail: harsh metal on metal, loudspeakers, the vibration of human despair. There were moments when Jack knew he was right and all he had to do was wait. Too bad he had no patience.

Len didn't disappoint. "That's why I did what Evan asked. I was afraid he was going to kill me. He said, 'Don't leave town,' so I didn't. He said, 'Get away from my mother,' so I did, sneaking out on her in the middle of the night. I didn't understand everything until you talked to me. Then it all fell together."

"Evan told you to lie."

"I'm afraid. And I didn't want Jessie to be mad at me and—" Len broke off and gave a bitter laugh. "I liked living in that house. She took me on trips, bought me clothes, took me out for fancy dinners. I was going to lose everything."

Jack looked down at Len's hands on the metal table and could see that Len had picked his cuticles until they bled. A good sign. A physical manifestation of the secret that had gnawed at Len on the inside for fifteen years. A secret Len was finally ready to share.

"It was a sedan. It was raining really hard so the other driver was using his wipers. I got a glimpse of his face. A good glimpse." Len glanced at Jack to gauge his reaction, then looked off to his left, remembering. "It was a Mercedes and I remember thinking how strange that was. You didn't see that many Mercedes out there in the country, and I remember thinking the most irrelevant thing: I wondered how that car did on the dirt roads."

CHAPTER SIXTY-FOUR

Morning. No. Not morning. Corie tried to move but couldn't. She groaned and fell back but the groan was muffled. Something was covering her mouth. She reached to pull it out, couldn't move her arms, and completely panicked. Where the hell was she? She tried to jerk herself to a seated position and couldn't do that either. Her head was spinning and there was a metallic taste in her mouth. Her head scraped the ground. It was dark. *Ground?*

A wave of nausea hit her and she fought it. *If I vomit I'll die.* Certain knowledge. Her heart pounded. She was restrained somewhere, somehow, and it was very dark. What was the last thing she remembered? Was she at Jack's? Was she home? Had she been in a car accident? It was so dark.

No. Jessie. She'd passed out at Jessie's. Fractured memories returned along with panic that hit full force. She gagged and furiously cleared her throat. *Can't be sick. Can't.*

Bread. Fire. Wine. *Oh no.* There must have been something in the wine. Corie forced herself to breath evenly through her nose. She moved her tongue around inside her mouth, which felt lined with cotton. Not a gag. Something on the outside, like duct tape. *Evan is getting creative.*

Her mind wasn't functioning. Corie whimpered, the sound tortured and muffled. Where was she? Why was it so dark? Why were they doing this to her? The nausea was utterly terrifying.

Breathe. Have to breathe. Even breaths. Count them. Corie thought about yoga, about the breathing exercises they taught you in class. Those yogis could withstand anything—hot coals, freezing cold, underwater. They could raise and lower their body temperature at will. If they could do it, so could she.

Wherever she was it smelled bad. Was it her? Had she messed herself? No, it was a musty smell. She moved a little, experimentally. Her hands were pinned behind her and her legs were bound together.

Corie flexed her feet and her wrists. Nothing hurt. Her eyes became adjusted to the dark and she saw some outlines. The space around her felt large. Not a grave then. That would be her worst nightmare, buried alive in a coffin when you're not dead with a straw to breathe through.

A toilet flushed and she heard water run through a pipe above her head. She was in a crawl space. Whose? A fresh wave of panic and sickness hit her.

There were rats in a crawl space. *Oh God.* She wriggled furiously but that made the nausea worse, so she stopped. *Think. Breathe.* Yoga breaths—four counts in, hold, four counts out. Miraculously a few of those calmed her. Maybe those Buddhists were onto something after all. Buddhists . . . Jessie laughing. 'I wonder what you'll come back as. Maybe a cow or a dog or a rodent. Yes, that's it. A rat.' Jessie's laughter. The last thing Corie heard.

Where was Jack? At work, of course, running down all the leads she'd dropped in his lap. She shouldn't have lied to him.

Well shit. She was on her own. She had to figure out what was she tied up with and what she was attached to. She had to get her mouth free. Where was her phone? Corie wriggled her fingers, as if that was going to provide answers. Obviously Jessie hadn't been thoughtful enough to bury her with her phone propped up nearby so it was handy. And how exactly would she dial it anyway? With mental telepathy?

She willed Jack to find her.

Where was her dog? She thought of Murphy's soft fur, the solid warmth of his body under her hand. Who would take care of Murphy if she died? *Jack, please.* Another futile whimper. *I can't cry. Can't. Plenty of time to cry about this later if I keep my wits about me now.*

Alone in the house Jessie paced the length of the kitchen, her feet in low-heeled, suede boots silent on the tile floor. She picked up a sponge from the sink and the harsh smell of bleach insulted her nose. Even though she'd already cleaned up, she wiped the low table in front of the fireplace a third time.

Evan slid open the atrium door. "Why does it smell like bleach in here?"

"I was cleaning up from lunch."

"What's with all the cleaning? First Corie, now you." He realized Jessie wouldn't know what he was talking about.

But she cocked her head and smiled at him. "Speaking of Corie, I have a surprise for you."

"It better be something good. Do you have any idea how goddamned hard it was to get here?"

Jessie scowled. "I think you owe me. And besides, it's something you really want."

CHAPTER SIXTY-FIVE

Like a bad dream on repeat, Jack found his house empty. Only this time when he let himself in the back door, a frantic Murphy made a mad dash for the backyard. Wherever Corie had gone she hadn't taken her dog. And she took that dog everywhere.

Now neither Corie nor Aranda were answering their phones.

Jack hated calling Roger D'Ambrose who instantly sounded panicked.

"I've been calling her, too." Roger sounded like he was going to cry. "She never came in to the office today. I figured she was working from home on account of the snow, but she's not there either. I drove by a little while ago."

"Does she have a boyfriend?" Jack asked.

"No. Not currently."

"Do you know the last place she was planning to go yesterday?"

Roger told him.

"Okay, listen to me. I'm calling dispatch right now. Do not go up there on your own. I know you want to, but don't. Wait for the police. I'll make sure it's a priority." As he spoke, his call waiting beeped and Jack stared at the display on his phone in disbelief: Evan Markham was calling him.

CHAPTER SIXTY-SIX

The hatch door opened abruptly and the sudden light blinded Corie. Jessie was back. *I haven't gotten free and now she's going to finish me off.* Corie had worked off a corner of the tape after what felt like hours of trying, but it wasn't enough.

The figure jumped down into the crawl space and, as Corie's eyes adjusted, she saw that it wasn't Jessie. It was worse. It was Evan.

Corie tried to scream but couldn't, the sounds that came out instead were high pitched and frightening.

"Corie." He hurried to her side and he looked concerned. "What did she do to you?"

Her heart hammered in her chest and the sudden panic caused a fresh wave of sickness. She fought to breathe. *Oh God, I can't be sick. God. Please.*

"This might hurt," Evan said, his voice kind.

That would have been funny in another context. Corie watched with wide eyes as her husband found the edge of the tape and, in one quick motion, ripped it off her face. That stung and Corie started coughing. She felt hot acid in her throat and realized how close she'd been to vomiting and choking to death. Her voice was a croak. "Are you going to kill me?"

"No. Of course not." Evan seemed shocked at the suggestion. He started to work on the knots at her feet. "I'm going to get you out of here."

"Evan?" Jessie's tremulous voice carried into the crawl space. Corie's breath caught.

"Don't say anything." Evan stopped working on the knots.

"Evan? What are you doing? You don't have time for anything fancy." Jessie's form filled the small opening, blocking the sunlight behind her. She was still wearing the fuzzy blue sweater.

Evan's eyes held Corie's for a moment and then he turned toward his mother. "It was you."

"You're welcome," Jessie said.

"Why would you do that to me?"

"Do what?" Corie's voice was low and hoarse.

"You were careless," Jessie said. "He found out. I did it to protect you, to protect our family. I couldn't have our good name dragged through the mud by some nobody."

"Does she mean Brice?" Corie whispered.

Evan focused on his mother. "You sent me the scrapbook."

Jessie's voice was indulgent. "Of course, darling. I sent you everything I found. Except the computer. Sorry about that. I dropped it because I was trying to hurry. It was dark and I was scared. Corie, you haven't found it, have you?"

Wildly, Corie shook her head from side to side. The movement made her nauseous again.

"Of course you haven't. Silly of me to ask." Jessie smiled, her teeth white in the dim light. "If you'd found it that cop would know everything by now."

"You mean to tell me it's been at our house the entire time? Show me." In a crouch, Evan started to move toward his mother.

"What about her?" Jessie motioned with her hand. She was holding something and Corie squinted to see what it was.

"Mother." Evan spoke in a warning tone. He scooted toward her but not fast enough.

A shot rang out and Corie screamed. It must have missed her because she didn't feel anything.

Evan yelled too. "No!"

"You always were weak." Jessie's voice dripped scorn. "I'll have to finish this myself. Like always."

A second shot rang out, and a third, and then everything went black.

"No!" Evan desperately scuttled in a crouch toward his mother. The thought that she might hit him never crossed his mind. He could see the gun in her hands, her arms held straight out in front of her. For a woman that abhorred violence she'd certainly learned how to shoot properly.

She managed to squeeze off three shots before he reached her. He yanked her right arm as she got off a fourth and the bullet went wide of its target.

"Son of a bitch," Evan said.

His hand closed around her wrist but she didn't let go of the gun. Her arm swung wildly as they struggled and the gun went off a fifth time; he heard a metallic sound, the bullet sparking off a cast-iron pipe.

Finally, not caring if he hurt her, Evan got a better angle and pulled as hard as he could on her forearm, twisting at the same time. Jessie gasped in pain and the gun flew out of her hands.

"What the hell is wrong with you?" Evan glanced back at Corie lying lifeless on the ground.

"How could you hurt me like that?" Jessie's voice was high with pain and stunned anger.

Evan shoved her backward so that she landed with a thump on her backside outside the hatch opening. Then he jumped out and struggled to get control of her.

"Let go of me!" Their breath fogged as they fought. Jessie screamed and tried to scratch him, going for his bruised eye.

Evan's fingers dug into her plump upper arms. Jessie writhed. The fabric of her sweater was slippery and he was surprised at her strength. He steered her roughly toward his car parked in front of the house. She dug her heels in and he wound up dragging her, leaving tracks in the snow. *What would the cops make of that?* he wondered. But he had no time to worry about it now.

"Get in." His voice was a snarl. In his mind he had the image of Corie on the floor, still half bound with rope.

"I don't know what's gotten into you." Jessie braced herself in the car doorway facing him, with one hand gripping the edge of the roof and the other holding the door open. She straightened her arms and tensed her body.

Evan punched her in the stomach and Jessie crumpled. He folded her into the car and slammed the door.

"Son of a bitch," he said again, shaking his hand which stung from the blows. He hit the lock button on his key fob to keep her from escaping in the few seconds it took for him to walk around to the driver's side. Once he climbed in, he took off so fast the rear end of the car fishtailed and Evan struggled to get the car back under control.

"Where are you taking me?" Jessie's voice rang with outrage. "How dare you?"

Using controls on the steering wheel Evan made a call. Jessie grabbed at his arm but he fended her off. The call went through via the car's Bluetooth and Jack's voice growled out of the speakers. "Corie's in Jessie's crawl space. Get her. Hurry." Evan disconnected before Jack could say anything or hear Jessie screaming.

"Why would you do that? Why would you help her? She's a slut and a liar."

"Shut up."

"You have horrible taste in women. I couldn't believe it when you brought her home. The girl who killed your sister! And then that other one. She was so stupid. She thought loaning me her gun would make me love her. We'd be best friends. Ha! I'm glad you killed her. Although I am sick of having to clean up your messes."

Evan stuck his right arm out and grabbed Jessie by the throat. "I swear to God, if you do not shut up I will throw you out of this car. I will kill you and I will revel in it." He shoved her away so hard that her head banged against the window glass.

Jessie gave a startled gasp. As if waking up from a bad dream, she looked at him and frowned. Her body went limp. "Evan," she said, her voice childish and timid. "What's wrong?"

"Your performances don't work on me." Out of the corner of his eye Evan saw her hand sliding slowly toward the gearshift lever. He grabbed her wrist and bent her hand back so hard she screamed.

"I don't understand why you're treating me this way." Jessie held her left wrist with her right hand and started to cry.

CHAPTER SIXTY-SEVEN

The drive up Downing was agonizing. Cars barely crawled on the slick road and the backup from the light at Alameda was three blocks long. Jack used his dashboard light and cars tried to move out of his way, but there was often nowhere for them to go with the piles of snow and slush and parked vehicles marooned at the curb.

Once he finally turned onto First Avenue, he sped up. First Avenue, through one of the richest parts of town, was six lanes wide and he was driving his personal car, his black Audi; as long as no one got in his way he could fly, even on the snow.

Jack hoped the other emergency vehicles were having a better time of it, but his heart sank when he skidded his car to a stop in front of Jessie's and realized he was the first one on the scene.

Fuck.

The car door closed with a solid thunk. Jack opened his trunk and, without taking his eyes off of the house, shrugged into his bulletproof vest, put his coat back on over it, checked his weapon, his flashlight, and called for backup again. Traffic was a mess, everything slowed down due to the snow. No one's fault.

His eyes scanned the house but he saw no sign of movement. It was so quiet he could hear his feet squeak on the fresh snow. There was parking around back on the alley and Jack made his way there, creeping around the exterior of the house, his gun drawn. Corie's car was parked in an outdoor space but the garage door was solid so he couldn't see if there were any other cars inside. No sign of the silver Mercedes.

"Corie?" Jack called her name, over and over. No answer. He stopped numerous times and listened but didn't hear anyone. He made his way into the secluded backyard and saw a small hatch door open, leading to the low, dark expanse under the house. "Corie?" Still no response. He called her phone but didn't hear it ringing.

His breath was ragged, as if he'd run a fast mile. 'Crawl space,' Evan said. Jack was well aware that it could be a trap. The open door taunted him. His training told him to wait for cover and his instincts told him to hurry. What if Evan was waiting for him, armed and dangerous? What if it wasn't a lie and Corie was in danger, or dying? It wasn't much of a decision.

Jack frowned at the overlapping shoe impressions and messy track marks in the snow leading away from the hatch. Like someone had been dragged. Had Jessie been taken against her will? Corie? Aranda?

"Police!" Jack yelled and inched closer, easing himself into the hatch opening. "Corie?" Still nothing. Then the arc of his flashlight illuminated a body.

Corie, lying motionless on the dirt floor in sizable pool of blood. Caution forgotten, Jack jumped inside and ran to her. "Corie. Oh God. No." She was filthy and unconscious but she was moaning. She was alive.

"Stay with me, Corie, it's Jack. You're going to be okay." He freed her hands and legs, then took off his coat and covered her with it. It was so cold and she'd lost so much blood. Was still bleeding. Her pulse was so weak he was afraid he was imagining it. He talked to her the whole time, told her she was going to be okay, told her she was beautiful, told her not to go away.

Where the hell was Jessie? Evan wouldn't kill his own mother, would he? Except there was no telling what Evan would do.

Two bodies on Jack's watch. So far. Not counting Monique. Or, God forbid, Aranda, or the others they hadn't figured out yet. Not counting Corie. And they never would count Corie, not if Jack had anything to say about it. He shouldn't have baited Evan; he should have kept his cool and done his job.

Jack reached for the radio again. "I need that goddamned ambulance yesterday." He made no effort to disguise the desperation in his voice.

"Two minutes out," came the response.

"Make it one."

Did he hear sirens in the distance? Pink foam edged her mouth. What did that mean? Jack should know. He kept talking to her, a stream of soothing nonsense, saying the things he'd recently begun to hope he'd have the chance to say. You're beautiful. I love you. Please don't leave me.

Jesus. She was down here in the dark and the filth, all alone, scared, and in pain. What kind of evil bastard could dump her like this and leave her to die?

"I'm here, Corie. You're going to be all right." With an agonizing sense of futility he tucked the coat tighter around her, touched her face, her hair, held her hand. What had Evan done to her?

Definitely sirens. And they were getting louder.

Jack turned his flashlight into the dark void around them, its arcing beam no match for the fetid darkness, its weak light soaking into the dirt floor like Corie's blood. It was so dim he wasn't sure at first what he was seeing.

"Christ."

Another body, or rather a skeleton, half buried in the dirt at the far end of the crawl space. Number three.

Car doors slammed. Voices. The reassuring chatter of police radios.

"Under here!" Jack yelled. Forms appeared in the opening. Uniformed officers, paramedics. Flashlight beams raked his face.

"You need to get a homicide team out here." Jack stopped as the paramedics loaded Corie on a stretcher and gave instructions to an officer. "Secure the entire property. There's a body under there. Looks old. Skeleton."

CHAPTER SIXTY-EIGHT

A male doctor called for a medication, machine alarms sounded, a female doctor said, "She's crashing, get the paddles."

They had asked Jack for Corie's name and used it as if she could hear them.

The male doctor injected something into an IV they'd hastily put in her arm in the ambulance. Epi, Jack thought he heard them say. He tried to remember his rudimentary first aid training and gave up. It was bad. That was all he needed to know. All that was relevant.

"Get another IV," someone said. "Tube her."

They'd brought her to Denver Health, a Level One Trauma Center, only a few minutes from Jessie's house. Usually. Precious minutes ticked away on the icy drive, and now Jack watched the doctors' frantic work from a narrow spot he'd found against the wall in between an unused IV stand and an ominous-looking piece of equipment with lots of dials on a cart. He'd flatly refused to leave and, since he was a cop, they let him stay, although they'd threatened him with forcible removal if he got in their way.

He could barely see Corie in the bed surrounded by doctors, nurses, and equipment. The female doctor injected something else into Corie's IV. Used gauze and bandages accumulated quickly in bloody heaps on the linoleum floor. He heard them say "clear" like in the movies and saw Corie's slight body jump from the charge.

"Three sixty," the woman said, a note of desperation in her voice.

"Charging. Clear."

"You're all right. Please be all right. You have to be all right. Please be all right." Jack's mouth moved and he whispered the words over and over, his own kind of prayer.

"Again," the woman called.

"Clear."

On the bed, Corie's body jumped.

"Got a rhythm," the male doctor said, wrapping his stethoscope back around his neck. "Notify the OR. Let's move." They started rolling the bed from the room.

"You're doing great, Corie," the female doctor said, walking next to the bed with her hand on the rail.

Jack followed. "Where are you taking her?"

"To surgery." The male doctor called more orders.

Jack tried to get on the elevator with them but they wouldn't allow it.

"You're almost there, Corie, you're doing great," he heard the female doctor say before the elevator door closed. "Hang in there. Stay with us."

Yes. Stay with us. Please, please stay with us. Jack's vision blurred as he stood there staring at the closed elevator door until it opened again and different doctors poured out. They stepped around him with some irritation. Eventually, Jack moved and found a seat along one wall. He leaned forward, elbows on knees, face in his hands. How could he have been so stupid?

CHAPTER SIXTY-NINE

"What are you going to do?" Jessie asked from the passenger seat. She'd finally stopped fighting and sat quietly, meek and confused. "Where are we going?"

Evan laughed shortly. "You tell me. This was all your idea."

In truth, there was nowhere to go. After his initial panic driving away from Jessie's he'd headed aimlessly south, sticking to side streets and picking his way carefully on the snow. He couldn't go home and look for the computer because the police would be watching the house. Hopefully the laptop was ruined after being outdoors, but Evan knew the police lab technicians might be able to salvage some of the information on it.

"I'm sorry." Jessie spoke in a little girl voice.

Evan glanced at her to see if she was going to try something, but she was slumped in the seat with her hands in her lap.

"Why couldn't you leave well enough alone?" Evan didn't ask 'how could you kill a man?' He knew exactly how she could do that.

"Brice was onto you. What was I supposed to do? Stand helplessly by while some stranger destroyed my family?"

"Corie wasn't a stranger."

"I can't go to jail, Evan. Maybe you should kill me too."

"Don't be dramatic."

"I thought I was helping you." Still in the small voice.

"By killing Corie?"

"That was . . . unfortunate. I thought you would know what to do about Corie. That's why I called you, that's why I waited for you and insisted you come over. Everything was perfect. Even the snow. The snow would slow everyone down."

"Thought it all through, did you?"

Malice crept into her voice. "I can't believe you're going to lose your wife to a cop."

Not to Jessie's bullets. No. He was going to lose his wife to Jack. If only Corie were alive to be lost to anyone. But Evan didn't argue the point.

Jessie's voice grew soft and dreamy. "I love it when it snows, when it's biting and harsh outside and warm and safe inside. I wasn't sure at first that I was going to do it. I decided to see her, to see how I felt. To see how she still felt about me."

"Corie loves you. She never stopped. She loved visiting you—most of the time she had to convince me. She loved your cooking, your clothes, she admired everything about you—God knows why. She would have done anything for you."

"You didn't see her face when she walked in. And her hair. That's when I knew: she'd left us."

"She left *me*."

Evan reached Washington Park. Front-end loaders were working to clear the northwest parking lot. He parked at the far end where they'd already finished.

"The roads aren't that bad," Jessie said. "You can keep driving."

"And go where?" Evan stared at the lake in the middle of the park. Not all that long ago the police had pulled a body out. A man down on his luck and friendless, the newspapers said. An apparent suicide. Evan compulsively checked his rearview mirror for police cars. He almost hoped for them. "I'm open to ideas. You're such an expert, after all."

"You'll figure it out. You always know how to handle these things."

Evan laughed again bitterly. *These things?* As if they were discussing paying a bill or hiring a gardener. "The police will have the cabin staked out, if we could even get there with all of the snow. Shaun usually plows the road but he's a bit indisposed at the moment."

"I hate it there anyway."

Evan wondered if Jack drove by the park, if he would spot Evan's car. But Jack was at the hospital with Corie. She wouldn't be alone as long as she was alive. If she was alive.

"I can't go to jail," Jessie said again. "I'm old. I wouldn't survive it."

How odd to hear his mother describe herself as old. She must be desperate.

"I'm not prepared for these kinds of things. I didn't mean what I said earlier, darling. I was upset. You're stronger than I am. I've always admired you and the way you can prevail over anything."

What she had always done was use him. He never had either her respect or her admiration. Let alone love. As long as he was useful she indulged him, but that was it. That had been Hennessy's undoing, refusing to be what Jessie wanted her to be. Refusing even to pretend. Hennessy had turned on herself and he'd turned on—no. It was too much of a cliché: *I did it because of my unhappy childhood.* He wouldn't reduce his life to psychobabble. Evan wasn't much but he wouldn't be a cliché.

"You have friends," Jessie said.

"I don't have friends," Evan said.

Jessie's voice was sweet. "You know people. That's even better. You get things done. I've always wanted to go to Mexico. I love the art, the ocean, the intrigue. I know. I'd like to go see the Mayan ruins."

Evan looked at his mother expecting the usual Jessie mask of delight and charmingly wicked humor. But her eyes didn't sparkle and she didn't press her hands together like a child in her usual manner.

Jessie's eyes were dull and opaque and she did look old. "There are ancient mysteries there in Mexico," she said. "Maybe I'll finally find some answers."

And he would sacrifice himself for her, as he always had.

CHAPTER SEVENTY

Someone sat down in the chair next to Jack and put a hand on his arm. Serena. He didn't know how long he'd been sitting there, and when he lifted his head to look at her he realized his eyes were moist. He didn't care.

"She's going to be all right," Serena said.

"It's my fault. I baited Evan. I shouldn't have said the things I did."

"You were doing your job."

"No." What Jack said to Evan at the wine tasting went way beyond the job. It was stupid, impulsive, egotistical. And possibly fatal.

"Evan's the bad guy here, Jack." Serena watched him for a moment. "They wouldn't operate unless there was hope." And then she sat with him in silence, although she left her hand, warm and soothing, on his arm.

One by one Jack's whole team showed up—Dani, Mike, Tiffany.

Mike asked questions; the women seemed to know better.

Jack looked at his old partner and tried to remember exactly what the doctor had told him. "Shot three times. Collapsed lung. Lot of internal damage. I don't know."

It had sounded brutal and hopeless. One bullet punctured her lung, nicked her spleen, and lacerated her liver. One shattered her ankle. The ankle would require reconstructive surgery later. For now they would only immobilize it, until she was out of danger. The ankle injury wasn't life threatening; the others were.

"I've, uh, secured the scene. At Jessie's." Mike paused as if waiting for something from Jack. "Frank says it'll take some time to remove the remains. They're old, he thinks ten maybe twenty years. It's gonna be almost like archaeology moving the bones. It was gonna take a while for them to get the right technicians out there with the snow and all, so I left Scalamandre in charge."

Jack nodded. Ten or twenty years. *Hennessy.* But that didn't make any sense.

Mike didn't seem to know what to do. He paced and finally volunteered to go get coffee.

Serena looked at the lieutenant. "Markham called Jack and told him exactly where to find Corie. And she was shot like Brice, not cut up. I know I'm new to homicide but I think we've got two killers."

"Evan could be playing you," Dani said.

Serena shook her head. "Uh-uh. Doesn't fit. Corie found Evan's office and helped us figure out the tax records. In essence, she led us to Evan's crimes. So why would he try to save her?"

"Changed his mind at the last minute?" Dani asked.

Serena arched an eyebrow. "A serial killer with a conscience?"

"You guys are overlooking the obvious." Jack was interrupted by his cell phone. He glanced at the display, said "D'Ambrose," and then answered in his customary way: "Fariel."

CHAPTER SEVENTY-ONE

There's a word for wounds that have been washed clean of blood, a scientific term, sterile, clinical, unforgiving. The word feels no emotion, has no awareness, and merely seeks to accurately describe a process. In forensic terms these wounds have undergone *lysis*. This is also the root of the word for the self-destruction a human body initiates on its own after death: *autolysis*. Our decay is coded in our DNA. Soft tissue is the first to go: skin, eyes, lymph, muscle. Our organs feast on themselves. Our bones become dust. Our disintegration is inevitable.

To lyse is to produce disintegration of a compound, substance, or cell. In this case, the substance that had disintegrated was blood. As Aranda's body lay on the cold, metal stairs, the running water from the hose did indeed cleanse. Her blood and bile mixed with the icy water and drained onto the ground below the stairs; rivulets of fluid snaked away from the trailer and, at the edges, froze into a biological slush.

Drained of blood she took on a grayish cast. A pale beauty melting into the sharp perforations of the stairs. Predators found her, hungry at the onset of winter, to them a piece of meat. Held in place by Evan's handcuffs, the mountain lion tasted but couldn't drag her away. Held tight and bathed in the icy water, she was preserved, forever asleep, food.

Roger thought of Aranda as a beloved daughter and doubled over in agony upon his discovery that frigid October afternoon. He was a man who demanded answers. The police took too long so Roger ignored Jack's advice and went to the construction site alone. His borrowed Lincoln Navigator sat in the lot, an ominous sentinel. Something lay on the stairs, some kind of debris Roger thought, or maybe some hapless animal that had found its way there to die.

Roger started to shake. His brain made no sense of the running water, and when he stepped out of his car he slipped and almost fell, confused and frightened by the icy, slushy parking lot. His reluctant gaze traveled to the form on the stairs again and he forced himself to take a closer look. It was far more evil than a dead animal. Roger's fingers, already numb from the cold, fumbled with the cell phone keypad.

To Roger, Jack's first instruction was counterintuitive and offensive: Don't touch anything, leave the water on.

"Aranda? When?" Serena hugged herself.

"Last time she was seen was late yesterday afternoon," Jack said.

Dani took a few steps away and barked commands into her radio.

"Evan's been busy," Serena said.

And Jack had been slow. He'd been sick while Evan was several lethal steps ahead. He had to close the gap. He had to go to Aranda. But he couldn't leave Corie.

Mike returned with a carrier full of coffee cups and took one look at their faces. "Is it Corie?"

"Aranda Sheffield," Serena said. "Roger D'Ambrose found her body a few minutes ago."

"Shit." Mike set down the coffee. "What do you want me to do?"

Dani said, "Warren's on his way there."

Jack stood. "No."

They all stared at him.

Dani recovered first. "Jack, we can handle this. You're not my only homicide detective. I'll get as many resources on this as I need to. You stay here."

"No," Jack repeated. "This is personal. I need to go up there. Corie'll be in surgery for a while. Mike needs to process the scene at Jessie's." He didn't tell the lieutenant how Aranda had tried to call him multiple times. Had Evan killed Aranda while Jack was at radiation or while he was a useless piece of shit on the couch?

"Jack." Tiffany touched his arm and looked up at him with kind eyes. He'd almost forgotten she was there. "I'll stay here. I'll let you know the minute I hear anything about Corie."

Tiffany's kindness was almost Jack's undoing. He managed to nod and not fall apart. Then he looked at Serena. "We'll take my car. It's good on the snow."

Serena picked up two coffees and followed her partner out the door.

CHAPTER SEVENTY-TWO

It was fully dark by the time Jack and Serena reached the construction site. Law enforcement vehicles clogged the icy, snow-packed road leading to the parking lot. At least they'd done that right. They were treating the parking lot as part of the crime scene.

When Jack stepped out of the car, an icy blast reminded him he no longer had his coat. And why. He set his teeth and walked toward the trailer with Serena, picking their way carefully toward the eerie glow of klieg lights illuminating the tent over the stairs.

It was hard to tell what the pale object was until you were too close to defend against the revulsion. Poor Roger. To have known her and then to find this. Uniforms swarmed the scene, and at one point, Jack noticed one young officer subtly slip away and head for the trees.

"Where's your coat?" Serena asked.

Aranda's smiling face when Jack bought her coffee flashed through his mind. Her flirtatious turn to let him see her naked back at the wine tasting. Corie at that same party in the silvery dress. Both of them so beautiful and so exquisitely alive a few short days ago.

A man in a dress coat was bent over the stairs. Warren. He motioned them closer and gave them a quick rundown. Between the flooded crime scene and the snow, tire tracks were long gone. Same for footprints or shoe impressions. DNA would be possible but difficult, with the likelihood of cross-contamination.

"Perp tried to destroy evidence," Warren said. He handed Jack an evidence bag. Inside was a muddy scrap of fabric. "Cut her clothes off. Raped her. Then cut her up, too."

Cut her. "Any idea yet on the time of death?" Jack asked.

Warren hesitated. "Found her phone propped on her hand. Look at the last number in her outgoing call list."

Jack looked. The last call was to him. *Fuck.*

"I doubt she made that call," Warren said. "I think she was already dead."

Jack stared, wanting to punish himself. Aranda's arms were still spread wide and her slim wrists had swollen so that the handcuffs cut a nasty channel into the decaying flesh. Animal activity was obvious, mostly on her legs and torso. Her head was turned to one side, her face somehow still beautiful, flawless pale skin that, when alive and pulsing with blood, was once the color of a mocha latte.

"Jack?" Serena's voice.

"You hear me?" Warren's.

Aranda's soaking wet hair hung limply. It used to be so shiny. Serena and Warren watched him as if he might keel over at any moment.

It pissed Jack off. "If you're right, she was killed more than twenty-four hours ago."

"The phone was a prop," Warren said. "She was already dead. The bastard's screwing with you. Don't let him get in your head."

"Too late." Jack wouldn't take his eyes off of Aranda.

Warren and Serena spoke as if they lived on some other, saner planet. One where missing a phone call didn't leave a beautiful woman mutilated and dead. If Jack had answered his goddamned phone they could have traced the call. If they'd traced it he would have found her. She may have already been dead, but she wouldn't have been out here for a day exposed to the elements and bait for animals. If Jack had done his fucking job, the water wouldn't have had twenty-four hours to destroy evidence. He wanted to hit something.

"Jack, it wouldn't have mattered if you got the call," Warren said. "It was snowing like a son of a bitch last night. The roads were impassable. We had trouble getting equipment up here as it is now. Had to call out a road crew to put down sand."

"When are you gonna move her?" Jack asked.

"I want to do as much processing as possible at the scene. We're bringing in some heaters to warm up the stairs so we can lift the body without pulling off too much skin. It's going to be damned near impossible not to damage it when we move it."

Jack's voice was a snarl and he looked at Warren with narrowed eyes. "Her body. When you move *her*. Not *it*."

"Anything else we need to know?" Serena asked.

Warren looked back at Aranda and a muscle moved in his jaw. "It's a construction site. Dozens of guys were through here on Monday before they shut down. There was a bottle of whiskey on one of the desks inside. Probably belonged to one of the workers. We're gonna test it for DNA."

"What kind of whiskey?" Jack asked.

Warren looked at him curiously. "Jack Daniels. Why?"

Abruptly, Jack turned and walked fast, back toward his car.

Serena caught up with him. "Why'd you ask what kind of whiskey?"

"Evan wouldn't drink Jack Daniels."

"Would it even matter if they find Evan's DNA? He'll explain it away like he does everything. He'll claim it got here while he was consulting on the project."

Jack succumbed to frustration and pounded on the side of the car with his fist.

Serena looked around. "I wonder where D'Ambrose is? Maybe they have him in a car or back at the station for questioning. I'll go find out."

When she came back, Jack could tell by her expression there was more bad news. "What now?"

She watched him, a little warily it seemed, as she spoke. "When they got here Roger was experiencing chest pains. They thought he might be having a heart attack, so they took him to the hospital to get checked out."

"Two birds with one stone. Nice work, Evan." Jack pounded on the car again.

Serena gave him a minute alone. When he finally got in the car and joined her she'd cranked the heat up to high. Her voice was kind. "You must be freezing."

Jack looked at her for a second in her parka and scarf but didn't really see her. His eyes traveled back to Aranda; he wanted the sight of Aranda's body burned into his brain for all eternity. Or at least for the rest of his miserable life. But he didn't have the time to indulge in self-loathing. All he could do was catch Evan Markham and he was goddamned well going to do it.

"You're human you know," Serena said.

Without a word, Jack put the car in gear and turned around.

"Where to?" Serena asked. "We gonna go talk to Roger?"

"I doubt Evan's gonna go visit him in the hospital." Jack exhaled and shook his head. No use taking this out on her or Warren or anyone. "Where do you think Evan would go?"

"Ordinarily? To see Mommy."

Jack looked at her in surprise. "Yeah." He thought about it and nodded. "Serena, you might make a good detective after all."

CHAPTER SEVENTY-THREE

Evan did, as Jessie stated, know people. The pilot he'd hired—paying triple the usual rate—would fly Jessie out of the country as soon as there was a break in the weather.

He drove Jessie to the airport himself, and when he said goodbye, she called him "darling" and touched his cheek in the way he used to relish. He tried to hate her for what she did to Corie but he couldn't.

And he was so tired. It wasn't like him and he didn't understand it at first. He prided himself on not needing sleep. And then he remembered; the nights when he played were exceptions. Nine, ten, twelve hours—as if he fell into a coma. It was the only time he could rest and the exhaustion was usually blissful. But this time he had nowhere to go.

Driving in circles, thinking in circles. Only one of them—Jessie or Evan—could escape. Not both and he'd known that all along. But he wasn't a whiner. Jessie was his responsibility. He'd taken care of her ever since his father died, since he was sixteen, back when he still idolized her. It didn't matter what she did. It didn't matter whether or not he still liked her. She was his mother. Evan had never disappointed her and he wasn't about to start now.

Saying his father died made it sound benign, as if he'd simply fallen asleep with no outside intervention. His father. Hadn't thought about him in decades, but all of a sudden Evan couldn't stop thinking about him. Perhaps because Evan now tasted failure. All his life Evan lived secure in the knowledge that he wouldn't end up like his father, that he was better, that he was stronger. Now, for the first time it felt possible that Evan was not so different after all.

What had his father's final failing been? Evan never asked Jessie, that was out of the question. Disappointing Jessie was dangerous and his father had known that better than anyone. He'd tried his best and given her everything but evidently it wasn't enough. Perhaps Jessie had simply tired of his father's health problems and physical limitations. She wanted someone strong; Evan could understand that.

Her solution, like all of Jessie's solutions, was dramatic. At the time, Evan hated his father for doing nothing more but sit there and die. He knew he'd never be that weak.

Driving in circles, thinking in circles. It wasn't that way at all. Evan gripped the steering wheel. He remembered it wrong. Jessie didn't purposely screw up the dosage. Evan had watched her help his father with his insulin dozens, hundreds of times over the years, marveling at the way Jessie could make even an injection seem tender. Evan was wrong. It was an accident. He was only sixteen after all.

What wasn't an accident, though, was the way Jessie sat there and waited. Evan put a dog to sleep once and it happened the same way, its breath became shallower, its chest moved less and less, the whole process was so subtle that it was hard to know exactly when it was over. When Evan begged his mother to do something, she laughed and gave him his first drink. She treated him like a grownup and wanted to celebrate with him. What were they celebrating? Evan didn't know but he couldn't refuse. He needed to show Jessie that she could rely on him. He needed

Jessie to be happy. So he sat with her and watched his father go while every fiber in Evan's body told him to run and get help.

Driving in circles, thinking in circles. Each memory in its own little compartment, like treasures in a jewelry box. Only now they tumbled out, crashed into each other, contradicted each other. Evan couldn't fall apart like this. He wouldn't. She still needed him. He had to think. He couldn't afford to be disorganized and melodramatic. Cold, tired, confused—it wouldn't do. But as Evan wrestled with his thoughts, one broke free and wouldn't stay contained: what if, in the end, Jessie was nothing but a silly, selfish woman and it had all been for nothing?

CHAPTER SEVENTY-FOUR

Jack watched the wipers move slush around on the windshield. During the drive back to central Denver it had started snowing lightly again. No word yet from Tiffany. He picked up his phone and looked at it so many times that Serena finally commented.

"It's probably—it takes a long time. Surgery."

Jack didn't say anything, focused on his driving, the white road in his headlights. Now that the sun was down, everything had turned to ice. He was driving slowly but his thoughts were racing. If Jessie went with Evan willingly, why were there drag marks in the snow outside the crawl space? Or was that from dragging Corie? He hadn't had time to take a thorough look and determine if the marks indicated someone being brought in or taken away. If Jessie had been dragged she was going against her will. Which meant what?

The bigger question was why had Corie gone there? She certainly wouldn't have gone to see Evan. But she might have gone if Jessie called.

Jack's phone buzzed and he grabbed it. "Tiffany. Speak to me." He heard her say the words and closed his eyes for a moment. Relief washed over him. Corie made it through surgery and was in recovery. She was alive.

"I told you she was strong," Serena said.

"Yeah." Stronger than anyone realized. "Tiffany said Corie would be out of it for a few hours still. It would be awesome to be able to tell her Evan was in custody when she wakes up."

"See, this is why I don't date cops." Serena's lips pressed into a thin smile and the mood in the car lightened a little bit. "They're always cops first and boyfriends second."

"That's not true. And besides, I'm not her boyfriend." But Jack was giddy with relief and the thought made him smile for a second, too.

"You might want to stop and get something warmer to wear," Serena said. "Your getting hypothermia isn't going to help us catch anyone."

"My house isn't that far from here. I'll grab a coat. I should let that damned dog out anyway before he destroys my carpet." Not to mention that it wouldn't do much to cheer Corie up if he killed her dog.

Jack took Washington south from Sixth Avenue. He turned left onto Kentucky and was beginning a slow right turn onto Ogden, his street, when he saw the Mercedes.

Serena saw the car at the same time and he heard her sharp intake of breath.

Jack cut his lights and slammed on the brakes; the Audi stopped. "Going to be easier than we thought." Jack looked over his shoulder and backed up quickly to the alley entrance.

Serena reached for the radio and Jack stopped her.

"No."

"Are you insane? That's Evan's car."

"Parked in front of my house." Jack turned into the alley. "I want to hear what he has to say."

"You really think he wants to talk to you? I know you don't want to talk." Her eyes went to his .45. "This is a very bad idea. I'm calling for backup."

"I said no." Jack slammed on the brakes again. "If it has to be an order, consider it an order. I don't have time to argue. Evan's made this personal from the very beginning. If he's after anyone, he's after me. You get out of the car here. There's no reason for you to put yourself in danger."

"What about you?"

"I'm not a dark-haired woman with full breasts." And it hit him. The answer had been right there in front of him all along. "Go on. He probably heard us. I don't want to spook him off."

Serena shook her head. "Mm-mm. I'm not leaving my partner, even if he is insane."

Jack drove a short way into the alley and parked. "I want him to think I'm alone. Give me ten minutes and then call for backup. Tell them no sirens."

"Jack—"

But he was out of the car.

CHAPTER SEVENTY-FIVE

In the dream Corie was doing laundry, hanging shirts on a line with old-fashioned wooden clothespins. She was outdoors and the sun was glaring. Corie wanted to shield her eyes but couldn't because she needed both hands to manage the wet clothes.

A man called her name but she didn't turn around. "You're going to be all right," the man said. "You don't have to worry."

But she did. She had a nightgown that really needed a hanger. Instead she used the clothespins and wondered if she was going to get caught.

"You don't have to be perfect," someone in the dream said.

They didn't understand. She would get caught and then everything would go all wrong.

She would like to think later that she knew when Jack was there. That she heard his voice. But in reality she didn't hear anything. It was like going underwater; there was no sound.

Her puffs of air were shallow, like a fish. She moved her mouth. *If only I didn't have the gag.* She moved her mouth again. *But I don't.* Her tongue raked the back of her teeth.

Like a dream, time was one large, dark, undefined mass. Like a dream, everyone from her past and her present talked to her and did strange things. She would swim to the surface of consciousness, see the light through the water, and then go down again.

In the dream she heard a man's voice. Felt him hold her hand. And then strangeness again, staircases, the laundry, houses she'd never really been in that somehow felt familiar. She took a bath in one of them in a large, claw-footed tub in the middle of an empty room with a wooden floor.

Beeping. Her head heavy on a pillow. Or was there a pillow? She licked her lips.

"She's thirsty!" a voice said, as though that was the most remarkable thing in the world.

In her dream the light was white and harsh. Corie tried to see what it was, but when she looked to her left she was overcome by pain. Instinctively, in real life, without knowing what to do, her slim hand groped for the call button. It pressed something, a click, and then came the merciful darkness again.

In the dream her hands swam next to her. She felt sand and heard the ocean and tried again to look into the light. Jessie walked toward her across the sand, still wearing the blue sweater, still smiling. She said something but Corie couldn't hear what it was, only heard the laundry flapping and snapping in the breeze.

Someone gave her water in a cup with a straw. She drank and drank.

"You're safe now," someone said, someone not Jack. "You're all right now, darling," the voice said.

In the dream someone touched Corie's arm, and in real life she flinched.

CHAPTER SEVENTY-SIX

Jack slipped between houses, gun drawn. It was late. People were asleep and lights were off. It was hard to see if anyone was inside the Mercedes. It was so quiet he could hear Murphy barking from inside his house across the street.

The snow made it easier to see but Jack was very cold. He willed himself to stop shivering so he could maintain a steady grip on his gun. The house he was next to had a large bush in front and Jack used that as cover. His eyes scanned his front yard up to the steps where Evan sat.

Slowly, his gun on Evan, Jack made his way across the frozen street.

"Don't move," Jack called.

Evan looked up. "I think the dog needs to go out."

"Let me see your hands." God, Jack wanted him to do something. Anything at all.

But Evan knew better. In slow motion, he pulled his hands away from his body and raised them, palms out. "Detective."

"Evan." Jack's breath fogged. Christ, it was freezing.

"Where's your partner?" Evan held himself perfectly still.

"Nearby. What do you want to tell me?"

"What makes you think I want to tell you anything?"

"You're at my house and this sure as hell isn't a social visit."

"Why aren't you with Corie?" Something resembling an emotion crossed Evan's face. "Did she—"

Roughly, Jack cuffed Evan, gratified to see him wince at the cold metal. "What a loyal, loving husband. Loyal to business, loyal to pleasure. Which one is Corie again?"

"She's gone."

"No. Not that you give a shit."

"No, Jessie. She's gone."

"You killed your own mother?"

Within Jack's grip Evan stiffened. "Of course not. I got her a plane. I got everything set up and it wasn't easy. She said she wanted to go to Mexico so I hired a private pilot to take her. He called me a few minutes ago. Jessie never got on the plane. She left and he doesn't know where she went or how. But I know where she'll try to go. That's why I'm here. Jessie's going to kill Corie."

It all tumbled out. A confused story about Evan's father, and insulin, and Brice's computer.

"Evan, what the hell are you talking about? Jessie dropped the computer? Where?"

"Near our house. She wasn't sure."

Jack's head was spinning. Inside the house Murphy's barking reached a frenzied peak. "Fuck. C'mon."

Jack opened the front door and pulled Evan inside with him. Murphy jumped excitedly on his master before Jack shooed him into the fenced backyard.

Jack turned on Evan. "Backup's on its way so if you're going to talk, you'd better do it."

"Jessie killed my Daddy. She's going to do the same thing to Corie."

Evan's urgency was completely out of character. Jack wondered if it was an act. "Any idea who that is in Mommy's crawl space?"

Evan held Jack's gaze, his eyes like chunks of polar blue ice. "Hennessy. But there's no time for this, Jack. You have to get to Corie. You have to believe me."

"Believe you?" Jack took Evan by the shoulders and slammed him into the wall, his forearm hard against Evan's throat. "I don't believe any goddamn thing you say. You're a fucking liar, a murderer, a sadist, a useless piece of shit."

"I've told you everything."

"Not everything." Jack took a step back and raised his .45. "Why Corie?"

"What do you mean? I love Corie."

Jack trained the gun on Evan from barely three feet away. "Why Corie?"

A sad smile crossed Evan's face. "You remember when Hennessy died? Corie came to the funeral with her loathsome mother. Afterward, Vi showed up at the funeral home as we were leaving for the cemetery."

Jack watched Evan through the sight of his gun. He could wait forever. He had waited forever. He was a thousand years old, ten thousand. He thought he'd wanted answers. He realized he already had them.

"My mother was already in the hearse. They'd loaded the flowers and everything but Hennessy. Vi came screeching up. I was relieved to see she wasn't drunk. She marched up to me in that way she has and said there was something she needed."

"Is there a point to this fairy tale?" Still with Evan in his sight.

Evan spoke as if he didn't even notice the gun. "It was family going to the burial. I couldn't imagine what Vi needed from me. Then she told me. While Hennessy was dying Corie had competed in a horseback riding event. And won. Corie brought the ribbons with her to the funeral home and slipped them into the casket so Hennessy could have them forever. And that vile woman wanted me to get them back."

Tears glittered in the monster's eyes. Jack shoved away his own emotion. No fucking way he'd let Evan see him react. But oh, Corie. He felt his cell phone vibrate.

Evan's voice was harsh. "You want to know why? You want to know why Corie? Because even though I may be a complete piece of shit, I realized at that moment that Corie was everything her mother was not, everything that most people are not."

Jack saw Serena pull up at the curb and get out of the car. "How'd Hennessy's body get into the crawl space?"

Evan laughed. "My mother decided that she wanted her daughter with her. Isn't that funny? Hadn't wanted her close while Hennessy was alive. Dead she was more compliant. And Corie's going to be dead too, unless you know where Jessie is. Do you want to know what she said? Right before she shot Corie? How nice it would be for the two friends to be together."

Jack held Evan's steady gaze and thought of the women who'd looked into those icy blue eyes. That face was the last thing they saw. Aranda. Vangie. Yvonne. Monique. Who else? Hennessy? Looking into those eyes you'd know you didn't stand a chance. Evan Markham only came alive when he spilled blood. Jack had stared evil in the face before. He never got used to it.

And yet . . . Evan's phone call nagged at him. It all fit together: Jessie's ring under the bed, her lie about losing it when she spent the night, engineering Brice's move to Colorado.

"It was Hennessy, wasn't it?" Jack lowered the gun but he kept it ready.

"What are you talking about?"

"The women. Dark hair. Young. Only plump and healthy, idealized versions of your sister."

"Don't be vile." Evan choked on the word and his face shattered. Decades of practiced composure failed in an instant.

Jack was so close. He was going to get the truth.

"Jack." Serena was at the door.

He ignored her. "I know when it started, Evan. Monique Lawson was killed right after Hennessy's funeral."

Evan's voice was harsh. "We don't have time for this. I thought you loved Corie."

"Jack!" Serena opened the storm door.

"Serena, not yet."

Her voice was urgent. "You'll want to hear this. Dani's been trying to call you. She pulled Corie's phone records like you asked. One of the last calls to her cell, at twelve thirty, was from Jessie."

Evan said, "I told you."

Jack cursed and, in two long strides, was halfway down the walk before he turned back. "Where the hell's the backup?"

"They should be here any minute."

"We don't have a minute." Jack grabbed Evan's arm and shoved him toward the car. "We're all going. You get in back."

Serena stood frozen in confusion on the front walk.

"You coming?"

Serena jumped in and Jack pulled away from the curb as fast as the Audi would let him on the ice. Which was plenty fast. "Keep an eye on him. If he so much as flinches, shoot him. I'll worry about the mess later."

"So she is alive. Damn it, Jack, why were you wasting time?"

"Shut the fuck up, Evan." Lights and traffic were irrelevant. Jack drove as fast as the laws of physics and the Audi's all-wheel drive would allow. All that mattered was getting to Corie. At one point he found himself on the wrong side of the road when people didn't move out of his way.

Serena fought to keep her gun steady on Evan. "They have a guard on her room."

"Come on, come on." Jack leaned on his horn, wove around one car, and almost sideswiped a second. "Goddamn people, get out of my way!"

"Jack, the way you're driving I might shoot him accidentally."

"Aw."

Jack skidded to a stop outside the emergency room at Denver Health and ran for the entrance. Two marked cars were there, so he left Evan for Serena and the uniforms to deal with.

But at that moment Jack didn't give a shit about Evan. He ignored shouts from the doctors and orderlies, found the stairwell, and took the steps two at a time up to Corie's floor.

No one had considered Jessie seriously as a suspect. No one thought the murderer could possibly be a dizzy sixty-year-old woman. They'd all made an assumption and they'd all been wrong.

A uniformed officer stood outside the door to Corie's room.

"Anyone try to get to her?" Jack asked.

"No, sir. The nurse just left. The only other person who's gone in is one of the volunteers delivering flowers."

Jack saw the cart parked outside the door to Corie's room loaded with colorful arrangements.

"One of the volunteers? I said no one."

"She was an old lady. She had flowers. I thought it was all right."

Fresh adrenaline coursed through Jack and he forced himself to steady his breathing. He put one hand flat on the door and slowly pushed it open. Behind him, the officer was still explaining and Jack motioned for him to shut up.

Inside the room was Jessie in the pink smock of a hospital volunteer, her hair pinned up and covered with a knit hat. She smiled at Jack from where she stood next to Corie's bed. With her left hand, she reached for the plastic tubing snaking its way into Corie's arm. Jack saw what she had in her right hand and realized Evan was telling the truth.

"Jessie, drop the syringe." Jack assumed his stance, arms extended, gun aimed at her head. He wouldn't, couldn't, risk shooting Corie. Which meant he had to aim high.

Jessie looked at Jack calmly, still with that same scary smile on her face. "I don't think so, dear."

Then she turned back to Corie, stuck the needle into the IV, and Jack took his shot.

Jessie crumpled to the ground, dead instantly.

Jack wasn't taking any chances. He apologized to the unconscious Corie as he pulled the IV needle from her arm and stepped over Jessie to sit on the edge of the bed. There was no way to put his arms around Corie without hurting her, so he held her hand and gently wiped away bits of Jessie's blood that speckled Corie's pale face with a tissue. Blood sprayed the wall, the nightstand, the sheets. On the floor, the smile was frozen forever on Jessie's face.

For once, Jack was in time.

CHAPTER SEVENTY-SEVEN

Hours blurred into days. The FBI arrived. The media went crazy. Everyone had questions. Jack lived in a chair in Corie's room, afraid if he took his eyes off of her she'd disappear for good. His back ached and even the nurses felt sorry for him. He got his mother to take care of the dog and let his cell phone die. If anyone wanted to talk to him they had to come to the hospital, so they set up a mobile command post right outside.

Serena came. So did Dani and Mike and Roger and special agents and even a repentant Vi. Serena had handled herself admirably, securing Markham and getting him processed. She took a serial killer into custody on her first homicide, watched out for Jack, and other than when he was driving, kept her cool. Jack thought when this was all over, he'd put her in for a commendation.

As he sat in the chair watching Corie, he remembered the night he brought her takeout from Del Friscos. Her delight when she bit into the burger. He vowed to take her there for dinner when she was better. If she let him. It seemed like an impossible daydream.

He remembered her eyes, that marvelous sparkling blue, bright with intelligence and laughter. Their smartass banter. The way she felt in his arms. The way she'd tasted like coffee that morning at his house. The way she'd moved in his bed, her passion, and the way she said his name.

Corie's responsiveness must have been addicting to a narcissist like Markham. She'd been so badly used by people who claimed to love her. The one thing Jack wanted most was impossible. He couldn't wipe away the painful memories and he couldn't restore her innocence. That was shattered forever, to be replaced by—what? Corie was artless, open, spontaneous, trusting. What would replace that trust? What would this do to her?

Machines made their accustomed sounds. He knew the difference now between the beeping that was meaningless and the alarms that brought people running. A thin blanket covered her chest, stopping just under her arms.

Wasn't she cold? He wanted to get a thick down comforter, tuck it around her like a cocoon, and keep her warm. More times than he could count, Jack reached for her hand and raised it gently to his lips. Did it matter that he loved her? Would he get the chance to tell her? Would he say it if he were given the opportunity? Would it change anything?

Jack found the waiting safe, like an old friend. Once Corie woke up, it would all start again.

Jack remembered Evan's face when he heard Corie was alive—first hope, then panic and the way he said, 'You have to get to her.' So the bastard was capable of emotion after all. Evan's lawyer sought permission for him to see his wife one last time and Jack told him to go to hell. Evan was done, in large part because of Corie. Because she found the locket, which belonged to Yvonne; because she delivered the tax records proving Evan had been in Charlotte and taken Monique to dinner; because those records and receipts also put Evan in New York at the time of another unsolved homicide and in the wrong place at the right time for a dozen others.

A search of Evan's car turned up a scrap of fabric that matched the cut-up cashmere sweater found at the scene near Aranda's mutilated body. Roger had identified it. Jack badly wanted justice for Aranda. So smart. So beautiful. So unnecessary. In his mind Jack still saw her smile. He had a dream where he was in Starbucks with her, and Aranda laughed and told him it was going to be all right. In the dream she said, "Thank you." Jack woke from the dream with renewed self-loathing.

He didn't go back for his last radiation treatment, even though everyone persisted in pointing out all of the ways answering his phone that night wouldn't have made a difference. But it made a difference to Jack.

And then there was Jessie. There was insulin in the syringe, the same thing she'd used to kill her husband. Corie would have been dead almost instantly. The woman Corie viewed as a second mother tried to kill her. Twice. Neither one of Corie's mothers had done her any damned good.

With a mother like Jessie it was no wonder Evan had turned out warped. Not that there was any excuse for murdering lovely young women. Defense lawyers would try and use it, though, and considering Jessie's murderous actions, they'd gain some leverage.

Of all the things Evan said at Jack's house, none of them was a confession.

Law enforcement didn't have enough yet and a long, legal road lay ahead of them. But it was only a matter of time. Jack would do whatever it took to get justice for Aranda and the others. They would find all of the bodies, solve all of the murders; Evan's killing streak had finally come to an end.

Special Agent Rogers from the FBI cornered him near a vending machine the second day. "You been here the whole time?"

"Yeah."

"Any change?"

"Not yet."

"She'll make it."

Jack watched Rogers put a bill into the slot on the machine and pound on the glass when his bag of chips didn't drop. You had to give him credit. The guy knew how not to have a conversation.

"Avoid it for as long as you need to, but when you're ready, we need to spend some time," Rogers said.

"What if I'm never ready?"

The agent gave a tight, closed-mouth smile. "Let me know if you need anything. Markham's in Canon City."

He referred to the Supermax federal prison known as "the Alcatraz of the Rockies."

"Good," Jack said.

Rogers looked like he wanted to say something else but didn't. Jack went back to the room and found Corie awake. Sort of. Her blue eyes looked dark, like the sky right before a storm, and he wasn't sure she even recognized him.

"She's in a lot of pain," the nurse said, the nice one with the Jamaican accent and the warm, tilted eyes the color of wheat. "It's better if she sleeps. Why don't you go home? Take a shower, tidy up."

"I look that bad?"

The nice Jamaican nurse smiled, turned on her silent shoes, and left.

But Jack couldn't leave the sanctuary of the chair. When he let Corie out of his sight, bad things happened. He dozed off. When he woke up, an orderly was wheeling in a second bed. Corie was getting a roommate. Jack was going to protest, but before he could do anything, the nice nurse came back.

"If you're going to stay, you might as well get some real sleep. We don't do this for everyone." She shrugged. "Up to you."

Jack wasn't going to accept any comfort, but she left and the bed stayed. Jack eyed it and finally lay down tentatively, fully dressed. The next thing he knew, he felt a hand on his arm shaking him. He must have passed out.

There had been a shift change because a different nurse stood by his bed—the short, dark-haired one, the one Jack thought was mean, but now she was smiling.

"She's awake."

"Jack?" Corie's voice. A miracle.

The dark-haired nurse let herself out.

"Hey."

"You look like shit." Corie looked at him through slitted eyes. Apparently she recognized him.

"Right back at you." He pushed himself off with his hands and lurched to her bed. "How are you . . ." Dumb question.

"I feel like I got run over by a train." Her eyes looked normal again. Alert. Intelligent. Beautiful.

Now that she was awake, all of the things he wanted to say had fled.

"How long have I been here?" she asked.

It was two thirty a.m. Jack scrubbed his scalp with his hands and tried to do the math. "Wow. Going on thirty-six hours."

"Have you been here the whole time?"

Jack smiled. "Off and on."

"Did you get her?"

"Who?"

"Jessie."

Maybe he was hallucinating. Maybe he was still asleep. *How could she know?* Exhaustion made him stupid. "Who?" he repeated.

"Jessie."

He got her, all right. "It's over. You're safe. Evan's in jail, for real this time."

Jack thought of Evan's weeping when he heard about Jessie. Jack had so wanted to shoot Evan. He should have. No one would have blamed him and it would have saved the taxpayers a lot of money.

He smiled and gently touched Corie's hot, pale forehead, her cheek, and what was left of her hair. She looked so small. "It's over," he repeated.

"Where's Jessie?" Corie asked.

Had she heard whispering from the nurses? There was no other way she could know. She'd been unconscious. He wasn't going to burden her with any of it until she was stronger, if then. "Just rest."

"No." She struggled to sit up and couldn't. With a frustrated whimper she gave up and closed her eyes.

"Corie, honey, you're safe. I'm here. Don't think about any of it right now."

With her eyes closed, she frowned like she was concentrating. She tried with great effort to take some deep breaths. Then she opened her eyes again and her face cleared. Her gaze was focused and she looked right at him, into his eyes. "She shot me. Didn't I tell you?"

Jack held her hand. "I know."

"Jessie. Shot me. In the crawl space. She almost shot Evan and she shot Brice, too." Corie was not confused at all. Although her breathing was that of someone in tremendous pain, her voice was surprisingly strong. "Where is she?"

"She's dead. I shot her."

"Really? You're not lying?"

"She's dead."

"Good." Corie's gaze held his. "Who found me?"

"I did."

"I knew it."

It must hurt that the woman Corie viewed as a second mother tried to kill her. But she didn't seem hurt. She seemed satisfied.

Then her hand moved weakly in his. "Pain."

He realized she was asking for pain medicine and guided her hand to the pump that dispensed it. "Go back to sleep. It's really over."

"Evan couldn't kill me after all." Her mouth twisted and her voice was a hoarse whisper. "I'm—not his type."

"You're mine."

Corie looked at him and her face relaxed. Or maybe it was the painkillers.

Although she looked right into his eyes when she asked, "Stay?"

"Forever."

She put her hand back in his. The blue eyes fluttered closed and then open again briefly. "Jack?"

"Uh-huh."

"Thank you." Then the medicine took her away again into its narcotic embrace.

Jack leaned down and kissed her forehead. He pulled the covers up over her thin shoulders and settled in to wait, for as long as it took.

ABOUT THE AUTHOR

A native New Yorker, Merit Clark now writes from the Rocky Mountains. Her short fiction has won awards and in her previous life as a software developer she wrote really boring technical documentation you'd have absolutely no interest in. KILLING STREAK is the first in a series featuring Jack Fariel and is her first mystery.

To find out more about Merit and her books please visit: www.meritclark.com

Made in the USA
Coppell, TX
23 March 2021